The Shadow
of
Simon Magus

The Shadow of Simon Magus

Samuel Spulman

iUniverse, Inc.
New York   Bloomington

iUniverse books may be ordered through booksellers or by contacting:

iUniverse
1663 Liberty Drive
Bloomington, IN 47403
www.iuniverse.com
1-800-Authors (1-800-288-4677)

Because of the dynamic nature of the Internet, any Web addresses or links contained in this book may have changed since publication and may no longer be valid. The views expressed in this work are solely those of the author and do not necessarily reflect the views of the publisher, and the publisher hereby disclaims any responsibility for them.

ISBN: 978-1-4401-2436-5 (pbk)
ISBN: 978-1-4401-2437-2 (ebk)

Printed in the United States of America

iUniverse rev. date: 2/17/2009

Introduction

The following is a fictionalized version of a true story. Approximately 90% of the story happened the way you will read it here. But for legal reasons the names had to be changed, some characters eliminated altogether and others created to keep the story coherent.

PROLOGUE

January 3, 1955, Fort Knox, Kentucky; Ireland Army Hospital

"Good morning Mrs. Michelson. Please come in and be seated." Dr. Neblett said as quietly and calmly as he could. He wasn't looking forward to this. He'd known Mrs. Michelson for some time. Her husband was a Captain on the base, but she lived in Louisville. Her husband went home on leave on weekends. The last time he'd seen her was ten years ago.

When he received her phone call he had gotten her old file out to review it. He'd also spoken to her family doctor, Dr. Bates in Louisville. Apparently she had made an appointment to see him last November when she was experiencing early morning nausea. She told him she was certain that she was pregnant.

A logical conclusion for morning sickness except for the fact that ten years earlier Dr. Neblett had performed an operation on her to remove five ovarian tumors. In the process one ovary was removed and half of the other one as well. It was Dr. Neblett who had to deliver the sad news that she could never have any more children.

He thought she had accepted that at the time, but now here she was in his office looking for all the world like a woman who was 5 months pregnant.

Dr. Neblett cleared his throat and put on his horn rim glasses. He opened Katherine Michelson's lab report and looked up into her beaming face. She was 36 years old but looked older than her years. She's not had an easy life and children seemed to be her one joy. So the news that she would never be a mother again must have been devastating to her.

Dr. Neblett ran his hand through his grey streaked hair and searched for the right words to let her down easily. "I've spoken with your family doctor, Mrs. Michelson. Dr. Bates tells me you began having episodes of nausea in September of last year, is that correct?" "Yes, but the morning sickness has passed now." Katie replied matter of factly.

Dr. Neblett decided to quit beating around the bush and just come out with it. Mrs.

Michelson," he said firmly but not angrily. "You cannot be pregnant. I'm sure I made that clear to you when I last operated on you."

"And I'm telling you, you were wrong! Look at me. How do you explain this?"

She stood up and opened her heavy winter coat and revealed her swollen abdomen." Mrs. Michelson you know that ten years ago I removed 5 ovarian tumors along with one ovary and half of the other one. Clearly you have another tumor. I recommend you allow me to check you into the hospital and operate immediately."

"Oh no you're not!" Katie replied, "You're going to wait until it's been 9 months anyway!"

"Mrs. Michelson please listen to reason." Dr. Neblett pleaded. "Every minute you delay the operation you risk the tumor going cancerous. I would not suggest operating if I thought for one second that you were really carrying a child. But I've seen your x-rays and all that can be seen is a white mass. Not a fetus. Nor can any heartbeat be detected. Therefore you must accept the truth for the good of your own health. You have an ovarian tumor."

"Well I'll tell you what I told Dr. Bates. If it's a tumor then it's got legs!" Katie replied with a half smile.

"Are you suggesting you felt it kick you?" Dr. Neblett said in surprise.

"I've had two sons already doctor. I know what it feels like to have a baby kick you on the inside. So I don't care what your tests show. I'm telling you I'm pregnant. I know I am! But since you don't believe me either, I'm going home." She rises to leave.

"Dr. Neblett tried one last time to convince her to be admitted. "Mrs. Michelson please listen to reason." I know how badly you want to believe this is a child, but it isn't. What you felt may only have been a gas bubble. You mustn't leave."

"Oh yes I am! I'm getting out of here. You doctors with all of your education and fancy equipment think you know more about a woman's body then she does herself! I'm sorry you don't believe me, but I know what I know! Goodbye!" Katie heads for the door.

"Mrs. Michelson at least promise me you'll come by to let me do a check up on you once each month." Dr. Neblett said as one last ditch effort to talk reason to his stubborn patient.

"Maybe. I can't promise you anything except that around June you'll be delivering my child."

March 15, 1955

"Good morning Mrs. Michelson." Dr. Neblett said. This was now Katie's third visit to his office since January.

"Well what did your tests show this time?" Katie was never one to mince her words. If she had something to say she just came out with it.

Dr. Neblett half smiled as he pushed his glasses back on his nose. "Well" he said, "I hope you're happy Mrs. Michelson. Your case has become the subject of quite a debate among the specialists who I called in on your case."

"What do you mean?" She inquired.

"One group of specialists believes that you are carrying twins and one or both of them are deceased. Another group thinks it is a tumor and a child and still another group, myself included, believes it is nothing more than ovarian tumors as before. My main concern is that you are going to delay the operation too long. The longer you wait the greater the chance of the tumors going cancerous." Dr. Neblett informed her.

He too was stubborn individual when he believed in something. He would never back down. But he had more than met his match in Katie.

"Dr. Neblett, are we going to have this same argument again? How many times do I have to tell you? No one is going to operate on me until I've reached full term!" Katie's brown eyes flashed with the temper he'd grown used to seeing.

Dr. Neblett sighed and took off his glasses. You're a stubborn woman, Mrs. Michelson. I sure hope you know what you're doing?"

June 13, 1955

"Get her to the O.R. stat!" Dr. Neblett said to the E.R. Nurse who had just phoned him to inform him that Mrs. Michelson had just arrived.

Dr. Neblett rushed to the O.R, stopping only to get prepped for surgery, his mind racing back to ten years earlier when he had operated on this woman once before. He'd learned then that Katie's heart could not tolerate gas without her going into cardiac arrest. This made operating on her very difficult as the most he could give her was a local anesthetic. Meaning Mrs. Michelson would be conscious throughout the operation.

"O.K., let's begin .... scalpel." The O.R. Nurse handed him his scalpel and Dr. Neblett began to make his first incision. "Mrs. Michelson, could you feel that?" He asks

"Yes" she replied. "It felt like a thorn scratch. But don't worry about it. I'm in such pain already that it almost felt good to me."

Dr. Neblett smiled beneath his surgical mask. Such bravery should be rewarded. How was she going to take the news that there was no child? All he could see was the white fibrous tissue of an enormous tumor. He kept cutting away at it and then in spite of himself he stopped and put his stethoscope to his ears.

Not because he believed he would hear anything, but because Mrs. Michelson's faith was so strong he felt he owed it to her to make one last attempt to verify her belief.

But to his shock, there it was! He kept listening just to make sure he wasn't imagining things. But no! It was real! The unmistakable sound of a child's heartbeat! Deep behind and encased in the tumor itself!

"My God!" he couldn't help but exclaim. "I. . .I can't believe it!"

One hour later Dr. Neblett leaned forward. "Mrs. Michelson, can you hear me?" "Yes." She replied weakly."Congratulations. It's a boy." Dr. Neblett told her. Katie smiled to herself.

CHAPTER ONE
Session #1

Paul Michelson sat nervously on the leather sofa in the beige colored office. He thumbed through last month's issue of Time Magazine but was unable to focus on any of the articles. His mind was on meeting Dr. Bornstein. He'd never been to a psychiatrist before, but knows he should have seen one years ago. What would he tell the doctor? Should he tell him everything? He puts down the magazine in anticipation and rubs his face. The anxiety of telling someone the secret that he has guarded for 23 years now makes even breathing seem labored.

Then he hears the receptionist call his last name. "Mr. Michelson, the doctor will see you now." Paul rises from the sofa and feels like a man walking the last mile when being taken to the electric chair. He fights the impulse to just bolt out of the door and never come back. But he promised his wife Susan he would try to get help. So he thumbed through the Bay Area yellow pages until he spotted Dr. Morris Bornstein's ad in Tampa, Fl. Just 20 minutes across the Gandy bridge that spans Tampa Bay.

Paul entered Dr. Bornstein's office and saw him seated behind a hand carved oak desk. He rose with a friendly smile on his face. Dr. Morris Bornstein was a distinguished looking man in his mid forties. He wore a moustache, which like his curly salt and pepper hair, had streaks of grey through it. He was reading something when Paul entered the office. But he took off his horn-rimmed glasses, smiled and stood to greet Paul, offering him his hand.

"Good afternoon Mr. Michelson. Please be seated." Dr. Bornstein said. "Now before we get into the reason that you're here, I always like to conduct a personal background interview. I'll be asking you a lot of questions, so just relax and answer as honestly as you can." Paul nodded "Yes" and sat in a large black leather chair that faced the doctor's desk.

"I always tape record every session. Just so you're aware." Dr. Bornstein presses the record button on his small pocket recorder. "Session number one, Thursday, June 1st, 1995. Patient's name Mr. Paul Michelson. All right let's begin with the basics shall we?

"When were you born?"

"June 13th, 1955."

"So you're 39 years old, is that correct?"

"Yes. I'll be 40 on the 13th."

"Your father's name?"

"Louis J. Michelson."

"Is he still living?"

"No, Paul shook his head, He passed away from a heart attack in 1983."

"I see, and your mother's name?"

"Katherine E. Michelson."

"Is she still living?" Dr. Bornstein asked.

"No. She passed away in 1979 of colon cancer."

"Any siblings?"

"Two older brothers. Donnie who is 15 years older than me and Pat who is 10 years older."

"Are they still living?"

"Yes. Yes they are?" Paul nodded.

"Are you married?"

"Yes sir. My wife's name is Susan."

"Her age?"

"She's 37."

"Any children?"

"No. She has a 17 year old son named Levi who lives with his father and step-mother though."

"Is this your first marriage?" The doctor asked.

"No, this is my second marriage."

"Your first wife's name?"

"It was Lavonne." Paul looked down at the floor.

"Divorced or widowed?"

"Both."

"I'm not sure I understand." Dr. Bornstein asked.

"She left me in 1988. She remarried and died in childbirth in 1989."

"I see. Any children by her in that marriage?"

"We had none."

"How long were you married the first time?"

"We were married 12 years."

"And how long have you been married to Susan?"

"Two years now. Since 1993." Paul smiled.

"Do your brothers live in Florida?"

"No. Donnie still lives in Louisville, Ky. Where we were raised and Pat moved out to Sacramento, Ca."

"So other than your wife Susan do you have any family living in Florida?" Dr. Bornstein asked.

"No sir."

"Ok tell me about your life growing up in Louisville? Were you close to your mother and father?"

"Well I was extremely close to my mother. My father came home only on weekends. His job kept him awake all week. "What did he do?"

"He was a Quality Control Inspector for the Federal Government. They would send him to inspect factories that had government contracts all over the country. Before that he was a Captain in the army, stationed at Ft. Knox. That's where I was born."

"How would you describe your relationship with your father?" The doctor asked.

"Cordial. He was always aloof. Not cold, but not really warm and friendly either."

"And your mother? You say you were closer to her."

"She was my whole world and I was hers."

"What about your brothers?"

"Well remember the wide age gap. By the time I was four years old my oldest brother Donnie was nineteen and he married his wife Barbara. Then by the time I was eight years old, Pat turned 18 and joined the Airforce." Paul explained.

"I see. So from the time you were eight years old it was only you and your mother, with your father coming home only on weekends?" The doctor asked.

"Yes. That's right."

"Which parent was the disciplinarian?"

"My mother was. My father put her in charge of raising the kids and taking care of the house. He felt his job was to bring in the money and pay the bills."

"What method did your mother use to discipline you?" Dr. Bornstein asked.

"We had these bushes growing in the yard and she would make me go out and cut my own switch. Then I had to strip all of the leaves off of it. All of that was worse than the actual beating."

"Do you feel you were an abused child?"

"Oh yes." Paul nodded.

"Describe the abuse."

"Well my mother had me late in life. She was born in 1919 and my father in 1913. So my parents were as old as most of my peers grandparents. My mother began to go into menopause shortly after I was born and because of it she was in a constant state of anxiety. She started to drink heavily by the time I was 13."

"Would you describe her as an alcoholic?"

"Yes, absolutely. If you've ever lived with an alcoholic no further explanation is needed. If not, no words can really describe it. She just got mean and the more she drank the meaner she got."

"Did she ever become violent?" Dr. Bornstein asked.

"Only if I disobeyed her or tried to "talk back" to her."

"What would happen then?"

"She'd explode into a rage. Flipping over furniture, throwing things."

"At you?" The doctor asked him.

"Oh yes. Luckily when she was drunk she had a bad aim! I remember a glass beer mug sailing past my head and putting a big hole in the wall. I think we kept the plaster manufacturers in business repairing the holes. If you made her mad enough whatever was in reach became a missile."

"What else would she do?"

"Well she would slap me on occasion as well. She shook a butcher knife in my face a few times and she kept her rifle in her closet. I remember having to wrestle it away from her once when she got into an argument with some contractors she had doing some job for her. They made her angry and she went to get the rifle to kill them and I had to delay her while they ran for their cars to get away."

"Do you really believe she would have killed someone?"

"Definitely." Paul looked the doctor straight in the eye as he answered.

"Did she ever threaten your life?"

"Frequently. She'd tell me that if I didn't obey her she would get the rifle and blow my head off and hers as well.

"Yet you describe your relationship to your mother as close?" Dr. Bornstein asked.

"Well I don't mean to make her sound like a monster. She wasn't. When she was sober she was the best person I ever met. Honest, loving, generous. But when she was drunk I just tried my best to stay out of her way. I spent most of my time downstairs in our concrete basement. It was my sanctuary away from her."

"Did your father ever stand up for you?"

"No. Her abuse was probably the only thing that we had in common. I used to look forward to the weekends because I knew that meant she would climb off of my back and onto his."

"Don't be upset by this next question, but I have to ask. Was there any sexual abuse?" Dr. Bornstein asked.

"Oh no. Nothing like that. My mother was the world's biggest prude. She wouldn't even get undressed in front of my father. Truthfully if I weren't the living proof of it, I'd swear she and my father never had sex. They slept in separate bedrooms the whole time I knew them."

"Did you experience any other type of abuse?"

"The physical violence only occurred if I stood up to her. But even worse was the psychological abuse."

"Explain." Dr. Bornstein asked.

"Well my mother carried the term over-protective to the insane level. Her first and main rule of our house was that I was not allowed to leave the yard, not unless she was with me. The only exception was of course going to school. But even then she would drive me there and pick me up afterwards. Now to make matters even worse, the school bus stopped right in front of my house. So every morning I had to endure the humiliation of driving past the row of faces, all of them glaring at me."

"How long did this permanent grounding go on for?"

"Until I was 18 years old. I can't really explain to you how devastating it was to me. I was too ashamed to tell anyone that my mother wouldn't let me out of my own yard. So consequently I could never allow any of my peers to get too close to me. I grew up practically friendless." Paul explained.

"Practically?"

"Yes. I did make one friend at school. His name was Larry Troutman. He was tall and skinny and wore horn rim glasses. He was nearly as unpopular as I was. He was the captain of the chess club and we met in the seventh grade. He was the only one I told about my mother keeping me a prisoner in my own home. So he would ride his bike over to visit me from time to time. Then there was my cousin Rick Murray. He was my Uncle Robert's son and only 9 months older than I was. My mother would drive to Fairdale to get him and make him come over and spend the weekend with me."

"She made him?" The doctor questioned.

"Yes. My mother not only ruled our home with an iron fist but she also controlled other families as well. She was always a control freak and everyone just did what she said rather than deal with the consequences. So every weekend she would go get poor Rick and drag him over to our place, where he was subject to the same weird house rules as I was. He couldn't leave the yard either. Which I guess was even worse for him because all week he had the same freedom's as any other kid. He rode his bike to school and so on. Plus every weekend he had to face the laxative ritual."

"Laxatives?" Dr. Bornstein asked.

"Yes. My mother got it into her head that both Rick and I kept getting sick so often because we needed a good "cleaning out." So every weekend she made us take laxatives and never being one who paid any attention to directions she gave us 10 times the dosage an adult was supposed to take. First it was the chocolate bar type of laxatives. The directions said break off two little squares for an adult. She made us eat an entire bar apiece. Later she switched to the chewing gum type and again the directions said for an adult to chew two pieces. She made us chew 15 pieces apiece. Still later she switched us to the liquid magnesia type of laxative. The directions for an adult were to take 30cc. She made us drink and eight ounce glass full apiece. I remember standing at the kitchen sink with her holding the glass to my mouth and making me swallow it all down in one long drink. A few times I almost vomited but she'd say "Don't you dare throw up! Keep swallowing!"

Well needless to say Rick and I spent most of our weekend in the bathroom. But at least Rick did not have to endure the enemas."

"The enemas?"

"Oh yes. At least once month she's march me into the bathroom and give me soap-suds enemas."

"How long did you have to endure this?" Dr. Bornstein asked.

"The enemas continued until I was 13 years old."

"It must have been embarrassing for a teenager to be seen naked that way."

"Oh I was used to that. She bathed me until I was twelve." Paul said matter of factly.

"Yet you don't believe that you were sexually abused?"

"Well I never thought of it that way back then, nor do I think that she thought of it that way either ... It was more like as far as she was concerned her children never got any older than 7 years old."

"You mentioned being ill often."

"From the time I entered the first grade, which in my case was 7 years old because my mother felt I was physically too small at 6 years old. Which made me a year older than my peers but still I was a head shorter than anyone else in my class.Between age 7 till 13 I was in the sick bed more than out of it. But the funny part was she kept rushing me to see my pediatrician. But she never told him about the laxative and enema routine. Now as an adult and a nurse I realize that the loss of electrolytes alone must have played havoc with my immune system. They wanted to put me in the hospital a couple of times but she wouldn't allow it. She felt that she could take better care of me than the doctors."

"You say these childhood illnesses stopped at age 13?" The doctor asked.

"Yes sir. Everything changed when I turned 13. It's because of the events of that year that I am here to see you today. Please understand that this is really hard to talk about. I've been guarding this secret for most of my life. I know how crazy it sounds and if someone were to tell me this story I would think that they were insane. In fact I've concluded that must be exactly what I am? It's the only explanation that makes sense."

"Well our time is almost up for today Mr. Michelson. I think this would be a good place to stop. I'd like to see you on a weekly basis for a time if that is acceptable to you."

"Uh ... No. I think monthly might be best." Paul quickly added.

"Very well, whatever is the most convenient for you. This ends our first session."

Dr. Bornstein clicks off his tape recorder. Paul rises and shakes Dr. Bornstein's hand. He feels a sense of great relief and he leaves his office. He stops at the receptionist's desk to set up his next appointment. She was a young girl in her mid twenties with long dark wavy hair, shoulder length and a lovely smile. Paul tried not to look at her form. He always had to be careful. He set up the next appointment deliberately on the 1st because on the 3rd was the night of the new moon when he knew it would be safest.

"Mr. Michelson" she smiled, "When would you like to see the doctor again? I have an opening on the 14th.". "Oh no ... no. Um, is July 1st open?" Paul asked. "Why yes it is. Would 4 o'clock be good for you?" She asked him. "Yes. That will be fine thanks." He said and then left the office.

Paul headed for the elevator. He made his way down to his van parked on the curb. The meter had nearly run out. He started it up and began his journey home. He'd always loved vans. This was his 3rd high top van that he owned. After fighting the traffic on the Gandy Bridge, he finally arrives home.

He lives at 1347 17th Ave. N. in St. Petersburg, Florida. Their house along with the house behind it is owned by the same landlord. Who divided it into 4 apartments, one upstairs and one downstairs in each home. This was actually the second time that he lived there. He rented the downstairs apartment in the other home back in 1991. He and Susan moved here a year ago. Regina who was only 14 years old the first time he lived here is now 18 and lives in the apartment above his and Susan's with her boyfriend Eric.

Paul pulls into his driveway and parks. He gets out and walks up to the front door. Susan opens it and one smile from her and all of his tension and fears melt away. "There you are!" She greeted him. "I was getting worried. So how did it go?" She asked. "Oh the traffic on the way home was bumper to bumper. But the session went fine. I was real nervous at first but once he got me talking about my past it all just flowed out. It felt very cathartic to get it all off of my chest."

He kept talking as they entered the living room, first passing through the glassed in front porch. Susan had filled it to the brim with her plants. It looked almost jungle like and she and Paul enjoyed sitting out there on their rattan furniture."Listen after you eat dinner you'd better lay down for a nap. You've got to work tonight." Susan reminded him. She then went into the kitchen to make his dinner. Then a knock came on their front door. "I'll get it." Paul said and rose from the sofa. He opened the front door and there stood Regina. "Uh, hello, sorry to bother you but have you seen my cat?" She asked. "He ran out of the door again did he?" Paul replied. "No, but if I see him I'll let you know." "Ok, thanks!" She smiled.

Paul went back inside and sat in the living room watching television. Susan made him her homemade pea soup for dinner. Paul believes Susan was the best cook who has ever lived. Getting married to her was the best thing he had ever done and the last two years were the happiest of his whole life. His life would be nearly perfect if it weren't for his "problem". But maybe Dr. Bomstein will be able to cure him.

About thirty minutes after eating Paul decided it was time to lay down for his nap. He knew he had to get up at 10pm and drive to work. Paul was a Licensed Practical Nurse and was currently working at a nursing home called "The Priory", where he worked on the 11-7 shift.

Paul laid down in his bed and in no time fell into a deep sleep. He dreamed he was back in Dr. Bomstein's waiting room. He looked up from his magazine to see the pretty receptionist sitting behind the window.

She was speaking to someone on the telephone. Paul rose from the black leather sofa and started to approach the window to ask when the doctor could see him. He spoke to the receptionist but she couldn't seem to hear him. Then he heard a low chuckle coming from behind him. He spun around in surprise because before he was the only one in the waiting room.

Someone, a man was sitting on the sofa where he had been sitting. The man looked up and Paul could see that he was now looking at himself. But his eyes looked different. They seemed wider and more piercing and now he could see that they were blue in color, cobalt blue.

Paul's eyes had always been hazel colored. As he watched his body rose from the sofa and walked up to the receptionist's desk. He heard his body speak. "Please hang up the phone and come out here to me." Paul watched as the receptionist obeyed like a woman in a trance.

She rose and walked to the door and opened it. Paul then watched his doppelganger reach out his hand and the receptionist took it. He then saw them walk over to the sofa. She sat down on it and his double next to her.

She did not blink or react at all as he saw his double begin to unzip the front of her uniform. "Leave her alone!" Paul shouted as his evil twin just smiled at him.

"I know who you are! Now leave her alone, please!" Paul begged as he helplessly had to stand there and watch his mirror self slowly undress the receptionist until she was completely nude. He then made her lie on the sofa and began to remove his trousers. Paul tried to yank his twin off the poor girl He tried to but his hand passed right through both of them!

Then Paul awoke with a start as his alarm went off. It was 10pm. He tried to forget the dream and just get ready for work. He put on his uniform and lab coat and came out into the living room. Picking up his wallet and car keys, he kissed Susan goodnight and left the house. On the drive to work he couldn't get the dream out of his mind. Should he tell Dr. Bornstein about it?

He arrived at The Priory at 10:45pm. He punched in and reported to Station 5. The older nursing home was divided into 4 nursing stations, each with 50 to 60 residents. The stations themselves were numbered 3, 4, 5, and 6. 1 and 2 were administrator's office and the director of nursing's office.

Both of which went home at 5pm so he rarely saw them. At night the RN on Station 6 was in charge. The 3-11 nurse named Judy was always glad to see him. Her green eyes shown through her glasses and she always greeted Paul with a big smile.

"Oh thank God!" Judy exclaimed, "It's been a hell of a day. Let's count." Paul and Judy stepped over to the medicine cart. The first duty to be performed was counting the narcotics by the off going and on coming nurses together before she handed him the keys.

Judy held the narcotic book while Paul unlocked the top drawer of the medicine cart. She would call off the numbers while he verified the number of pills in each plastic cassette. "Darvocet-N fifteen." Judy stated. "Fifteen" Paul verified. "Morphine twelve" Judy stated. "Twelve" Paul replied. "Hold on a second. I want to re-order this one."

Paul interrupted her as he pulled off the label and stuck it to the pharmacy re-order sheet. Later that night he would fax the re-order sheet over to the pharmacy who would deliver the medications needed the next day.

After counting all of the narcotics, Judy handed Paul the keys and they sat down at the desk while she gave him shift report. She ran down the room list and reported on any new problems he would need to know about and report to the next shift in the morning.

There were 3 incident reports of falls by residents. No serious injuries noted. Two residents were on antibiotics. One for the flu and the other had a urinary tract infection. There was one new admit, a 72 year old male recovering from hip replacement surgery. His admission examination revealed that he had two stage 4 decubitus, one on each heel, both necrotic.

Paul replied, "That figures. I wonder why nursing homes get all of the bad press for bedsores when it's really the hospitals where most people get them? We're the ones who heal them up!"

Judy smiled and said, "Yeah but I don't think we'll be healing these two. They're both stage 4, to the bone."

Paul raised one eyebrow and replied, "What a pessimistic attitude. Personally I love a challenge. I'll get them healed up. Provided he lives long enough of course. You'll see."

After report Judy left and Paul got out his C.N.A. assignment sheet. There were now 60 patients on Station 5 with the latest admit. That meant 20 patients apiece per each C.N.A.

Paul wrote the vital signs on the sheet that he would need before morning. But he usually got his own vital signs anyway. Then he looked up to see only Mary standing there. He looked at the clock and it said 11: 15pm.

"You're it!" Paul said, "It looks that way." Mary replied. "This is the second night in a row Tina and Jackie have been no call, no show. I guess they must have quit with no notice." "Ok, I guess we'll just do what we did last night. You take rooms 1-10 and I'll take the other two assignments myself."

Paul informed her. "I'm so glad you're on tonight. I don't know what I would do if I had the whole unit. You're the only nurse I've ever worked with who would take one assignment, let alone two." Mary informed him. "Well I don't believe you should be punished because someone else didn't show Mary."

Mary was only 5 feet tall and almost 60 years old. Paul's conscience wouldn't let him sit at the desk and watch this poor old black woman try and clean up 60 incontinent residents every two hours.

"There's more good news." Mary said. "Let me guess. We're out of linen again." Paul replied. "You guessed it!" Mary laughed. "This is really getting old. I'm going to write the director of nursing another note.Maybe if she gets tired of hearing from me, she'll do something about this."

Paul stated. "Ok let me go down to the laundry and see what I can rustle up for us." Mary follows him and he goes out into the hallway and begins to push the laundry cart. It was on wheels and made of PVC pipe and had 3 shelves to hold the linen.

He pushes it down the long hallway past the station 6 nursing station. "Good evening Kwan." Paul greeted the LPN on station 6. "What? No laundry again?" She said with exasperation. "Well you know the laundry people leave at 5pm and they leave this cart for the 3-11 shift and us. But 3-11 always uses it all before we get here. But don't worry. I'm getting to be a pro at washing linen."

Paul laughed as he continued to push the laundry cart down to the laundry room at the end of the hallway. He used his keys to open the laundry room and he and Mary began filling the cart with fitted sheets, top sheets, towels, wash cloths, patient gowns and the large rubber backed incontinent pads.

"This is all the clean pads we've got, about enough for one round." Mary stated. "Ok, I'll wash us enough for the other two rounds then." Paul informed her. He let himself into the room with the washers and dryers and all the barrels of dirty linen. Putting on rubber gloves Paul began going through each barrel of dirty linen picking out as many incontinent pads as he could find. He loaded them into the washer and after adding detergent started it up. Then he and Mary started pushing their now full cart back down the hallway to station 5.

"Ok, it's almost midnight now. I've got to get my 12 o'clock meds passed." Paul muttered to himself. He pushed his medicine cart out into the hallway and opened his medication book. He had 11 tube feeders on this station. Each one must have their gastric tube flushed with 30cc of water to keep it from plugging, twice a shift.

He checked to see how much feeding was left in each bottle as he flushed them and hung a new bottle if needed beside the old one on the feeding pump. Each pump had an alarm which would begin to beep whenever the feeding bottle was empty. Fortunately there were only a few midnight medications to give out.

Usually the antibiotics were every 6 hours so he had to give them at midnight and 6am. Then he had 3 residents who got around the clock pain medications. Two cancer patients and the new admit who was recovering from hip surgery.

Most of the residents on station 5 were not alert and oriented to person, place or time. Most were very confused and required their medications to be crushed and placed in applesauce. Room by room he goes down the hallway until all the medications are given and all of the tube feedings flushed as ordered.

When he gets to 89 year old Mrs. Schroeder's room he sees that she has managed to take her mittens off and has pulled out her nasal gastric tube. Patients who have not had a gastric tube inserted directly into their stomachs via surgery and will not eat must have an NG tube inserted into their nostril, all the way down into their stomachs and be fed by tube feeding.

But Mrs. Schroeder being very confused has pulled hers out and now Paul must replace it. Her pump was still running so she is also laying in a pool of tube feeding. Paul calls for Mary and together they clean her up and change her bed linen and gown. Then Paul goes to the supply room and gets a new NG tube, some KY jelly, a stethoscope and a 30cc syringe.

Then he returns to her room. While Mary holds the patients hands Paul cranks the old fashioned hospital bed up to a 45 degree angle. Then placing KY jelly on the end of the end of the tubing he inserts it into her left nostril until he feels it hit the back of her throat.

Now comes the tricky part. Paul waits until he sees the patient swallow and then shoves the tube into her throat. Feeding it down until he is sure it is now in her stomach. But he must check. Because if it's in the lung and he starts the feeding she'll drown.

So he puts the stethoscope in his ears and using the 30cc syringe he draws up air and blows it to the tube while listening to hear the sound of it in her stomach. Which he hears loud and clearly. He then draws up on the plunger and sees gastric juices in the tubing which is the second method for checking placement of the tube, he then re-connects the tube feeding and starts the pump. Mary and he place the safety mittens back on Mrs. Schroeder's hands so she cannot pull out the tubing again.

Paul hates having to insert NG tubes. He was told by someone he knew that had one, that it feels like having a tree branch inserted into your nose.

But those were the doctor's orders. Returning to the nursing station it was now l2:30am. Time for Paul to go do his treatments. He takes his treatment cart and book and heads back down the hallway.

He asks Mary to assist him as he goes to each room that requires a dressing change. But this was actually the part of the job that Paul enjoyed. He took great pride in healing up wounds and he had gotten very good at it in the 14 years he had been an :LPN.

One patient had a bad rash under her left arm so he applied Mycolog cream to it. Another had a reddened coccyx, a sign he was getting a decubitus, so Paul made sure he was turned every 2 hours side to side only and sprayed it with Granulex spray. Still another whose skin was a thin as tissue paper, had multiple skin tears on her forearms. She was forever banging them on the side rails and would receive skin tears despite the heavy padding on them.

He checks each skin tear to see if the tegaderm needed replacing. It was like an artificial skin that protected the wound while allowing air to flow in as well. On this night two of the pieces need changing.

Then Paul enters the room of the new admit, Mr. Sullivan. He unwraps both of his heels and cleans them one at a time with normal saline. He applies silvadene cream and 4x4 gauze and wraps each one in Kling.

Finally finished with his treatments he returns to the nursing station. Now it was l am and time for Mary and he to begin first rounds. It was also time for Paul's favorite radio talk: show.

From l am until 5 am each night on AM radio there was a talk show that dealt with paranormal topics, Paul's favorite genre. So he always carried a portable radio with an earphone attached so he could listen to it while he worked. Each night the host Art Norry would interview authors and experts on subjects such as ghosts, ufo's, Bigfoot, witchcraft and the rest. Then he would turn over the microphone to the audience who would call in with their questions and stories of their own. It was right up Paul's alley and he wouldn't miss it for the world.

Mary pushed her laundry barrel to the end of the hallway and went from room to room on her assignment. She had 20 residents in rooms 1-10 and Paul took care of the other 40 himself. He'd go in and turn on the light. He would take off the top covers and turn the patient so that they would not be lying on the same side for more than two hours.

No adult diapers were used at night, they used large rubber backed incontinent pads. Usually 2 would cover the whole bed. All of the patients on

Station 5 were incontinent of bowel and bladder. So Paul put on his rubber gloves and went to work cleaning the residents.

Even though Paul was a very fast worker it still took him until 2am to finish his first rounds. Then he headed back to the laundry room to put the washed pads into the dryers so he and Mary would have enough pads for the next two rounds at 3am and 5am.

But the Art Norry show took his mind off of his grueling job. Tonight's subject was "Shadow People."

[Radio] "What are shadow people?" Art's baritone voice intoned.

[Art] "We're going to devote tonight's entire show to the topic. It all started quite by accident when one of my callers mentioned seeing a dark form out of the corner of his eye. We dubbed this entity a shadow person and ever sense I have received an avalanche of e-mails from people all over the world saying that they have seen the same thing. Are they ghosts? Aliens? What are shadow people?

Some people claim to have seen them straight on and not just out of the corner of their eyes. Some are formless but most seemed shaped like human beings. Some are wearing clothes and hats but remember that unlike ghosts, no details can be seen, only the black silhouette of a person or persons. Some wear capes and one of the more common descriptions is that they see the shadow person wearing a hood ... "

Paul stopped in his tracks when he heard that. "Can it be?" he thought.

Art continued, "The descriptions that really creep me out were the ones who claim that their shadow people have red eyes." "Oh my God! I can't believe it!" Paul exclaimed audibly to himself in the laundry room. Looking around to make sure no one heard him speaking to himself.

Paul returned to the nursing station and between 2am and 3am he managed to do all of his nightly charting. At 3am it was time for his second rounds to begin. He once again began to turn and clean his 40 residents while still riveted to his radio program.

[Art] Good evening this is Art, you're on the air.

[Male voice] Am I on the air?

[Art] Yes. Go ahead. Do you have a story to share with our listeners about Shadow people? But first give us your first name only and tell us where you're calling from?

[Male voice] Ok ... My name is William and I live in Augusta, Georgia now. But I grew up in Jacksonville, Miss. This story happened to me when I was 7 years

old. But I remember it as clearly as if it happened yesterday. Anyway, I had just gone to bed. My mom was still up watching the tv in the living room. My dad had gone to bed. I had just crawled under the covers. The only light was the light from our bathroom across the hallway from my room. The light shined in my open bedroom door. My bed faced the closet.

Anyway I was lying there wide awake I could still hear the tv set in the living room. Well just then the figure of a man slid into my room. He was all black like a shadow and you couldn't make out any features. Just a man in a coat of some kind. What really got to me was the way he seemed to slide in sideways. Not walk in. He slid in and was facing me. Looking at me in bed. Well I don't have to tell you I was frozen with fear. I was so scared I couldn't move or speak. He just stood there a minute and then slid back out the door just the way that he had come in.

After a minute or so, I found my voice and I screamed so loud that it woke Dad and he and mom both ran into my room to see what was going on? After I calmed down enough to tell them what I had seen they thought I was just dreaming of course. But I know that I wasn't even asleep.

[Art] Ok next caller. This is Art Norry. What is your name and where are you calling from?

[Female voice] This is Sharon. I'm calling from Scottsdale, Arizona.

[Art] Do you have a shadow person story for us?

[Sharon] Oh yes ... A few months ago before my mother died. She and my sister started talking about some weird happenings in our home. Mom stated that she had seen a dark shape come out of the closet a few times. My sister was shocked to hear this as she had seen the very same thing. When they finally started describing it they said it was all black but wore a black hood like a monk would wear. Well when I heard that I spoke up and told them that when I was real little I used to see a man in a hood like that. He would stand over my crib and look down at me. I would see him almost every night.

Paul listened to the show unnerved by the description of the black hooded figure. "It can't be." He thought.

[Art] This is Art, who are you and where are you calling from?

[Female voice] Good evening Art. This is Angela and I'm calling from Columbus, Ohio. This happened about 5 years ago. I had just gotten married and moved into my husband's house. He was gone to work one day and I was in the house alone. I was reading a book when something caught my eye. You know how you see something out of the corner of your eye? I turned and looked and froze in terror. There at the end of the hallway was the silhouette of a man. A big man, almost 6 feet tall. He just stood there staring at me. He was solid black but his eyes were red. We both froze looking at each other for over a minute when he turned and went into my son's room. My maternal instincts kicked in and I ran in there. My son was asleep but no one else was in the room.

[Art] Ugh ... I hate it when they have red eyes.

[Angela] Oh but there's more. My son started having nightmares frequently. He would wake up screaming. He was only 6 years old at the time. He refused to sleep in there unless the dog slept with him. So we allowed that to give him peace of mind. Then it started happening to me. I would wake up in the middle of the night terrified and I would see the same shadow man standing at the foot of my bed. His eyes looked brighter red this time. I closed my eyes hoping he was not real but when I opened them I could still see him.

Then he turned and went out the door. I jumped out of bed to see if it was really somebody alive. I turned on every light in the house but no one was there and all the doors and windows were all locked. My husband asked me what I was doing and I told him he had a bad dream. About a month later it happened again. But this time he was standing by the side of the bed. I turned to wake my husband but he wouldn't wake up and he's a light sleeper. The man leaned down with his face only 2 inches from mine. All I could see were those red eyes.

His body was blocking the light from the hallway. I just could not move. I was so scared I had trouble breathing, I shut my eyes again and when I opened them he was gone. Then fate stepped in. My husband got a promotion and we moved to another state. After we moved, I never saw it again.

[Art] Ok next caller. This is Art Norry. You're on the air.

[Male voice] Hello Art, long time listener, first time caller.

[Art] Tell us your first name and where you're calling from?

[Male voice] This is James and I'm calling from Trenton, NJ.

[Art] Good evening James, have you got a shadow person story to share?

[James] Yes. When I heard what the subject was I just had to call. This happened to my wife and me. I woke up one Sunday morning and I could see a shadowy figure standing at the foot of my bed. Behind the silhouette of the man was my bedroom window. It had the curtains drawn but there was still plenty of light shining through. It stayed there for a second and then appeared as if it knew I was looking at it. It seemed to take a step backwards and then darted to the left. It seemed to pass right through the bedroom wall! Well I sat straight up. I know this is on the air so I can't tell you exactly what I said, but it was like "What the blank was that?" You'll have to fill in your own blank."

[Art] Yeah I probably would have said the same thing if it had happened to me. Go ahead.

[James] Well my wife just thought I was dreaming of course. Until one night she got up to go to the bathroom and when she came back to the bedroom she saw what she thought was me leaning over the bed. But then she realized I was still asleep in the bed. She said she saw a dark figure of a man leaning over me. She screamed and her eyes went closed and when she opened them it was gone. It woke me naturally when she screamed and after I got her calmed down she told me what she saw.

[Art] Did you ever see it again?

[James] Are you kidding? We moved out of there!

[Art] Ok next caller. This is Art, you're on the air.

[Male voice] Uh ... Hello?

[Art] Yes, you're on the air.

[Male voice] Oh, uh, I have a story that happened to me about 10 years ago.

[Art] First give us your first name and tell us where you are calling from?

[Male voice] This is Andrew and I'm calling from Gary, Indiana.

[Art] Ok tell us what happened?

[Andrew] This happened in 85 when I was 21 years old. I was unemployed and still living at home with my mom. I was just getting ready to go to sleep when I got the feeling that I was not alone in the room. Then I heard breathing sounds in my room.

Paul almost felt faint when he heard that. This story like all the others were hitting a little too close to home to suit him.

[Art] Breathing sounds?

[Andrew] Yeah. It sounded just like it was coming from the corner of the room. That corner is always dark so I didn't see anyone. But then I saw the shadow of a man step toward me. I was so afraid that I couldn't move. He came over and sat on the bed and I felt it go down where he sat. He didn't do anything. He just kept watching me and me him. Well I began to pray to the Lord to make this thing go away and when I did that he stood up like I had insulted him and just disappeared. Well I jumped out of bed and sat up the rest of the night. I never did tell anyone what I'd seen until tonight.

Paul continued to listen to the astonishing stories about shadow people while he continued to work until 5am when the program ended. For others the show was just light entertainment, but for him it was more verification that his problem was far more than mental. But he would ask Dr. Bomstein about that in his next session.

At 5am he had to pass his morning medications. There were always considerably more of those than his midnight meds. He f lushed all 11 of his feeding tubes as he went. He finished his med pass at 6am and then began his final round of patient care. The last round was the hardest because he had 15 people to diaper, dress and lift into their wheelchairs. Mary had 5 of her own to also get up for breakfast. Finishing that at 6:45am he then met the on coming 7-3 nurse Cynthia. They counted the narcotics and he gave her shift report. Finally at 7: l5 am it was time to punch out and drive home.

The moon was still out just as the sun rose. It was still in it's first quarter phase. On nights like this Paul felt so normal that seeing a psychiatrist seemed like a waste of money. But he knew it wouldn't last. The first night of the full moon this month would fall on his 40th birthday on June 13th. He dreaded that time of the month. He used to enjoy watching the old Universal horror film, "The WolfMan" as a child. He remembered how Lon Chaney Jr was always cursing the full moon. But that was just fiction. Mark Twain once said, "Of course truth is stranger than fiction. Fiction has to stick to the possibilities."

Paul arrived home at 7:30am. He opened the door as quietly as possible trying not to awaken Susan. She was such a light sleeper. He loves to watch her sleep. No matter what his problems, they don't seem so important anymore since she came into his life. He first met her at work 9 years earlier. She was a cna who worked for a nursing agency. He believes he fell in love with her the moment he first saw her but he was still married to his first wife Lavonne back then so he couldn't tell her of course. Then he had to change jobs again.

His average length of stay in any facility was 6 months or less, due to his secret problem.

Then in 1988 when Lavonne left him because of it, he swore he would never marry again. It just wouldn't be fair to ask anyone to live with this. So he stayed single for 5 years. The worst 5 years of his life, he felt. Then one day while working at still another nursing home, who should walk through the door but Susan Egan. He couldn't believe his eyes. She didn't recognize him at first. His hair was longer and in a pony tail and he had a beard.

He was at lunch and she walked into the break room and sat down in front of him. He said, "You don't know who I am do you?" She said, "No, have we met?" He replied, "Maybe this will ring a bell." He then reached into his pocket and pulled out a small black enameled pocket knife. He said, "Watch this." He showed the knife to be black on both sides and then pushed it though his fist. It changed into a white pearl handled knife.

"Magic man!" She grinned. He had shown her this same trick when they met previously so many years before. They began talking and he learned that she was now engaged and had been for 2 years. Once they began working together again it didn't take long for the embers of Paul's old infatuation with her to be fanned into a flame.

It was 1993 and Paul was living in a garage apartment at the time on 11th Avenue N. He had finally gotten out of debt for the first time in his adult life. His van had broken down and he had gotten rid of it. He took a job at St. Mary's, a Catholic nursing home. There he had worked 12 hour shifts on the weekends from 7pm-7am. Susan worked there 5 days a week on the 3-11 shift. He never looked forward to going to work as much as he did then. Just being around her filled him with joy. Not only did he think that she was physically beautiful but she had the most delightful sense of humor.

Growing up he had always been the class clown, making others laugh. Of course it was only a mask for the fears and depression he suffered from, but no one knew that. But now he had found someone who made him laugh. He found it impossible to be depressed around her.

As their friendship grew at work he began to get to know her and to his astonishment they seemed to share every opinion on virtually every topic. Every word that she uttered seemed to come from his own thoughts. To find someone with whom he has anything in common would have been a treat, but everything? This was a new experience for him completely. He'd never had the slightest thing in common even with the members of his own family.

But now here was this stranger who seemed to be like him in every way. He found himself asking her, "Do you think that we were separated at birth?"

Well before he knew what hit him, he realized that he had fallen madly in love with her. He'd never really been in love before. He met his first wife Lavonne in High School and it was she who made no secret of her infatuation for him. Since no female had ever shown any interest in him before he asked her out and they dated for 2 years before she turned 18 and he 21. Then they eloped. But that was prompted mostly by his desire to get away from his alcoholic mother and her alcoholic father. He loved her as a girlfriend and grew to love her as his wife, but the love that he felt for her was nothing compared to this tidal wave of emotion that just being in Susan's presence evoked in him.

But he'd sworn to himself that he'd never get involved with anyone else once Lavonne left him. His secret problem and trying to hide it from her forced him to lie to her over and over again. Eventually the lies caught up with him and she left. He never blamed her, nor could he explain to her what was really going on? Then she died the next year in childbirth and he swore that he would never get involved with anyone ever again. It wouldn't be fair to any woman to ask him to share the torture that is his life.

So what happens? Five years later he meets Susan, the woman of his dreams. But at least she was engaged to be married to someone else. Although it hardly seemed like a blissful engagement. Every weekend it seemed like Susan spent a considerable amount of of time venting her frustrations about her fiance'. Paul listened as she complained about her interfering mother in law to be and how her fiance' always let her lead him around by the nose.

Every time she would start complaining about how unhappy she was in her current relationship, Paul could not help but think that if only there was someway they could end up together. If only she was his, he would be the happiest man on earth. But just because that could never be did not mean that they couldn't be friends at least.

So one day around the beginning of September 1992, Paul gave Susan his phone number and told her to call him sometime. He told her that they have such a great time talking at work and even though she was engaged there was no harm talking on the telephone. She agreed with him. Then one night she did call him and they spent hours on the telephone talking like two teenagers. But then came the most astonishing coincidence of all. He was currently living in a garage apartment on 11th Ave. N and so was she! Of all of the places that she might have lived, she lived only 5 blocks from him on the same street.

Despite himself he found himself saying, "Look if you are ever in the area please feel free to stop over sometime." To his utter shock she said that she would be over tomorrow! What had he done? But still it was too late to back out of it now. The next day at 6pm, she road her bicycle over to his place. Neither of them had a car at time. He let her in and they sat around laughing and talking for an hour. He showed her his photo albums and all of the handwritten books he'd written and illustrated. Then before either of them realized what happened, the talking stopped. They ended up making love for the first time and she did not leave until midnight.

The next day she called him and told him she had broken off her engagement with her fiance. What Paul had never suspected was that his infatuation with her had been mutual. After that either she would visit him everyday or he would go visit her. He couldn't get enough of her. He only felt happiness when she was around.

From September until December they lived in bliss and grew more and more in love each day. But now Paul had a very important decision to make. Keeping his problem a secret from his first wife destroyed their marriage. He wanted nothing more than to marry Susan, but it would not be fair to not tell her the whole truth up front. But he feared how she would take it? What if by telling her about his problem she found it too much to be asked to live with? He may lose her as well.

Finally in January of 93, Paul proposed to Susan and she accepted. But now came the moment he dreaded. It was time to sit her down and tell her the truth. If she chose never to see him again, then he would just have to live with it. He couldn't go through another marriage built on lies. So he calmly and quietly sat her down and just told her the truth about himself. She sat stunned for a time, not knowing what to say? What do you say to the person you love when you find out that they are mentally ill? But to his surprise she wanted to marry him anyway. So great was their love that nothing mattered to either of them except that they were together.

With no more obstacles in their path, they were married in March of 1993. As with his first marriage his problem seemed to disappear for many months and he believed that her love had cured him. Unfortunately it slowly returned.

Now with her mother and aunt living in an apartment not far away, her mother insisted that Susan come over each day to help care for them both, the time she spent each day doing so grew in length until she found herself there up to 8 hours a day. It was like having a full time job but with no pay.

Susan's nerves began to fray and Paul watched helplessly as the wear and tear on her began to take its toll. It was around then that Paul's secret problem returned full time. But his wife was already under so much stress that she was about to pull her hair out, that he just couldn't bring himself to tell her that his problem had started up again. So he kept it to himself.

That was two years ago now. The aunt passed on but her mother fell ill and Susan was still going over to her place on a daily basis, cooking and cleaning for her mother. Paul had changed jobs four times in the last two years out of necessity but still did not tell Susan why, as she was still under so much stress.

When he proposed going to see a psychiatrist, she naturally asked if his problem had returned and he lied and said that he felt that it might be. So she gave her blessing. "Now if only Dr. Bomstein can help me somehow." He thinks to himself as he slips beneath the covers and lays beside his sleeping wife. "Only two more weeks until the moon is full again. I sure hope that I don't have to change jobs again." He thinks as he drifts off to sleep.

CHAPTER TWO
Full Moon Madness

Two weeks pass by all too quickly. On June 13th Paul awakens at 2pm. He gets out of bed and gets dressed. When he enters his living room Susan yells, "Happy birthday!" She brings him a birthday cake with candles. "Oh thank you angel." He says, "You spoil me rotten." Paul sits on his sofa and Susan bends down to kiss him and places the cake in front of him on his tray table. "Don't forget to make a wish." she says and he blows out the candles. His wish, unknown to her, was for an uneventful night at work. For he knew that tonight was also the first night of the full moon.

At 6pm after dinner Paul lays down for his nap before he has to go to work. He falls into a deep sleep. He dreams he is back at his childhood home, in Louisville, Kentucky. In his dream he awakes in his old bedroom feeling terrified for no reason. His alarm clock says 3am. Then he hears footsteps. They're in the hallway outside of his room. He can hear them plainly stop right outside his bedroom door. Paralyzed now with fear, Paul sees the doorknob slowly begin to tum.

Then a crack of light as the door begins to open. The opening grows wider and Paul can now see the silhouette of someone standing there. It looks like a man in cape and a hood like that of a monk's robe. Only the black outline of him is visible. Then to make matters worse, Paul can see that he has no shadow. He himself is blocking the light behind him but on the floor is the full rectangle of light from the open doorway. The shadow of the man that should be there is not.

Paul lays in his bed too afraid to move as the hooded, caped man slowly enters his room and now stands facing him at the front of his bed. He just stands there staring at Paul who cannot take his eyes off of the black hollow space of the hood. No features can be seen inside the hood with the light behind him. Then the man leans forward and places one knee on the end of the bed. Paul feels the weight of it as it sinks into the mattress. Then he sees one black gloved hand reach the bed and then the other knee as the man is now crawling on all fours making his way on top of Paul.

Paul realizes for the first time that he cannot move! His whole body is paralyzed, except for his eyes. He wanted to jump out of the bed but he cannot. He watches helplessly as the monk climbs on top of him ever so slowly. His face is now inches away from that awful black hood. Only now he can see eyes inside of it.

Two red, glowing eyes, wide open and staring into his. The weight of the man seems enormous. He was so heavy that Paul is having difficulty breathing. He feels he is suffocating! Just then his alarm clock goes off and he awakens! It was only a nightmare. He looks at the clock and it is 10pm. Time to get ready for work.

He kept trying to put the nightmare out of his mind as he got dressed for work. He put on his white uniform pants and blue scrub top, followed by his white lab coat. He places his stethoscope in his pocket. He slips on his white shoes and opens the bedroom door.

Susan is sitting on the sofa watching tv. "Have a good night at work, birthday boy." She says as she rises to kiss him goodnight. He goes out the front door and gets in his Dodge van. Pausing only to look at the orange, full moon just coming up over the horizon.

He says a silent prayer and then checks his eye color in his rear view mirror. His eyes are his usual greenish-brown hazel color. He starts up his van and heads for work. Once he arrives at work he punches in and heads for Station four. It's the Alzheimer's floor.

It's a locked unit which means you can push the button to ride the elevator up to it from Station three, but once up there you must have a key to open the elevator door. There were only 30 residents on this floor which was made in the shape of a square around the nursing station.

He counted the narcotics and received shift report from the off going 3-11 nurse named Chyrll. There were no tube feedings and only a few treatments on this floor. Usually minor skin tears on the forearms of one patient grabbing another one. Physically the residents on this floor were much healthier than on the other 3 nursing stations.

But mentally they were very ill. Most had Alzheimer's in the advanced stage but others had schizophrenia, bi-polar or manic-depression.

None of them really had the capacity to know where they were, what time or day it was or often, who they were? Nor did they know who these strange people were who were coming into their rooms at night and trying to change them out of their urine soaked clothing.

It was a kind of hell they were perpetually in and it was not much better for the workers who had to care for them. Some of the men particularly could become quite combative if not approached just right during patient care. Sometimes even if you did everything just right you could still be seriously injured.

In the last 14 years that Paul has been a nurse he has been often hit, slapped, kicked, scratched, spit on, hit with canes and bedpans, you name it! He remembered one time when an Alzheimer's resident once grabbed his thumb and put it in her mouth and tried to bite off his thumb! It was the worst pain he ever felt.

Another six foot, male resident who suffered from schizophrenia once picked him straight up off of the floor by the collar and shook him like a rag doll. So even though there were less residents on this floor, it was in many ways the hardest to work.

Jennifer came off of the elevator. She was a 25 year old black female, with her hair straightened and dyed red. "Jennifer" Paul said, "I'm sorry to tell you that Nadia called in sick tonight. But don't worry, I'll do rounds with you." "Ok" she smiled. "She didn't feel too good last night. I thought she might call in."

"They called all of the agencies but they couldn't get a replacement." Paul informed her. He had been working with Jennifer for the last 6 months and like all of his other CNA's she really appreciated the way Paul would jump in and help on the floor when they had to work short.

"I'm sure glad you're on tonight!" she beamed. "Any other nurse would just sit behind the desk and not lift a finger to help us."

"Well that's just not me." Paul replied. "Ok, while you go down to get us some linen, I'll pass my 12 o'clock meds and then we'll do first rounds together at 1am. Here's the key to the elevator."

He handed her the key and she said, "Ok I'll be right back." She then left the floor.

Paul took his med cart and got his container of applesauce out of the refrigerator. All of the meds on this floor had to be crushed and put in applesauce to get the residents to take them. Many tranquilizers were given. Haldol, Valium, Restoril and Ambien were quite common but most had little effect on these residents.

They had little sense of day or night on this floor and slept off and on at will. So while some were fast asleep others were up wandering the hallways. Paul guided each of them back to his or her room. Some were continent and if directed to the bathroom could use it on their own. Others were completely incontinent and had to be cleaned up every two hours.

He found Mr. Perkins wandering the hallway looking for the bathroom. So he guided him back to his room and into his own bathroom. As he did he passed by the mirror over the sink and leaned forward to check his eye color. Still greenish brown hazel. Paul felt a sigh of relief. Maybe it wouldn't happen tonight. Sometimes it didn't happen. Maybe it would never happen again. He always had those hopes.

After he finished passing his meds he began doing his nightly charting at 12:30am. One of the things he liked about this floor was there wasn't as much paperwork to do. One am arrived. Paul took out his portable radio and placed the ear jack in his left ear. "Ok Jennifer, let's get started."

Paul said. "Do we have to?" Jennifer asked, already knowing the answer. "Yes" Paul stated. "I'm afraid so." So she got up from the chair she was sitting on, in the small dining room where the tv set was playing.

Room by room Paul and Jennifer began to work. Checking each resident. Taking the continent ones to the bathroom and assisting them on and off the toilet. Washing and changing the gowns and bed linens of the ones who were not. Periodically Paul would secretly check his eye color in the mirror, unbeknownst to Jennifer.

So far there was no sign of the change. Except instead of getting more tired as the night was wearing on, he was feeling more energetic. That was always the first symptom of the change. His peers always marveled at the speed at which he could work. Some even went as far as to ask him if he was on speed?

But Paul was extremely anti-drug due to his being raised by his alcoholic mother. He abhorred all forms of drugs or alcohol. He had never had a drop of alcohol, nor any drugs, nor even smoked a cigarette in his entire life. But he had his own cross to bear none the less. One so bizarre he'd kept it a secret from nearly everyone.

As he worked he took his mind off his problems by listening to the Art Norry show on radio.

[Radio] This is Art Norry. Tonight's topic is the real Entity case. Most of you are familiar with the 1981 movie. Which was a filmed version of the semi-fictional book released in 1977 by Frank DeFalletta. But what a lot of people are unaware of is that his book was based on a real life case. Our guest tonight is Carl Warner. Carl is a parapsychologist and when he was a student he was fortunate enough to be part of the team which investigated the real life Entity case. Good evening Carl. Are you there? [Carl] Yes Art. It's wonderful to be here. I'm a long time fan of your show.

[Art] What year did the event occur?

[Carl] It was 1974. In Culver City,California.

Paul listening thinks back. He graduated from High School that year and spent his first summer away from home. He had landed a job at an amusement park called Gunsmoke Mountain in Cave City, Ky. Where he performed his magic show 3 times a day.

[Art] And how old were you then?

[Carl] Oh I was 21 that year.

[Art] So tell us what happened?

[Carl] I was actually living in Los Angeles at the time. I was a friend of Barry Taft, one of the two main investigators. The other being Terry Gaynor. As I understand it, Kerry and Barry were in a bookstore in the paranormal section, naturally and were having some kind of discussion regarding ghosts vs poltergeist activity, when this young woman overheard them and surmised that they seem to know a lot about the subject. She was there trying to find some books that might help her. Once she introduced herself she confessed that she was experiencing a haunting that involved both apparitions and the physical movement of objects.

[Art] Did she tell them about the rapes?

[Carl] No, not yet. She held that back. Kerry and Barry said they belonged to a team who would be very interested in investigating the case. Both Kerry Gaynor and Barry Taft were working under the auspices of Dr. Thelma Moss who granted them permission to check out the woman's story.

[Art] And what did they find?

[Carl] Well the first standard procedure is to conduct an interview. So they visited the woman's home. Kerry later said that he could tell that she was holding something back and he kept pushing her to tell him more. Finally she broke down and told them

the ghost would rape and beat her.

[Art] Did they believe her?

[Carl] Well ... as scientists, we try not to judge nor take the stories we hear at face value. We don't discount it either. Their story is just the beginning of the investigation. Our job is to try and document any phenomena that occurs during the course of the investigation.

[Art] But what did they originally think when they heard her story?

[Carl] Well frankly, they thought that she was probably out of her mind. After all nothing like this had ever been reported in the history of parapsychology! I mean, a ghost rapist? Come on now!

Paul remembers watching the movie in 1981 when it came out. He later read the book. For others it was only another horror film but for Paul it was still another piece of the puzzle in his own real life horror movie. Can a ghost rape a living woman?

He already believed that the answer was yes. The film and book just verified to him that others are experiencing things that he has lived. But like the woman in the film, played by actress Barbara Hershey, he wondered if he wasn't just insane. If one is truly mad then once can experience anything inside your own mind. Maybe Dr. Bornstein will be able to help him.

[Art] So what was it that made Gaynor and Taft certain that there really was something paranormal about the case?

[Carl] It was at their second visit to the home. That's when they began to witness things for themselves. Kerry was standing in the kitchen talking to the woman's 16 year old son when all of a sudden a lower kitchen cabinet door flew open and a pan came flying out! It flew and landed about 3 or 4 feet from the cabinet.

[Art] What did he do when he saw that?

[Carl] Well the first thing any investigator has to watch out for is trickery. So he immediately began a thorough examination of the cabinet. Looking for any type of strings, springs or what have you that might have been set up. But he found no evidence of any trickery.

[Art] Were you present as yet?

[Carl] Oh no. Me and the others were called in much later. At the time it was still just Gaynor and Taft investigating. I heard about this first hand from Barry when he recruited me later. But there's more. Because right after that was when things really started happening.

[Art] Ok, tell us what happened?

[Carl] Next the woman herself shouted "It's in the bedroom!" So everyone rushed in. They said they kept seeing these little pops of light that would zip past them. They were armed with a 35mm camera and a Polaroid but it would happen too fast to shoot it. Then the woman shouted "It's in the corner!" They both snapped their cameras in that direction but didn't see anything themselves.

The Polaroid just came out all bleached white looking. So thinking the camera wasn't working Kerry took two control shots. Both came out just fine. But then she shouted "It's right in front of my face." So they snapped again. Still not seeing anything themselves. Now in that photo you can clearly see the curtains and even the buttons on her dress but her whole face is obliterated. Just a white bleached out appearance like before but isolated to the very spot she claimed to see the spirit. Then she said it again.

"It's right in front of my face!" Amazingly her face in the Polaroid was obliterated again, but you could see details in the rest of the photo. But every time she said "The ghost is gone" the photos came out normal.

Paul and Jennifer finish their rounds. Paul returns to sit at his desk and Jennifer went back into the small dining room. You weren't supposed to sleep on duty naturally, but it was 2:30 in the morning. None of the residents on this floor knew how to use their call lights.

It was agreed that only two rounds should be made, at 1am and 5am because once you woke up some of the more disturbed residents they would keep the rest awake with their wandering or shouting.

So it was for everyone's benefit to let them sleep as much as possible. Plus knowing that Jennifer had two little boys to take care of at home with her mother, Paul allowed her to put her head down and nap between rounds. He would wake her if he heard the night supervisor coming up the elevator for some reason. But she never did except at the end of the shift to get report. So Paul continued to listen to his program while Jennifer tried to catch 40 winks.

[Art] So when did you get involved directly?

[Carl] On the 3rd night of the investigation. Barry called me and about 15 others and we brought all of the equipment to the house. I noticed that the walls had a lot of uneven paint chips that might create false images in the photos. So what we decided to do was to cover the walls entirely with black poster boards with a different magnetic orientation and a number. So there would be no confusion to what wall we would be seeing in the shots.

[Art] So one wall would say North-number one and another South-number two. Is that correct?

[Carl] Yeah exactly.

[Art] Ok so now tell us what you observed first hand?

[Carl] Ok. We were all gathered in the bedroom when the victim began to call out to the Entity and we saw the little lights begin to appear. Kerry began to try and communicate with it. He would say "Blink 3 times on board number two for yes. Blink twice on board number 5 for no."

[Art] Did it respond?

[Carl] Yeah it did. At that point the level of excitement really increased because it seemed like we were communicating with something intelligent. It would blink on the exact board that Kerry asked it to. Kerry later said he was concerned that maybe somebody was faking it by projecting light onto the wall. So then he said to it. "If you really are here, come off the wall?"

[Art] Did it?

[Carl] Yes. We all saw it. It dived right off of the wall and floated in the middle of the room. It started spinning, twisting and expanding in different directions simultaneously. We all began snapping photos.

[Art] How many cameras did you have at that time?

[Carl] We had nine different professional photographers shooting every angle of the room. It was extraordinary because it was floating in the middle of the room and the light was dimensional. It would have been very difficult to fake something like that.

[Art] How would someone fake it?

[Carl] Well the only way to project a light in mid space like that would be if you had a very sophisticated laser system.

[Art] And that wasn't very likely.

[Carl] Oh no way. Remember this house had been condemned by the city twice so it was a pretty old place. Plus we had the entire bedroom sealed off. So that nobody could go in or out during the photo session.

[Art] What did the light look like? Can you describe it for us?

[Carl] It was 3 dimensional and greenish yellow to white in color.

[Art] Did the cameras capture it?

[Carl] Yes and no. What showed up on film was these strange arcs of light. We never saw any arcs but they were in all of the photos. One of the better photos showed these two reverse arcs over the woman's head. In fact this photo was published in Popular Photography magazine. They've never published any other ghost photos before or since. But they published that one.

[Art] I think I have seen that one on the television show "Sightings".

[Carl] Yes, that's the one I was talking about.

[Art] Well lights and arcs are interesting enough but what about the Entity itself?

[Carl] Ok, now one major difference between the movie version was in the film the Entity was like an invisible man. She could feel him but not see him. But in the real case she saw him. He was described as a male figure that she did not recognize.

[Art] How did she know it was a ghost then?

[Carl] Because after he assaulted her he faded away. Plus the film implied only one attacker I think but in the real case she actually saw 3 apparitions. Two held her down while the third would rape her. It was horrible.

[Art] So did you actually see the Entity yourself?

[Carl] Yes. Yes we all did. The victim got angry with it and began taunting it, calling it a coward. She told it "We don't want to see your light show. We want to see you!" Well she no sooner said that than we saw the formation of the head and shoulders. The light continued on down to the floor until it became a full humanoid figure of greenish-white light. Then it just vanished. Almost as if somebody had pulled the plug. It didn't fade away it just vanished.

[Art] What did you think of that?

[Carl] We were all in awe and silent as we watched this happen. When it vanished two of our crew passed out and had to be carried from the room.

[Art] I remember a scene in the film where the woman's 16 year old son was attacked and broke his arm, I believe ..

[Carl] Yes that really happened. The attack happened at night and one night the woman's 16 year old son heard his mother screaming. He ran into her bedroom and saw his mother being thrown around in the bed. When he went over to help her, something hit him on the head and threw him across the room. He broke his arm. Now here is a bit of trivia that most people aren't aware of. When the young actor who was portraying the role of the woman's son was filming this particular scene he too broke his arm during the shot.

[Art] That is a strange coincidence.

Paul while sitting at his desk suddenly becomes aware of an all too familiar feeling. Suddenly he feels detached from his body. It was getting hard to think straight. Jumping up from his chair he runs into the bathroom at the nursing station and looks into the mirror. His eyes are now bluish-grey. It was starting to happen! He begins to fight the change. He has to stay focused. He begins to splash cold water on his face.

Then he begins to recite the rosary to help him keep focused and also to pray for help. He begins to recite The Apostle's Creed. "I...I believe in God ... the Father ... the Father almighty, creator ... creator of...the heavens and the earth ... and I believe in Jesus Christ.His only son ... our Lord ... " By the time he finishes the long prayer he feels the attack subside. He looked in the mirror but his eyes are still blue-grey. But at least he can think straight again. That was close. Maybe it went away for tonight, he silently hoped. He returned to his desk and placed his ear jack back into his ear.

[Art] How many times was the woman attacked?

[Carl] At least 15 times during the 10 week investigation. But she did get stronger. She was finally able to realize that she wasn't crazy and that there really was something going on.

[Art] Did she try moving?

[Carl] Oh yes. As I understand it, she moved 5 times but it always followed her. She kept moving further away. The phenomena diminished and after about two years the attacks stopped altogether.

[Art] Ok let's go to the phones ... Hello ... You're on the air.

[Voice] Am I on the air?

[Art] Yes. This is Art. Who is this?

[Voice] My name is Kristen. I'm calling from Little Rock, Ark.

[Art] Ok go on.

[Kristen] This happened to me last year. .. I was home alone laying on the couch. I'd like to think I drifted off to sleep, but I know that I didn't. I just know. I felt a presence in my room. All of a sudden a man's arm wrapped around my shoulders. I was terrified! Then he started groping my breasts and started rubbing me in a very sexual way. I kept trying to turn around to see who it was, but he would flip me back over.

Physically flip me to face the wall. All I could see was a man's arm holding me in place. he was wearing a black watch. I could even see the hair on his arm. I fought with everything in me to get a look at him. What I saw was that he was translucent. Hazy. The only thing that was clear was this one arm. I could see the wall, the tv set, etc. But he was not shaped like a man. He really had no shape at all. I fought with him as he touched me. Then it was over. Just like that. I sat on the couch shaking. I felt like I had been raped.

Then Paul's own attack returned! It came on harder and faster this time. There was no time to even get out of his chair. Reality seemed to be moving away down a long tunnel and then as he watched, his own right arm reached up and took the ear phone out of his ear. No one can ever know the horror of being trapped inside your own body which has begun to move on its own! With no more control over your actions than if you were watching television.

He helplessly watched his body rise up from the desk. He spotted the time on the clock as it passed by. 3am. His body left the nursing station and walked softly and slowly towards the dining room. As he stood in the doorway he could see Jennifer with her head down on the table. Her eyes were closed. Paul watched himself walk up to her and just stand behind her, watching her.

Then he saw his head turn to look and see another dining room chair nearby. He pulled it up behind Jennifer and sat down. His hands reached forward and began kneading her neck and shoulders. She awoke. "Oooooh ... That feels good. Thank you" She said softly. "You know you're not going to believe this, but I just had the most wonderful dream. It was about you."

Still only able to helplessly observe what was happening Paul knew that Jennifer had had the dream. How many times had he'd seen this same pattern? First the victim had an erotic dream about him to put them in the proper mood and then began the seduction.

Even as he was thinking this, he watched as his automated hands left Jennifer's shoulders and moved down her back. First her upper back and then make their way to her lower back. Without a word the hands slipped up under her smock, now kneading the bare skin on her lower back. Then slowly working their way upwards. Up to her bare shoulders.

She made no protest, only moaned in pleasure. Up and down his hands now roamed, passing her bra strap again and again and then stopping slowly to unfasten it. Still she made no sounds of a protest as his hands now unimpeded by the bra strap began to work feverishly over the muscles of her back. It felt so good she surrendered completely to it.

Then the left hand slipped down to her rib cage while the right one continued to message her neck. Ever so slowly she became aware that his left hand was slipping around under her bra making its way toward her left breast.

Paul heard Jennifer's breathing become slightly more rapid and shallow and she audibly swallowed hard once in nervousness. But still she made no protest as his fingers now made no more pretenses and slipped completely under her bra cup. His fingers kneading the warm flesh of her ample left breast and then the right hand joining it cupping her right breast. The last thing Paul heard was Jennifer letting out a gasp and then blackness.

Instantly he was back in his body and he could move again. He was standing at his desk at the nursing station. He looked at the clock. It said 5am. Two hours were missing! Rushing to the restroom he looked into the mirror to see that he still had cobalt blue eyes. Just then someone came up behind him and touched his cheek. It was Jennifer! "Oh my God!" he thought as his cheeks flushed. "What was he going to say to her?"

He reached up and took her hand away from his face gently. "Jennifer ... we .. we have to make rounds now." He said and turned to walk past her without looking her in the eyes. "Oh ... yeah. I guess you're right." She said with a tone of resignation.

Together they went room to room and cleaned and dressed all of the residents. Then Paul had to pass his morning medications and Jennifer had two showers to give. At 6:30am the night supervisor came up and picked up the shift report. Then at 6:45am the day nurse arrived and she and Paul counted the narcotics and he gave her shift report.

The day cna's began helping Jennifer. Paul walked to the elevator and left the floor. He punched out at 7:15am. As he was leaving, he passed Jennifer getting off of the elevator. She gave him a knowing smile. He forced himself to smile and then headed for his van. He drove home. Should he tell Susan or not?

Just before they were married he sat her down and told her he had another personality. That he had been hiding from everyone for years. That there was no way he could stay faithful because of his other self who he had no control over. But Susan was no ordinary woman. All she knew was that she and Paul were meant to be together and that for the first time in her life she was really happy. He felt the same way.

So even though he'd swore to himself that he would never get involved with anyone ever again, because it wouldn't be fair to ask anyone to share the burden of living with someone as mentally ill as he was, it was already too late. Neither he nor Susan could imagine life without the other one. So she told him she wanted to marry him anyway. No matter what problem he had. She said all she wanted was his heart. If his other self was determined to share his body with other women then so be it. It wasn't really him doing it anyway.

But once into the marriage Paul realized that Susan's nerves were way too bad for her to worry constantly about what his alter-ego may do next? At first he was honest with her and told her up front that he had another one of his spells. But then her mother entered their lives. They weren't even married 3 months yet when her mother called. She asked Susan to fly up to Somers, Connecticut to help her take care of her elderly Aunt. She was gone 6 weeks.

Paul had been free of attacks for their 3 month marriage and Paul had believed that Susan's love had cured him. But on the night of the first full moon while she was gone he awoke at 3am. He heard the neighbors dog howling. He got up and stumbled to the bathroom. Looking in the mirror he saw his eyes had changed to ice blue. The next thing he recalled he was on a strange street with no idea where he was or how he got there? All he knew was two hours had vanished from his life.

When Susan returned she told him her mother was moving down to Florida and bringing the aunt with her. She was so exasperated about the news because she knew that her mother would expect her to come over everyday and take care of them both. So Paul did not tell her about his attack. Hoping of course that now that she was home he would never have it happen again.

Susan's prediction came true and her mother and aunt moved into an apartment not far away and she had to go over at 9am and she was usually not able to come home until almost 8pm at night. So with her hands full, Paul again did not want to add to her stress by telling her his problem had returned.

Then about 6 months into their marriage nature seemed to deal Susan another blow as she went into early menopause. She was only 37 years old but she began to suffer from the hot flashes, the severe anxiety attacks, the bloating and worst of all she almost completely lost her sex drive.

Paul did all he could to be supportive and understanding. But once again his attacks returned monthly. With Susan exhausted mentally, physically and emotionally he decided not to tell her his problem had returned. He just didn't have the heart to add to her stress and anxiety.

So this morning when he returned home and saw her angelic face sleeping so peacefully he once again decided to keep it to himself. He undressed and got into the shower and broke down. Silently sobbing to himself and praying to God to free him from this curse. He said nothing whatsoever to Susan. She got up and showered and made them both breakfast and at 8:30 he drove her over to her mother's. Then came home and went to bed.

All he had told her last month was that he felt a spell coming on but had fought it off and then told her he was considering seeing a psychiatrist about his problem. Now he felt that Dr. Bomstein could be his only hope to ever lead a normal life. June 14th, 1995- Paul had awakened at 6pm. He watched tv until it was time to go pick up Susan at her mother's.She got to leave at 7pm tonight. On the way home they stopped at the grocery store and she bought two more plants for their front porch. Which now was starting to resemble a jungle

Once they came home she made him dinner and they ate while watching tv on their tv trays, but his mind was elsewhere. He knew that tonight the moon would be full once again. He hoped to God nothing happened that would cause him to get fired again. Jennifer was the fourth secret lover he'd acquired at work. He now had one on each nursing station who thought of him as more than just their supervisor.

He'd been in this same awful situation every place he had ever worked. What usually ended up happening was that one of the girls he had been with would find out about another one and they would both become angry with him and report him to the office. He would be fired for sexual harassment which was automatic termination. Usually though he could see it coming and would quit his job and move on before disaster struck. It looked like it was getting time to move on again. With 4 secret lovers all working in the same place it was like a time bomb waiting to go off.

At 8 :30pm it was time to lay down for his nap. At 10pm his alarm went off and he rose and dressed in his uniform for work. He kissed Susan goodnight and drove off in his van. He looked over to see the moon. It was already up, blazing brightly in the sky. He arrived at work and learned that tonight he would be working on station 3. That was the easiest of the 4 stations. All of the residents were alert and oriented and continent of bowel and bladder.

Thus on this floor only one cna was required at night. Denise was on tonight. She smiled at Paul when he was getting his shift report. It was only last month that she too became one of his secret lovers at work. Denise, like Paul was married. She had 3 children and she was 36 years old.

But her husband of 10 years had lost interest in her sexually. He preferred his porn films she told him, to coming to bed with her. Paul was surprised that any man would rather look at photos than lay next to such a lovely woman. She had brunette hair, curly and shoulder length. her face and arms were covered in light brown freckles and she had large blue eyes and a beautiful dimpled smile.

After he'd gotten shift report and passed his 12 midnight medications Denise approached him from behind while he was charting. She began to play with his ponytail. He hated these awkward moments. What was he supposed to say? "I'm sorry Denise that wasn't me you had sex with last month. That was someone else in my body?" No... sometimes honesty is not the best policy. So he stood and tried to get past her.

"What's wrong?" she said. Looking worried. Not wanting to hurt her feelings he said, "Nothing" and smiled. "Nothing's wrong. I...I'm just afraid one of our residents night see us. You know they aren't asleep yet." As if on cue Mr. Wiles knocked on the nursing station door. He was 86 years old and came to the nursing station nightly to ask for his laxative before bedtime. Paul was relieved to see him. It gave him an excuse to get past Denise.

After he gave Mr. Wiles his laxative he asked Denise to check on each resident while he went to go get the linens. When he got to the laundry room he saw Jennifer from Station 4 and Belinda from Station 5 filling up their linen carts. They both turned to look at him simultaneously. Both gave him a knowing smile. He smiled back nervously. Trying to act as normal as he could he asked if their were enough fitted sheets.

Then he gathered up his linen and headed back toward Station 3. On the way he spotted Carol. The LPN who worked on Station 6. "Hello stranger" she smiled at him. "Hello" Paul said and smiled back. "Maybe we could have lunch together tonight." She said and licked her lips suggestively and then giggled. He turned away involuntarily. "Shh!" he cautioned. "You have to be more careful. The walls have ears around here you know."

"You worry too much." She replied. He returned to Station 3. He finished his nightly charting while Denise finished her first rounds. The residents on this floor were continent except for occasional accidents, but most needed assistance to go to the bathroom.

Four lovers in one building. All lovely sweet women. I suppose most men might envy Paul his problem. But they had never walked in his shoes. First there was the fear of not being in control of your body. True so far his alter ego was only a womanizer and seducer. But what if he turned into a rapist or murderer? But it was bad enough having no control over your life, nor even being able to tell a soul what was going on?

The missing time was the worst of all. It was not always so obvious what had occurred while he was out. How many times had he awakened in a strange place? His car, on the beach, on a strange street with no idea where he was, how he got there or what he had done?

He wasn't sure which was worse. Knowing what had happened, like turning a co-worker into a lover or not knowing what had happened and no way to ever know? Then there was the fear of being arrested because his alter ego often picked up prostitutes. Paul had awakened more than once to find them getting dressed in the back of his van.

Add to all of that the fear of catching some horrible disease like HIV and bringing it home to Susan and spreading it to who knows how many people?

Aside from his fears there was the constant pain of guilt. Guilt for cheating on Susan, his soul mate and the one person he loved more than anyone in the world. Plus the guilt of committing adultery with many married women. Seducing them and causing them to cheat on their marriages and worst of all the guilt of breaking so many hearts.

How many had fallen in love with him? How many believed that he loved them too? How many were crushed to find out he was having simultaneous affairs?

Then there was the pain of the humiliation of having to stand before the Director of Nursing or Administrator when they told him they were firing him. It never got any easier. No, I don't think Paul's condition should be envied by anyone. Dr. Bornstein seemed like his only hope to ending this insane duel existence of his.

It was now 1 am and time for his favorite program. He took out his pocket radio and placed the ear jack in his ear. Unlike station 4, on station 3 the residents knew all too well how to use their call lights. From 11 pm- till nearly 2am they kept Denise hopping asking for water or another blanket or help going to the bathroom. Meanwhile Paul tried to forget his problem listening to his show. Still during commercials he would get up and go to the bathroom at the station to check on his eye color.

[Art] Good evening. How many of you saw the movie "The Exorcist"? Most of you I imagine. What did you think of it? Can a person really be possessed by demons in real life? Do all of the supernatural events portrayed in the film really occur in a real exorcism or was that just Hollywood exaggeration?

Our guest tonight doesn't think so. In fact he says what you saw on the screen was nothing compared to the real thing! Who is he? He's the Rev. Dipietro and he's an exorcist. Good evening Father. It's an honor to have you on the show.

[Dipietro] Thank you the honor is mine.

[Art} Father Dipietro is the author of several books. His latest is titled "Satan Begone"and is an eye witness account of an exorcism of a 40 year old woman in Earling, Iowa in 1928. Is that correct?

[Dipietro] Yes Art. I was a young seminarian then. Only 21 years old.

[Art] So you're 84 years old today?

[Dipietro] Yes Art.

[Art] You've authored several books, what did you want to convey to the reader by writing this book?

[Dipietro] Well I wanted to let the world know that possession is a reality, not just the stuff of Hollywood horror films. But a harsh reality.

[Art] What did you think of the film?

[Dipietro] Well guess I had a unique perspective on it. Having seen the real thing I found it to be rather tame.

[Art] Really? Well let's discuss the 1928 exorcism.

[Dipietro] Very well. Of course the real identity of the woman in question must remain anonymous for legal reasons and to protect her privacy.

[Art] Of course.

[Dipietro] This unfortunate woman suffered from her possession since her 14th birthday and she was 40 years old before she finally was freed through exorcism. Even though she is no longer with us her identity will be kept secret to protect her family's privacy.

Paul smiles at himself knowing that his own condition began when he was 13 years old and now he was 40 as well. Perhaps Dr. Bomstein will be able to cure him somehow. Of course Paul is not sure what is wrong with him? He has always drifted back and forth believing that he is possessed or suffering from a mental disorder like multiple personality disorder. What is the real difference between the two? Does anyone know?

[Art] So what brought on this condition? In the film the young girl was playing with a Ouija board and became possessed. Was that true in this case as well?

[Dipietro] No it wasn't. Now it is true that playing with a Ouija board can indeed lead to possession. But this was not the situation in this woman's case.

Paul cannot help but think back on his own Ouija board experiments when he was 13 years old.

[Dipietro] No in fact she lived a very pious life. She was a devout Catholic who attended church weekly. So you see sometimes the Lord allows even the best people to become possessed as a test of their faith and also to test the faith of those who perform the exorcism.

The woman's mother was already dead but her troubles began after the death of her father. He was an alcoholic who abused her constantly. He even tried repeatedly to seduce his own daughter, but she would have nothing to do with him?

It was after his death that she began to experience her trials. It became harder and harder for her to pray. After a time it became impossible for her to go anywhere near a church or to recieve the sacraments. She felt some inner power was holding her back. As time passed the situation grew worse instead of improving.

Words cannot express what she had to suffer. She could not help herself in any way and seemed to be in the clutches of some mysterious power. Thinking she was mad, she went from doctor to doctor. Over the years she saw specialist after specialist. They never found any physical cause for her condition.

[Art] Now that much was indeed like the film. The poor child is subjected to every medical test in the world and they could not find anything wrong. Only then did they recommend exorcism.

[Dipietro] Yes, that much parallels this case. But in the film it happened way too fast. Real doctors do not give up that easily, as in this woman's case. She spent almost 20 years in their care before she and they gave up. The only option left was exorcism. [Art] I would think that she would have tried it sooner.

[Dipietro] Well that's just it. She did turn to the church for help early on. But before the church grants permission for an exorcism all physical and mental diagnosis must be eliminated and that takes a lot of time.

[Art] But eventually the church agreed to it. How does the church differentiate between mental illness and possession.

Paul sat riveted to his radio. He felt like they were talking about him.

[Dipietro] When a person can read or speak languages that they have never studied. When they can distinguish between blessed objects or food brought to them from unblessed by merely looking at it. Possessed people have a revulsion toward holy objects or places.

Paul has read this before and has never displayed any of the symptoms mentioned, which is one reason why he still leans toward mental illness. But the victim in the movie and in the case being discussed tonight were both demonically possessed. But what of those who are possessed by a spirit?

Not a demon but the ghost of a human being. In those cases would you still find any of the supernatural gifts or revulsion toward holy objects? If only Paul could get through on the phone tonight once they open the phones to callers. He would love to ask the exorcist that question.

[Art] Who performed the exorcism?

[Dipietro] The exorcist was a Capuchin monk named Father Theophilus Ratsinger.

[Art] And where was the exorcism held?

[Dipietro] The site chosen was a convent in a rural section of Earling, Iowa. Father Ratsinger had been a missionary and had performed several exorcisms in the past. Thus the bishop chose him for this assignment. But despite his experience nothing could have prepared him for the ordeal he was about to endure. I remember when I watched the film "The Exorcist" the actual exorcism takes no more than 15 minutes of screen time and those who watched this simulated exorcism felt it was almost unbearable to sit through. Now imagine if it were not on the screen but in the room with you and it lasted not 15 minutes but went on day after day for 23 days.

[Art] Twenty-three days!!

[Dipietro] Yes, I'm afraid so.

[Art] That's incredible. And you were there. Did you observe anything like the things we saw on the screen?

[Dipietro] I assure you the film paled by comparison.

[Art] Please describe what you saw to our listeners.

[Dipietro] I'll try Art. On the very first day the woman was placed on a mattress on an iron bed. As in the film her hands were bound to prevent her from attacking the priest. Once Father Ratsinger began to recite the opening prayers of the Roman Ritual of exorcism the woman sank into unconsciousness and she remained in that state throughout the exorcism.

Her eyes were clamped tightly shut and then without warning her restraints flew off and the woman flew through the air and landed above the door and clung there to the bare wall like a fly. She had to be pulled down and brought back to the bed. This time she was held down by the nuns as the exorcism continued.

[Art] Incredible. What else happened?

[Dipietro] As in the film strange noises began to erupt from the woman. Animal sounds like a horde of hyenas and lions were set loose, The meowing of cats, barking of dogs and bellowing of cattle were all heard simultaneously. The horror of the scene was so intense that the team had to take turns leaving the room to get air and rest before returning. The most unflappable was Father Theophilus. Like Max Von Sydow in the film, he seemed a tower of strength.

[Art] What about the vomiting?

[Dipietro] Oh yes. The poor woman vomited buckets of the most vile emesis. Despite the fact that she took in so little food each day. Her weight dropped daily and we feared she might die in the course of the exorcism. From 10 to 20 times a day she wretched even though she took in no more than a teaspoon of water or milk each day. Yet she seemed to produce volumes of fluid that seemed impossible to lodge in a normal human being.

[Art] I have to ask this. What about the famous head turning scene?

[Dipietro] No that did not happen. But her body underwent such horrific changes that a turning head would have seemed trivial. At one point her body became so swollen her head looked like an inverted water pitcher. Only blood red. Her eyes protruded from their sockets and her lips became as large as hands. Her abdomen grew large and as hard as a rock. Her weight increased until she was so heavy she actually bent the iron rails of the bed to the floor.

[Art] What was her normal weight?

[Dipietro] She was a small woman. 96 pounds. So when her body would expand suddenly it was quite frightening to see. We feared she might burst open at any moment.

[Art] You mentioned one of the signs of true possession was recognizing blessed from unblessed objects.

[Dipietro] Yes Art. On her first day when she was brought to the convent, a well meaning nun sprinkled holy water on her tray and when it was brought to her she immediately flew into a rage. Another unblessed tray had to be brought as a replacement. On one occasion a priest had a small relic of a saint in his pocket and she immediately knew it was there. Even the exorcist was unaware.

Paul was listening intently to the show when suddenly he felt the same familiar feeling of detachment. Like suddenly he was not anchored in his own body anymore. He had to focus on staying inside.

But no matter how hard he fought it. It always returned stronger than the first attack. So finally he just gave in to it. He saw his body rise up once again from his chair. The clock said 2:30am. Once again he left the nursing station and saw himself walking down the hallway.

Denise had just entered a room to assist a resident to the bathroom. The bathroom adjoined two rooms. The room next to it was empty. Paul saw himself go into the room and stand by the bathroom door. He could hear Denise helping Mrs. Rosen off of the toilet and then out of the bathroom. The sound of her walker was clear against the linoleum floor. Then in a few moments Denise returned to the bathroom to wash her hands. Paul's body opened the door from the adjoining room and entered the bathroom with her. He locked the door.

She watched as he then locked the other door that she had just come in. She turned to face him and he reached up and began un-zipping the front of her uniform. Her back was to the sink and Paul could see his own eyes in the mirror which were now cobalt blue.

Then blackness and he awoke. Which for him seemed instantaneous. He could move on his own again and the clock now read 4:30am. Denise stepped out of the bathroom at the nursing station. She smiled at him and adjusted her skirt. He turned away unable to face her, but she walked up behind him and embraced him.

Knowing he mustn't pull away or she would be hurt, he gently took her hands from around him and said almost in a whisper. "Not here. Someone will see us." She smiled and said, "You worry too much." Just then the elevator door opened and it was Jennifer from upstairs.

Paul said, "Did you get me Mr. Bowen's vital signs?" Loudly enough for Jennifer to hear it as she passed by. "No, not yet." Denise replied, understanding he was saying that for Jennifer's benefit. As Jennifer passed by the nurse's station she smiled knowingly to Paul. He wished he were dead. His life was one big lie. He had to lie to Denise and pretend he really loved her and the others as well.

Then go home and lie by omission to the one who his heart truly belonged to. He was tired of living a lie. Tired of trying to put on the mask of normalcy for the world. Tired of covering up the truth. But what else could he do? If only the doctor would be able to help him.

Paul kept busy until 5am to avoid Denise and after that it wasn't necessary. She was taking care of the residents till 7am. Paul counted the narcotics and gave shift report to the on-coming nurse. Then he punched out and headed home.

Not only did he hate himself for not being normal, he also lived in fear of the consequences of his involuntary promiscuity. What if one of his victims became pregnant?

What if one of them had HIV? Not only would he carry it home to Susan but since he couldn't stop his alter-ego's actions he might cause the deaths of not only his lovers but all of their boyfriends and husbands. He tried not to think of anything right now. The stress of it just left him numb. Especially since he knew that the moon would be full again tonight.

For now he had to shrug it off and put on his happy face for Susan. He must not add to the stress that she was already under due to her mother. Not that Susan minded caring for her mother. But it might not be so bad if her mom lifted a finger to help. The woman left everything as is, everyday for Susan to clean up. She never washed a dish, nor even bothered to use the garbage can. She just tossed her trash on the floor.

To her Susan had always been her free maid and the fact that she got married did not deter her in the least from using her own daughter as a legalized slave to do her bidding. Paul did not like his mother in law in the least. He found her conniving, deceitful, manipulative, and bent on doing her best to destroy her own daughter's marriage just so she could have her live in maid returned to her.

But although he vented his opinions to Susan she felt duty bound to care for her mother. A lifetime of jumping to do her bidding was a hard thing to break. Since Paul had been similarly tied to his mother's apron strings he completely understood. So he did his best not to put any pressure on Susan. The last thing she needed was to be caught up in a tug of war between him and her mother.

So he came home, showered and Susan awoke and made them breakfast. Then it was time to take her over to her mother's again. She dreaded it but did not know how to get out of it without standing up to her mother. They went out to his van and he started to drive her over there. "I can't tell you how much I hate seeing you get used like this.

Your mom sold your aunt's home in Connecticut, kept the money for herself, then moved down here so she could have you do all of the work taking care of the poor old alzhiemer's lady and do all of her cleaning as well.

While she sits on her fat can in her lazy boy drinking beer all day. Your aunt died and suddenly she takes ill just to keep you coming over. It's just ridiculous. She's perfectly capable of taking care of herself." Paul vented to Susan on the way over to her mother's condominium. "I don't even want to talk about it. Besides my mother does have a lot of her own medical problems you know?" Susan responded.

"Yeah I know" Paul countered "But all of them are brought on by her alcoholism. Her diabetes could brought under control if she would quit drinking, lose weight and quit eating whatever she pleases. She chugs beer and shoots up with insulin." "Don't you think I know all of this?"

Susan said, her voice filled with exasperation. But you might as well talk to the wall as to her. Let's not talk about it anymore. Listen since I won't get home until probably 8 o'clock I need you to run to the grocery store,ok? I made you a list." She asked him. He dropped the subject. There was no sense discussing it any further. Nothing he said would change the situation. It would only stress Susan out even further.

They arrived at the condominium and he kissed her goodbye and dropped her off. Then he drove over to the grocery store which was right across the street from her mother's place. Parking the van he got out and went inside. He was at the meat counter trying to select the best deal on chicken thighs when he heard a female voice call his name.

He turned around and saw a young woman across the store shouting and waving at him. She was practically running to greet him. As she neared he realized that he had never seen this woman before in his life. He had no idea who she was but clearly she knew him.

"Paul is it really you? I can't believe it!" She gushed. "Um ... yeah ... How are you?" He said while pretending her knew her as well. "You know I shouldn't even talk to you the way you stood me up!" The pretty redhead replied. :"What happened to you anyway? Why didn't you show up? You could have at least called me?" "I...I'm sorry. It's a long story." Paul lied. "I can't believe I finally found you. Oh I've moved since we ... well you know. Let me write down my phone number."

She rumages through her purse and finds a scrap piece of paper and pen and scribbles her number down and hands it to him. "Now there's no excuse for you not to call me. So call ok?" She then kisses him on the cheek and leaves. He stands there looking at the number before he wads it up and drops it on the floor.

How many times has he been through this same scenario? Running into people who seem to know him intimately but he hasn't the first idea who they are? He's glad Susan wasn't with him. But if she had of been the redhead probably wouldn't have approached him anyway.

Paul drove home and put the groceries away and then slipped into bed. He set his alarm for 7pm so he could wake up to go get his wife. He slept fitfully. In his dream he arrived at work and Jennifer met him in the parking lot. She screamed at him "You bastard! You used me! Didn't you? Didn't you?"

He was backed up against his van and he didn't know what to say? Tears were streaming down her face and then there was another voice behind him. "He used all of us." He heard a woman state. He turned around to see Denise, Carol, and Belinda and standing there glaring at him.

Carol said, "How could you do this to me? What kind of heartless monster are you?" Then Denise said, "He used us. He used us all!" Finally Belinda chimed in saying, "I left my boyfriend over you! ... You've ruined my life."

In his nightmare Paul couldn't take it anymore and broke down himself. "I...I'm s-sorry. I'm so sorry." He woke up then and got out of bed for awhile until he felt he could get the nightmare out of his mind. Was it really just a nightmare or a premonition? If any one of the girls talked to the other about him it would become a reality.

No doubt about it. It was time to move on. But he hated quitting another job and starting all over again somewhere new. Maybe he should just go back to working for the nursing agency.

The agencies were set up so that if a nurse anywhere in the city got sick and called into work the facility could call the agency and have them send a nurse over. It was a bit like being a substitute teacher.

You were in a different place every night. It was harder to walk in cold and do the work of a staff member. Not every nurse could do that. But Paul was used to thinking on his feet and was good at it.

The advantage of being in a different place every night is that you would think it would make it harder for his alter-ego to seduce total strangers in the one night he had to work with them, but believe it or not he managed to do it anyway.

Paul was always amazed by that. He was never a ladies man type at any age but somehow his alter ego could walk up to a total stranger and seduce them in minutes. Well at least with the agency work Paul did not have to face the person the next day. It was 1 pm and Paul went back to sleep. Hoping he would not have anymore nightmares. He slept until 7pm when the alarm went off and then he got up and drove over to pick up Susan.

They were home by 8pm and she made dinner for him. He watched tv until she served him pork chops, mashed potatoes, mixed vegetables and a glass of milk. "I believe you must be the greatest cook on earth. "Paul complimented her. "Ah shucks. I bet you say that to all of your women." Susan teased. He pretended to laugh but really the comment made him sad. She was the only woman he wanted in his life, not any of the others.

If only he could be himself all of the time like everyone else. At 9:45pm he got dressed for work and kissed his wife goodnight. He wished he did not have to go to work tonight. He started praying that he wouldn't have to go through the change again tonight.

He arrived at work and discovered that he would be working Station 6 tonight. Carol was off so at least he wouldn't have to worry about avoiding her. Plus the 3 cna's who worked on Station 6 were all elderly. Hattie and Agnes were black and Estelle white and all were in their late 60's and had been working there for years.

So they were safe from his alter-ego's advances. Belinda was working on Station 5 with Mary, Denise on Station 3 and Jennifer as usual was upstairs on Station 4 with Nadia. So it appeared as though he should have a quiet night with no one close enough for his alter-ego to seduce should he come out.

That alone put Paul in a better mood. He counted the narcotics and received shift report from the 3-11 nurse. Station 6 was the busiest of the 4 stations, nursing wise. Not only did he have 9 tube feedings but 2 people were getting IV anti-biotics. If the feeding pumps weren't beeping demanding attention then the IV pumps were.

He kept quite busy until 1am passing his medications and tending to his IV's and tube feedings. Then he sat down to do his charting. He turned on his pocket radio and placed the ear jack in his ear in time to hear the Art Norry show. He began to do his charting while he listened.

[Art] Good evening. Art Norry here. Our guest tonight is para-psychologist Dr. Robert Buchanan. He has written a book that will fit in well with our possession theme this week. It's called "The Bell Witch of Tennessee." Good evening doctor are you there?

[Buchanan] Good evening Art. It's a pleasure to be on your show.

[Art] Doctor who or what is the Bell Witch?

[Buchanan] The story of the Bell witch is the most famous haunting in America. Plus it's the most heavily documented.

Paul thinks aloud, "I'll bet you it had nothing on our old place on McCawley Road."

[Buchanan] In brief, in the early 1800's John Bell moved his family from North Carolina to the Red River bottom land in Robertson County, Tennessee that today is know as Adam's county. John Bell purchased some land and a log house and the Bell's gained prominence in the community. Their troubles began in 1817 when one day John Bell and his son Drewery Bell were out hunting.

At first they thought what they were seeing was a huge turkey and they shot at it. But then they saw that it looked human but didn't have a face like a human. It was terrifying. It then vanished into thin air.

A few days after this they saw another weird animal. This one had the head of a rabbit and the body of a dog. They tried to shoot it but it too vanished.

Paul thinks, "Weird animals...Yep. We had those too."

Shortly after that, in the orchard near the house Drewery and his younger sister Betsy saw an old woman walking slowing. When Betsy started to speak to the old woman she disappeared.

"Apparitions too. This does sound familar." Paul thinks.

[Buchanan] It was after that the haunting began. The first thing that occurred was the sounds. Like someone beating on the outside of the house. John Bell and his sons kept jumping out of their beds in the middle of the night and running outside trying to catch the culprits. But they never saw anybody. In a day or so the noises outside were accompanied by strange noises inside. The Bell children began to complain of sounds like rats gnawing at their bedposts. Then the terror began to escalate when the bedcovers kept getting pulled off of the children by unseen forces.

Paul is shocked to hear this. "Amazing. It sounds just like our old place so far."

[Buchanan] Then their pillows kept getting tossed off of their beds. Time passed and the Bell's began to hear what sounded like faint whispering, voices too weak to understand. Then they heard an old woman crying or singing hymns. Then the physical attacks began. It seemed to center on their youngest daughter Betsy.

Whatever it was began to brutally pull her hair and slap her face. Often leaving visible prints that would last for days at a time. The Bells suffered in silence with this bizarre and frightening activity for over a year.

Then they sought help. John Bell decided to confide in his closest friend and neighbor, James Johnston. Johnston and his wife spent the night in the Bell home and they too were subjected to the same terrifying disturbances. Johnston had his bed clothes yanked off of him several times and then was slapped by the invisible being.

Word spread not only throughout the county, but throughout the state. When the news got to Nashville, Andrew Jackson became interested.

Betsy Bell became interested in Joshua Gardner, a young man who lived not far from her. They became engaged. But the spirit repeatedly told Betsy not to marry Joshua Gardner. Betsy's school teacher Richard Powell was noticeably interested in Betsy and was hoping to marry her when she became older.

Powell was believed to have been a student of the occult. On Easter morning 1821 Betsy met Joshua at the riverside and broke off their engagement. The encounters began to decrease. Although the spirit continued to express it's hatred of John Bell, calling him, "Old Jack Bell" and "Old sugar mouth." It continued to vow to kill him.

From the time of the attacks on Betsy Bell, her hair being pulled and face being slapped and beaten, John Bell's health began to deteriorate. Something seemed wrong with his jaw and tongue. He became increasingly ill as time passed.

On December 20, 1820 John Bell died as predicted by the witch. A strange vial of liquid was found and when some of it was given to their car it fell over dead. The witch was heard to laugh and say, "I finally fixed old Jack for good." At his funeral the witch was heard laughing. She remained with the family for weeks afterwards and then she left and promised to return in 7 years.

[Art] Did she?

[Buchanan] Yes, according to legend she spoke to John Bell Jr and his friend Frank Miles. She promised to return again on 107 years.

[Art] And what happened?

[Buchanan] Well according to urban legend she did return in 1935 when she appeared to several soldiers who were camping in a cave for the night. This is the same cave that was on the original plantation.

[Art] That's a pretty amazing story.

[Buchanan] What makes it so fascinating is the incredible number of witnesses. The witch began to bother other neighbors and was even heard in various churches around the area.

[Art] Ok in your book you not only site the well know facts of the case but attempt to examine the possible causes.

[Buchanan] Yes that's correct. What fascinated me as a para-psychologist is that usually most hauntings are sharply divided between poltergeist phenomenon, things being tossed about or unexplained noises and actual apparitions, the misty or fully solid looking beings that appear to us.

Paul thinks, "Well not always."

[Buchanan] But this case began as a typical poltergiest case. In every poltergeist case there is always a young child involved that the activity seems to center around. Usually one about to enter puberty.

Some parapsychologists have suggested that the hormonal changes being triggered in the brain of the young child somehow activates those mysterious powers that we all possess but have no conscious control over. This the rappings on the wall are really being caused by the adolescent's unconscious telekinesis.

Paul adds, "That's what I used to think too."

[Buchanan] But in the Bell Witch case it didn't stop there. The phenomenon changed. It seemed to take on a personality that grew stronger and behaved like an invisible human being capable of violence.

Paul thinks, "Maybe my case is not as singular as I thought."

[Art] Just two nights ago we dicussed the real life Entity case. I'm sure you're familiar with it. It too was like an invisible man who could hit and beat on the living.

[Buchanan] Yes, I was listening to that program. Yes indeed it was similar but in the Bell Witch case the entity grew so powerful that it could carry on lengthy conversations for hours. Plus it demonstrated many psychic abilities. It used telepathy to read the thoughts of those present. It demonstrated precognition by predicting the future.

[Art] Any theories on what the Bell Witch really was?

Now they have Paul's complete attention.

[Buchanan] Yes as a parapsychologist and a practicing magician, I think I have a rather unique perspective on the case. Have you ever heard the term "Eggregore"?

[Art] No. I can't say that I have. What is it?

[Buchanan] It's an old term that sorcerers use to describe a created spirit?

[Art] A created spirit?

Paul listens closer.

[Buchanan] Yes. According to many old texts, just as a musician or artist taps into the creative power of the God force to create their works of art, so too can a magician tap into the same creative power to create a new spirit. One that will serve the creator's will. Usually an eggregore is given a set time to live and then ritually destroyed. If this is not done the eggregore will grow stronger and take on a will of its own.

Paul thinks, "I didn't know that was possible. I wonder if that's what happened with me?"

[Art] But who in the area would have the expertise to know how to create this eggregore?

[Buchanan] There are actually 3 suspects. The first is a woman named Kate Batts. Kate was rumored to be a local witch. What few know is that in her youth, Kate and John Bell kept company as they used to say in those days. But he jilted her to marry Lucy Bell.

[Art] Hmm ... Well that would provide a motive.

[Buchanan] Yes but there is more. There was a legal dispute between the two. She took him to court because he over-charged her for some slaves and he was found guilty of usery and excommunicated from the local church. The most common explanation for the Bell Witch case at the time was that the Entity was something that Kate Batts had conjured up and sent after John Bell for revenge. It was often called "The Kate Batts Witch".

[Art] But you suspect others in the area.

[Buchanan] Yes. Betsy Bell's teacher Richard Powell was 20 years her senior but clearly he was smitten with her. What few know is that he was a student of the occult.

[Art] Are you suggesting he conjured the entity?

[Buchanan] It's a possibility. I point out that the entity repeatedly warned Betsy not to marry Joshua Gardner and would not let up until Betsy formerly and publicly broke off her engagement. Yet when she became engaged to Richard Powell it made no protest.

[Art] So you're saying he may have conjured it to break off the engagement.

[Buchanan] It occurred to me. But there is one more suspect that I lean toward even more. Betsy Bell herself. You see there were rumors of John Bell abusing his children.

Of course I don't wish to besmirch the man's good name, but let's say hypothetically speaking, that he sexually abused Betsy secretly. Now Betsy was the right age for the poltergeist effect to take place.

Sexual abuse comes in two forms, assault and seduction. Of the two I lean toward seduction. For one thing the entity attacked Betsy first violently. Now if indeed it was a creature born of her own subconscious she may have been going through a lot of silent turmoil for participating in sex with her father. Therefore she may have felt that she needed to be punished.

[Art] Why him? She also had many brothers. Why don't you suspect them?

[Buchanan] Two reasons. One, the entity itself focused on punishing Betsy and John Bell and secondly, don't forget the entity's favorite name for John Bell was "Old sugar mouth".

[Art] Oh my! I hadn't thought of that.

Just then Paul began to feel the first sense of drifting. He got up from his chair and went into the restroom at the nurse's station. He looked in the mirror. His eyes were bluish-grey. He began to feel despair.

"Oh God...Please don't let this happen to me again..." He prayed in a whisper. "Please help me Lord. Please help me. I can't go through this again. I can't!...I can't!" Then it happened. He was no longer in control of his body. He watched his own head rise up from it's position on his chest. He saw himself stand erect and look at himself in the mirror.

His eyes now cobalt blue. He saw his face break into an evil smile. He watched as his body left the nurse's station. It looked down the long hallway toward Station 5. It was 3:15am and all of the CNA's were busy doing their second rounds. He spotted Belinda coming out of one of her rooms on Station 5 to get some linens off of the linen cart.

He watched her go back into the room she just came out of. He began to walk toward the room, always fighting mentally to regain control of his automated body. Pausing before he got to the room, he saw his head double check to make sure the nurse on Station 5 did not see him enter. But she was out of sight at her desk.

Once inside he saw Belinda trying to pull up a heavy male patient up in his bed. His body went over and helped her lift him up. "Thanks" she smiled. Belinda had brown shoulder length wavy hair and big brown eyes. Finished with that patient's care she pulled off her rubber gloves and went into the bathroom to wash her hands.

Paul saw his body follow her. He too washed his hands. As he was washing up he heard himself say, "Lock the door." She smiled and did so. Then he locked the other door to the adjoining room. "Take down your panties." He asked her quite calmly. Wearing a short skirt she complied.

He then embraced her and they kissed. As they were doing so he lifted her up and sat her bare buttocks on the cold sink, which put her at just the right height to penetrate. He quickly did so and then things went black.

Paul awoke with a start and found himself back at his own nursing station. Only 20 minutes had passed. The most time his alter ego would take over his body seemed to be 2 hours. But thankfully most of his spells were much shorter. He figures his other self didn't want to risk getting caught or perhaps Belinda didn't. Whatever the reason he was just glad to be back in control of his body.

The only reason Paul had not committed himself to an insane asylum years ago was that his alter ego never actually hurt anyone. Not physically anyway, although he's certainly caused a lot of emotional pain.

But at least he never had to worry about waking up and reading about his murders the way the Boston Strangler did. Once again he said a silent prayer of thanks that no one had discovered his awful secret and he also prayed that Dr. Bornstein would be able to help him somehow.

Paul finished listening to the Art Norry show while he finished working. At 7:30am he punched out and began to drive home. At least he now had 30 more days of normalcy before the next full moon cycle. This was why he had scheduled Dr. Bornstein's appointments during the cycle of the new moon.

That was when he would be sure that his alter ego would not come out. He's still unsure how much he should reveal to Dr. Bornstein? Should he tell him everything? How it began? Should he tell the doctor that he doesn't really believe that he has a true mental illness. That down deep he truly believes that he is possessed!

CHAPTER 3
Sessions #2 #3 #4

(The following is a compilation of the transcripts of the past six sessions with the patient Mr. Paul Michelson. Today is August 26, 1995. Once the seriousness of his illness became apparent to me during our second session on July 1 st, 1995, I insisted that he see me weekly after that. The patient has been very cooperative. Due to his admitted memory losses he requested to be hypnotically regressed back to the year 1968. Specifically the months of September and October.-Dr. Morris Bornstein)

Session 2, July 1st, 1995

Dr. Bornstein rises from his seat. He takes a silver metallic pen from his pocket.

He goes behind Paul's chair and reaching to the side of it he pulls the wooden lever, causing the head to recline and the foot rest to extend. Then stepping back to the side he holds the pen about a foot away from Paul's eyes. Bornstein starts his tape recorder.

"Now Mr. Michelson, I want you to take a couple of deep breaths and try to become relaxed." Dr. Bornstein begins to twirl the pen between his fingers so that the light reflects off of it.

"I want you to look at the pen." Dr. Bornstein instructs him. "See how the light from the window is reflecting off of it. Keep watching the pen Mr. Michelson and as you do you will start to feel more and more relaxed.

First your feet are relaxed ... relaxed ... relaxed. Now your legs are relaxed ... relaxed ... relaxed. Now your torso is relaxed ... relaxed... relaxed. Now your arms and hands are relaxed ... relaxed. Now your eyelids are becoming heavy ... You want to close them. In a moment you will be asleep, but you will still be able to hear the sound of my voice ... Do you understand? Now you are asleep. Can you hear me Mr. Michelson?"

"Yes."

"We're going to take a trip together. A trip back in time. Do you understand?"

"Yes." Paul says calmly.

"Let's go back now. It's 1968. September of 1968. Where are you now?"

"I'm in school. I'm heading for the front doors. The hallways are full of students. Everyone is leaving the school. It just let out."

"What is the name of the school?" The doctor asks.

"Southern High School."

"What city is it in?"

"Louisville, Kentucky."

"What grade are you in?"

"I'm in the seventh grade. It's my first year in Junior High School."

"What day is it?" Asks the doctor."

"It's Monday."

"What is the date?"

"September 23, 1968"

"And how old are you"

"I'm thirteen years old."

"Describe to me what is happening?"

"I made it out the front doors. I see my mother's car in the semi circle driveway out front.

What kind of car is it?"

"It's a 1963 Ford Galaxy 500." Paul responds. "It's light blue with a white roof. I see my mother. She's motioning for me to hurry. I'm running as fast as I can. I've reached the car. She said "Get in!" I jump in as fast as I can and I shout "Go! Go!" She hits the accelerator and we turn right onto Preston Hwy. She's driving 10 miles over the speed limit.

We caught the green light at South Park Road and hang a right. I'm looking at my watch. I say, "We'll never make it!" She says, "Oh yes we will!" She drives even faster. Now we're turning left onto Blue Lick Road. We're almost home. We live at the corner of Blue Lick and Maynard Drive. At 9409 Blue Lick Road.

We're almost home now. I can see our house. She's turning left onto Maynard Drive and now she's whipping into our gravel driveway and slamming on the brakes.

I'm climbing out of the car before she has even cut the engine off. I'm racing to the back door as she's getting out of the car. I'm jumping up and down now saying "Hurry! Hurry!" She's putting the keys in the back door now. It's open!

I race inside and through the kitchen. Now I'm in the living room. I'm turning on the tv set. I hear the familiar theme music of the tv show "Dark Shadows". I yell "We made it!" as my mother joins me in the living room and we watch it together."

"Is this a typical day in your life in 1968?" Dr. Bornstein asks.

"Yes. We raced home from school every day to watch it. It was my favorite show."

"Ok I want you to fast forward the images now until after the show."

"Ok. I'm talking to my mother. I asked her if she ever saw any real vampires back home?"

"Where is back home? I thought you were at home." The doctor questioned.

"I mean our old home. The one we moved away from when I was four years old. I still call it "back home"."

"But you are now thirteen, not four. Do you really believe in vampires?"

"I grew up hearing so many weird stories about our old place back home that vampires seemed tame by comparison. My mother is laughing now. She said "Oh Hell no! We'd have been getting out of there even faster than we did if we'd had of!"

"Now I'm asking her to tell me some more of her ghost stories from back home." Paul explains.

"She's saying "Oh Paul! Not again!" She says," You must've heard them a million times by now." Now I'm begging, "Oh come on! Please!" "Alright,

alright!" She says. "But only after you do your homework." I say "Ok" and then tell her I'm going downstairs to the basement."

"Why the basement?"

"It's where I spend most of my time. All of my books are down there. We even have our old refrigerator and kitchen table from back home down there. I open the basement door and Lucky comes running up the wooden steps as fast as he can go."

"Is Lucky your dog I presume?" Dr. Bornstein asks him?

"Yes. He's only 6 months old. We found him on the back porch when he was a puppy. I take him outside to our backyard and fasten him to the long chain so he can run all over the yard but not leave it. Then I go back downstairs."

"What do you do down there?"

"Oh I listen to the radio, read comics and books, draw pictures and do my experiments.

"What kind of experiments?"

"Psychic experiments." Paul says matter of factly.

"Describe them to me."

"Today I am going to try and levitate again".

"You're seriously trying to levitate?" Dr. Bornstein asks.

"Oh yes ... I'm laying on the cold concrete floor with my arms and legs spread eagle. I'm trying to lighten my body by imagining it has been transformed into a helium balloon."

"How long do attempt this?"

I get discouraged after 15 minutes. So I get up and walk over to the kitchen table and record the time and the results in my journal. Now I'm taking out a deck of Rhine ESP cards and dealing 5 of them face down on the table. I write on a pad of paper. 1. Red square. 2. Blue Cross. 3. Yellow wavy lines. 4. Black circle. 5. Green triangle.

Now I turn over the cards and see that I missed all 5 predictions. I write in my journal again the time and results of the experiment. Next I take a bowl and fill it with water from the facet on the wall. I set it on the table and place a cork in it. I attempt to move the cork with my mind.

After 10 minutes with no results I give up and record the time and results of the experiment in my journal. Now I hear my mother calling me to dinner."

"Let's fast forward now until after you've eaten." Dr. Bornstein instructs him.

"I ask my mother to tell me one of her stories about McCawley Road. She says, "Which one?" I ask her to start at the beginning. Then I ask her to wait a moment. I say "I'll be right back." I go to my bedroom and open my dresser drawer. I get out my small cassette tape recorder that I received on my birthday last June.

I check to see that it has a fresh tape in it. I put it under my sweater and go back into the kitchen. My mother is standing at the sink doing the dishes. I see that she is distracted. I hit the record button and ask, "How did you find our old house and why did you move back there in the first place." She says, "Well at the time me and Dutch were living in a duplex ..."

"Stop. Ok let's fast forward through your mother's story." Dr. Bornstein instructs him. "What happened next?"

"She says "Is that enough for tonight?" I say, "Yeah. That was great. Thanks." She tells me to bring Lucky in and feed him. I go outside and unchain him and he runs to the door. We go in and I get a can of his dog food and the can opener and he runs to the basement door. I go downstairs and feed him. Then I sit down and read my new library book on Harry Houdini. After that I practice my sleight of hand."

"You're a magician?" Bornstien asks.

"Yes. It's my hobby. This is why I am obsessed with finding the secret of tapping into my psychic abilities. If only I could really read minds or move objects mentally. I could then become the greatest magician the world has ever known." Paul explains.

"What makes you believe psychic powers exist?"

"Oh, because my mother has them. She's amazing, She seems to know every thought you have and finishes your sentences for you. Or answers questions that you haven't yet asked. Nine times out of ten when the telephone rings she knows who it is before she answers it." Paul explains.

"That never ceased to amaze me. I'd say "How did you know it was Donnie calling?" She'd say, "Oh, I just know his ring." Know his ring? "What does that mean?" I'd ask. Once when Pat was still in the Airforce and was stationed in Goosebay, Labrador, she and I were over at Aunt Lizzie's house.

She lived right down the street from us. We were only there about 30 minutes when my mother said, "You know I have to go home."

Aunt Lizzie said, "How come?" My mother replied, "I have the feeling Pat is going to try and sneak in for a visit." So we went home and she started getting his room ready. Sure enough at midnight the front door bell rang and there stood Pat! That was only one instance but she did that kind of thing all of the time. The funny part is I would always be astonished but she never thought anything about her abilities.

As bizarre as her psychic abilities were, even stranger were her visions. Sometimes she would have them when she was asleep and other times while she was wide awake. But once she started having them she said they were an omen of an impending death. I remember once she was sitting at the kitchen table and I saw her look up suddenly. She was looking down the hallway. I looked around and saw nothing there.

I said, "What did you see?" She said she saw a silver casket come out of her room and go down the hallway. Three days later we got the news that my cousin Bobby had been killed in Vietnam. Every time there was a death in the family, she always knew it was coming. She never knew who it was going to be but she knew someone was about to die. She hated having her abilities but I would have given anything to have even one genuine psychic experience. I admit I was envious of her powers."

"Envious?" Dr. Bornstein asks him.

"Oh yes. I was green with envy. Grandma had psychic powers, my mother had them, Donnie had some also. But I didn't seem to inherit any psychic ability at all! I felt cheated. I suppose that was why I chose magic as a hobby. If I had no real powers I could at least fake it."

"What happened next on -Septernber 23, 1968?"

"After a while I went back upstairs and watched tv until it was time for bed."

"Let's fast forward then to September 24, 1968, where are you now?" The doctor says.

"I'm in the school library. It's 2:30pm. I'm in study hall. I just finished my homework. Someone is approaching me. It's my friend Larry Troutman. He's speaking to me. He says, "Hey Pablo! Got any new tricks?"

I said, "Sure. Check this out." I pull out a pocket knife. It has black enameled sides. I show it on both sides and pass it through my hand. Now it has changed into a white pearl handled knife. I say, "If it were real magic

I could just snap my fingers and it would change in front of your eyes." It changes from white to black when I snap my fingers. "Here let me give you one of each." Passing it though my hand again I now show him that it has one side of each color.

I hand it to Larry for inspection and he says, "That's far out! How'd you do that?" I say, "Magic of course. How else?" He laughs.

At 3pm the final bell rings and I dash for my mother's car again. We race home to watch Dark Shadows. On this episode the Collins family holds a seance."

"Alright let's fast forward through the show. What happened afterwards?"

"I asked my mother if she had ever participated in a seance?" Paul replies.

"What was her answer?"

"She said that when she was a little girl her mother sent her down to the local saloon to make her father come home. She was about 10 years old at the time. When she got there all the guys in the bar were trying to talk this one guy into doing some trick that he did. He didn't want to do it because he said it caused him to have nightmares whenever he did it.

But they kept at him and he gave in. He spotted my mother in the crowd and asked her father to sit her atop of this card table. Then he stood back and held out his hands and the card table rose up on two legs while my mother was still sitting on it. She had to hold on to it to keep from falling off!

Paul continues, "Once she told me this story I thought, "If only I could do that! I excused myself and ran downstairs to my basement. I began combing through all of my books on the history of magic. I found what I was looking for. "Spiritualism". I began reading about automatic writing, seances and ouija boards. I thought, "This may be the answer I've been looking for."

I took out my pad and pen and tried my hand at automatic writing. I just let my mind go blank and let the pen just scribble on the paper. After a time I looked at the scribbles but could not make out a single word.

I wrote in my journal. "Sept. 24, 1968- My first attempt at automatic writing was a failure. I played at it awhile until my mother called me upstairs for dinner. Afterwards I recorded another one of her stories about McCawley Road."

"Let's fast forward now through her story. What happened after that?" Dr. Bornstein instructs him.

"I said, "Mom, I was wondering if you would buy me a ouija board?" Then she said, "A what? Oh Hell no! Those things are witchboards. I don't want you messing with those." So I lied and said, "But mom, I. .. I need it for a new trick I'm working on." She said, "What kind of trick?"

I said, "Well, I have somebody take a card and then instead of just telling them what it is, I have the board spell it out. It's a lot spookier that way?" She laughed and said, "Well alright. If it's for your hobby I guess it's alright. We have to go to Woolco tonight anyway to buy you some new shoes."

"Let's fast forward now to after you got home that night. Did she buy you the board?"

"Yes. It was in the game section. I couldn't wait to try it out but she insisted I go to bed."

"Very well, let's fast forward then to the first time you used it."

"It was the next night." Paul continues. "September 25, 1968. I brought it to the dinner table after I ate. I said, "Come on, let's try it.""

She said, "Oh Paul, I told you I don't like those things. They're evil."

I said, "Oh good grief! It's made by Parker Brothers. It's just a game. They sell millions of them." I said, "Come on, please. I can't do it alone. It takes two people to make it work."

She said, "Oh alright. What do you do?"

I said, "We both put our fingers on the planchette and then ask a question." So we both put our fingers on it and I asked "Is anyone there?" The planchette moved to "Yes".

I said, "You're pushing it."

She replied, "I am not!"

I said, "I felt you!"

She said, "Look I have to wash the dishes. Put that thing away."

I said, "Ok. I'm going downstairs for awhile ok?"

She said, "Ok."

So I went downstairs to my basement and placed the ouija board on the kitchen table down there and tried to work the board alone. But of course it wouldn't move. Then there was a knock on the back door. I heard my mother answer it. Then I heard footsteps approach the basement door.

It opened and my mother said, "Paul! Larry's here!" Then I saw him walking down the stairs.

"Pablo! What's up?" He said, "What that?"

I said, "It's a ouija board. Want to try it?"

He said, "That's for kids." I started making clucking sounds like a chicken.

"Funny! Oh alright. Alright!" he said.

So we placed our hands on the planchette and he said, "Now what?" I said, "We talk to the dead! Ooooooh!" He said, "Give me a break." So then I said, "Is anyone there?" The planchette began to move to "Yes". Larry said, "You pushed it." I said, "No way. You did!" Larry said, "This is boring."

I said, "You really didn't push it?" I thought, "Everybody can't be cheating. Maybe there is something really is going on here?" Larry pushed his horn rim glasses back on his nose and said, "Look Brainiac. These things have been around since my Grandmother's days. Everybody knows that they work by tapping into your subconscious mind. There's nothing supernatural about it. Parker Borothers sells millions of them. Do you want to play chess or not? I brought my board.

I said, "Sure." So for the next hour or so Larry beat me 3 times. He wasn't captain of the chess club for nothing. Then he had to be getting home.

After he left I got out the ouija board and placed my fingers on the planchette. "Is anyone there?" I asked. Nothing happened. So then I came up with an idea. "What if I use it like the pen in the automatic writing experiments? Push it, but don't control it. I said, "Is anybody there?" I pushed the planchette slightly and it slid around on the board.

After a minute or so it seemed like it was moving on it's own. Then it slid over to "Yes". I said, "Hmm ... Larry's right. I must be subconsciously pushing it." But that alone is kind of interesting.

So I gave it a little push and it slid around in a circle for a minute and then it spelled out W-H-O A-R-E Y-O-U? So I started talking to it. I said, "Who am I? My name is Paul, what's yours?"

It slid around and spelled out "H-O-W O-L-D A-R-E Y-O-U?" I said, "I'm 13. How old are you?" Then it spelled out "W-H-E-R-E DO Y-O-U L-I-V-E?" I said, "I live in Louisville, Ky. Where do you ... " Before I could even ask it spelled out "I W-I-L-L A-S-K T-H-E Q-U-E-S-T-I-O-N-S!"

I laughed and said, "Stupid board. You're supposed to answer questions." The planchette slid to "Goodbye." I said, "Hey! Wait a minute. Don't go. I'll answer any questions you'd like. It spelled out "W-H-A-T D-O Y-O-U

S-E-E-K?" I said, "I seek the secret of real magic powers. It spelled out, "W-H-Y?"

So I said, "I want to be the greatest magician the world has ever known." It spelled out, "I C-A-N H-E-L-P Y-O-U." So I said, "Can I ask a question now?" It slid to "Yes".

So I asked "Who are you? What is your name?" It spelled out "S-I-M-O-N." I said, "Simon?" How weird? Where did that come from?" I said, "Well Simon. I'm going upstairs to watch tv. Can I talk to you again?" It slid to "Yes".

I wrote in my journal, "I played with the ouija board tonight by myself and it seems like I was really talking to someone but most likely it was just my imagination. But it is still kind of fun." I then went upstairs and watched "Batman" on tv. Then it was time for bed.

"Let's fast forward now to September 26, 1968. It is after school and you have gone down to your basement. What is happening?" Dr. Bornstein instructs him.

"I tried an experiment in telepathy, then telekinesis and after that clairvoyance. I'd stare into a glass of water as a make shift crystal ball. I'd look for 30 to 40 minutes hoping to see something ... anything. Then I gave up. I wrote in my journal, "I'm getting nowhere fast with my esp experiments. I guess I'm about as psychic as an oyster."

I then went upstairs to watch tv for awhile. The telephone rang. My mother was busy vacuuming, I hear her yell, "Paul! Get the phone! It's Donnie calling!" I picked up the telephone in the kitchen and said "Hello Donnie." Donnie laughed on the other end and said "Is the witchy woman there?" I said, "Yeah. Here she comes." She took the reciever.

I said, "I'm going downstairs for awhile." I went down to the basement and opened my journal. I wrote, "Mom did it again. She always knows who it is when the phone rings. Why can't I do that?"

I closed my journal and took out my ouija board and placed my hands on the planchette. I said, "Is anybody there?" As before I gently pushed the planchette. It moved in a circle for a moment and then slid over to "Yes".

I said, "Is that you Simon?" Again it pointed to "Yes". I asked "Why do I have no psychic abilities?" It spelled out, "Everyone does." I said, "Not me." It began to spell faster and easier and I was always surprised by the answer. It said, "If you believe you can do something or you believe that you cannot, either way you are right."

I laughed at that and said, "That's pretty profound for a figment of my imagination. Ok Simon. Do you feel like answering some questions now?" The board replied, "What would you like to know?"

I asked, "What is your last name?" It said, "We had no last names." I asked, "Where on earth do people have no last names?" It replied, "Samaria." I said, "I don't know where that is." It replied, "It no longer exists."

I said, "Were you once alive?" It said, " I still am. There is no such thing as death." I asked. "When were you born?" It answered "13 BC by your calendar." I said, " 13 BC!! You've got to be kidding! Tell me more."

It said, "What would you like to know?" I said, "Tell me your life story."

Here is the answer I received, "I Simon, know as Simon of Samaria, Simon of Gitta or Simon the Gnostic was born in the nation of Samaria, north of Judea and south of Galilee from the small village of Gitta. My father's name was Antonius. He was a Roman soldier. My mother's name was Rachel. She was a Jewish whore who was barren all of her life.

She was troubled and shocked by her pregnancy. For the penalty for any woman sleeping with a Roman soldier was death by stoning."

The message was coming so fast now I could barely keep up with it. I kept thinking, "Where is all of this coming from?" The message just went on. " ... She decided not to tell my father. She disappeared and moved into the home of her aunt Miriam until she gave birth. I was born with blue eyes. A dead givaway to my Roman blood.

Her aunt came up with a plan. She knew a wealthy merchant from Alexandria and made arrangements to sell me into slavery to him. From the time I was able to walk I had to work. But I knew that someday I would run-a-way. My chance finally came when I was seven years old.

While helping to load wool onto a ship I dove off the gang plank and into the water.

I swam to shore and escaped into the city streets."

I asked, "How did you eat? Where did you sleep?" It answered, "I was but one of many street children. Alexandria was ripe with gangs of children. It didn't take long for one of them to locate me. It was from them that I learned how to steal and thus I grew up in the streets.

When I grew older I became the leader of the gang. Then when I was the age that you are now, I was caught stealing in the sacred temple by the high priest whose name was Tanaim. The price for simple theft was to lose one's hand but to steal from a Holy place meant death. Knowing that I was caught, I knelt before him and offered him my head. Saying "Do what you must. As I have." So impressed was he with my bravery that he spared my life.

But made me his slave as the price for my crime. I thought secretly that I would soon escape again. But I was so well treated that all thoughts of leaving soon fled me. It was the first real home I had ever known and Tanaim was very pleased with me. I became the son he never had. So it was there in the temple that I began to learn the secrets of high magic." I said aloud, "So you were a magician then?" "I still am." Was the reply."

Just then I heard my mother calling me to dinner. I put the board away and went upstairs. I ate my hamburger and fries in a daze. I couldn't get over the bizarre story that flowed out of me. Oh I was aware that I was moving the planchette. But it seemed like each letter would pop into my head, before I moved it. I tried to be rational about it all. Larry told me the board taps into your subconscious mind. Perhaps this was all from a story I had read somewhere.

After I ate I went to my room and did my homework. Then I watched tv in my room until it was time to go to sleep. By then I had convinced myself that I was just letting my imagination run away with me."

"Let us fast forward to the next day." Dr.Bornstein instructs him. "Now it is September 27, 1968. Where are you now?"

"It's Friday. I'm in study hall. It's 2:30pm in my High school library. I started looking in the reference section trying to see if there was any info that could verify any of the strange story I had received on the ouija board. Then Larry came up to me. "Hey Pablo, what's up?" I said, "Larry have you ever heard of a magician named Simon of Samaria?" He said, "You mean besides the Biblical one?"

I said, "Whoa! There's a Biblical one?" He laughed at me and said, "You know for an honor roll student you need to go back to Sunday school." I said, "Hey! I'm Catholic. We never had Sunday school!"

He walked over to the Theology section and pulled out a copy of the New Testament. "It's in Acts, I think ... Here you go? So what's your interest?" I said, "Oh ... uh ... I have a report to do on him is all." That was only the first of many lies I would have to tell in my lifetime to keep my secret. But I didn't know that then. Larry said, "Whoa! Look! There's Sharon Smyth! Check out those ta tas!"

But I didn't even hear him as I couldn't believe what I was reading? He looked at me and said, "You kill me! You're so pathetic! You'd rather read a book than check out the hottest chick in Southern High School!" I said, "I'm sorry Larry. What did you say?" He just rolled his eyes and said, "I give up!"

He walked away but I barely noticed for I was reading Acts; chapter 8; verses 9-25. "But there was a certain man called Simon, which before time in the same city used sorcery and bewitched the people of Samaria. Giving out that he himself was some great one! To whom they all gave heed, from the least to the greatest saying, this man is the great power of God. And to him they had regard because of that long time he had bewitched them with sorceries.

But when they believed Phillip preaching the things concerning the Kingdom of God and the name Jesus Christ, they were baptized both men and women. Then Simon himself believed also and when he was baptized he continued with Phillip and wondered, beholding the miracles that were done.

Now when the Apostles which were in Jeruselem heard that Samaria had received the word of God, they sent unto them Peter and John. Who when they were come down prayed for them that they might receive the Holy Spirit. And when Simon saw that through the laying on of the Apostle's hands the Holy Spirit was given, he offered them money saying, give me also this power, that whomsoever that I lay my hands, he may receive the Holy Spirit.

But Peter said unto him, "Thy money perish with thee. Because thou hast thought that the gift of God may be purchased with money. Thou hast neither part nor lot in this matter; For thy heart is not right in the sight of God. Repent therefore of this wickedness, and pray God, if perhaps the thought of thine heart may be forgiven thee. For I perceive that thou art in the gall of bitterness and the bond of iniquity.

"Then answered Simon and said, "pray ye to the Lord for me that none of these things which ye have spoken come upon me." And when they had testified and preached the word of the Lord, returned to Jeruselem and preached the gospel in many villages of Samaritans ... "

I closed the Bible and put it back on the shelf. I was certain that I had never heard of Simon Magus before this and yet the message spoke of a magician named Simon from Samaria. But then my logic fought its way back in control and I thought, "Well since this is a Biblical character I no doubt had heard this passage some time in the past and simply had no conscious recollection of it. I must be pulling it out of my subconscious mind somehow. But still I found that alone to be amazing."

"Let us fast forward now to after you came home. Did you receive any more of the message that day?" Bornstein asks.

"Yes. I said, "Simon are you there?" He replied "I am always here." I said, "You were telling me your life story. You left off when you were age 13 and were caught stealing in the temple."

He said, "I spent the next ten years of my life there studying the secrets of high magic." I said, "I am a magician as well. But only a trickster who does magic tricks for my friends. I have always longed to do real magic." He said, "The tricks as you call them had their roots in Egypt. They are real magic to the one who observes them. It is the lowest form of magic, but magic nonetheless. It is psychological magic."

I said, "Yes, but I want to be able to really make things float. Not depend on strings." He said, "You have to crawl before you can walk. In the temple the first thing I had to learn was the art of illusion. While Egyptian magicians believed wholeheartedly in the reality of their magic, true ceremonial or high magic can take months of preparation and sometimes days to perform.

But the general populace expected instant miracles from their magicians and thus the illusions were created to satisfy the instant gratification of the people."

I said, "Simon I read about you in the New Testament today and a few things are bothering me. For instance, if you're the real Simon of Samaria, how is it you speak fluent 20th century English?" He replied, "The messages you are receiving are telepathic. It is your mind which translates it into language.

I said, "Ok but why would Simon Magus, one of the most famous magicians of all time contact a 13 year old kid from Louisville, Kentucky of all places?" He replied, "I am not yet ready to reveal that to you. But in time you shall know." I said, "Very well. Go on with your story then."

He replied, "As I said, I spent the next ten years in the temple, studying magic. Then on my 23rd year my real father Antonius finally located me. He had been searching for me all of those years. He gave me my citizenship papers. I was now a free man and a citizen of the Roman empire. Free to travel anywhere in the empire I wished. I learned from my father that my mother Rachel had been murdered by one of her patrons not long after she had sold me into slavery.

On her death bed she sent for Antonius and informed him that he had a son. So it was then that I began my journeys. I traveled to Persia, India and the far east. Learning from the Persian magi, the Hindu Yogis and the Buddhist monks in their own mystery schools. Wherever I went I astonished the locals with my magic. I became the most celebrated wonder-worker of my day. My fame preceded me and I received invitations from Kings and Emperors."

My mother called me to dinner at that time. It took me hours to get the message one letter at a time on the ouija board, because I had to keep stopping to write it down. So I only received a small portion of the message a little each day. But I found it quite fun. I was not taking any of it seriously of course, It was just a game I was playing with my own subconscious as far as I was concerned.

It was Friday night and my father came home and went to his bedroom. My mother and I drove out to Fairdale to pick up my cousin Rickey. He was still being forced to come over on the weekends. We made the best of it though. I couldn't do any of my occult experiments or use the ouija board around him of course.

He would not have approved. Uncle Robert and all of Rick's family were devout Baptists. He stayed until Sunday night and we took him home. My father got up early Monday morning and hit the road again. As usual I went back to school."

(The following is the transcript from hypnotic session number 2. From Paul Michelson's 3rd appointment on July 8, 1995. We will forgo the repeat of the process of putting Mr. Michelson in a hypnotic trance and focus on the text of the actual hypnotic regression. Dr. Bornstein)

"It's now September 30, 1968 Mr. Michelson. Did you continue with your ouija board experiment after school that day?" Dr. Bornstein asked.

"Yes I did. I said, "Simon tell me more about your life." The planchette began to move. It spelled out, "During my travels I kept hearing of the astonishing miracles of a rival wonder worker called Rabbi Yeshua Ben Yosef. Known to you as Jesus of Nazareth." "Did you meet Jesus?" I asked.

"No. Sadly he was put to death just after I arrived in Judea. I met a man named Dositheus who now led the followers of the late John the Baptist.

From him I learned of the career of Jesus and his untimely death. Had I arrived early enough to meet him I would probably have warned him not to perform his wonders for the Hebrews. For they were famous for killing their own prophets. I stayed with Dositheus but a short time when I received word from Samaria that my father Antonius had died.

I had inherited his estate in Gitta. So it was that I left for home. Once there I claimed my estate and had every intention of settling down there. As with everywhere else I went I began to perform my magic in the streets of Gitta and was soon being clamored to perform for the rich and powerful in Samaria."

Just then my mother called me to dinner. I put the board away and went upstairs to the kitchen. After I ate and did my homework I watched tv until it was time for bed. That night was the first time I heard the walking sounds."

"Tell me about that?" The doctor asks.

"I went to bed at 9pm." Paul continues. "I vaguely heard my mother go to her room at around 10pm. I slept soundly as usual but at 3am I awoke with a start. I felt terrified but did not know why? I looked at the clock to see what time it was. I tried to roll over and dismiss it. The house was so quiet you could hear a pin drop. That was when I first heard the footsteps, distinct footsteps. Just as though someone were walking in the hallway outside my room in their socks only.

You could hear every floorboard creak in the hardwood floor. I heard it near the bathroom. Then I could hear it pass my mother's room and then turn the corner. It was getting closer to my room. I heard it stop right outside my bedroom door. My heart was in my mouth. I waited for over a minute and then I heard it go back the way it came. Then more silence. But somehow I felt relieved like I knew that it was gone. I got out of bed and opened my bedroom door. I peeked around the corner. No one was there.

I walked to my mother's room and listened at her door. She always ground her teeth in her sleep. She was definitely sleeping. I thought, "If it wasn't her, then who was it?" I went back to bed and eventually calmed down enough to go back to sleep.

I mentioned it the next morning at breakfast and my mother became very worried. She told me they all used to hear that same sound back on McCawley Road. She told me she thought someone was trying to bewitch us. I just rolled my eyes when she wasn't looking of course. By now I was sure it was all just my imagination working overtime. So I went on to school."

"Let's fast forward in time now to the afternoon of October 1st, 1968. Did you continue your ouija board experiment after school?" Bornstein asks.

"Yes it was Tuesday and I could hardly wait to get home to see what message I would get today?" Paul continues. "It was so much fun. So I went downstairs and got my board and began to talk to my imaginary friend Simon.

I said, "I read about your encounter with the Apostles in the New Testament but I would love to hear your version of the story." The planchette began to move. "That took place in the Samaritan city of Sabaste. I was in the middle of performing street magic to quite a large crowd when one man shouted, "Come quickly! We are doubly blessed this day! Two disciples of Jesus are here. Down by the river!" So the crowd began to rush to the river out of curiosity. I too, was delighted to hear the news.

I'd always wanted to meet his followers ever since I learned of him. So I too accompanied them. As I listened to Phillip and Thomas I was moved by the words of Jesus and when I saw them cure a blind woman I knew that this was a magic that I had never seen. Many at the end of their sermon went down to the river to be baptized by them. I joined them and was baptized as well.

I waited patiently until the crowd had dispersed and then introduced myself to Phillip. We sat through the night talking of God and the Kingdom of God. In him I found a kindred spirit and one who also thirsted for more knowledge. So it was that he invited me to travel with them and I eagerly did so. Phillip told me that the things I had witnessed him do were nothing compared to what Simon Peter, the leader of the Apostles could do.

I confess that I was a bit relieved to hear that he no longer went by the name Simon. I feared two wonder workers traveling about with the same name could cause much confusion. I spent six weeks with Phillip and Thomas and then we received word that two of the Apostles were coming to Samaria.

When I first saw Peter, he was a short stocky man and John was tall and lean. I admit I was a bit shocked by their appearance. They looked more like beggars to me than men of importance.

Nevertheless I stood silently by and watched as they conversed with Phillip and Thomas. Then I heard Peter ask them to kneel down and as I watched he placed his hands on their heads and prayed that they would receive the power of the Holy Spirit. "So that's it!" I thought. That is the secret to their magic. The power is transferable by touch!"

Now as a brother magician you know full well that when one magician sees something that another magician does, that he himself wishes to do, he should never copy it or worse steal it. The proper etiquette between magicians is to offer to buy the secret. So quite innocently I spoke up and offered Peter a considerable sum in silver if he would pass on this power to me.

But Peter became red in the face upon hearing my offer and bellowed "Your money perish with you for believing you could buy the power of the Holy Spirit!" Now I was offended. But realizing I had offended the Apostles and embarrassed my new friend Phillip I made my apologies and left their company. I never went back."

Then my mother called me to dinner. As I ate I thought about what Simon had said. I realized that had I been there or any other magician we would have offered them anything to pass on their powers to us. So his actions that day were perfectly understandable from a magicians point of view.

Still as always, I had no preconceived idea of what the answer would be when I asked my questions? So I was as surprised as ever by the details of the story."

"Very well let us move forward now in time to October 2nd, 1968. It is Wednesday. Where are you now?"

"I'm back in the school library . I'rn trying to find more information on Simon Magus. I found material in four sections. First in the theology section. Most of the material on Simon seemed to have been written by the Christian fathers who hated him. Then in the occult section I found many books that mentioned him.

Those written by spiritualists seemed to portray him as a misunderstood medium. In the entertainment and arts section I found many books on the history of stage magic that describe Simon in glowing terms.

He is seen as one of the first magicians who brought the illusions out of the temple and into the streets to the common man. They see him as a brother trickster who made his living playing it mysterious for the gullible. Also in the theology section I found books by modern practitioners of the religion of Gnosticism. These books hail Simon as their founder and call him an incarnation of God.

So to the Christians he is in league with the Devil. To the Gnostics he is a god. To stage magicians he is a brother performer and to parapsychologists a man with mediumistic powers. I had to wonder just who was the real Simon Magus?"

Dr. Bornstein instructs him, "Let's fast forward to your ouija board experiment of that day."

"I asked Simon to continue telling me his story. Simon replied "Although rejected by the Apostles I was not soured on the teachings of Jesus. I returned to Judea where I sought out the cult of John, now led by Dositheus. Since I had left Dositheus had proclaimed himself to be the true Messiah and so I challenged him to a duel of magic and soundly defeated him in front of his followers. I now assumed leadership of the group.

Like myself, Jesus was an intellectual. From the stories I heard from Phillip he had been a child prodigy who confounded the scholars in the temple at age twelve. By adulthood he was so far ahead of his peers intellectually he seemed almost to be speaking another language. His followers like Peter were uneducated fishermen and did not understand what Jesus was saying half of the time when he lived among them?

With Jesus cut down early in his career by the jealously of those who considered him a threat to their position in the community, who was left to carryon his mission? Fishermen and uneducated rabble who had inherited his powers but not his wisdom. So I took it upon myself to spread the true ministry of Jesus. Being a scholar of every religion of the day I felt I was far better suited to teach it than Peter and his ilk. So in the beginning there were now two branches of Christianity. Although it was not yet called that nor seen as separate from Judaism.

Peter was determined to first convert his fellow Jews before spreading the message to the gentiles. So I had a free reign to spread Christianity to the gentiles and was as responsible for it's spread as was the Apostle Paul who would come later. Though I was never given any credit for it. Later Paul, another scholar also rejected by Peter followed my path and converted a lot of my followers to Pauline Christianity. He started the third branch of Christianity.

When I traveled to Tyre I met the great love of my life. Her name was Helena and she was but a beautiful dark haired teenager when I first beheld her. She was the slave of a wealthy merchant and the moment I saw her I knew that she must be mine. I nave no doubt that if anyone else had asked to purchase her he would have refused.

But one advantage of being the most famous sorcerer in the world was that people feared me. So when I offered him a tidy sum in silver for her he reluctantly relented. Helena was my devoted companion until my death."

That was all of the message I received that day." Paul explains. "I went up to supper. Then after I ate and did my homework I watched tv until bedtime. Then at 3am I once again woke up feeling frightened for no reason. I tried to go back to sleep when once again I heard soft footsteps out in the hallway. My fear kept growing as I could hear it coming closer and closer to my door. I heard it stop outside my door again. I held my breath as it seemed to stand there for an eternity.

But really it was only a minute or two. Then I heard it leaving again. It went back up the hallway. Just as I started to feel relieved I heard the footsteps coming back down the hallway. Much louder this time! Anger dispelled my fear and I leapt from my bed and stood by my closed door waiting for it to arrive.

Just when I was sure it was there I jerked open my door. My mother was standing there and we both screamed at the same time. Then we laughed so hard I had to sink to the floor in hysterics. After I got up I followed her into the kitchen.

I was still giggling when I said, "That must have been you I heard the first time." She said, "No! I heard it too! I thought it was you! That's why I got up to see what you were doing awake?" Well that worried us both. But we both eventually relaxed enough to go back to bed."

"Very well, let us fast forward now to the events of Thursday October 3, 1968. Where are you now?" Dr. Bornstein asks.

"Back in the library reading more about Simon in the encyclopedias."

"I want you to focus on the page. Can you see it? Try pausing the memory like a video."

"Yes." Paul says.

"Read it to me."

"Simon Magus; 1st century sorcerer mentioned in Acts of the Apostles for whom the term Simony was named. According to other writings the magician Simon had God like powers. He could reputedly become invisible, move objects with his mind, change his form to other people or animals, be unharmed by fire, walk though walls and fly through the air ... " I became very excited when I read this."

"Why is that?"

"If it turned out that I really was in contact with the spirit of Simon Magus then he may be able to teach me how to do all of these things. I would then truly become the greatest magician the world has ever known." Paul explains.

"I see. Let us fast forward now to your ouija board message of October 3rd, 1968." Bornstein instructs him.

"I said, "Simon you were telling me about your death." He replied, "In the year 66AD I received an invitation from Rome. I had been there years before under Claudius and had started my own mystery school there.

In my absense the Apostle Paul came to Rome and also started his own rival church. But Claudius had died and Nero had become Caesar. He had begun to arrest philosophers and persecute Christians.

He was a very jealous Caesar who didn't appreciate a lowly Samaritan subject receiving so much adoration and praise. Paul himself was arrested and thrown into prison. I was of course, unaware of this and so the moment I arrived in Rome I too was seized and tossed into prison.

My execution was to be by beheading in the Roman forum. But I wasn't finished yet. I still had many followers in Rome. At my instructions they bribed the guard who was watching me and replaced him and the executioner with my men.

One of the prime illusions I used was called "The Floating Head Illusion". It involved a trick ax and chopping block that enabled me to create the illusion that my head had been cut off. So I had my men substitute the trick ax and block for the one used in the forum.

The date of my execution had come and I was led out in chains into the Roman forum. It was packed with people who had come to watch the famous sorcerer die. I knelt down and placed my head on the block and my assistant swung the ax. To the audience it looked exactly like my head had been chopped off.

But the cheers from the crowd were suddenly cut off into shocked silence when my "headless" body stood up, reached into the basket and put my head back on! The silence was followed by cheers and the crowd began chanting my name. "Simon, Simon, Simon" echoed through the forum.

Nero who was present was horrified, shocked, fearful and amused all at the same time. Seeing my popularity he decided to play to the crowd and appointed me Imperial Court Magician. It was my greatest and proudest achievement. I was the one and only person to ever hold such a title in the history of the Roman empire. But it would ultimately lead to my doom.

Months passed and Helena and I enjoyed my new position. I was furnished with a beautiful home in which I moved my school. There I taught philosphy and religion. But near the end of the year I was summoned to the Imperial Court. Nero who despised this new Jewish cult called Christians because they denied his God-hood had already caught and executed hundreds of them and beheaded the Apostle Paul.

Peter who received word that Paul had been beheaded and that I had been converting many Romans to my beliefs chose to come to Rome himself. But Nero had now captured him as well.

But simply executing Peter was not good enough for Nero. He needed to humiliate him. So it was that I was summoned to the Imperial Court. Nero declared that there would be a duel of magic between myself and Simon Peter to demonstrate that my powers in the service of Nero were far superior to Peter's powers in the service of Jesus.

Now I don't have to tell you that I did not like this idea at all! First of all I had witnessed Peter's powers myself all of those years before and knew that he was powerful indeed. Worse yet there was no way to really win.

If I refused an Imperial order Nero would have be crucified right next to Peter. If I won the duel Peter and Paul's followers would assassinate me and of course if I lost the duel I would embarrass Nero and he would have me killed.

Nero was very crafty and he didn't like me much more than Peter and he saw this as an opportunity to be rid of us both. Nero feared my powers and secretly hoped to use this rival wonder worker to destroy me and be free of us both.

As for Peter, despite our initial misunderstanding I wished him no harm. Remember I still considered myself a Christian of sorts. But I really had no choice in the matter. I had to do my utmost to win this duel of Nero would have me executed.

Now over the years since I had last seen him I had learned the secrets of magic in all the cultures of the world. I was certain that my powers were superior to his but there was an easier way to win this contest, because I was also a master of illusion as well.

The contest was to be held in 3 days. I spent my time setting up a little surprise for everyone. The day of the contest came and once again the forum was packed with people. Peter was led out in chains. I bowed to him. We'd not seen each other in so many years and his hair was now as white as my own had become.

I announced to Nero and the crowd that I would now perform a miracle that even Jesus had not done in his day. I would fly through the air. I spread my arms which was the cue for my assistant backstage to begin to turn the crank which was connected to the thin wire which ran to a harness beneath my robes.

I felt it grow taut and to the astonished crowd it looked as though I was rising into the air. Higher and higher I rose and then my assistant began to turn the second crank which caused me to spin in the air in an ever widening circle. To the crowd I appeared to be flying around the forum.

But Peter at that moment dropped to his knees and in a loud voice cried out for God to end this spectacle. Now unbeknownst to me a Roman centurion who was backstage was also secretly a Christian.

When he discovered my assistant turning the crank he yelled "cheater", drew his sword, killed my assistant and cut my wire. I started to fall of course. I dropped like a stone. I tried to land on my feet but broke both of my legs.

"There was a riot and the crowd rushed the stage. In the confusion my assistants smuggled me out of there and hid me. Peter was taken away and crucified upside down. I lived for 3 more weeks, I was 79 years old at the time and I grew increasingly weak and died."

"It was then that my mother called me to dinner. After I ate I went to my room and did my homework. Then I couldn't find anything on tv so I put on one of my Beatles' album. The Magical Mystery Tour. My mother yelled at me to put on my headphones so I did. Later that night my mother came to my room and sprinkled me with Holy water. I said, "Hey! What was that for?" She said, "Protection.""

I went on to sleep. Then I awoke again at 3am and heard the walking sounds in the hallway. But I had lost my fear of it by this time and rolled over and went back to sleep."

"Alright let's fast forward to October 4th, 1968. It's Friday. Where are you?" Bornstein asks.

"I'm in the library again" Paul says, "But I'm not alone. I see Larry approaching me. I'm showing one of my magic tricks to two girls. I say, "Ok watch this closely. Here I have two balls made of sponge." I set them on the library table.

"Ok hold out your hand." I say to Barbara. She does. "Now you take this one." I place one sponge ball in her hand, close her fingers around it and turn her hand palm down. "And now I'll take this one." I pick up the other one and place it in my own closed fist.

"Now watch." I snap my fingers and open my hand and my sponge ball is gone. I say "Open your hand," She does and screams because now she is holding two sponge balls. Barbara says, "Oh my God! How did you do that?" "I told you he was weird!" Phyllis said as they giggle and run off.

Larry said, "Well Pablo! Maybe there's hope for you after all." I said, "Well I finally found a way to get girls to notice me but now they are afraid of me!"

"If nothing else pertinent occurred then let's fast forward in time. Did you continue your ouija board experiment that afternoon?" Dr. Bornstein asks.

"Yes. I said, "Hello Simon." He replied, "Greetings little one." I said, "Simon you left off with your death in 66AD. What is it like to die?" He said, "Not as fearful as you believe. I died in my sleep and did not know for a moment what had happened to me?

Suddenly my pain was gone and I was euphoric. It was only after I had risen from my bed that I realized what must have happened? My followers buried me secretly in the catacombs and my remains are there to this day." "Can I visit them someday?" I asked. Simon replied, "That would be most difficult to do little one."

I said, "Why is that?" He said, "My bones lay directly beneath the main altar of the Vatican." I said, "What? But that's where the bones of St. Peter are supposed to be!" Simon replied, "So they believe. But common sense should have told them that as a devout Jew, Simon Peter would never be buried in a pagan cemetery. His body was taken back to Jeruselem by his followers."

I said, "So how did this legend get started?" Simon said, "The Christian church did not become the legal religion of Rome until Constantine was converted to Christianity some 300 years after Peter, Paul and I died in Rome. Now as I said my followers in Rome were also believers in Jesus, so when I died, the Gnostic Christians as they were to be called later began visiting my grave and it became a pilgrimage site.

Remember that both Peter and I were named Simon. So as time progressed some Gnostic Christians converted to Pauline Christianity. There were also many marriages between families and the line blurred between the two sects. By the time of Constantine the legend of Simon Peter, the Christian being crucified on Vatican Hill had merged with the legend of Simon the Gnostic Christian being buried in the catacombs."

I said, "Oh my God! So the Vatican is built over your gravesite not Peter's?" He replied," Personally I find it most amusing. The same church which branded me as everything from a black magician to an anti-Christ has built its Holiest shrine over my bones."

Just then I heard my mother calling me to dinner. As usual my mind was on the information I had just received. Where was all of this coming from? I was just getting comfortable with the idea that my subconscious had retained everything I had ever read and that this board was like a self hypnosis tool that enabled me to retrieve that information.

But this latest bombshell really flipped me out! I know that I've never read that it is the bones of Simon Magus under the main alter of the Vatican, not Simon Peter's. Where the heck did that come from?

After dinner we went to Fairdale to pick up Rickey again. He spent the weekend with us and we took him home on Sunday night as usual. I was tempted to tell him about the ouija board experiment but I was always afraid he'd tell me mother and I knew she would break it in half if she found out. So I kept it to myself.

Sunday night at 3am I awoke to a new sound. I heard scratching sounds coming from the wall that my head rested against. I got up and turned on the light. I still heard it. I thought, "We must have mice."

(This ends the transcript of the second hypnotic regression session. The following is the transcript of the 3rd hypnotic regression session on Mr. Paul Michelson's 4th appointment with me on July 15th, 1995)

"The day is Monday October 7th, 1968. Where are you now?" Bornstein asks.

"I'm back in the school library looking for more information on the historical Simon Magus." Paul replies. "In a book on the history of magic I read, "Simon Magus; controversial figure of the NT. Described variously as a Christian, Jew and Pagan, the founder of a new religion, am magician, a sorcerer, a religious philosopher, and an arch-heretic; A pseudo Apostle, a pseudo Messiah and a pretended incarnation of God. Often called "The father of all heresies."

I thought, "My goodness. Simon seems to be the only character in the New Testament that is more controversial that Jesus himself." I checked out six books with references to Simon Magus. I was walking down the hall looking like a stack of books with legs, when one of the many bullies who picked on me daily, named Bradley Walker, stuck his foot out and tripped me deliberately. I fell flat on my stomach and books scattered everywhere.

I heard a chorus of laughter and giggles as I got up and started picking up my things. "What's the matter short stuff? Walk much?" He laughed and his gang of thugs laughed with him. They moved on and Larry showed up to help me pick up my books, He said, "Pay no attention to that creep. He'll get his someday."

'Were you bullied frequently?" The doctor asked.

"Almost daily. My poor health had stunted my growth and I was a head shorter than my entire class. It didn't help that my mother wouldn't let me leave the house. I was never seen outside of school. Only Larry befriended me and would visit me at home."

"Let's fast forward then to your ouija board experiment that afternoon."

"I said, "Hello Simon."

He replied. "I am here."

I asked, "If you died way back in 66AD why are you earthbound?"

Simon replied, "Unfinished business."

I said, "Explain."

Simon said, "I felt that only I understood the true meaning and message of Jesus. Peter and Paul couldn't seem to agree on anything.

But both seemed determined to turn Christianity into a religion about Jesus rather than the religion of Jesus."

I said, "I'm not sure I understand either."

Hesaid, "Rabbi Yeshua was a Jew. All of his ancestors were Jews and 99% of all of his followers were Jews. He never left Judaism, nor asked any of his followers to leave it."

His entire ministry he always pointed people towards God, never himself. He never said, "When I die I want you to stop praying to the father and pray to me instead."

He never said, "I want huge cathedrals built in my name and golden statues of me placed inside for people to bow down to." As a Jew he would have been horrified at the thought.

I ask you. If Jesus was so pleased with the job Peter was doing in carrying on his mission, then why appear to Paul? Because Paul being a scholar like me was better equipped to teach than a fisherman. But Paul also seemed determined to deify Jesus. Jesus became more important than the things he taught.

But I was a student of all philosophies and religions. I was as versed in Greek philosophy as I was in Persian Zoroastrianism, Hinduism of India or Buddhism as well. Mine was a universal religion that accepted all other religions and merged with them.

That was why my teachings were so much easier to accept for the pagans. They weren't asked to abandon their old gods only to see them in this new way as manifestations of the one true God. So I felt bound to stay on earth so that the truth of my teachings would not be lost.

For nearly 300 years my sect of Christianity was a close rival to Pauline Christianity. Until the Emperor Constantine was converted to Pauline Christianity. Once in power they set out to destroy all other faiths. Most of the Gnostic writings were burnt and most of the Gnostics with them. What would Yeshua have thought of that?

Jesus was not a Christian, he was a Jew. Buddha was not a Buddhist, he was a Hindu monk. Martin Luther was not a Lutheran, he was a Catholic priest.

History always repeats itself. Each of these men were not revolutionaries and had no intention of starting a new religion at all. They were reformers trying to change their own religions from within. Always it is the followers who start the new religion based on their teachings and against the will of their founders."

I asked, "So what did you teach exactly and did you believe that Jesus was the Son of God?" Simon replied, "I taught that Jesus was an incarnation of God but that so is every single human being. I believe that the only real difference in people like Jesus or Krishna or the Buddha was that they knew exactly who they were and acted accordingly. If you believed even for a second that you were one with God, you could perform every miracle that they did and even more so.

This is what Rabbi Yeshua meant when he said "That if you had faith the size of a mustard seed you could say to a mountain, cast yourself into the sea and it would be done." Here is another example. When Yeshua walked on the water. He asked Peter to get out of the boat and do the same. For a moment Peter was able to do it, but then he doubted and began to sink."

I asked "So exactly what is your unfinished business then? To correct the errors of Christianity." Simon said, "Yes. For if the world had followed the true teachings of Jesus they would not be a group of Jesus worshippers but a group of Jesus like beings. This knowledge has been surpressed by the Church for 2000 years now.

But even in death I have found a way to keep the flame of truth burning still. It has been passed down in secret. For I became the spirit guide to many mystics and magicians down through the ages who have preserved the true path to salvation." I asked, "Can you name some of them?"

Simon replied, "Apollonius of Tyana, Albertus Magnus, Cornelius Agrippa, Paracelsus, Nostradamus, Alessandro Cagliostro, Edward Kelly the associate of Dr. John Dee, Eliphas Levi, Gregori Rasputin and Aleister Crowley to name only a few of the more famous ones."

Just then my mother called me to dinner. I was thinking about my latest message and now I had more names to look up. Clearly my subconscious already knew the names. So what must be happening here is that my subconscious remembers everything I have ever seen, touched, tasted or smelled from birth till death.

Since I have read a mountain of books on the occult in my short life, perhaps this information that I am receiving is just something that I may have glanced at and now I am pulling it up to create this tale. That must be it.

I went to my room and watched tv. All the while hearing those scratching sounds again. I went and got my mother but every time she'd come in to my room it would stop. At 9 pm I went on to bed.

At 3am I awoke feeling terrified again. Then I heard a sound that made my blood freeze. Something was breathing in my room! I was laying in bed so that my back was to the wall. Yet I was hearing someone breathing behind me. Long, slow, open mouth kind of breaths. Hoping it might be my own breathing behind me somehow, I held my breath.

The sound stopped a moment later. I began to breathe normally and then the sound started up again. So I held my breath again and again it stopped. So when I started breathing again it started up too a moment later. I was starting to breathe easier thinking it must somehow be me.

But I held my breath one more time to be sure. This time the sound continued. My terror tripled now. Not only was it not coming from me but whatever was doing it was playing games with me. I was so terrified now I began to pray. I thought, "Lord if there really is something in this room with me please give me a sign!" Well I no sooner thought that then it sounded like someone rapped hard once on my bedroom window! One loud rap!

Man! I flew out of that bed and ran to my mother's room. My mother said, "What is it?" I couldn't get the words out fast enough. She couldn't understand what I was saying for a minute until I calmed down enough to tell her about the breathing and the rap on the window. She took her bottle of Holy Water and went to my bedroom and began sprinkling my bed and the room. We both sat up for an hour until I felt calm enough to go back to sleep."

Dr. Bornstein instructs, "Let us fast forward now to October 8th, 1968. It's Tuesday. Where are you now?"

"I'm back in the school library trying to look up information on the names I received on my ouija board."

"Very well if nothing pertinent happened let us fast forward to your ouija board message that afternoon." The doctor said.

Paul contines, "I said, "Simon it's me. I have some more questions.""

Simon said, "Ask them."

I said, "You stated yesterday that your teachings bring enlightenment but then you named some famous magicians and mystics who you say passed down this secret knowledge. But from what I've read Cagliostro was a famous fraud, Rasputin an evil manipulator and Aleister Crowley so evil that he even named himself "The Beast". So how do account for associating yourself with such historically evil men?"

Simon replied, "History is always written by the victors. When Constantine was converted to Pauline Christianity this put them in the power seat. Once in power they set out to obliterate all other religions save their own. Nor was even any other version of Christianity tolerated except for the official version.

Needless to say my followers teachings were branded heresy. 300 years of writings burned and anyone who did not convert was put to the sword. I was labeled "The Father of all Heresies" So to this day you will read nothing positive about me nor those who followed me.

Let us review the mystics one at a time." I said, "The first one you mentioned was Apollonius of Tyana." Simon said, "Yes. After my death in 66AD I knew that the best way to correct the errors being spread by Pauline Christianity would be to present to the world a new wonder worker.

One that would rival Jesus himself in power and yet be a pagan. As a disembodied spirit I could now communicate only with those who had the power of clairvoyance. Fortunately at that time in 66AD Apollonius of Tyana had come to Rome due to the persecution of philpsopher's by Nero. He had come to defend a good friend of his, a philosopher who had been arrested.

As a spirit I can easily see the energy of the human aura, which is composed of the same higher energy as my own spiritual body. Apollonius glowed like a bonfire amongst candles. I came to him while he slept. I had already met him once in life. Just before Nero had come up with his foolish magic duel.

So when I came to him in his dreams he knew me. I told him that I could not rest in peace until my mission was completed and bid him to help me. He saw the wisdom of my mission and vowed to help me.

I showed him that it would take a wonder worker on the level of Jesus to so capture the world's imagination that they would follow him and then the world could be placed on the road to salvation through his teachings.

I told him the first step in the plan was to capture the world's attention by showing them a pagan could work miracles just like Jesus. This was the opposite of what the Pauline Christians were teaching that miracles could only be worked by invoking the name of Jesus.

I told him I would teach him all that I knew through dream revelations and between my magical knowledge and his natural psychic abilities his power would be staggering. And so it was.

But my plan backfired. I did not take into consideration that Apollonius like Jesus before him would become the subject of jealousy and lies. This time spread by the Christian leaders, just as the Jewish clergy had done to Jesus ironically enough. As Apollonius fame as a miracle worker grew. The Christians began to conspire against him

Christians had already infiltrated the highest ranks of the Roman Senate. When word reached their ears of this pagan performing God-like miracles they knew that it contradicted their beliefs and what they were teaching? That Holiness and salvation came only from worshipping Jesus.

So they began to whisper gossip and lies about him. They said that he had conspired to assassinate the Emperor Domitian. He was arrested and tossed into prison. His long hair which he had never cut in his life and which reached to his feet was cut off. For Domitian was falsely told that it was the source of his powers.

But his enemies had not taken into account his immense wisdom. For once he was standing face to face with the emperor at his trial his answers were so brilliant and so profound that Domitian became impressed with him and acquitted him.

But the experience so disheartened Apollonius that he abandoned our mission. He vanished right before the eyes of his accusers. He then traveled to India in secret and lived out his life in solitude there. Rumors spread that he was Jesus who had survived the cross.

Thus when he died he was entombed in Kashmir, where to this day his grave is venerated as the tomb of Christ. But even after his death his reputation was attacked by the Church fathers who attacked me. By the 4th century the Church fathers had to explain Apollonius and his miracles for it conflicted with their teachings of Jesus as the only Son of God. So they labeled him a charlatan and some called him a black magician. Just as they had done to me."

I said, "The next mystic you mentioned was Albertus Magnus. But he lived in the 13th century. Why the big gap between Apollonius in the 2nd century and the 13th century? What happened in between?"

Simon replied, "For the first 3 centuries my teachings and followers were a serious rival to Christianity. But then in the 3rd century when Pauline Christianity became the official religion of Rome following the conversion of Constantine, the Christians who had once been so persecuted became the persecutors. Gnostic Christians were at the top of their list.

To survive my followers sought refuge in the city of Harran. Located in what is now northwest Iraq. There they remained safe from Christian persecution and later Muslim persecution by posing as neo-Platonists. The city fell to the Muslims in 633 but atypically was not forcibly converted. Just as the previous Byzantine government had not suppressed it.

But the truth would not be extinguished. It was kept alive by one secret society after another all down through history. The Knights Templar, the Cathars, the Rosicrucians, the Freemasons, all did their part to preserve the secret path to true salvation, the Kabbalah. All of those I mentioned to you were Kabbalists."

I said, "Yes, I've heard of the Kabbalah. What is it exactly?" Simon said, "The Kabbalah is a psychic religious system that has been handed down in Judaism for centuries. It is so old that its origins have been lost in time. If practiced properly it is like a spiritual exercise course. It promotes growth and purification of the spirit. All of a person's Karma can be eliminated in a single lifetime and avoid the endless cycle of reincarnation."

I said, "Well I don't really believe in reincarnation." He replied, " That is because you have been brainwashed since birth by Catholicism. Which teaches only the Heaven/Hell concept.

What you were not taught is that Jesus himself believed in it. In fact all of the Jews of Jesus' time believed in it and the Hasedic Jews, the ultra orthodox Jews of today still believe in it. Reincarnation was not tossed out of Christianity until some 300 years after Jesus died. Origen, one of the greatest thinkers of the early Christian era, second only to Augustine believed in it. But once Origen fell out of favor with the Hierarchy all of all of his teachings including reincarnation were tossed out."

I said, "Wow! You're telling me that most everything I have learned in Church is false. That's a lot to accept but I'll try and remain open minded."

Just then my mother called me to dinner. After dinner I watched tv. "The Red Skelton Show". My mother came to my room at 9pm and sprinkled my bed with Holy water. Then she hung a rosary on the headboard of my bed. I heard the walking sounds again but I just chose to ignore it all and went back to sleep. I had completely lost my fear of it and just dismissed it as my imagination."

"Let's fast forward then to October 9, 1968. A Wednesday. If nothing pertinent happened during the day let us focus on your ouija board message of that day." Dr. Bornstein instructed him.

I said, "Good afternoon Simon'." He replied, "Greetings little one." I said, "Tell me about Albertus Magnus." Simon answered, "Like Apollonius who lived so long before him Albertus' aura glowed like the sun. Seeing his potential I began to visit him in his dreams. Unable to reveal my true identity due to my blackened reputation by this age, I claimed to be his Guardian Angel. I told him to keep our dream revelations a secret.

As time passed I had so inspired him toward spirituality he chose to join a Dominican monastery and become a monk. I continued to inspire him and revealed to him the gift of the angels, the Kabbalah. Which he studied in secret. He grew spiritually, mentally and impressed his teachers and peers so that he eventually rose to the rank of Bishop. By this time he had advanced so far in his secret study of the Kabbalah that he was able to work miracles."

I said," Whoa. Are you telling me that the Kabbalah is the secret to developing psychic abilities that I have searched for all of my life?" Simon said, "Yes. For a long time I have watched you. The answer has been under your nose all along. Always you sought to understand why your mother is such a powerful psychic? Yet you see yourself as being devoid of gifts."

I said, "I still don't understand it. Can you explain it to me?" Simon said, "There are two types of people on the earth, those who are ruled by their hearts, the emotional types, and those who are ruled by their minds, the intellectuals. True psychic powers are actually gifts of the spirit, not secret powers of the mind as you believed. If they were mental abilities then would not those with the highest intellects like Einstein or Edison display the most powerful psychic abilities?

But that is not the case is it? The ones who display the greatest psychic abilities are the ones who are the most spiritual. It is always the Holy men of every society who perform the miracles. Be they Native American Shamen, The Kahunas of Hawaii, the Buddhist monks of Tibet, the Hindu Yogis of India, the saints of Catholicism. In short, those who practice the development of the spirit are the ones who display the miraculous abilities."

I said, "But my mother has never practiced any form of mediation." Simon said, "But she is highly emotional is she not? Emotions are aspects of the spirit. People who are emotional are in touch with their inner voices. All of us start out with our hearts wide open but in time some learn to dismiss our inner voices or instincts in favor of our logic.

The Shadow of Simon Magus

Unemotional intellectuals, like you and your father are text book examples of those who are ruled by their minds. But your mother and your older brother Donnie remain emotional and ruled by their feelings. This is why they never fully lost touch with their inner voices. This is why women are as a rule more psychic than men. Why homosexual men are always more psychic than heterosexual men, why little children and animals are the most psychic of all?"

I said, "Of course. You make it seem so obvious. So you are saying that if I study the Kabbalah I can learn to grow spiritually and finally develop my psychic abilities." Simon said, "There will be no limit to your potential." I said, "Wow! That's wonderful news. I read a strange account about Albertus Magnus in the encyclopedias. About him creating some kind of android that could move and talk." .

Simon replied, "So powerful a Kabbalist was Albertus Magnus that I was able to reveal to him the secret of creating a golem." I said, "A golem! You know I once saw a silent movie on tv about a Golem. It was a man made of clay and brought to life." Simon said, "Yes. Albertus created his out of wood. It took years of preparation but he was able to master the ritual. It was into this artificial body that I had him infuse it with my spirit. After 1300 years I had a body once again." I said, "I read that it was destroyed by Thomas Aquinas."

Simon said, "Yes. I was like an infant at first having to learn how to speak and walk again. Once I was able to speak I began to express my opinions on Christianity, Jesus and the true nature of God. Thomas Aquinas was a student of Albertus Magnus and once when he was out, Thomas and I became embroiled in a heated theological debate.

Needless to say he did not appreciate my beliefs on any of these subjects. He grew to fear me and believe I was a creation inhabited by demons. So he broke a chair over my android form destroying Albertus' lifetime of work.

Once Albertus died the Church declared him a saint so they could explain away his magical feats which had become legendary."

I put the board away as my mother called me to dinner. I couldn't get over today's message and it was getting harder and harder for me to dismiss this as coming from my own subconscious. I went into my room and watched tv. I noticed that the rosary my mother had hung on my bed was broken and laying on the floor.

I took it to my mother who fixed the chain. I reasoned that I must have done it in my sleep. So this time she hung it on the back of my headboard, between the headboard and the wall. I watched tv until it was time for bed. I watched "The Beverly Hillbillies." I kept hearing the scratching sounds again behind the wall. That night as usual I heard the walking sounds again but just ignored it."

"Let's fast forward to the events of October 10, 1968. Where are you now?" Dr. Bornstein asks.

"Back at school." Paul replies, "Still researching the names Simon had given me. I was looking at information on Cornelius Agrippa and Paracelsus. While I was at school my mother told me she found the rosary broken and laying on the floor again. This time she replaced it with a larger one with a heavier chain. She hung it too on the back of the headboard of my bed. Once I was home I rushed downstairs to contact Simon."

"Tell me about today's message." Dr. Bornstein says.

"I said, "Simon today I read about a disturbing account of Cornelius Agrippa. I read that a young student of the occult begged the key to Agrippa's study from his wife and entered it. There he found a book and read a passage and a demon appeared and strangled him."

Simon replied, "The truth is often stranger than the fiction. I had inspired Cornelius from birth. He became a most powerful Kabbalist and his 3 volume'work about occult philosophy became a cornerstone of Kabbalistic study down to this day. The incident you mentioned is partially true.

A student of the occult did indeed sneak into Cornelius' study. He began touching sacred objects and reading aloud dangerous passages. It was no demon, but I who appeared before him to frighten him off. But he had a weak heart and died from fright. When Agrippa returned and found the body he feared a murder charge. Remember this was during the height of the Inquisition and there were already too many townspeople whispering rumors of witchcraft against him.

The rumors of witchcraft abounded. Agrippa fearing the worst, packed up and fled town. He abandoned magic after that and rejected me as his spirit guide. So I turned to my other student of the times, Paracelsus. He had the most brilliant mind of his day."

I said, "I read that he created something called a humunculus. But I don't know what that is?" Simon answered, "I tried to convince him through dreams to recreate the experiment of Albertus Magnus. To create and artificial

The Shadow of Simon Magus

body for me. But before he would create the full size fugure he created a miniature life form.

He used the bones and skin of a bat and brought it to life using the ritual I had taught him. But he was so repulsed by the sight of it. He burned it. He too feared what the inquisition would do to him if they found out he was dabbling in magic. No amount of coercing could convince him to create the golem for me after that."

I said, "Those are pretty fantastic tales Simon. I'm not sure what to make of it?" It was then that I put the board up and went upstairs to dinner. These stories sounded so fantastic to me that I began to lean toward the whole thing coming from my imagination again as the source of this bizarre message. So I went to my room, did my homework and watched tv until bedtime as usual. That night I had a terrible nightmare that I was fighting with something.

It was too dark to see what it was but it felt like I fought with it all night. When I awoke at 6am I was so exhausted that I told my mother that I did not feel like going to school. She told me I could stay home then and to go take a shower, it would make me feel better. When I got into the bathroom and undressed I found weird scratches on my back and bruises on my arms and legs I couldn't account for. After my shower I did feel better and so I decided to go on to school. Once in study hall I used my time to look up more info on another Kabbalist.

"Then if nothing else pertinent occurred let us fast forward in time to your ouija board message of Friday, October 11, 1968."

"I said, "Hello Simon. I'm looking forward to hearing your views on this next character. I've been fascinated by the predictions of Nostradamus most of my life. What can you tell me about him?"

Simon said, "As I explained I was drawn to those with the brightest auras for I knew that they would likely develop clairvoyance and thus I could communicate with them in dreams. His real name was Michel de Nostradame. He was born Jewish and thus was already familiar with the Kabbalah. His family converted to Catholicism when he was but four years old to avoid the persecution of the Jews by the church."

Once again I came to him in dreams and it was I who led him to discover the book "De Mysteris Egyptorum". That prompted his early interest in the occult sciences. He became most interested in astrology and all forms of divination." I asked, "Could he really see the future?" Simon said, "Yes. He was the most powerful clairvoyant who ever lived." I said, "If you were looking for a wonder-worker to capture the world's attention you could not do better than him. What happened?"

Simon replied, "In his youth when I came to him in dreams I once again feared using my real name as my reputation as a black magician would frighten off most adepts. Especially since the church had declared that I had gone to Hell. So I once again claimed to be his Holy Guardian Angel. But by the time he was your age his powers of clairvoyance had grown so that he saw through my deception. Once he knew who I really was he would have nothing whatsoever to do with me."

He used what magic I had taught him though to see into the future and write his famous quatrains. So though he had more raw natural power than any psychic since Apollonius, he wanted nothing to do with my plans. I had far more success with Cagliostro."

I said, "You say that Cagliostro was not the fraud that he was labeled." Simon said, "That is correct. Cagliostro had the natural gift of healing by touch. Even better for my plans he loved the limelight and so in short time his fame spread across Europe like a bonfire. He cured millions of people and I was certain that I had finally found the one I had searched for. The wonder-worker that would inspire the world to learn the ways of the Kabbalah for themselves.

Indeed he did spread his Masonic lodges and converted many to join them. But it was not to be. He became embroiled in the political intrigue of the French Revolution. He became a favorite at the Court of King Louis XIX and was arrested in the famous "Affair of the Necklace" scandal. The enemies of Marie Antoinette became his enemies as well and once acquitted he had to flee from France. He went to Rome after that, to the very heart of Christianity and once again drew flocks of people to him seeking cures.

Cure them he did and converted thousands to his Masonic Order. Which he founded in Rome. The Vatican was not amused. They simply could not have a pagan healer running around curing the sick. So he was arrested and tossed into prison to die. But that was not enough to suit them. They needed to destroy his reputation as well. So they began to spread rumors and lies about him. He has been labeled a fraud by the Church and that label has stuck with him all through time as mine has as well."

I put the board away for the day and went upstairs to dinner. After which I went to my room and found the broken pieces of the rosary on the floor behind my bed. I called my mother and she saw that not only was it broken in several pieces but part of it was missing. So it could not be repaired. "I knew it!" She said, "I knew someone was trying to bewitch us again!" I wasn't sure what she meant by that?

But my father got home from the road just then. A little later we drove to pick up Rickey again. He stayed until Sunday night as usual and then we took him home. It was then that I noticed that I never heard the walking sounds when either he or my father was there. I only heard things when it was only my mother and me in the house alone. No scratching sounds either.

On Sunday night while my father was eating his dinner I decided to get his opinion on what was happening? My mother was outside doing something. I said, "Has mom mentioned to you the strange walking sounds we've heard at night?"

He said, "She has. But I fail to find it as mysterious as she does. Your mother is a wonderful woman, but she grew up deprived of a formal education. She is forever seeking a supernatural explanation for ordinary events." I said, "Still. .. I've heard it myself. It sounds just like someone is walking in the hallway. But no one is there."

He said, "Really, I am quite surprised at you. You mustn't allow your mother's superstitious nature to effect you. I knew immediately what it must be the moment she told me about it? Observe the hallway. Note that it consists of hardwood flooring. Boards that we walk on all day. At night the temperature changes. The house expands and contracts. No doubt what you are hearing is simply the floorboards expanding and contracting."

I said, "Hmm ...I hadn't thought about that. That does make sense. Thanks." My father said, " Your mother means well but at times her superstitions outweigh her common sense. Still it is not your place to correct her. That would be disrespectful and rude. Instead try and see the world from a more educated point of view." I said, "Yes. You're right. I will."

So I went to my room and watched tv. I heard the scratching sounds and said to myself, "It's only mice." My father left for work at 9pm. I had to take a shower because tomorrow was a school day. While I was in the shower my mother went to my room and sprinkled my bed with Holy water. I got out of the shower, dried off and put in my pajamas.

Then I went to my room. But when I got to my doorway what I saw stopped me in my tracks! My pillow on my bed was swollen up in the center like there was a head of cabbage inside! I yelled for my mother and when she saw it she said, "By God! I knew somebody was bewitching us!" She grabbed my pillow off of my bed and tossed it outside on the carport. Then she gave me one of her extra ones to sleep on.

I laid down but I couldn't get the sight of that swollen pillow out of my mind. Eventually I fell asleep. I heard the walking sounds at 3 am but just smiled. I was now sure it was only the floorboards settling like my father said.

At breakfast my mother said, "As soon as I take you to school. I'm going to cut that pillow open and see what's inside that swollen area." I said, "No! Let me do it before I go!" She said, "Oh alright. Here's the scissors." So I went out on the carport and picked up the pillow. The lump was still there. I was kind of afraid to touch it at first.

But I removed the pillow case and then stuck the scissors into the foam rubber pillow and started cutting. Inside the lump it looked like someone had stuck the pillow in a meat grinder. But only in the center of the pillow. The rest of the pillow was normal. I said, "I have to admit, this is pretty weird." My mother said, "Just toss it in the garbage can. It's time to take you to school."

(The ends the transcript of the 3rd hypnotic session with the patient Paul Michelson.)

CHAPTER 4
Sessions #4 #5 #6 and #7

(The following is a compilation of sessions 4, 5 and 6 with the patient Paul Michelson. Session 4 took place on July 22nd, 1995- Dr. Morris Bornstein)

Once again Paul Michelson reclines in the black leather recliner as Dr. Bornstein has him focus his eyes on the silver metallic pen. Once again he is instructed to relax each muscle in his body beginning with his feet and legs and working his way up his entire body, until once again he is instructed to close his eyes and sleep. Dr. Bornstein hits the record button on his pocket tape recorder.

"Mr. Michelson, the date is October 14, 1968. It's a Monday. Where are you now?" Bornstein asks.

"I am in my school library looking up more information on the next Kabbalist on my list. But all day my mind has been on what happened to my pillow?" Paul replies.

"If nothing else pertinent occurred, let us fast forward to today's ouija board message." The doctor states.

I said, "Simon, I have more questions." Simon said, "Please ask them." I said, "Tell me what you remember about Edward Kelly?" Simon replied, "The psychic associate of Dr. John Dee. Dee was a brilliant scholar but as we discussed, most intellectuals have no psychic abilities because they have lost touch with their inner voices in favor of their logical minds.

Although Dee had amassed the largest occult library of all time and had accumulated a vast knowledge of magic, he had no psychics talents whatsoever.

He would hire psychics and mediums to talk to spirits for him. The most gifted one was Edward Kelly. He and Dee were opposites in every way. Kelly was a crude, uneducated, uncouth Irishman. But he did have the sight. Through him I was able to impart much of the lost knowledge of the Simonians.

But as always due to my blackened reputation I could not say who I really was or they would not have listened to me. So I said I was the Archangel Uriel. Through Kelly I was able to reveal the Enochian language, the written language of the angels. It had been lost since the library of Alexandria had burned down. The writings of Dee and Kelly inspired many Kabbalistic magicians down to this day. Including Eliphas Levi."

I said, "I read that Eliphas Levi once conjured the spirit of Apollonius of Tyana." Simon said, "Not quite. The real spirit of Apollonius went into the light after his death where he rejoined the God-force. But I was still earthbound. Determined to bring the truth to mankind.

When Eliphas attempted his evocation ritual, it was I who appeared to him, not Apollonius as he had hoped. We met face to face in this manner on 3 occasions and I was able to impart to him still more lost knowledge of the Simonians. But he grew suspicious that I was not truly Apollonius and ended the sessions.

Once again I dared not say that I was the spirit of Simon Magus since the church had branded me the most evil black magician of all time for Eliphas Levi was a Christian magician and would have rejected me."

I said, "Are you aware of what-happened to my pillow last night?"

Simon said, "Yes."

I said, "Can you tell me what happened?"

Simon replied "Yes."

But just then my mother called me to dinner and I put up the board. After dinner I went to my room and watched tv. I was watching when a movie came on. The announcer said, "Tonight's film is "The Silver Chalice." The credits rolled by and it starred Jack Palance, Virginia Mayo, Lorne Greene and introducing Paul Newman.

Being a big fan of Jack Palance I started watching the movie when suddenly it became clear that this was an old Hollywood religious film and starred Jack Palance as Simon the Magician!

I said, "I don't believe it!" As I watched the movie unfold I saw Simon become Imperial Court Magician under Nero. In another scene, Paul Newman's character, who is a slave, is found by his Roman centurion father who gives him his citizenship papers and his freedom.

Simon's great love, Helena is played by Virginia Mayo. At the end of the film, Simon has Nero use Christian slaves to build a high tower from which he has promised to fly to prove that his powers in the service of Nero were superior to Peter's in the service of Jesus. But he goes power mad and decides not to wear his secret harness connected to a wire and believes he can really fly. He leaps off to his death.

When the film was over I had to laugh at myself. I wrote in my journal, "I just saw the film "The Silver Chalice" on tv. So that's where it all came from! Larry was right. I do now recall seeing this film when I was very young.

It must have been in my subconscious all of this time and the ouija board helped me to bring it back. It wasn't an exact match but it was close enough. Well case closed on this mystery. I don't know whether to be relieved or disappointed."

Dr. Bornstein says, "Let us continue to the next ouija experiment." Dr. Bornstein says.

"After school I rushed home to watch "Dark Shadows" on tv. Then I went down to my basement. It had snowed last night so Lucky only went out for about 30 minutes. Then we let him back in. I looked at the ouija board and said, "Forget it Simon. I've got you figured out." I picked up one of my books on Houdini and was reading it when I saw Lucky cocking his head back and forth. He was looking at the ceiling. He was following the sound of footsteps upstairs. I said, "Lucky that's just mom."

But just then I saw someone go by the basement window. I stood on a trunk and looked out the basement window. I saw my mother outside. She was talking to Donnie who just arrived. I said to myself, "If she's out there who was just walking in the hallway upstairs?" I went upstairs and looked around but no one was in the house. I dismissed it and went outside to see Donnie. My mother yelled at me to go back in the house and put on my jacket. "You've been lucky not to catch pneumonia this year", she reminded me. So I went in and put on my heavy jacket.

Then Lucky and I bounded out in the snow. Donnie was shoveling out our driveway. I asked, "Can I help?" Donnie said, "Sure." But mom said, "Donnie! You know how sickly he is. I don't want him out here working!" Donnie said, "Oh mom! You baby him too much!" I said, "Yeah mom! You're always telling me to go outside and get more sunshine." My mother said, "Alright! But just don't stay out here too long!"

Donnie and I finished shoveling out the driveway and we went on inside. My mother made us her "famous" vegetable soup. She never did learn how to cook for only 3 people. So when she made it, she made enough for an army.

Donnie stayed till after dinner and just as he was leaving I sneezed. Katie shot him one of her "I told you so" looks and he rolled his eyes and left. As the afternoon became evening my head cold got rapidly worse. My mother insisted I take a hot bath and go to bed early. I did but my stuffed up sinuses kept me awake most of the night."

"Let us move on the events of October 16, 1968." Dr. Bornstein states.

"By morning my head cold had moved into my chest. I coughed continuously. My mother kept me home from school. I stayed in bed most of the day. She made me a bowl of vegetable soup, but I could barely taste it. My mother said, "If you're not better by tomorrow you're staying home from school again."

I said, "Oh mom (cough cough) I'll be alright. (cough cough) She said, "You must be the only little boy in the world who gets disappointed if he can't go to school."

I sat around all day feeling worse and worse. I read a little between naps. For dinner my mother made me a chicken sandwich and more vegetable soup but I couldn't finish it. Then she felt my head and said "Oh oh! You're burning up." She gave me two aspirins and I went and laid down.

Then she stuck a thermometer in my mouth. "103!" She said. Then she went and got a bucket and filled it with ice water and began putting cold rags on my head. She changed them every 30 minutes. I drifted off the sleep. I didn't even wake up when she changed the rags. I began to dream."

"Can you recall the dream?" The doctor asks.

"Oh yes." Paul relies, "Vividly. I was walking down a gravel road with woods on each side of me. It looked familiar and then I realized where I was. "I must be on McCawley Road." I said. Then I heard footsteps walking behind me. I turned around and saw a tall man.

He was dressed in robes. Kind of like the style like Jesus wears in the paintings, except instead of being the traditional white tunic with red cloak, this man wore a black tunic and maroon cloak. He had a white beard and olive colored skin. On his head was black turbin of the Arabian style which hung down to his shoulders and had a silver band around his head. It looked like a snake biting it's own tail. His eyes were blue. The deepest blue I had ever seen, and he had sandals on his feet. His voice was deep and he said, "Greetings little one." "Simon!!" I shouted and ran to hug him like I was greeting a long lost relative.

"I've missed out talks." He said."Yeah, me too." I replied. "Do you still wish to learn how to use the Kabbalah?" he asked. "Oh yes! Please teach me!" I said. "Very well but we have to take a journey." He said.

Then he picked me up and placed me on his top of his shoulders and we rose into the air. I could see the tops of the trees and houses. It all seemed so real. Higher and higher we rose. There were clouds now below me, beside me and above me. The ground below us looked blue in color. Higher we rose until we were now above all of the clouds. They looked like a fluffy white blanket beneath us. Then down we went through them. We broke through the clouds and it now felt like we were falling, not flying! I hung on for dear life. I was terrified as the ground began to rush up at us. But then we slowed down.

"Where are we going?" I asked. "India" Simon replied. We landed before a temple in the mountains. "I spent years at this temple studying all forms of Yoga." We entered the temple and I saw an old Indian man sitting with his legs crossed beneath him. His eyes were half closed. Next to him another Yogis takes a long, sharp steel spike and shoves it through the man's cheek. The yogis does not even blink. Nor do his cheeks bleed very much.

"What is Yoga exactly?" I asked. "It is the union between man and the higher planes. The goal is to train the mind, body and spirit as a whole. To unite the 3 elements is to become one with the God-head. There are 4 types of yoga. Hatha yoga, Raja yoga, mantra yoga and the one I was the most interested in. Kundalini yoga."

Simon replied. "What is that exactly?" I asked. "It teaches integration through the physical and mental control of a dormant energy that lies at the base of the spine, near the sex organs. This energy is called Kundalini, which means "Fiery serpent." So called because it feels like molten metal when climbing up the spine in a helical pattern around the 7 chakras." Simon explained.

"Ok what's a chakra?" I asked.

"In Sanskrit it means "Wheel of light." A chakra is a vortex of energy found in the spiritual body that circulates the life force energy. You have 7 major chakras. Behold!"

As I watched his whole body grew dark like a silhouette. Then I saw 7 pinwheels of light appear one at a time. Each a different color.

At his groin level I saw a red pinwheel of light. "This is the root chakra" He said.

Next an orange pinwheel of light appeared just below his navel. "This is your spleen chakra." He said.

Then I saw a yellow pinwheel of light just above his navel. "This is your stomach chakra." He said.

Then a green pinwheel of light appeared in the center of his heart. "This is your heart chakra."

Then a blue pinwheel of light appeared at his throat. "This is your throat chakra", Simon said.

Then an indigo pinwheel appeared on his forehead. "This is your brow chakra", Simon said.

Then finally a violet pinwheel appeared on top of his head. "This is your crown chakra", Simon said. Then he resumed his normal appearance.

"So what does the kundalini energy do?" I asked. "Once it charges each of the chakras and reaches the crown chakra the owner reaches a state of ecstasy. The benefits of raising your kundalini are many. Your mental state will grow to genius level. You will understand languages without study.

You will become impervious to disease. Be able to heal the sick by touch. You can defy gravity. Move objects with your mind. Read thoughts and see the future."

"Wow! How long does it take to raise your kundalini?" I asked. "It can take a lifetime of practice." Simon replied. "I don't think I have the patience for that." I told him. "Neither did I. That was why I sought a shortcut." He replied.

Then I awoke. It was daylight. My mother slept in a chair beside my bed all night.

"Good morning." She said. "Your temperature is down. How do you feel?"

"I (cough cough) feel better." I said.

"Well you don't sound any better. I'll make you breakfast."

"Let us continue with the events of Thursday, October 17th, 1968." Dr. Bornstein states.

"I stayed in bed most of the day. Getting up to go to the bathroom. I felt so dizzy I had to hold onto the wall to walk straight. I watched tv and napped between meals. I still had no appetite. My head was still stuffed up and I coughed continuously. My temperature seemed to go up at night. My mother slept next to my bed again and put cold compresses on my head to keep my temperature down.

That night I once again dreamed of Simon. This time I dreamed I was walking on a strange street. From everyone's dress I could tell that I was somewhere in the middle east. It was some kind of market place.

Then I saw a large circle of people. I could hear the crowd saying "Oooooh" and "Ahhh". I pushed my way through the crowd to see what they were looking at? It was Simon.

He was performing magic for the crowd. I saw Simon hold out a red silk bag. He turned it inside out to prove it was empty. Then he reached inside and pulled out a white dove. The crowd said, "Oooooh" again and he let it fly away. He turned the bag inside out and another dove appeared.

He let it fly off as well. Then turning the large silk bag upside down he shook it and a dozen birds all flew out and went in every direction. He bowed to the audience and I smiled because I already knew how that one was done?

Amazing how little magic has changed in all these years. Simon's assistant passed a bowl to the crowd to accept gratuities. Then the crowd disperses and I stayed.

"Greetings little one. I have much to show you. Come with me." We walk through the streets. I see camels and horse drawn carts. "Where are we?" I asked. "Alexandria, Egypt." Simon replied. "When are we?" I asked. "The first century A.D. Behold!" Simon said.

We turn a corner and saw a magnificent structure. Simon said, "The Library of Alexandria. It housed more than half

a million volumns. The collective wisdom of the Greeks, the Jews, the Hindus, the Egyptians, the Persians, the Babylonians and more. All the collective knowledge of the known world." Simon explained.

"Amazing! I've read of it. What really became of it?" I asked. "The Patriach of the 3rd century was a man named Cyrill. He ordered all of the Jews in Alexandria banished from the city. The Roman Prefect, a man named Srestes objected to the order. So Cyrill sent his army of monks who murdered the Prefect and ordered the pagan writings burned. Cyrill was canonized a saint for this action.

The library was partially rebuilt over the years and then it fell under Muslim rule. They were no better. They used the remaining books as fuel for their bathhouses. The Caliph Omar was quoted as saying that books that contradicted the Koran were heresy and books that agreed with it unnecessary." Simon said.

"Why are we here?" I asked. "It was here that I grew up studying all of the world's religions and here that I first learned of the Kabbalah." Simon told me. Once inside I saw him pull a great scroll from a shelf and unroll it on a marble table. I saw a series of 10 circles and lines connecting them. "What is this?" I asked. "This is called the Kabbalistic Tree of Life. Ten circles connected by 22 lines." Simon explained.

"What do they represent?" I asked. "When the Divine source decided to create the universe he used the only substance he had to work with, namely, his own Divine energy. As steam condenses to form water and ice, so the God force condensed his own essence to form the physical universe. This action took nine stages to complete. Each of the circles represents a level of the God force.

Each is a separate dimension and also a level of consciousness within you." Simon said. "The tenth and final sphere of existence is called Malkuth, which is Hebrew for the Kingdom. It is the world of physical matter in which your body exists. Because it is the densest level it contains all of the energies of the 10 spheres within it and thus within you. Each of these levels can be reached within you as a level of consciousness."

"I see. What benefits would be gained by doing that?" I asked. "By doing work on each level, you can eliminate your vices and magnify your virtues. You can eliminate your bad karma in a single lifetime and end the cycle of reincarnation." Simon explained. "What is this top level called?" I asked him. "That is Kether and it was the first level to be manifested in creation and the closest to the pure God-force.

It is the white light of Kether that those who are dying see at the end of the tunnel." Simon said. "What is this level just above Malkuth?" I asked. "It is called Yesod and is the astral plane. It is where you are now in your dream state and where I am condemned to stay until my work is complete," Simon said.

I said, "Yes. I am dreaming this. How can I know that I am dreaming?" I asked. "It is called lucid dreaming and one day I will teach you how to do it deliberately." Simon said.

Then I woke up. It was morning."

"What were the major events of Friday October 18, 1968." Dr. Bornstein asks him.

"I was starting to feel better, a little stronger, but still coughing my head off. My mother made me breakfast and I was starting to get my appetite back. Still I just watched tv and tried not to exert myself. I was watching the 4 o'clock movie. I was "Houdini" with Tony Curtis, one of my favorites. While it was on I kept hearing the scratching sounds behind the wall again. I couldn't help but wonder why I only heard them behind this one wall? The one behind my bed. Why haven't we seen any mice or even any evidence of mice?

With my fever broken my mother was able to sleep in her own room. My father arrived at 6pm. We didn't go get Rickey that weekend. Much to his relief I'm sure.

I fell asleep early and before long I was dreaming again. I found myself outside and it had snowed. The snow was real deep and I was having trouble walking through it. It was snowing so hard I couldn't see my surroundings. Then I stepped in a snow bank and sank up to my chest. I was having trouble breathing and starting to panic when I felt an arm reach down and grab mine. I was pulled free and I saw that it was Simon. "Watch your step." He warned. I said, "Simon where are we?" "Tibet. High in the Himalayas." Simon replied. "We are at a secret monastery where I once studied. Come with me." He said.

As if from nowhere I found myself now in front of gigantic brass doors that were now swinging open. Inside I see a million candles along the wall and at the end of the corridor a gigantic statue of the Buddha. As we begin walking down the hallway toward the statue, I notice the walls have carvings on them, thousands of carvings on them. Each depicting men and women engaged in various sex positions.

I said, "Uh ...I think I'm too young to be seeing this." Simon replied, "Nonsense. In my time you would be considered a man at the age of thirteen." I said, "I thought all Buddhists abstained from sex." He replied, "Most Buddhist monks do but this sect seeks enlightenment through the embracing of the sex act. They see the body itself as the ultimate shrine.

They teach certain meditations that they use during the sex act and it enables them to reach nirvana during their climax. But still it takes a lifetime of practice.

But it was here in this temple that I reached my epiphany. For here it all came together, my studies of the kundalini yoga, the Jewish Kabbalah and Tantric Buddhism. I discovered that if I first used the kabbalistic rituals to tap into the energy of Kether and while in that higher consciousness state performed these Tantric sex rituals, the higher energy level of my spirit would cause the dormant Kundalini energy of my partner to be released.

It would then flow into my body via the root chakra and for a time I would be endowed with all of the powers that would normally take a kundalini yogis a lifetime to achieve. I'd found the secret that changed me into the most powerful wonder-worker in the world.

But the best was yet to come. For while in that super-charged state astral projection was child's play for me now. My spirit was able to soar through the world. There was no where I could not now go, invisibly, while my body stayed safely at home in my trance state. I noticed that my astral eyes could easily see the energy of other people's auras.

Then I saw her, a woman whose aura glowed like the sun. She lived in Tyana in the Roman province of Cappadocia. I realized that if her aura glowed this brightly then she must contain a wealth of Kundalini energy. But I was thousands of miles away in India. Only my astral form was there and it was invisible to her.

Then it occurred to me to try something that had never been attempted. I knew that my astral body was composed of the higher energy of Yesod, the astral plane. While this woman lived in the physical plane of Malkuth. But aside from the higher vibrational rate of Yesod the two spheres are identical.

While still in the astral I performed the kabbalistic ritual of entering the sephira of Malkuth. What occurred was that my astral body began to duplicate the process of Divine creation and slow down its vibrational rate and as a result it became as visible and solid as my physical body.

The woman said, "Who are you? Are you the god Proteus whose temple lies just over that hill?" I said, "I am." For I knew she could not refuse the honor of mating with a god. When I mounted her, while still in my astral body I was able to drain her of her Kundalini energy through the tantric sex act.

But something unexpected occurred. She became pregnant from my astral seed!"

I said, "Tyana? Was this Apollonius' mother?"

He replied, "It was. I was his true father. A fact that I revealed to him only after my death. It made it much easier to convince him to allow me to share his body.

Furthermore, you should know that even after my death I was able to use this same method to father offspring."

I said, "Are you saying that you are the father of all of those famous mystics and magicians down through history?" Simon replied, "I am and many more besides them."

It was then that a chilling thought came to me as I looked into his face and for the first time I noticed our resemblance. I had to ask him.

"Oh no! No no, Simon ... are your trying to tell me that you're my father as well?"

Simon smiled down at me. "Yes little one. I am."

The shock of the news woke me from my dream and I sat straight up in the bed. I looked at the clock and it said 3am.

"It can't be! Can it? Simon is only a figment of my imagination. Isn't he?" Then I kept thinking about how my mother said that the doctor's had told her that she couldn't have any more children after she had Pat. Yet here I am.

Both Dutch and Katie have brown eyes and brown eyes are dominant genes. Pat's eyes are brown. Donnie's are blue but he had a different father, so that doesn't count. My eyes are hazel and my hair is brown. The rest of the family has black hair.

Then I just blew it off. I thought, "Come on Paul. It was just a dream. Get over it." So I rolled over and went back to sleep.

"Let us fast forward to the events of October 19, 1968." Bornstein says.

"I slept until noon and then I woke up and got out of bed. I felt weak but I could tell that I was on the mend. I phoned Larry. He answered, "Pablo? Alright! I heard you were almost dead."

I said, "Rumors of my death were greatly exaggerated. I need a favor. If you're not busy I could use some help catching up on my homework."

Larry said, "Sure Fine, I'll help you catch up. I'll come by this afternoon."

I said, "Ok thanks. Bye."

I hung up the phone and went back to bed. I watched tv. Then after a time I told my mother I was going downstairs.

She said, "Oh alright. But I'm going to watch you all the way down the steps."

I said, "Oh good grief. Like you weren't over protective before." ,

So I went over to my table full of books and turned on my radio. I glanced at the ouija board and then laughed at myself. I started reading the latest issue of Spider-Man instead. About an hour later Larry arrived on his bicycle.

My mother let him in and I heard him coming down the steps.

"Pablo! Hey you're looking pretty good for someone I heard was a goner."

I said, "I feel fine really. You know how my mother exaggerates."

He said, "Yeah. Mom's do that. Oh I brought our math book and my chess board. That way I can teach you two lessons at the same time."

I said, "Hey! I'm getting better at chess. One of these days I might beat you."

Larry said, "No one can say that you don't dream big."

I said, "You want a soda?" I went to the refrigerator and got one for us both.

"Yeah. Thanks."

Larry opened the math book and began to read, "Ok if a man gets on a train in New York, going to Miami at the speed of 175 mph and travels half of the way. Stopping at Nashville. Then takes a bus the rest of the way to Miami traveling at 45 mph. How long will it take him to make the 5000 mile trip?"

I said, "Arrgg! My brain hurts! I think I feel a relapse coming on!"

Larry said, "Don't worry. I figured out an easy formula to beat all of these tricky word problems. Here I'll show you."

We studied for the next two hours and then closed our books.

"Thanks ... I think! Ok, set up the chess board now. It's time for my revenge." I said.

We sat in quiet contemplation for awhile. It was my move.

Larry reached over for his soda bottle and it wasn't there! He looked around and found it sitting on the floor beside the table leg.

I said, "Ok. Let's see of you can get out of this one." I moved my Bishop to take his Knight and placed his King in check. "Check!" I said.

"Not bad, Pablo! You are getting better at this. But not good enough yet."

Larry's Queen took my Bishop. Then Larry reached to take a drink out of his soda and his bottle was missing again. He looked around a found it next to his foot on the floor again. He stared at it for a moment and then picked it up. Looking at it in puzzlement.

"Ah! But see that's what I wanted you to do! Because now I have your Queen!" I said and took his Queen with my Knight.

"Hmm ... Not bad. But I'm not the Captain of the chess club for nothing you know." Larry responded He took my Knight with his Rook and simultaneously put my King in check. "I believe you'll find that's checkmate."

Larry reached for his soda and once again it was gone! He looked around for it and now it was not by his foot but on the floor way over by the refrigerator!

"Oh I get it! You and your magic tricks! You're trying to distract me so you could beat me at chess! Very clever, but it didn't work. Sorry." He said.

I had no idea what he was talking about at the time? It was years later when he told me what had happened?

I said, "Have you been smoking that stuff again? I don't know what you're talking about?" He said.

"Yeah right! No problemo, Pablo. All's fair in love and chess. Hey, I gotta be running. I'll see you Monday in class."

I said, "Ok thanks. I appreciate you catching me up to speed."

He left and I went up stairs. I was still not feeling all that great. I watched tv. "Forbidden Planet" was on. Another one of my favorites. Once again I heard the scratching sounds but I ignored it I went to sleep early. No weird dreams this night though."

Dr. Borstein continues, "Let us move on to Sunday, October 20, 1968."

"My day was quiet. I had dinner with my father that night." Paul replies.

"Did anything significant occur?

"I asked him questions about some things that had been on my mind. He said, "How are your grades?"

I said, "I'm still on the honor roll."

He said, "I hope this unfortunate bout of illness doesn't effect your grade average."

I said, "Don't worry. I've learned from past experience to stay 6 weeks ahead of the class. Except for math, but Larry helped me get caught up with that."

He said, "It's good that you have such a close friend. Your mother feels that you spend too much time alone in the basement."

I said, "It's quiet down there and I read a lot. Besides you saw what happened to me when I did go outside?"

He said, "That's a good point. Perhaps you will outgrow your unfortunate debilitation."

I said, "Something has been bothering me. How much do you know about the history of the Library of Alexandria?"

"What is it you would like to know?" He asked.

I said, "Is it true that the Christians were responsible for the burning of the library?"

He scoffed, "Rubbish. Is that the sort of anti-Catholic propaganda they are teaching you in history class?"

I said, "No ... I uh, read it somewhere."

Dutch replied, "I see. Well remember that most history is slanted by the opinions of the author. I'm sure if the author was Muslim or more likely Protestant, it should come as no surprise that he should blame the Catholics for such an atrocity. From all have read, it was the Romans who were responsible. But any history that old is always subject to misinterpretation as there are no records to support the facts."

I said, "I see. I'm finished eating. May I be excused?"

"Certainly." He replied and continued to eat his soup.

I went to my room and watched tv. Ed Sullivan was on. I always watched it hoping they would have a magician on. I went on to sleep. My father left for work at 9pm. That night I heard the walking sounds once again. But ignored it."

(This ended the transcript for this hypnotic session. Paul Michelson returned for his next appointment on July 29, 1995. He was then hypnotically regressed and we resumed reviewing the events of 1968. The following is the transcript for this session.)

Dr. Bornstein says, "Tell me the events of October 21, 1968."

"I'm back in the school library during study hall. I'm looking up the Library of Alexandria in the school encyclopedias. Well I'll be .." Paul says as though he is looking at something..

"What is it?" Dr. Bornstein asks.

"There's an artist rendition of the library. It looks a lot like the one in my dream. Except there was a big statue of Zeus over here ... But that doesn't mean anything. We have these same encyclopedia's at Blue Lick Elementary and I thumbed through them no telling how many times doing reports for school. So I probably saw it before and it just stuck in my subconscious. Then out of habit I decided to look up Simon Magus to see what this set had to say about him."

"Can you read it to me?" The doctor asks.

"Simon was born in the Samaritan town of Gitta to parents named Antonius and Rachel!" I can't believe I'm reading this! Those are the very names I received in my ouija board message and there was no mention of that in the movie "The Silver Chalice"! Incredible. Just incredible."

"What occurred next?" Bornstein asks.

"I couldn't wait to get home. I watched Dark Shadows as usual but I couldn't focus on it. All I could think about was finding those names. After it was over I rushed downstairs and got out my ouija board.

I said, "Simon are you there?"

"Welcome back" He replied.

I said, "When we left off you were telling me about Rasputin and Crowley."

Simon said, "With Rasputin history truly repeated itself. Like Cagliostro before him he was a most powerful psychic healer and also like Cagliostro he became embroiled in the political intrigue of the Russian revolution, just as Cagliostro had done with the French revolution.

Both made powerful enemies in the church and state and both were destroyed by their enemies."

I said, "Are you saying that Rasputin was not an evil man?" Simon replied, "If he were evil, how is it he could stop the bleeding of the Czar's hemophiliac son, Alexi? Such miraculous healing power can only come from a true Holy man, not a fraud."

I said, "Still from what I've read he was also a notorious alcoholic."

Simon said, "Yes that is true. But alcoholism is a physical illness and one's spirituality is not diminished by a physical illness."

I said, "Ok then, what about Aleister Crowley? What can you tell me about him?"

Simon said, "Crowley had a will of iron and a thirst for knowledge that surpassed even my own. I watched him with fascination as he ascended the ranks of the Golden Dawn Society so quickly.

I was certain his vast knowledge of the Kabbalas would turn him into the greatest wonder-worker of all time. So I appeared to his clairvoyant wife Rose Kelly. I called myself Aiwass and through her I was able to dictate "The Book of the Law."

I said, "So you were Aiwass. So what happened? You tell me that knowledge of the Kabbalah will make one Holy and bring forth their latent psychic gifts. But Aleister Crowley was an expert in Kabbalistic magic and he became as unholy as one could possibly get?"

Simon answered, "That is because the Kabbalah is like a two edged sword. If used for the purpose of spiritual growth it will indeed make one Holy and the gifts of the spirit will blossom accordingly. But if the Kabbalah is used to gain power over others it will have the opposite effect. It will wither the spirit and one will become increasingly evil and mad."

I said, "I see. So you're saying that Crowley's ambition was his undoing."

Simon replied, "Yes. There was little I could do but watch as he destroyed his fine mind with Gin and Heroin."

I said, "The last time we spoke, I asked you if you knew what had happened to my pillow? Do you know why we seem to be experiencing all the strange phenomenon around here lately? My father says it is all in our imagination, but I'm not so sure. In fact it recently occurred to me that the phenomena began to occur just after we began our communication on this board."

Simon answered, "Because we began to communicate in this manner you have opened a crack into the astral plane allowing other undesirable entities to come through. The strange phenomenon will only grow worse the longer we speak in this manner."

I asked, "Is there anyway to stop it?"

Simon said, "Yes. Only two ways. We can break off our communication which would close the door or if you are willing, I can teach you a way to bring me over to your side of the veil."

I said, "How can that be done?"

Simon replied, "It is called the spell of invocation and it will enable us to share the same body."

I said, "I'll have to think it over."

Just then my mother called me to dinner. I ate in silence. My excitement had grown to fever pitch. Truthfully I didn't need any time to think about it at all! By now I was a firm believer that I was really communicating with the Biblical sorcerer Simon Magus. One of the most powerful sorcerers of all time was offering to share my body.

I kept thinking about all of the powers I read that he possessed. He could become invisible, walk through solid walls, pass unharmed through fire, transform into other people or animals, move objects with his mind and fly though the air. If I let him share my body then I too will be able to perform all of those miracles as well! My dream of becoming the greatest magician of all time was guanteed. What was there to think about? I'd give anything for powers like that!

That night I could barely sleep I was so excited. I heard the walking sounds again. The downside to believing in Simon was that meant that there really was something walking in our hallway. All the more reason to do the spell of invocation. To put a stop to all of this madness.

"That brings us to Tuesday October 22, 1968" Dr. Bornstein states.

"I awoke feeling drained again. I thought maybe I was having a relapse. I didn't tell my mother because I didn't want her keeping me home from school and I'd missed enough already. In the bathroom that morning I noticed I had big bruises on my inner thighs. I wondered how I had gotten them? I went on to school, but I had trouble concentrating all day. I couldn't wait to get home."

"Let us move forward to your ouija board message of that day."

"I said, "Simon, I've made my decision. I want to perform the spell of invocation. Only I'm a little concerned about performing an actual magic ritual. I always thought all sorcery was evil.

Simon replied, "Yet you attend Mass regularly do you not?" I said, "Sure. I still go to church. Not as often as I should but what has that to do with sorcery?"

He said, "The Catholic mass is a gigantic white magic ceremony. Observe that they use an alter, white candles, incense used in a magic circle to bless the alter, special colored vestments to symbolize the intent of the ritual. Do they not also call upon their God to invoke himself into the sacrificial items they offer up to him? They then consume the possessed bread. Is the term priest not identical to the practitioner of a ceremonial magic ritual?"

I said, "You know, I never thought about it like that before? But you have a good point."

Simon said, "Where do you suppose they learned these things? Jesus taught none of this. They learned them from the pagans of course. When Constantine the Emperor of Rome was converted to Christianity, all of the temples that were previously dedicated to the Roman gods like Jupiter were converted to Christian churches. The reenactment of the last supper by the Roman Christians, which before had been performed only in secret was now able to be celebrated inside the temples.

To make the ceremony seem less strange to the pagans who were forced to convert, all of the trappings of the previous ceremonies performed to the Roman gods were kept. Thus the Christian reenactment of the last supper became blended with the ancient magic rituals."

I said, "That's a pretty startling revelation. So you are saying that my performing the magic ritual of invocation will be little different than the mass that I've been participating in most of my life."

Simon said, "That is correct. Now here is a list of items you will need. 5 violet colored candles, some honeysuckle incense and a piece of chalk."

Just then my mother called me to dinner. I put the board up and went upstairs. After dinner I phoned Larry. I said, "Larry I need a few things and I was wondering if you could get them for me and bring them to school. I'll give you the money. I don't want my mother to know.

He said, "Sure. What do you need?"

I told him the items I needed and he said, "I already have the incense. I'll just give you a stick."

I said, "What are you doing with incense?"

He said, "It covers up certain scents in your room if you know what I mean? What are you planning on doing with it? Finally joining the cool people?"

I said, "I don't think smoking that stuff is cool Larry. But to each his own. I'm ... uh ... getting into some eastern meditation."

He said, "Really? Like TM?"

I said, "Yeah sort of. Ever heard of the Kabbalah?"

He said, "Nope. But it sounds weird enough for you to like it though. Ok I'll buy your candles at this head shop I go to and put them in my locker. I'll give them to you tomorrow in study hall."

I said, "Perfect. Thanks."

I watched tv the rest of the night. "Get Smart" was on. As usual I heard the scratching sounds and that night I heard the walking sounds again. I started saying the rosary to calm down enough to go to sleep."

"Let us fast forward then to the events of Wednesday October 23,1968." Says Dr. Bornstein.

Paul continues, "As promised Larry delivered my supplies. I gave him 5 dollars to cover his expenses. After school I rushed home to watch Dark Shadows on tv and then downstairs to contact Simon.

I said, "Simon I am here."

He replied, "If I am to be your teacher then you must address me as master from now on as a sign of respect."

I said, "Yes master. When will we attempt the spell of invocation?"

Simon said, "Seven nights from tonight. If you can be ready."

I said, "That's October 30th"

He said, "Yes the ceremony must be performed exactly at midnight."

I said, "Can you explain why exactly?"

He said, "Because that will be when the veil between our two planes of existence will be at it's thinnest."

I said, "Oh I see. Just as we move into Halloween."

Simon said, "Yes. The celts referred to it as samhain."

I said, "I'll be ready. Tell me what I must do?"

Simon said, "First you must practice your visualization. You do it naturally when you daydream. You will now learn to control your daydream. Although your eyes and ears will be open you will see and hear nothing that is around you, but only what you are focusing on. Today I want you to lay on the floor and pretend you are standing in each corner of the basement. Try and see the room from that perspective in as much detail as you can. Then do likewise in every corner of the room. That will be enough for today."

So I put up the board and began practicing my visualization as he had instructed me for an hour, until my mother called me to dinner. After dinner I worked on my homework. Once again I kept hearing the scratching sounds behind the wall. That night when I went to bed I began practicing myself standing in each corner of that room as well. Until I drifted off to sleep."

Bornstein says, "Then let us fast forward to the events of Thursday, October 24th, 1968. If nothing pertinent occurred let us proceed to your ouija message for that day."

"I said, "Master I am ready for my next lesson."

Simon said, "Today you will attempt a different visualization exercise. Lay on the floor and pretend to rise out of your body. Go wherever you choose but resist the urge to look back at your body for you will be pulled back into it. Try to experience the visualization with all of your senses. Not just sight alone. That will be all for today."

I put up the board and lay on the floor. Closing my eyes I imagined myself becoming lighter and lighter. I pretended I was drifting upwards like a balloon. I reached the wooden rafters of the basement ceiling. Then I passed right through the ceiling and was lying on the living room floor upstairs. I continued to drift up and saw the plaster ceiling growing closer and closer and then I passed through that. Now I was in the darkness of our attic and still I floated upwards.

Then as I passed though that ceiling I was now laying on the tiles of the roof and the sky was above me. I sat up. I could feel the wind on my face as I looked out from our rooftop. I stood up and I could feel the warm rough shingles of the roof. Now standing I could see the row of rooftops down Maynard drive. Then I rose into the air. I could feel the wind blowing all around me. Up, up past the telephone polls and higher still until now I am looking down at the tops of the walnut trees that flanked each side of our driveway.

Just then my mother called me to dinner. As I started upstairs, I was impressed by the 3 dimensional feeling that I was able to achieve in today's exercise. That night while laying in bed I practiced it again.

This time rising into the blackness of the night sky. I soared like Superman over my home and on into downtown Louisville, visualizing all of the bright lights of the city. My imagination turned into a dream and I slept soundly until 3am when I awoke feeling terrified again for no reason. I said the rosary until I calmed down enough to go back to sleep."

"Let us fast forward now to the events of Friday, October 25, 1968. Unless something eventful occurred let us move on to your message for that day." Bornstein says.

I said, "Master I am ready for today's lesson."

Simon said, "Today you will learn how to enter the Holy Sephiroth of Yesod, the astral plane. It is the next sphere of existance just above the level of Malkuth the physical plane that you reside in. It is also a level of consciousness within you for Malkuth contains all of the energies of all of the higher sephiroth.

Each sephira is associated with a different planet. Yesod is associated with the moon. Each level has a symbolic color. Yesod is violet. It is the foundation of the astral and etheric planes of existence. It is that level in which our mind can build the images that connect us to all of the others planes. It is here that we can touch our subconscious mind. Where we can build thought forms and images.

The aspect of God that operates at this level is called Shaddai EI Chai. Pronounced Shah-Dye-EI-Kye. Which is Hebrew for Almightly Living God. The vice that we must beware of on this level is idleness. The virtue to be cultivated is independence. The Archangel Gabriel guards this sphere.

He is the angel of truth. For Yesod is the gateway to all other levels of consciousness. He brings us the gift of hope, no matter the circumstances. Under him are the Cherubim. They are the angels of light and glory. Also keepers of the Akashic records, which contain all the information of the past, present and future. By walking with them we can attain greater knowledge from the records made available to us.

Each sephiroth has it's own symbolic color and incense. So your first step is to light your violet candle and honeysuckle incense. Now be seated and close your eyes. Relax each muscle until you are relaxed all over. Begin to visualize a ball of violet light before you. Draw it closer to you. Visualize it filling the room. Surrounding you, permeating you.

Step two is to picture a doorway in the light. It is the door to your subconscious. See it open and picture the light inside and color even more brilliantly as you move though it.

Step three. Take a deep breath and as you slowly exhale, utter aloud the name of the God force at this level. Say Shaddai EI Chai each time you slowly exhale. As you inhale slowly think the name. Each time you repeat the name visualize the light glowing brighter. By alternating the outsound with the insound, you are setting up a resonance between the two spheres. Linking the inner world to the outer world. Repeat step 3 until you can no longer see the light any brighter.

Step four. Now begin to chant the name of Gabriel. Alternating the outsound with the insound on each exhalation and inhalation as before. But this time as you utter the name visualize the light soften. Becoming less intense to your senses.

Step five. Chant the name of the Archangel until you see the colors begin to shift and wave. As it clears you will see an alter before you standing between two pillars. On the alter is a lamp and the flame burns violet in color. This is the temple of your consciousness. These temples exist at each level.

Step six. You will begin to feel that you are not alone. Then as if stepping from behind an invisible curtain a being will appear. Each level has a different magical image. At Yesod it is traditionally that of a beautiful naked man. It is more of a thought form than an actual being but it will serve to transmit messages to you.

He will speak to you. Be mindful and respectful of what you are told. When he finishes speaking ask if you may come again. This ritual takes much time. Do not attempt it today as time is short."

Just then I heard my mother calling me to dinner. My father arrived home from the road and I knew that after we ate, my mother and I would drive to Fairdale to pick up Rickey. So I would have to wait until Sunday night after we took him home to attempt the ritual."

"Fast forward then to your attempt of the ritual on October 27, 1968." Says Bornstein.

Paul continues his narrative, "We got back home on Sunday night at about 7pm. That was when I went downstairs. I lit my violet candle and honeysuckle incense and began my relaxation exercises. I performed the ritual chanting the God name and Archangel name as instructed. I eventually reached the temple and the man appeared. I knelt as he spoke to me of how idleness had affected my life and how I could overcome it by becoming more independent. When the ritual was over, I felt more energized. I can't really explain it in words. It was like I was glowing. I went upstairs and did my homework and watched tv until it was time to go to bed."

(This ends the transcript of this session. Paul Michelson returned for his next appointment on August 5th, 1995. After undergoing his hypnotic regression the following is the transcript of this session.)

Bornstein says, "Let us proceed to the events of Monday October 28th, 1968."

"I'm in the library at school." Paul states, "Larry approaches me. He looks concerned like something is bothering him.

"Hey Pablo." He said.

"Are you ok Larry? You look like you've seen a ghost?" I asked him.

He said, "It's funny you should say that. You're not going to believe this, but I have to tell somebody and I know you're into this supernatural crap."

I said, "What's going on? Has something happened?"

He said, "Well. .. ever since that day I came over to help you catch up on your math homework, something weird has been going on. I hate to talk about it because it sounds so nuts!"

I said, "It's alright. I promise not to laugh."

He said, "Things keep moving around by themselves ... I mean I don't see them move. But if I set something down and go to pick it up, it's not there and I find it someplace else. But that's not all. .. "

I said, "What else?"

He said, "I keep hearing footsteps. But no one is there. Especially at night!"

I said, "I believe you Larry. It's been going on at my house too."

He said, "It has! Oh thank goodness! I was afraid to tell anyone. What's going on?"

I didn't want to tell him about Simon or the ouija experiments so I said, "This sort of thing falls under poltergeist activity. Most parapsychologists believe that the activity is caused by the subconscious psychic abilities of a teen or pre-teen. So bottom line is I think I am somehow causing this."

I said, "Here look." I pull a book off of the shelf entitled "The Encyclopedia of Parapsychology". I look up "Poltergeist" and hand it too him. He reads, "From the German "polter" which means noise and "geist' meaning ghost. Always associated with an unseen force credited with creating disturbing phenomena such as inexplicable noises, movement of household items, or in extreme cases spontaneous fires, objects being thrown, or worse.

Such phenomena are attributed by some parapsychologists to being connected to the latent psychic abilities of a pre-teen or teenager. Such activity is always of short duration ... "

I said, "I've read of cases of stones raining down on houses and spontaneous fires. So I guess it could be worse."

Larry said, "Well I still think most of this stuff is crap, but I guess this beats believing in a ghost."

I said, "Keep a log for me of the activity at your place. Times, dates and events. If it happens anymore."

He said, "Alright. That's a good idea. But if my clothes catch on fire, I'm suing." He could always make me laugh.

I only told him it was poltergeist activity to set his mind at ease. But secretly I was worried. I was sure that the entities at my house had followed him home. The sooner I performed the ritual the better for us all."

"If nothing else pertinent occurred let us fast forward to today's ouija board message." Dr. Bornstein says.

"I said, "Master I am read for today's lesson."

Simon said, "Today you must learn to draw a very special pentagram. Get a piece of paper and pen. Draw a 5 sided star in a circle." I did as he instructed then put my hands back on the planchette. " Now look at the right lower point of the star. See how two lines of the lower point could be two sides of a smaller pentacle connected to the larger one."

I drew it and said, "Ok, how does that look?"

Simon replied. "Yes that is correct."

I said, "Master what is the meaning of this pentagram?"

Simon said, "Both the 5 pointed star and the 6 pointed star come from the Hebrew religion. The 6 pointed star or hexagram is the symbol of God. Two triangles inverted represent the reconciliation of opposites, good, evil, light, dark, male, female, etc.

But the 5 pointed star represents man. This double pentagram as you have just drawn represents the joining of two men or in your case a man and a young boy. For today practice your visualizations."

I said, "Yes master."

So I practiced my astral projection and visualized entering the sephiroth of Yesod until my mother called me to dinner. After I ate and did my homework and then listened to my Beatles' albums. But my mind was on my invocation spell. How perfect that it should fall on Halloween. The anniversary of the death of Harry Houdini and the birth of ... what should I call myself? Simon Magus. Yes. What better name could I take? I'll ask him if that would be alright with him. But I am sure he will agree to it.

I went to sleep dreaming of being world famous. Nothing disturbed my rest that night."

"Very well, then let us fast forward to the events of Tuesday, October 29,1968." Says the doctor.

"I could barely focus on my school work. I was so excited about the invocation ritual to take place tomorrow night. As usual I went home and watched Dark Shadows on tv and then went downstairs for my lesson.

(Mr. Michelson then recounted the exact instructions that he received that day on how to perform the spell of invocation. To avoid repetition we shall skip over it and continue with the rest of the events of October 29,1968-Dr. Morris Bornstein)

Then my mother called me to dinner. Just after I finished eating I heard a car pull into the driveway. I looked out the kitchen door. "Donnie's here!" I shouted. I rushed outside to greet my big brother. Barbara and little Ricky who is 7 years old were with him.

Donnie said, "Well! You're pretty lively for somebody I heard was nearly dead." He got out of the car and assumed a boxing stance. "Ok put um up! Now you're going to get it for scaring everybody to death!"

I tried to box with him but it looked just like that scene from Disney's "Jungle Book" I'd seen last year, when Mogli is boxing with Baloo the bear!

Donnie said, "Come on! Let's see what you've got?" I swung my fist as hard as I could and my fist just sank into Donnie's big gut like a giant pillow.

Donnie said, "Oh ho ho! That tickled! You trying to tickle me to death?"

Barbara meanwhile went to the house with little Ricky and my mother was busy kissing his face all over saying, "There's my little Grandbaby!" When suddenly she spotted the boxing match in the driveway!

"Donnie!!! Are you out of your mind! He just got out of the sick bed! Stop that you two this minute!" Katie yelled.

"Oh mom, you baby him too much!" Donnie said.

"That's what you said when I told you not to let him shovel snow with you remember?" Katie reminded him.

"Who me?" Donnie said, "I'd never say anything as stupid as that. Would I?"

I said, "Nope! Never!"

Katie stood there with her hands on her hips and a frown on her face as we immediately obeyed and headed for the back door.

"You go first!" Donnie said.

"Thanks a lot!" I said.

We went inside and they sat around the kitchen table while I played with little Ricky. Around 8pm we put Ricky to bed in mom's room. Then at 9pm I went to bed myself. After they thought I was asleep I heard Donnie talking to mom.

He said, " I had a bad dream about Paul last night."

Katie said, "What kind of dream?"

Donnie said, "I saw something. It was some kind of demon and it was about to grab him and I woke up."

" Katie said, "I don't like the sound of that. There's something strange going on around here too."

She then told him about the walking sounds, the breathing sounds I heard, what happened to my pillow and rosary and the scratching sounds.

Since I knew that Donnie was nearly as psychic as Katie, his dream worried me. I was glad the invocation spell was tomorrow night so the door to the astral plane would be closed and we'd be safe from these entities. I went on to sleep after that. I heard Donnie and his family leaving at 11 pm."

Dr. Bornstein says, "Very well, let is fast forward to the events of Wednesday, October 30th, 1968."

Paul continues, "I went to school as usual. But my mind was not really on my school work of course. I was just counting the minutes until midnight. At 3pm the school bell rang and I made my usual dash for my mother's car. We rushed home and I watched "Dark Shadows" as usual. Then I went downstairs. Simon told me to rehearse the ritual. So I did that over and over. Going through the motions of it until my mother called me for dinner.

After I ate I did my homework and watched tv until it was time for bed. I went to bed at 9pm, but there was no way I was going to sleep. I laid there awake watching the clock and waiting for my mother to go to bed. At 10:30 she finally turned out the lights and went.to bed. I sat up in my bed, got dressed and watched the clock. It seemed to take forever to reach 11:45pm.

I crept out of bed and slowly opened my bedroom door. I looked down the hallway and could see that my mother's bedroom door was closed. The basement was midway between my room and my mother's room. I tip-toed to the basement door trying to open it without any noise.

I stepped onto the first step and carefully closed the basement door slowly behind me. I waited a moment to make sure that I didn't wake my mother. Then I flipped on the light switch. As I made my way down the wooden steps I saw Lucky walk over to greet me. I could tell that I woke him up. He was wagging his tail. I whispered for him to follow me.

I took down his walking chain and collar and put it on him. I said, "I'll have to chain you over here boy. I can't have you licking my face in the middle of the ritual."

After chaining him up on the other side of the basement and telling him to "stay" I went over to the kitchen table and got the items I needed that Larry had given me. I then walked over to the side of the basement beneath our living room upstairs. There was a large circular area rug there. I folded it back. I felt that if I heard my mother coming I could pull it quickly over the pentagram and erase it later if I had to.

Then kneeling down on the concrete floor I took the chalk out of the bag and drew a large circle around myself, one big enough to lie down in. I then drew the giant pentagram with the apex point facing east as Simon had instructed. Now in the lower right point I drew the second smaller pentacle.

I then took out the 5 violet colored candles and placed one on each point of the large pentacle. I then lit each one with the lighter. I then took out the honeysuckle incense and the incense holder Larry loaned me and lit the incense. I then placed the holder which I sat between the bottom two apex points.

Standing facing east I next performed the ritual called the "Mystic Pentagram" as Simon had taught me.

Saying "In the name of ... " I touch my forehead with my right hand, "Earth".

I touch my left knee. "Water", I touch my right shoulder. "Air", I touch my left shoulder. "Fire" I touch my right knee and "Spirit", I touch my forehead again. "Amen" I say.

Now I must perform the protection ritual Simon taught me to prevent any interference from any spirits drawn to the ritual. I pick up my box of salt and say, "By the power of earth" and I walk around the perimeter of the circle sprinkling the salt as I go.

Then I say "Water" and pick up a glass of water and again walk the perimeter of the circle sprinkling it as I walked. Then I say "Air", and pick up the stick of burning incense and walk around the perimeter of the circle once again.

Then I say "Fire" and pick up the apex candle and walk around the circle and then place it back where I got it. Finally I said, "And spirit." I then point my finger at the apex point and I visualized a beam of light shoot out of it. I trace it around the circle.

Now I sit in the center of the pentagram. I look at the clock on the wall. 11 :55pm. "Perfect' I thought. I lay down with my arms and legs spread eagle to match the points of the large pentacle. I close my eyes and begin my astral projection. I visualize myself rising out of my body until I am hovering above it. While keeping my consciousness in my astral body I must perform the ritual for entering the Holy Sephiroth of Yesod.

First I visualize the ball of violet light before me. Then I bring it closer until it engulfs the whole room. Now I picture a doorway in the light and open it seeing the brighter violet light within. I step through it mentally.

Now for the hard part, I take a deep breath and while exhaling intone the God name "Shah-Dye-EI-Kye". All the while visualizing it coming from my astral body not my physical one lying on the floor. I did it and now I have to mentally intone the name as inhale. Each time I intone the name I picture the light glowing brighter.

I continue until I can no longer see the light any brighter. Next I begin to intone the name of the Archangel Gabriel. Again verbally with the outsound and mentally with the insound. Each time the light grows softer.

After a minute of this the light begins to shift and wave. It clears and now I am standing before the temple. The flame on the lamp sitting on the alter is burning violet in color. I step up and go behind the alter and part the curtains. I see a door with an old fashioned cross beam on it. I lift the beam and open the door.

Inside is a violet fog. Then I see a hand emerge from the fog. Then another hand. I reach in without stepping inside and take hold of the man's hands. I pull him through the doorway. It is Simon looking just as he did in my dream.

Now I visualize the ball of light leave us and we are both hovering above my body on the floor. Without a word I see my astral body become white smoke and his black smoke. My body inhales and both spiral down into my lungs.

It is over! My eyes snap open. I look at the clock. One minute past midnight.

I sit up and blowout the candles and incense. I erase the chalk pentagram and pull the rug back into place. I stand there a moment. I feel a little foolish. I don't feel any different at all. I went over to unchain Lucky. I hung his chain and collar back up. I felt a chill go through me which I attributed to laying on the cold basement floor at midnight. I then tried to levitate but of course nothing happened. Feeling really stupid now I went on upstairs to bed.

Then at 3am I awoke hearing a strange sound. What was that? It sounded like a dog howling low. It's Lucky! But he's never howled before. Barked sure, but never howled. I jumped out of bed and put on my pants. I met my mother coming out of her room.

"Is that Lucky?" She asked.

I said, "Yeah." We both went down the basement steps. Lucky came over to us with his tail tucked between his legs. He was whimpering and sounded frightened.

I said, "What's the matter boy?" I petted him and he seemed alright after that.

My mother said, "I don't like the sound of this! He's never acted this way before."

I said, "Yeah. I know." We both went on back to bed."

"Let us fast forward then to Thursday, October 31, 1968." Dr. Bornstein said.

"I went to school as always and came home in time to watch "Dark Shadows". After which I went downstairs and got out my ouija board.

I said, "Master, are you there?" I got no response. I kept trying it but I got nothing. So I put the board away. I wrote in my journal.

"Simon's not responding on the board. Looks like it all turned out to be just my imagination after all." I read some comic books until it was time for supper."

After I ate my mother said, "Would you like to carve the Jack 0' Lantern?" Of course I said yes. I went out on the carport and carved it with a small knife and spoon.

"Ok it's ready!" I said. My mother brought out the candle and put inside it.

She said, "Are you sure you just want to stay home this year and pass out the candy? It'll be the first year you haven't dressed up and gone out to get candy like the other kids."

I said, "Mom, in some cultures I am considered an adult at age 13."

"Well alright. Have it your way." She said. I went inside to watch tv. My mother set up a large bowl of candy by the door. I was enjoying all of my favorite Universal horror films. "Dracula, Frankenstein, The Wolfman, Dr. Jekyll and Mr. Hyde. I had to plead with my mother to stay up late to watch "Diary of a Madman" with Vincent Price. She watched it with me. I went to bed at 11 :30pm."

"Were you able to contact Simon after that?" Dr. Bornstein asks.

"No." Paul replies, "There was no sign of him for 5 days."

"Alright, let us fast forward to November 5th, 1968. Where are you now?"

"I'm in school. I'm sitting in Mr. Chappell's English class. I am staring discreetly at Sharon Smyth. She had platinum blonde hair and I thought she must be the most beautiful creature on earth. She had no idea I was even alive of course.

But then I began to feel light-headed. It was getting hard to think straight. I felt detached from my body. Reality seemed to be moving away down a tunnel, then blackness.

I awoke with a start. I was standing at my locker. How did I get here? I was just in English class.

Then I heard Larry. He said, "Pablo? You ok?"

I said, "Uh .. Yeah. Sure. Why?"

He said, "I called to you earlier and you just kept walking."

I said, "I ... uh ... didn't hear you. Sorry ... I don't seem to be myself today."

I had no idea yet just how true a statement that was. I opened my locker and took out my history book.

Larry said, "What are you doing with that? We just came out of tv history class, remember?"

I said, "What did you say? What time is it?"

He said, "It's 2pm. It's time for study hall of course. Are you sure you're alright?"

I put my hand to my mouth involuntarily when Larry told me the time. Two hours disappeared from my life! I had no memory whatsoever.

I said, "I'm fine. I just realized something is all. Let's go to study hall." I walked to the library in shock. I could barely feel my feet hitting the floor. I was totally confused. If I had fainted how could I still be walking around? Was I sleep walking? I did stay up late last night, but still?

The 3pm bell rang and I went home. I said nothing whatsoever about what had happened to me? I could just see my mother rushing me to the doctor if I did. I watched "Dark Shadows", I went downstairs and got out my ouija board.

"Simon I have to talk to you! Where are you?" No reply. Frustrated I just tried to read and forget about it. My mother called me to dinner and after I ate I watched tv. Then I heard the scratching sounds! Either it really is mice or the ritual failed to get rid of the entities. "Maybe I did it wrong", I thought.

That night I went to bed. At 3am I awoke feeling terrified again. The room was pretty bright. It was the first night of the full moon, although I did not yet understand the significance of that. Then I heard the walking sounds. It wasn't over. I tried to roll over and just ignore it. Eventually I went back to sleep."

"Let's fast forward now to Wednesday, November 6th, 1968. Where are you?" Bornstein asks.

"I'm back in school, in the library at study hall. Sharon Smyth comes in and she sits at one of the tables. I am quietly watching her when suddenly I feel light headed again.

But this time I do not black out. But to my horror I saw my own right arm open my notebook. It was only then that I realized that I was no longer in control of my body! It was moving all by itself!

I could only watch what was happening like it was on tv. It was horrible! I saw my own hand take my pen from my shirt pocket and write on the notepad. "I can get her for you. I can get you anyone you want." Then blackness!

I woke with a start. It was now 2:45pm. Thirty minutes had disappeared this time. The full horror of what I had done to myself set upon me like a load of bricks!

My mother picked me up at school like always and took me home. Then she had to go to the grocery store. I ran straight downstairs. I got out the ouija board. But it wouldn't move!

I said, "Simon! Simon! I have to talk to you! Please talk to me! Please!"

"Remain calm Mr. Michelson. You are only watching the past. You are a detached observer. What happened next?"

"I lost my temper. I kept talking out loud to Simon. I stood the ouija board against the concrete wall at an angle and smashed it with my foot. Breaking it in half.

I kept shouting "Simon! I know you can hear me! I didn't know it would be like this! I want out. .. Simon. Simon! Talk to me!" I tossed all of my candles and magic supplies in the garbage can.

I said, "You listen to me! You're not going to get away with this! I'll tell my mother everything. She can call a priest or somebody to help me!"

The moment I said that Simon instantly took over my body. It happened instantaneously. In the blink of an eye. I was no longer in control of my body but could still see and hear what was happening!

I had a small hand held mirror on my table that I used to practice my sleight of hand. I saw myself calmly walk over and pick up the mirror and hold it up to my face. My eyes! My eyes were different looking. Wide and staring. But it was the color that completely freaked me out. They were blue! Cobalt blue! My eyes are hazel!

Then I heard myself speak. Simon was speaking through me. His voice was very calm and icy. He spoke to me in almost a whisper.

He said, "Silence. Enough of this. From this moment on, you will do everything that I tell you to do and you will tell no one of my existance, unless I allow it. I can see everything that you see, hear everything that you say. Anyone who learns of my existance and tries to interfere with my plans must die. Remember that I have complete control over your body now. Do you understand? But you tell me you want out. I told you from the beginning that once we merged it was until death do us part."

He put down the mirror and looked over at Lucky's walking chain hanging from the wooden beam. He slowly pushed one of the chairs from the kitchen table over under the loop of chain. He stood my body in the chair and placed my head into the loop. He then said, "This is your only way out!"

He then stepped off the chair into space. Just as my toes hit the floor the chain slammed into my throat. It was the worst pain I have ever felt in my life!

I fell to the floor immediately. I could not move again.I just lay there for a moment, holding my throat. Tears welling up in my eyes, I covered my face with both hands. Slowly I got up and walked to the table. I picked up the hand mirror and looked at my throat. The chain marks were clearly visible and the bruises were already starting to form. If my legs were one inch shorter or the chain one inch higher. I would be dead right now.

The reality of what I had done to myself sank in! I realized I could never tell anyone because there was no telling what he would do to them? I went upstairs and changed my shirt and put on one of my turtle neck shirts on. Luckily I owned 3 or 4 of them because I knew the bruises would take weeks to heal.

My mother was still not home. We had a painting of the Sacred Heart of Jesus hanging in our living room. I sank to my knees and began to pray.

"Oh Lord please help me. Please help me Lord. Please. You're the only one I can turn to. Cast him out of me. I've ruined my life. I've sold my soul... Worse, I've given it away for the promise of power. Now I've lost everything! He has stolen my life Lord. Please help me. Please help me! I don't know what to do? I can't even tell anyone except you! Please save me. Please!!"

"Remain calm Mr. Michelson. The past is gone. It was long ago. You are only an independent observer. Do you understand?" Dr. Bornstein reassured him.

"Yes. I understand." Paul said more calmly.

"What happened next?" The doctor asked.

"I went to my room and laid on my bed. I heard my mother come home. I helped her with the groceries. She fed me dinner and afterwards I went to my room to watch tv to try and take my mind off of my problem.

There was an old movie on. I began to watch it. It was called 'The Three Faces of Eve." As I watched it I couldn't believe what I was seeing? The movie was about a woman who had 3 personalities all living in one body. They could take her over at will and she had no memory of what had happened?

When it was over I said another prayer. "Thank you Lord for hearing my prayer. Now I know what is really wrong with me? I must be suffering from a split personality. It's all starting to make sense. Those high fevers I had may have caused some brain damage. I see the truth now. Simon is just part of me. He's a handicap, but that is all. I suppose if Helen Keller, who was blind and deaf could go on to become a teacher, then I'm sure I can live with this. But still I'd better keep it a secret because they'd probably want to put me in an asylum if anyone ever found out."

"I'm going to awaken you now Mr. Michelson. As we count backwards from ten to zero you will gradually awaken. You will remember everything. Do you understand?"

"Yes." Paul replied.

"10, 9, 8, 7, 6, 5, 4, 3, 2, 1, 0. Wake up Mr. Michelson."

"Wow! That was amazing. It was just like being there." Paul said.

"Yes. Hypnosis is a very useful tool. So you tell me that to this day you still experience these blackouts and another personality takes over your body." The doctor asks.

"Yes sir. That's correct." Paul tells him. "I don't know how to describe the full horror of it to someone who has never experienced it. Most people can imagine sleep walking. Your body acting out some dream. But imagine if you woke up in the middle of it and still had no control over your body? It just kept moving and acting on its own and all you could so was to watch helplessly from inside."

"How often does this happen to you?" Bornstein asks.

"At least once a month, but more often than that usually. He can come out anytime, day or night. Asleep or awake. I noticed over the years that it seems to revolve around the full moon cycle. He seems to be stronger then for some reason."

"You were 13 when this started. What would happen back then when he would take you over? What would he do?"

"Not too much really. It was all very strange. Usually he would come out at school. He would pick out some girl in class and just stare at her. He would stare a hole though her for 20 to 30 minutes and then it would be over. I never did figure out what the purpose of that was? It got me beat up once though when the girl noticed and told her boyfriend. He looked me up between classes and hit me in the gut. But other than that it seemed harmless enough. Believe it or not I just got used to it."

"You say sometimes you had no memory and other times seemed more like a spectator in your own body."

"Yes. Actually the attacks came in four types. The complete blackouts were the rarest thankfully. The spectator types were the most common. Then sometimes he would take me over when I was asleep. I'd go to bed in one place and wake up somewhere else. Like in my car or on a strange street with no idea where I was or how I got there?

Then there was what I call the "us" stage. I could feel his presence like he was standing right behind me. When that happened I knew he was waiting to see how I handled things. If I did what he wanted, he did not take me over. But I knew that he could at anytime."

"I think that will be all for today Mr. Michelson. Please come see me again next week." Dr. Bornstein says and clicks off his tape recorder.

(This ended the transcript for this session. Mr. Michelson returned to my office on August 12,1995. The following is a transcript of that session.)

"Good afternoon Mr. Michelson, there will be no need for hypnosis this session. I'd like you to summarize the rest of your life from age 13 to present."

Very well. In 1969 I turned 14. My secret problem continued but I had actually grown used to it. The longest he seemed to be able to take over my body was 2 hours at the most but usually must shorter spells. It would generally happen at school and he would do that staring thing. It seemed harmless enough."

"What about the summer months?"

"Yes he would take me over while in the basement back then and would sometimes perform some strange meditation rituals. I never really understood what he was doing? But again it seemed harmless enough, so I kind of got used to it." Paul says.

"Did you ever communicate with him via the ouija board again?" Dr. Bornstein asks.

"No. But he still came to me in dreams."

Bornstein says, "Tell me about that."

"I will be having an ordinary dream and suddenly he appears in it. It's strange but in my dream state I am always glad to see him. Like greeting a long lost relative. I sure don't feel that way about him when I'm awake. But usually we end up going for a walk and he teaches me things."

"Such as?" The doctor asks.

"Magic mostly, illusions and ceremonial magic. I actually received full blown illusions in my sleep. Like "The floating head" illusion which I later used in my show. So not only did I get used to my strange condition, but God help me, I was starting to like it."

"You implied that the walking sounds and other strange phenomenon you experienced did not stop after the spell of invocation as promised."

"That's right." Paul explains, "I could only conclude that he lied to me about the cause. Somehow it was all coming from him. But other events at my house soon made me forget all about Simon. He seemed pretty trivial by comparison.

"What events?"

"My mother began to change. From the time I was 13 until 19 she began to drink more and more. She no longer even looked like the loving mother I was used to. She turned into my worst nightmare. I didn't understand then why she was drinking so much? Now looking back on it, I realize it was because she was in pain. The tumors had returned and she drank to kill the pain.

It's obvious now but then all I knew was that she turned my world into a living Hell of screaming, ranting and raving. I spent most of my time trying to stay away from her.

Her appearance began to change too. She's always been so thin and now she had begun to swell. Her abdomen in particular and her color grew jaundiced. She quit fixing her hair and walked around in a bathrobe all day.

She was going through a case of beer a day and sometimes she chased that with whiskey. So like I said, Simon seemed pretty trivial compared to being trapped in a house with a mad woman who threatened to kill you constantly."

"Did you grow to hate your mother?" Bornstein asks him.

"No. No I couldn't. She was my whole world. I blamed it all on the alcohol and I can't stand to be around drunks to this day. But one good thing did happen during my teenage years. I stopped getting sick.

From age 7 till 13 I caught every cold, flu and childhood disease imaginable. But right after the ritual I never had another sick day. Oh I'd catch the occasional cold like everyone else but instead of having it 7 to 10 days like most people, it would only last 24 to 48 hours tops.

The weird part is when Simon would take me over, the cold symptoms would disappear. Then they would return when I was back in control. So I went from having almost no immunity to diseases to having a super-immune system."

"Let us proceed with your biography. What was the next major turning point in your life?"

"Meeting Lavonne. I was in my senior year. I was now 18 but still subject to my forced imprisonment at home. I had intended to leave home after I graduated in June but while in school that year I met a Lavonne who was a sophomore. She sat in the desk in front of me in Anatomy and Physiology class. My reputation as the school magician had grown and I showed her a few magic tricks. I could tell after awhile that she had become infatuated with me.

This was a new experience for me. As most of my class hated me like poison. Because no one had ever seen me date anyone rumors spread that I was gay. Which fueled the bullies hatred of me even more. So now for the first time a young lady was showing interest in me. But still I was not even allowed out of my house so dating was out of the question.

Then one month Simon took me over in class. He scooted my desk forward until my knees were brushing against Lavonne's buttocks. Then he left me and after class she kept trying to follow me to talk about it. I kept avoiding her because I didn't know what to say?

"Sorry Lavonne it was my alter ego who made a pass at you!" Well she didn't give up easily. Knowing Larry was my only friend she got my address from him and rode her bicycle over to my house one Saturday. When my mother opened the door Lavonne said, "Is Paul at home? I was hoping we could go for a ride."

My mother said, "Yes, he's at home, but he's not allowed to leave the yard." Lavonne said, "Why not?" My mother said, "Because I said so!" and slammed the door in her face!

I was in my bedroom at the time. I called Larry and he confessed that he had given her my address. He also had her phone number. So I called her to ask her to please not tell anyone about my embarrassing home life.

Well we got to talking and it turned out that she lived alone with her father who was also an alcoholic. She was his adopted daughter and he'd had 7 wives already because no one could live with his drunken rages. So she completely understood. We talked on the phone everyday after that. This was in 1974. I had one more month until graduation. Then I was planning on leaving home.

So in June I graduated and turned 19. The time had come to defy my mother's imprisonment. I got up way before dawn and left a note on the kitchen table. "Gone for a walk!" Then I stepped out the door and walked out of my yard for the first time in my life. I walked to Lavonne's house. She had already told me that her father was out of town on business. Her mouth flew open when she opened the door and saw me standing there.

"Come in!" she said and pulled me inside. Well the door hardly closed before the clothes started flying."

"So you had your first sexual experience at age 19".

"Yes, but something odd happened. For a few minutes during our lovemaking, Simon took over my body. I was no longer in control, he was. Lavonne of course never knew the difference.

Well afterwards I was afraid to go home. I didn't know what my mother would do? When I got home she was standing at the kitchen counter cutting up chicken with that butcher knife of hers. But when I walked in the door, instead of exploding in rage like I expected, she very coldly said, "Where have you been?"

Not wanting to put Lavonne in danger, I lied and said that I was out looking for a job and that I was moving out. That was the day my imprisonment ended. She finally realized I was over 18 and there was she could no longer keep me at home.

Shortly after that I did get my first job. I went to work at the only Magic and Novelty store in Louisville. It was my dream job. Selling magic tricks. Lavonne and I began secretly dating. Her father knew but I didn't tell my mother of course, as I knew that she didn't like Lavonne.

Simon all but disappeared. He came out only during sex, but otherwise it was as though he didn't exist. But then in July of 1974 I took a call at work. An amusement Park in Cave City, Ky called "Gunsmoke Mountain" called because they were looking got a mid-season replacement for their magician. The one they had quit suddenly.

So I had my father drive me there. I auditioned and got the job. It meant living at the park through the summer. I did 3 shows a day and lived in an apartment behind the stage. I loved it.

But then Simon returned. He took me over on the first night of the full moon in July. I awoke in a motel room in Cave City with no idea how I had gotten there? Two hours were missing from my life. It happened all 3 nights of the full moon and again the following month in August.

At the park my co-workers started talking about seeing a ghost there. Many of the girls said that they were hearing walking sounds in their room at night and one said she saw a black form in her room. I said nothing about Simon of course. But I was sure him.

In September the park closed for the winter and I came home. Since I was invited to come back next summer. I knew all I needed to do was to book enough shows for the winter and my dream of becoming a full time professional magician would come true. I told my father I needed a car and he cashed in a life insurance policy he had been keeping for me and I bought my first car with it. It was a 1974 Vega.

With a car I was now completely independent. Lavonne and I began dating openly and I began training her to be my assistannt in the show. I went to see several local malls trying to book some shows and I thought I had booked 3 but two of them backed out at the last minute. I learned to get things in writing after that.

I kept trying to book elementary school showsbut learned that Jefferson county where I lived would not allow shows during school hours. I tried Bullet county but learned that most of the schools were already booked by a local magician who performed there annually. I did get a few that he missed. But it would not be enough to support me alone, let alone two of us. Lavonne and I planned on being married as soon as she turned 18 in 1976.

In June 1975 I called "Gunsmoke Mountain" and discovered that the magician who I had replaced decided to return and since he had been there for years they decided to rehire him. Which means I was out in the cold. I still had not seen any sign of Simon once I returned home and Lavonne and I had gotten back together. I felt that her love had cured me. He still came out briefly during sex but otherwise it was as though he did not exist. I could live with that.

But then Lavonne began hearing the walking sounds at her house. I heard them there too. She lived in the furnished basement of her father's house. On the steps that led down to the basement each step had this metal strip on the edge of it. You could plainly hear the clacking sound of shoes on those metal strips. It sounded exactly like someone was coming down the steps. Well that caused us a fright a few times. We didn't want her father to catch is in bed of course. But no one was there.

Then one night Lavonne called me at home. She was hysterical and talking so fast I couldn't understand her at first. But she finally calmed down enough to tell me what had happened? She said that she had just gone to bed and turned out the light. The only light that was on was the one in their laundry room. She was laying there with her back to the doorway when she felt like someone was watching her.

She slowly turned over and her heart nearly stopped beating, because standing in her doorway was the silhoutte of a man! All she could see of him was his eyes, which seemed to glow. They were blue eyes staring at her. Ever so slowly she reached for the lamp beside her bed and searched the whole house, but no one was there. That was when she called me. I talked to her on the phone until she calmed down enough to go to sleep.

But the next night it happened again. Once again she was in bed and felt like someone was watching her. But this time she was facing the doorway and did not see anyone. But when she rolled over she saw the same two eyes looking at her through the basement window. She screamed and her eyes went closed. When she opened them it was gone.

The activity began to increase at her house. We both heard the toilet flush upstairs when no one was in the house but us. It kept happening and we kind of got used to it. But one day Larry came over and we were all talking downstairs when suddenly we heard the toilet flush upstairs.

Larry said, "Who's upstairs?"

We said, "No one." We told him about what was going on? He thought it was all pretty weird."

"Were you married the next year then?" Bornstein asks.

"Yes. Lavonne turned 18 so we eloped. My mother was devastated. She didn't consider you married unless it was a church wedding. So to keep peace in the family we were married again in the church the next month in August.

Her father bought us an old trailer in a trailer park. We got odd jobs. We both went to work at a fast food place. She waited tables and I was a dishwasher. Meanwhile I kept trying to book us enough shows to turn professional.

I met an older man named William Stevens. He was a professional ventriloquist and had been working the school show circuit for years. He came to watch our show and liked what he saw so he proposed that we combine our shows. We mailed out brochures to every school in Kentucky and booked ourselves in over 200 schools that year. I felt that my dream of becoming a professional magician was coming to pass. That was in the winter of 76-77.

But something began happening to Lavonne's health. She had always been healthy all of the life but starting about six months into our marriage she began having these coughing attacks. They would last from 15 to 45 minutes. She'd bring up volumes of phlegm. The doctor's did not know what was wrong with her?

All the money we made was eaten up in doctor bills and medicine for her. When winter hit she got pneumonia and began to lose weight. She dropped down to 96 pounds and she got so weak I'd have to carry her to the bathroom. In the summer months she would get better. No pneumonia at least.

That year I learned that my mother had colon cancer. She was operated on and was getting chemo and radiation treatments. My folks moved from Blue Lick when the new expressway took our old home. I was so broke from Lavonne's medical bills that we couldn't pay our fuel oil bill for our furnace. Our pipes froze up and burst under the trailer forming a large ice burg. So we had to move in with my folks. My mother was ill downstairs and my wife was ill upstairs.

Then in the summer of 78 "Gunsmoke Mountain" called me. Their magician quit on them again, so they offered the job to me. We took it of course. Lavonne and I did 3 shows a day there and lived in the apartment above the stage. While we were there my mother's health grew worse.

We returned in September of 78 when the park closed. Once again I was invited to return the next summer. My uncle repaired our trailer while we were gone. That winter Lavonne caught pneumonia and her condition grew too bad for her to be able to work. The peanuts I made working as a self-service attendant barely fed us and paid the rent. She rallied for the shows when I needed her.

But it became clear that her health was not going to improve nor was my mother's. My mother's weight began to drop and she started looking like a walking skeleton. She asked us to move in with her to help her. So we did. Everyday I watched my mother slowly disappear.

In January of 79 my mother passed away. There was a blizzard the day of her funeral but I didn't even feel the cold. I was too numb with grief.

Lavonne and I moved back into our trailer. Her condition kept growing worse. Naturally our sex life took a nosedive. It was no problem for me, but it seemed to be for Simon. I was working as a janitor now at a college. Simon once again began to take me over monthly.

He would introduce himself to some college girl by doing magic tricks for them and somehow within minutes he convinced them to have sex with him in one of the storage rooms or wherever he could get them alone.

Now I had the guilt of cheating on my sick wife to live with. Plus just when I thought my split personality was over, now it was back and I had to worry about Lavonne finding out about it.

In April of 1979 my best friend, Larry Troutman was diagnosed as having a cancerous tumor in his nose. He began getting chemo-therapy and radiation.

In August of 79 he died on the operating table. I went over to my father's house to ask him if he wanted to attend Larry's funeral and I noticed that my dog Lucky could barely stand. I rushed him to the vet and he also was eaten up with cancer. I gave the doctor permission to put him to sleep.

I went to the vet and picked up his remains. I took them over to my father's house and began digging a grave for Lucky in his backyard. I kept thinking, "What is going on here? Why was everyone I loved dying of cancer the same year? Katie in January, Larry in August and now even my dog! Who was next?"

In 1980 Lavonne discovered that the Ceta program would pay for us to go to LPN school. She had always wanted to be a nurse as I had always wanted to be a magician. So we went for it. Simon kept taking me over monthly.

I kept waking up in my car in our trailer park, 3 rows over from where we lived. One day while driving through the park I saw a blonde woman standing in front of that trailer I kept waking up in front of. She waved when she saw me and I knew that Simon had found a mistress.

So to break that up, I talked Lavonne into selling the trailer and we moved into an apartment by McNeely Lake. Her health declined even further that year and I had to rush her to the emergency room when she could barely breathe. They admitted her with pneumonia but she only stayed 3 days because she wanted to graduate from nursing school.

In April of 81 we graduated LPN school and obtained our first nursing jobs. Lavonne worked when her health would allow it. I took my first nursing home job. But like being the only rooster in a hen house, I worked with 99% women.

Simon had a field day. Every month he seduced someone at work. There was nothing I could do to stop him and I had to just live with the guilt and the fear that Lavonne would find out and leave me. With more income than we had ever had, we decided to rent a house on Barbee street in Louisville.

In the winter of 82 Lavonne had to be hospitalized again for her deteriorating lung condition. But this time I had health insurance and so we called in a lung specialist who wanted to do a lung biopsy to determine what was really wrong with her? In the meantime my father's health took a nosedive. He ended up in the hospital because of his diabetes, which went out of control.

My friend William Stevens met a young girl named Janet. They came over to our house. Lavonne and William went out back to work on the Winnebago that we used to travel around and do our shows with. I'd bought it with the money that we had made at Gunsmoke Mountain.

While they were gone Simon took me over and made a pass at Janet. But just then Lavonne came back in and Janet asked William to take her home. That pretty much ended that friendship and I was never able to explain what happened? Who would believe me anyway?"

"What result did the lung specialist find when he performed the lung biopsy on your wife?" Bornstein asks him.

"He was stumped. He saw she' had massive interstitial inflammation in her lung tissues but could not identify the cause. Meanwhile I now had a 15,000 dollar bill because Blue Cross and Blue Shield decided that they would not pay for it because it was a "pre-existing condition". The hospital demanded payment so we had to take bankruptcy.

Meanwhile when my father got out of the hospital he was too weak to take care of himself. The doctors recommended a nursing home. But it was killing us to see him in there. So Pat proposed that I move in with him and take care of him. I said I couldn't just quit my job because I was so deep in debt. The bankruptcy had not gone through as yet. So he offered to pay us a 200 dollar allowance each week out of Dutch's pension to care for him at his home. So I agreed to it.

We moved in with him in January of 83 and I took care of him around the clock until mid November. It was a full time job, as he could not even walk when he went home.

Simon became furious that I had quit my job in the nursing home. He came to me in dreams and insisted that I leave there. I refused.

Then he threatened to force me out. I wasn't sure what he meant by that? I figured there was nothing he could do about it. Unfortunately fate dealt me a blow because my nephew little Ricky and his new wife Becky moved into my father's house with Lavonne and me.

That was all the ammunition that Simon needed. It didn't take long for Simon to live up to his threat. He took me over and made a pass at Ricky's wife Becky. She told Ricky and he told Lavonne and I had some explaining to do.

So I just came out and told them I had a split personality and the strain of taking care of Dutch brought it out. I left out all of the mystical stuff as I figured it was hard enough of a story to believe as it was.

Well they all forgave me and I figured I had checkmated Simon's attempt to drive me out. Now instead of being angry with me they all felt sorry for crazy old Paul. Unfortunately in October of 83 Simon upped the ante. I had a dream in which he showed me that his next move was going to be to go after my niece Tammy.

I knew if that happened and Donnie found out he would kill me, no questions asked. So I announced to the family that I could do no more for Dutch and I feared one more winter in Kentucky would kill Lavonne. That was only a partial lie as I was worried for her.

So we packed up our Winnebago and left for St. Petersburg, FI. She and I were staying a KOA campground and waiting for our Florida nursing license's to arrive. I called home to check on Dutch. I'd only been gone a week and he had a heart attack and was rushed to the hospital. He died before I could get back home.

We stayed for the funeral and then headed back to St. Petersburg, FI. More guilt to live with. Would he have died had I been there? I couldn't help but feel that I'd let him down.

We both got jobs in a nursing home. Lavonne had to quit after 6 months. Her health was too poor to work full time. Simon began his flings again at work. I had to switch jobs roughly every six months because of his antics.

The next major turning point came in 1988. I lived in fear that Lavonne would find out about his affairs. How would I ever explain it? Who would believe me? I didn't even really understand it myself.

All really wanted was to live a normal life but with Simon that was impossible. Lavonne's illness improved only slightly without the harsh Kentucky winters. She at least was spared catching pneumonia. But rumors about me eventually caught up with me.

For her birthday in 1987 I bought her a plane ticket home to visit her father who was dying of cancer. While there she ran into her old high school boyfriend who had just left his wife. So they made plans. She came home and told me she was planning on moving home to live with her sister for awhile.

She left on a Friday in March of 1988 and I said, "Please call when you get there."

She called at 6pm to say she was as far as Nashville and she was going to drive straight on through.

I said, "Call me when you arrive. I'll wait up." I waited all night and no call came. By 6pm Saturday I finally reached her sister who said she hadn't seen her. Well I freaked out. I was sure she was off in a ditch or a Ted Bundy type had gotten her.

I called the police but they said they couldn't do anything until she had been missing 48 hours! There was nothing I could do but wait.

Saturday night passed. I walked the floor all night. I was so sick I was throwing up in the toilet. Sunday morning, no call. Sunday afternoon, no call. Sunday evening at 6pm she had been missing 48 hours so I called the police. I had the state police out in 4 states looking for her.

At 10pm, a man calls. He tells me Lavonne has been with him and she wants a divorce. I said, "Well I don't think that's going to be a problem." I hung up and sank to the floor. I couldn't even be angry with her. I felt she was right to leave me.

After two weeks of living alone, I decided I had to move. Too many memories in that place that we had rented for 3 years. So I went to the nursing home I was working at and placed an ad on the bulletin board listing all of my furniture for sale. I was practically giving it away.

People came from everywhere the next day. I had sold my lamps, so to see to read by I lit my oil lamp. I left it burning when I went to the bathroom to take my shower as I had done a million times before. When I got out of the shower, I dried off and got dressed.

I opened the bathroom door and black smoke hit me in the face. I rushed around the corner and the whole living room was on fire. I ran out of the house and across the street to the neighbors and banged on their door to ask them to call the fire department. What the fire did not destroy, the fire department did with their axes and water hoses.

I lost everything I owned. A few weeks later I moved into efficiency apartment. On the plus side I discovered the BayArea Renaissance festival.

I already had the perfect costume. Simon led me to a shop in Louisville called Hollywood's and I found a Greek Orthodox priest cape and tunic. I changed the Christian Cross on the back to the double pentagram symbol I'd used in the invocation spell so long ago.

The plan at the time was to perform my act under the name Simon Magus. But with everyone growing sick and dying around me my magic career had to be put in cold storage. But now with the festival I found an outlet to get back into it. So I performed street magic there each year as Simon Magus.

In August of 88 I met a nurse named Debra S. at a nursing home the agency sent me too. She turned out to be a fan of the Renaissance festival and we hit it right off like old friends. So I worked up the courage to ask her out. We dated for 30 days but she turned out to have a bad drinking and drug problem.

Still we tried to make a go of it. But as always Simon came out and seduced two other women at work. I realized I could never have a real relationship with anyone as long as he dominated my life. So I told her it was over.

But she didn't take it very well. She showed up at my efficiency apartment at 3am stoned out of her mind. She was ranting and calling me names and I was afraid the old couple I rented from would toss me out.

I let her in. But things got worse as she began tossing my stuff around. Then Simon suddenly came out and slapped her 3 times. Then left me! I came to and saw her nose bleeding and I tried to comfort her but she was inconsolable. She slammed my door so hard she broke several panes of glass in the door.

My landlords kicked me out the next day. I went to the apartment of Deborah B. One of the girls Simon had cheated on Debra S. with.

Simon had seduced Deborah B. years before when I was still with Lavonne. Curiously Simon had actually told Deborah who he was and so she was the only living person who know about my alter ego."

"Let me get this straight. You're saying that Simon told this Deborah B. that he was your other self?" Bornstein asked.

"Yes" Paul said, "So I told her what had happened with Debra S and she took me in. I stayed there 3 months. I felt horribly guilty though, for I knew that Deborah B. loved me dearly and all I really felt for her was friendship and gratitude.

When Simon would come out she allowed him to use her for sex because she wanted to be with me. This went on for months and then I decided that perhaps I could find a home there.

She already knew about my alter ego and was willing to live with it. Maybe I could learn to love her more than just as a friend. I was certainly grateful to her for helping me in my darkest times.

While I was still trying to decide whether to stay or move out, one night she had some friends come by unexpectedly. Unfortunately it was the first night of the full moon. The couple brought their little dog with them. We were all watching a movie on tv when I felt the change coming over me.

I looked over and their little dog was staring a hole through me. He began to cock his head back and forth. He was somehow sensing the change as it was happening to me! That was the last thing I remember.

Simon rose from the chair. He excused himself and left the apartment. He drove off in my van to the puzzlement of Deborah's friends. I woke up two hours later on the beach. I had no idea where I was? No idea where my van was? It took me some time to find it. Then I called Deborah to tell her I was all right.

I decided I wasn't doing Deborah any favors by letting her get increasingly involved with me. It was clear I was going to end up either in prison or an asylum eventually. So I moved out and into my van. But she followed me. She did not want to let me go. I thought I'd just live in my van and make a hermit out of myself. But when the full moon cycle hit Simon would always knock on her door and she would always let him in.

So I took a job in Largo, Florida hoping that I would be too far away from Simon to reach her in his allotted 2 hour time limit. I was still living in my van. I was allowed to live in the parking lot of the nursing home. I worked 12 hour shifts on the weekends.

As usual Simon managed to seduce many of my co-workers there. Still during the week he frequently drove to Deborah B.'s to be with her as well. I was just getting numb to the whole thing by now.

Then one weekend in April of 89 I got a call from Lavonne. She told me she was pregnant and I wished her well. The next month in May I got a call from her new husband who told me that she went into pre-mature labor. They rushed her to the hospital and her lungs collapsed on the table.

The baby girl lived but Lavonne was on a respirator and not expected to make it. So when I got off work I drove to Deborah B.'s and asked her to watch my van and to please drive me to the airport. I caught a flight to Louisville and arrived at 4pm. I took a taxi to the hospital and went straight to the Intensive care unit.

But now I had a problem. Because only the next of kin was allowed in and even though we had been married for 12 years and her current husband only a few months, I was not allowed in. So I was determined to get inside somehow. I was still in my nursing uniform from working the night before.

Who should happen to come down the hall right at that moment but my cousin Rick Murray? Who was now a minister in the Church of Christ.

He said, "Look as a minister they have to let me in. So I'll go in the entrance and when I come out the exit you slip in."   We tried that and it worked. I got in, but my God! I had to look at the name on the door twice to make sure it was really her! She was so swollen I didn't even recognize her. She had a trach and couldn't speak.

I sat on the bed and held her hand. I could see by her eyes that she knew it was me. I told her how sorry I was and that if I had only known this was going to happen I wouldn't have let her leave. Just then the nurse caught me and made me leave. When her husband found out he had me banned from the hospital.

I asked Rickey to drive me to Donnie's and he already knew I was in town. Apparently the nurse had called Lavonne's husband to tell him Mr. Michelson had sneaked into Intensive Care. Donnie and Rickey insisted on driving me all the way back to St. Pete.

They didn't want me to leave of course. But I couldn't stay there. Not ever knowing what Simon was going to do next? So I went back and lived in my van in that nursing home parking lot. About 10 days later I got a call from Donnie. Lavonne was dead. I decided that it was time to end my pact with Simon as well. The only thing that I couldn't decide was how to do it?"

"You decided to commit suicide you mean?" Dr. Bornstein stated.

"I didn't consider it suicide. I considered it an execution. Simon's. My life ended the day he took over my body as far as I was concerned. I was only Simon's puppet. His slave. Well enough was enough!

I knew that since it was June in Florida and the temperature was in the high 90's in the daytime and inside the closed van it rose to way over 120 degrees.

I decided when I got off work on Monday morning I would just roll up the windows and go to sleep and never get up. How long could anyone last in an oven?

I awoke around noon and could barely breathe. I resisted the temptation to open the door or windows. I just lay there and hoped dehydration would kill me quickly. It did not.

3 days later I was still lying there. My tongue now felt like a piece of wood in my mouth and my eyes burned like fire. But still I just wouldn't die! I had no idea dehydration was such a painful death.

On the 4th day I couldn't take it anymore and I drank some water.

I thought, "Well I'll drink water but I won't eat any food. It will take a lot longer but I will starve eventually.

Saturday night came and I had not eaten in 7 days and I had to go into work at 7pm. Part of my job was to help feed the patients. That was more torture. I made it through Saturday but my head was killing me and I was so weak from not eating that on Sunday I just said, "This is really stupid." I gave up and ate something and decided that Lavonne would not want me to do this anyway.

In August I met a girl I really liked at work. Her name was Deborah H. What is it with that name anyway? But she would come out to my van every night and we would talk before she had to go home. I became infatuated with her and one night she came to see me and told me that she had broken up with her boyfriend.

Somewhere in the night the talking stopped. We dated for 3 weeks. One night after we made love in the van she said to me "You have the bluest eyes"! I said, "Blue!!"

I sat up in the van and looked at my eyes in the mirror. She asked me what was wrong? I probably should have just told her I had a headache. But I blurted out the truth. She went back to her old boyfriend shortly after that and moved away. I never saw her again.

Meanwhile Simon started up his old tricks at work and I ended up leaving that job. Simon kept dropping in on Deborah B and my van started breaking down and she was the only one I could call for help. She was always there for me and that made me feel guiltier than ever. I felt like I was just using her and as long as I was in her life she would not look elsewhere for love.

In 1990 I finally got Lavonne's last hospital bill paid off and so I decided to move out of the van and into an apartment. I met another nurse I liked a whole lot. Despite myself I became infatuated with her.

Her name was Brenda R. one night at work I learned that she had just gotten a divorce. So I asked her out. I know I shouldn't have but one can take only so much lonliness. We only dated for 3 weekends.

One evening she arrived at my apartment in near hysterics. She said that on the drive over to my place she felt invisible hands touching her all over. She nearly had an accident because of it. I told her that strange things like that always happen to people I am close to. She moved to Tallahassee the next weekend and wrote me a month later to tell me she had gotten married.

In 1991 Simon kept on seducing women at work and visiting Deborah B. in between, who was still carrying a torch for me. I gave up trying to avoid her, for her own good and let her back into my life. We went to the movies and saw each other weekly at least.

In 1992 I met a young girl at work named Tanya M. Simon came out and gave her my phone number and she called me. While we were talking on the phone he took me over and invited her over.

She came over and he seduced her. I woke up while we were still lying in each other's arms. I was pretty lonely and asked her to move in with me. She did but only stayed 30 days.

Simon drove her off. He levitated in front of her and she freaked. I ended up telling her about my other self. It was too much for her. She went back to back to her "normal" boyfriend.

Then in September of 1992 I met Susan Egan at work and fell madly in love with her. We started dating in November of 92. I moved in with her in January of 93 and we were married in March of 93.

So I've come full circle. Six months into this marriage my wife who was only 36 began showing the symptoms of full blown menopause. Between her anxiety attacks and the additional stress her alcoholic, diabetic mother and her bi-polar drug addict son put her through, our sex life all but vanished.

That was when it hit me. Lavonne became physically ill also six months into our marriage. Neither wife had been sick a day hardly until they married me. In both cases I ended up in a sexless marriage and Simon began his seductions of my coworkers.

I just don't believe in coincidence. I think somehow he is responsible for not only their illnesses but perhaps all of the illness and death that seems to occur to everyone I love most.

Now I've come to you doctor. I'm hoping you can help me free myself of this duel existence. Whatever Simon really is, I want him out of my life. Can you help me?'

'Yes, I can help you Mr. Michelson. But our time is up this week. Come see me next week and we will discuss your diagnosis and treatment." Dr. Bornstein tells him.

"Thank you Dr. Bornstein. You've given me hope at least. Plus it really felt good to get all of that off of my chest. It's been bottled up for so long." Paul tells him.

CHAPTER 5
The Diagnosis

(The following is the transcript for the August 22, 1995 appointment with the patient Paul Michelson.- Dr. Morris Bornstein)

"Good afternoon Mr. Michelson, please be seated." Dr. Bornstein says.

"Thank you doctor. Have you come to any conclusions about what is wrong with me?" Paul asks.

"I have. Let's re-cap the highlights of your autobiography and deal with the case one issue at a time, shall we? In October of 1968, when you were 13 years old, you performed a magic ritual on Halloween and after which you've come to believe that you were possessed by the ghost of a 2000 year old sorcerer. Is that correct?" The doctor asks.

"Yes...You know it sounds even crazier coming from you." Paul says.

"We do not use that word in here. To begin with, no one is completely sane Mr. Michelson. We all have issues and baggage to deal with. But let us continue. From the age of 13 you believed yourself to be either possessed or a case of multiple personality syndrome.

You should know that there have been very few cases of multiple personality syndrome throughout history Mr. Michelson. I have not ruled it out but I suspect that you are suffering from a paranoid delusion. A delusion is a fixed, false belief.

You've taken great pains to point out all of the activity and occurances which you've deemed supernatural, and therefore provide you with circumstancial evidence that Simon exists outside of yourself. That he is not a part of you and thus you need accept no guilt for his actions. But I am sure that you will not blame me if given a choice between a natural explanation and a supernatural one to choose the former and not the latter." Bornstein tells him.

"Not at all. I'd be very relieved to hear a natural, logical explanation for this." Paul says.

"That's good to hear. Let us then look at this Simon personality you've created as a paranoid delusion. Simon then, would be a convenient scapegoat for not only everything bad that's ever happened to you, but everything bad that you've ever done.

Let's look at him from the beginning. You were 13 years old when he came into your life. Now I will ask you a question. At what age did you reach puberty?" Bornstein asks him.

"Also age 13." Paul states.

"Did you masturbate often?"

"Oh yes. I spent so much time in the bathroom my parents probably thought I had diarrhea." Paul says.

"How often did you masturbate?"

"Oh, I don't know. Probably 3 or 4 times a day." Paul answers.

"How did your mother and father feel about masturbation? Bornstein asks.

"Well they were devout Roman Catholics. The church teaches that masturbation is a mortal sin." Paul explains.

"Did you always obey your parents?

"Yes always." Paul states.

"But for the first time in your life you were hiding and deliberately disobeying them." Bornstein points out.

"Yes, that's true."

"How did your parents feel about sex in general?"

"They believed that all sex outside of marriage was sinful and even in marriage except for the purpose of procreation."

"Did you believe that too?"

"No. Not really." Paul says, "I just thought that teaching of the church was old fashioned thinking."

"So for the first 12 years of your life you believed everything your parents and the church taught you and now at age 13 you believed that they were wrong about something." Bornstein states.

"Yes."

"Can you not see that this set up a conflict within you? You had to put on one face for your parents, that of a good little Catholic boy that they wanted you to be, and then you had a secret face didn't you? A face that you never showed to them. Nor dared to. The face of a lustful teenage boy who couldn't get enough sex.

Now it was about then that you began to play with your ouija board. I happen to agree with your young friend Larry that a ouija board taps into your subconscious mind. I believe that is all you were doing here. For evidence I point out that Simon's messages always seemed to point out error's in church dogma. I believe that you were seeking to justify your natural urges to masturbate which is also against church dogma. If Simon provided you with examples where the church was wrong about some of their teachings, then perhaps they were also wrong about their teachings regarding sex and masturbation, you see?

Now later Simon offered to become part of you didn't he? And you were delighted by this offer, were you not? Why do you think that any young boy would want a stranger to share his body? Why would that appeal to you?" Bornstein asks.

"Because Simon was so powerful." Paul comments.

"Exactly and you were not. You were powerless and helpless to fight either the bullies at school who tormented you or your domineering mother who controlled every aspect of your life. You had no autonomy at all. You had to obey her without question.

So subconsciously you wished that you had power. Simon empowered you. You desired him to become part of you, didn't you? But in reality he was already a part of you. He was your subconscious incarnate. Through him you now had permission to do all of the things that you always wanted to do but couldn't face about yourself." Bornstein states.

"But Doc ... what about all of the supernatural occurances?" Paul asks.

"There wasn't any. I haven't heard a single unexplainable event." Bornstein tells him.

"What about all of those things my mother saw? Her visions for instance and the things she told me about on McCawley Road?" Paul asks.

"You grew up hearing all of your mother's tales about your former home, which instilled in you early on a belief in the supernatural. But you received them second hand from your mother who by her own admission often saw and heard things that were not there. She called them psychic visions, but in psychiatry we refer to it as schizophrenia, a disease in which the victim suffers from auditory and optical hallucinations." The doctor explains.

"Ok ... That's possible. But what about things like the walking sounds?" Paul asks.

"I thought your father did an excellent job of explaining that by telling you that it was the house settling."

"Yes...but others heard it as well in their homes. Lavonne and Larry for instance." Paul states.

"Ok you see what you do? You connect dots and apply supernatural connections to ordinary events. If more than one person's imagination runs away with them, then what they imagined must be real. Do you not see the illogic of that?" Bornstein asks.

"Very well, but what about all or the sickness and deaths that seem to surround me?" Paul asks.

"As a doctor I must tell you that there are two rules to medicine. Rule number one is that everyone is going to die. Rule number two is that all of the doctors and medicine in the world is not going to change rule number one. Mr. Michelson all of the illnesses and deaths of your loved ones was tragic, but that's all it was. You had nothing whatsoever to do with their deaths.

You are suffering from a guilt complex that goes all the way back to your childhood. You'll grab at any straw to blame yourself for all of the ills of the world. Even to the point of creating a fictional monster. It is no coincidence that you grew up a fan of both comic book super-heroes and horror films.

Let's examine them closely. What do characters like Superman, Batman and Spider-man all have in common?" Bornstein asks.

"Um ... they all have secret identities." Paul answers.

"Precisely. They are ordinary people by day and yet secretly they have powerful other identities do they not? Bornstein asks.

"Hmm ... yes." Paul agrees.

"You were feeling subconsciously powerless but you knew that you were also this secretly powerful character. One who had his own symbol, this double pentagram and later you even created a costume complete with cape to wear at the Renaissance Festivals. By day ordinary, boring Paul Michelson secretly transforms into the all powerful 2000 year old caped sorcerer, Simon Magus. Isn't that right?" Bornstein explains.

"Heh heh ... yeah. It sounds pretty silly when you put it like that." Paul tells him.

"Now let's turn to look at the movie monsters you loved to watch as a child and I think we can shed some light on the origins of this character your subconscious has created. You're in luck that you chose me for your doctor. As it so happens, I too am a fan of those old Universal horror films.

First take a look at "Dracula". A centuries old monster who walks around unnoticed by ordinary people. He wears a cape too doesn't he? Wherever he goes people grow sick and die, do they not?" Bornstein asks. .

"Yes" Paul is forced to agree.

"Next let's look at "Frankenstein". Is it not the story of a man whose ambition created a monster that destroyed all of those he loved most?" Bornstein asks.

"Yes."

"Then there's "The Wolf-Man". Lawrence Talbot is a good man but when ever the moon is full he transforms into a monster. Sound familiar?"

"Yes. Yes it does." Paul says.

"Need I even point out the similarities in your own case and that of "Dr. Jekyll and Mr. Hyde?"

"No, that one is pretty obvious."

"What about the movie "The Exorcist"? The story of a young girl who becomes possessed by an evil spirit by playing with a ouija board." Bornstein asks.

"Yes and even though it did not come out until 1974 and my tale takes place in 1968 I still knew all about possession from reading about it." Paul adds.

"Another movie called "The Entity" was about a spectral rapist, just like Simon. Even though they came out later than 68 you still connected the dots to your case once you viewed them."

"I see."

"You mentioned seeing the film "Diary of a Madman" starring Vincent Price? It was based on the story "The Horla" by Guy de Maupessant. It's about an invisible being that takes him over at will and makes him do horrible things." Bornstein points out.

"Yes ... That's true." Paul agrees.

"The list goes on. You mentioned the movie "Forbidden Planet" in your hypnotic regression. It was the story of a Dr. Morbius whose subconscious ID takes on a life of it's own and becomes an invisible monster who kills all of those close to the Doctor.

Can you not see how your subconscious mind has created this Simon Magus who has traits that resemble very closely bits and pieces of all your favorite film and literary characters?"

"I can't deny any of that Doc. But still there are some things that bother me about your theory. For instance the way Simon seems to show up sometimes in photos taken of me. I don't know if I even mentioned that, and also the way my eyes change color from hazel to blue. The way animals seem to sense my transformation, like that dog I mentioned at Deborah's." Paul interjects.

"I've not seen your photos but I'll bet you that I can describe them. Most ghost photos I've seen look like cloudy white mist or dark blobs in the photo are they like that?" Bornstein asks him.

"Yes. Exactly."

"Most believers in such things like to call them proof of ectoplasm, but a more logical conclusion is that they are simply flaws in the film. Remember that if evidence can have either a natural or supernatural explanation it is more rational to accept the natural explanation. Wouldn't you agree?" Bornstein says.

"Yes I would. But what about the eye color change and the animal's reactions?" Paul asks.

"Allow me to read something to you Mr. Michelson. "Dissociative Identity Disorder; Or DID is described as the existence in an individual of two or more distinct identities or personalities, each with its own pattern of percieving and interacting with the environment. At least two of these personalities are considered to routinely take control of the individual's behavior and there is also some associated memory loss. This memory loss is often referred to as "losing time"."

"Wow! That does sound exactly like me! What's the difference between multiple personality syndrome and DID?"

"Yes, I was just coming to that. Dissociative Identity Disorder that was intitially named multiple personality disorder, but there is a difference. True multiples are at best extremely rare and there is much debate as to their existence at all. But in MPD the distinct personalities have no knowledge of each other. The victim experiences amnesia or missing time but is unaware of his/her other self or selves."

But Dissociatiation is a complex mental process that provides a coping mechanism for individuals confronting painful and or traumatic situations. Dissociation describes a collapse in ego integrity so profound that the personality is considered to break apart. The difference between a psychotic break and a dissociation or dissociative break, is that someone who is experiencing a dissociation is technically pulling away from a situation that he/she cannot manage.

Some part of the person remains connected to reality. While a psychotic breaks from reality, the dissociative disconnects from it, but not all of the way. North American studies show that 97% of adults with dissociative identity disorder report abuse during their childhood. Children are not born with a sense of unified identity. It develops from many sources and experiences. In overwhelmed children its development is obstructed and many parts that should have blended into a relatively unified identity remain separate.

Human development requires that children be able to integrate complicated and different types of information and experiences successfully. As children achieve cohesive complex, appreciation's of themselves and others, they go through phases in which different perceptions and emotions are kept segregated. Each developmental stage may be used to generate different selves. Not every child who experiences abuse or major trauma has the capacity to develop multiple personalities. Patients with dissociative identity disorder can be easily hypnotized." Bornstein says.

"Oh man! One thing I left out of my narrative was that when I was doing all of those ESP experiments, I tried self-hypnosis as a method of trying to tap into my psychic powers. I literally trained myself to be suggestible. But none of this still explains the eye color change or the animal's reactions." Paul adds.

"Yes. I highlighted this next part that you should find most enlightening. "Another unusual but fascinating feature of DID is that each personality possesses a different brain wave pattern. Each has his own name, age, memories and abilities. Often his own style of handwriting, gender, cultural and racial background, artistic talents, foreign language fluency and I.Q.

Even more noteworthy are the biological changes that take place when they switch personalities. Frequently a medical condition possessed by one personality will mysteriously vanish when another personality takes over ... " Bornstein reads.

"Like my cold symptoms that would vanish when Simon took over." Paul states.

"Precisely. But there's more ... "In one documented case in Chicago all of the patient's personalities were allergic to orange juice, except one. If the man drank orange juice when one of his allergic personalities was in control, he would break out in a terrible rash. But if he switched to the non-allergic personality the rash would instantly start to fade and he could drink the orange juice freely". Other conditions that might vary from personality to personality include scars, burn marks, cysts, and left and right handedness. Visual acuity can differ and some multiples have to carry two or three different pairs of eyeglasses to accommodate their alternating personalities. One personality can be color blind and another not and even eye color can change."

"Oh wow! Ok ... Ok I'm convinced. If everything else about a person can change no doubt his scent can as well, which would account for that dog's strange reaction to me." Paul adds.

"I'm glad you agree Mr. Michelson. The first step to getting well is understanding what your problem is? So you see Simon does not exist outside of yourself. He's a coping mechanism. A way for you to face pieces of yourself, namely your sexuality that you don't want to face. Once you learn to accept that you and Simon are one and the same, you won't need to black out every time you have a sexual thought.

For instance, you tell me that Simon all but disappeared when you and your first wife Lavonne had a regular:sex life, but once she became too ill, you were cut off. You couldn't cheat on your sick wife with a clear conscience, but Simon could. Simon can do all of the things you really wanted to do. Go to topless bars, pick up prostitutes, seduce women, etc. He's free to do it all and then vanish. He gives you the excuse to act as you please. He's a crutch. A psychological crutch that you've created to allow yourself to feel sexual.

Well our time is up for today. I'm going to write you a prescription for some antidepressants. We'll begin with a low dosage and see what effect it has. Then increase it as necessary." Bornstein tells him.

"Thank you Dr. Bornstein. I feel better already. To think that maybe all I need to do is to take a pill and Simon may vanish for good." Paul says.

"I'm afraid it won't be as simple as that. This may take months or years of therapy. But let me know what effect the antidepressants have on you?" Bornstein tells him.

"I certainly will. Thank you." Paul says to him.

(This ends the transcript of this session on August 22, 1995- Dr. Morris Bornstein)

Paul found himself smiling all the way home. He kind of felt foolish for not seeking help years ago. He got home at 7pm. Susan was still over at her mother's. Her mom had gotten out of the hospital 6 weeks ago and Susan went over everyday to clean her home and make her meals. Then she would take a cab home. So Paul warmed up the meal she left for him in the fridge. He ate and watched a little tv and then decided to lay down for a nap before work tonight.

Paul begins to dream. In his dream he sees Dr. Bornstein in his car. He's heading home. He doesn't live in the city but in a town house on the outskirts. He arrives home and goes inside. He takes off his jacket and hangs it on his coat rack by the door. He loosens his tie. Then he picks up his mail off of the floor where the postman dropped them through his mail slot.

He walks to his desk in his study and turns on his desk lamp. He begins to thumb through his mail when his telephone rings. He picks up the receiver and says "Hello?" He receives no reply. "Hello?" he repeats. All he hears is heavy breathing. He says, "I don't know who this is but as a trained psychiatrist I suggest you get help." He hangs up angrily.

He reaches down to get the letter from his attorney regarding his current lawsuit that he was just reading, and now it's gone! He looks all over the desk and the floor but can't find it. He then sees a paper sticking out of his jacket pocket which is now draped on the back of his chair. He looks at it in disbelief and walks back into his living room to look at his coat rack. He could have sworn that he just hung his jacket there but now it's on his desk chair. How? He decides to laugh it off. He starts to talk to himself. "My goodness ... I'm starting to get as bad a some of my patients."

He goes into his living room and sits in his favorite chair as he turns on his television. He channel surfs until he gets to "Turner Classic Movies". "Casablanca" is playing. Suddenly the channels begin changing by themselves. "What's going on?" Dr. Bornstein mutters. He reaches for his remote and now it is gone as well. He just sat it on his coffee table and now it's not there! The television continues to flip channels on it's own. Then it stops on AMC. The movie "The Silver Chalice" is playing. Dr. Bornstein finds his remote control on the floor on the opposite side of his chair. He tries to change the channel but it won't change.

Then the power goes out. His whole town house is in darkness. "Oh great! Another power outage! That's it! I'm going to bed." He fumbles his way to his bedroom striking his shin on his coffee table on the way. He gets undressed and gets under the sheets. He tosses and turns but is having trouble relaxing. The house is just too quiet. But just then he hears a new sound. It sounds like someone is walking in his living room. He sits up in bed and he still hears it. He creeps out of his bed, his heart is in his mouth. He keeps a loaded revolver in his nightstand drawer. He takes it out and then he tip toes into his living room. He can still hear the walking loudly. Almost stomping. For a prowler he seems unconcerned about getting caught.

Just then the power comes back on and his lights with them. No one is there! The room is empty. Thinking they must have hidden he begins to search the room and then the rest of the house. No one is there. Feeling foolish he turns out the lights and goes back to his bedroom. He places the revolver back in its holster in his drawer and closes it. Then gets back under the sheets. He is no sooner in bed than he hears it again! Only much closer this time. The footsteps sound like they are in his very bedroom. Lying on his back he tries to sit up but now realizes that his body is paralyzed.

He cannot move anything except his eyes. Then he sees it. A dark shape in the corner of his room. It comes closer and closer. It leans forward. Twin red eyes come down out of the darkness as something grabs his hair. It feels like bony fingers. He is beyond terrified now. Then he feels something incredibly heavy climb onto his chest. He cannot breathe it is so heavy. He panics even more. A voice whispers in his ear. "Believe in me now?"

Paul sits up suddenly in bed! It was just a nightmare. Thank God! It was all just a nightmare. Susan hears him and opens the bedroom door. "Are you alright?" she asks. He nods "yes" and looks at his clock. 9:50pm. Only ten minutes until he has to get up for work anyway so he might as well get dressed. He puts on his uniform and shoes and goes into the living room to talk to Susan before he has to leave. He tells her what the doctor said and she tells him about her trying day at her mother's and then it is time for work.

He gets in his van and starts it up. He remembers his nightmare about Dr. Bornstein. He tries to dismiss it but he can't get it out of his mind.

He arrives at work and finds that he is on Station 5 tonight. Judy greets him with a big smile. "Am I glad to see you!" she says and then they count the narcotics and she gives him shift report. "Oh by the way, there's a note for you." Judy says. "What? From whom?" Paul asks. "From the D.O.N." Judy remarked casually. "Oh great!" Paul said. "Why is she leaving me notes?" "I have no idea. Hey, don't worry about it? She probably just wants you to do some overtime. Well gotta run. Have a good night." Judy left the station and Paul opened the envelope from the Director of Nursing.

She wanted to see him in her office after his shift. That was all it said. "That doesn't sound good." Paul muttered to himself. He put it aside and gets busy doing his job. He makes out his assignment sheet for 3 c.n.a.'s. He has 3 of them tonight so at least he only has his own work to do.

He passes his midnight meds and begins his treatments. Mr. Sullivan's heels are starting to improve. After doing his treatments Mary told him that they were running out of laundry again. "Ok" Paul said and got up from his desk. He started pushing the laundry cart down toward the laundry room. As he passes Station 6 he saw that Carol was on tonight, not Kwan. Paul smiled and waved at Carol who looked away suddenly when she saw him. "That's odd" he worried. "She usually greets me with a big smile." He stopped at Station 6 and still she refused to look at him. She just kept charting. "Um, Carol, I just got a note from the D.O.N. tonight. You wouldn't know anything about why she wants to see me in the morning? Would you?" "No" she said icily and kept charting. So Paul continued on to the laundry room at the end of the hallway.

As he pushed the cart full of linen back to Station 5 he saw Belinda coming out of a patient's room. The minute she saw him she ducked back into the patient's room. Something was definitely up. He'd been down this path so many times before.

So he went back to his nursing station and turned on his radio to listen to the Art Norry show. Tonight's show is about "Bigfoot". Paul listens to the people who call in with their Bigfoot encounter tales. It helps him to take his mind off of the meeting with the D.O.N. in the morning.

Morning comes all too soon and Paul passes his 6am meds. At 6:45am he counts the narcotics and gives shift report to the on-coming 7-3 nurse. Then he walks to the D.O.N's office. The door is open and he sees the Director of Nursing, the Assistant Director of Nursing and the Administrator all sitting there looking at him like the Spanish Inquisition. "Come in Mr. Michelson and be seated. I'll get right to the point. I've had two different employees come to me and accuse you of sexual harassment. As you know it is the policy of this facility that anyone even accused of such a thing is automatically terminated. Do you understand?"

"Yes" Paul said. "Please mail me my final paycheck." "I'm sorry but I have no choice in the matter." The D.O.N. said matter of factly. Paul walks out of the office. He punches the time clock for the last time. "Fired again. How many times does this make?" He thinks to himself. On the drive home he hopes that Dr. Bornstein's antidepressants will make a difference. He's not worried about finding work. There are over 300 nursing homes in this county alone and they are all begging for nurses. But still it hurts to be fired again and for such a shameful reason. He pulls into his driveway and Susan comes out the door. He has to take her over to her mother's again this morning. He decides not to tell her that he was fired again, at least not yet. She has enough on her mind right now as it is. So he drops her off and heads on home.

He goes home and goes to bed. He tosses and turns but cannot sleep. He can't seem to put that meeting out of his mind. After a couple of hours he is lying on his back and suddenly felt his body rise up by itself and realizes to his panic that Simon has taken over again. Helpless to do anything but watch from inside he sees his body put on his clothes and then shoes. He stands and walks out of the bedroom. He turns toward the front door. He watches his arm turn the doorknob and step outside. "Where is he going?" Paul wonders.

He sees his body turn to the right and walk over to the side of the house. Then he begins to climb the metal steps to Regina's apartment. Paul knows that Regina's boyfriend Eric leaves for work at 7am and that means Regina is alone all alone. When Simon reaches the top of the stairs he turns the doorknob and to Paul's horror the door opens! He sees Simon casually walk over to the closed bedroom door. He turns that doorknob as well and just walks in.

Paul sees Regina laying on her back sound asleep. Paul is really panicking now. What is Simon thinking? If she wakes up and sees him there how will he explain it? Simon steps over to the side of her bed and passes his hand over her eyes three times in a downward motion. He then slowly pulls the top sheet off of her sleeping form.

She does not awaken. Somehow he was keeping her from waking up! It's like she's hypnotized or drugged. She is wearing a thigh length white satin nightgown and little else. Simon reaches up under it and begins to pull down her panties. In one motion he pulls them off and tosses them aside. Helplessly Paul watches from within his body as he sees Simon lift her gown up to her neck exposing her nude body. Then Simon parts her legs. Paul is now screaming at Simon from inside his head. "Leave her alone you bastard! She's just a kid!"

He's known Regina since she was 14 years old and thought of her as a sweet kid and good friend. Simon then removes Paul's pants and underwear and crawls on top of her. He then penetrates her and still she does not awaken.

But then disaster strikes as the bedroom door suddenly opens. It's Eric! He came home early unexpectedly! He freezes a moment in shock and then screams "Get off of her! You son of a bitch!" Just then Simon leaves Paul's body. Eric has him in a choke hold and pulls him off of Regina and onto the floor. Paul cannot breathe as Eric continues to strangle him. Regina awakens and seeing the scene she screams at the top of her lungs.

Then Paul awakes in his own bed!!!! It was only a nightmare!

"Oh thank God! Thank God!" He says and sits up on the side of the bed. He must have drifted off to sleep and not known it when he got home. Too shook up to go back to sleep. He decides to get up and he goes to the bathroom. On his way out he hears the mailman deliver his mail. He puts on his shoes and goes outside to get it.

Then he sees Regina's cat. It is winding around his legs. He pets it. Then picks it up. "How did you get out again?" He asks the cat. So Paul walks around to the side of the house and begins to climb the steps to Regina's apartment. His intention is just to knock on the door and give Regina her cat. But when he reaches the top he freezes in horror. The door to Regina's apartment is wide open!

"Oh my God!" He says to himself. "What if...that wasn't just a dream?" He sticks his head inside and yells for Regina. He calls her four times as loud as he can shout but no response. He starts to put the cat inside and close door and leave but he has to know if she is all right? He steps inside and closes the door behind him. He puts down the cat and again shouts "Regina" at the top of his lungs! Still no response.

He can now see her closed bedroom door. He decides to go knock on it. He can always explain that the door was open and how worried he was and Regina would forgive him for entering uninvited. All that matters is making sure she is ok. He knocks on her bedroom door. "Regina!" He shouts. Still no answer. "How could she sleep through that?" he thinks. This time he really pounds on the door and shouts her name again. But still no response!

"Maybe she isn't even at home." Paul thinks. So he turns the doorknob and opens the door and Regina sits up in her bed! Paul freezes for just a second and says, "Uh .. .I can explain." Regina says, "I hope so!" So Paul explains how he found the door open and feared someone had broken in. Regina explains that she sleeps with a pillow over her head and didn't hear a thing. She wants to be mad at Paul for his intrusion but he is so flustered and embarrassed she begins to chuckle at him. He apologizes a million times and then leaves. His face is beet red.

But on the way back down to his apartment he makes a decision. That was no ordinary nightmare. Simon is going to try and get Regina somehow. Paul makes up his mind not to wait for the real disaster to strike.

At 6pm the telephone rings. It is Susan she is ready to come home. Paul drives over to get her and she gets in the van. She is furious. "What's wrong?" Paul asks. "My mother was drunk and she accused me of stealing her laundry basket! Can you believe it? After all I've done for her she calls me a thief! We both have the same type of baskets. I bought mine when she told me where she got hers and now thinks my basket is hers." Susan is beside herself with anger.

"Listen" Paul said, "There is something I want to talk to you about. . .I would like us to take a vacation."

"A vacation!" Susan repeated. "Well Lord knows we could use one. But we can't afford a vacation right now." Susan explained.

"Well we could take a working vacation. I have a current Kentucky Nursing license. We could put all of our stuff in storage down here and just pack up the van and go. I'll get a job when I get there. I've been really homesick lately and my family's never met you." Paul explained.

"Well if you're sure we can do this? My mother is back on her feet and I definitely need a break from her ... Ok, sure! Why not? Let's do it!" Susan says.

CHAPTER 6
Return to McCawley Road

September 1st, 1995. "There it is!" Paul exclaimed as soon as he saw the green exit sign that said "Cave City, Ky." It sure felt good to get off of I-65. It had been a long journey from St. Petersburg, Fl. They only stopped once in Nashville, Tenn. to sleep. Now they were almost there.

The first stop they make in Kentucky is the amusement park Paul spent two summers working at performing magic. But that was way back in 1974 and 1978. Gunsmoke Mountain looked the same. He and Susan rode the chair lift up to the mock western town and played tourist. They watched all of the shows and met the new magician there. After a few hours there they left.

Paul drove Susan to a special nearby motel called Wig Warn Village. The motel rooms are shaped like Tee Pees. They spend the night there. Early in the morning they tour Mammoth Cave, the world's largest cave. After that they also tour the nearby Crystal Onyx Cave as well. Then it was time to leave.

Before they go on to Louisville, Paul makes a detour to Edmonton, Ky. Once there he stops at the local cemetery and he and Susan visit the grave of his first wife, Lavonne. He says a silent prayer for her and then they leave.

Hours later they are back on 1-65 and see the exit sign that says "Ft. Knox, Ky." So he makes another detour there. He shows Susan the Gold Vault and then Ireland Army Hospital where he was born back in 1955.

Then it was back on the interstate once again and now they were finally exiting 165. They get off at the Lebanon Junction exit. This was the town his cousin Rick Murray now lived in, but he would visit him later. So he turned right and began heading north on Blue Lick Road. Of course he was still in Bullet County, still a long way from Jefferson County where he'd grown up.

Blue Lick Road was actually part of the Wilderness Trail blazed by Daniel Boone. Paul remembered reading that on a marker they posted on the road not far from his boyhood home. As they were driving down the narrow two lane road enjoying the beauty of Kentucky in autumn, the trees were ablaze in magenta, gold and brown, Paul suddenly spots a sign on the right that says, "Hebron Cemetery". He turns in.

"Where are we going now?" Susan asked. "You'll see." Paul replied. First they stopped at a grave marked "Troutman". "Who's this?" Susan asked.

"This is the grave of my only high school chum, Larry Troutman. He died in 1979 of cancer, the same year as my mother. He was only 22 years old."

"How awful."

"Well let's walk up here. I have another grave to visit." They walk up the gravel road until they come to a great tree. "Here's the one." Paul said. "This is the grave of my grandparents on my mother's side."

Susan reads the headstone. "Richard T. Murray-Born September 29th, 1873-Died July 2nd, 1954 and Emma J. Murray-Born September 5th, 1877-Died November 26th, 1952 ... My goodness! 1873?" she exclaimed.

"Yes" Paul replied. "I looked it up once. Ulysses S. Grant was the President when my Grandfather was born. I only played a Gunfighter type character at Guntown Mountain but he really was one. As you can see he died one year before I was born and my grandmother died 3 years before I was born. Yet I grew up hearing so many stories about them from my mother, I feel as though I knew them.

Grandpa was raised on a farm and was helping to hitch up the horses at 4 years old. He grew up riding horses and shooting guns like the western heroes I grew up watching on tv. He made and sold whiskey during prohibition and was a professional gambler. He was so good at cheating that my mother said gangsters used to pay him to gamble for them. He used to mark his own cards.

She told me a story about him I would like to share with you. She said once when he was gambling in this saloon, one of the men who lost called him a dirty cheating son of a bitch and then drew his gun on Grandpa.

The Shadow of Simon Magus

Grandpa jumped up from the table and slapped the gun to the right just as the man fired. Then he slapped it the second time to the left as he fired the second shot. Then the last time Grandpa slapped the gun straight down as he fired and the bullet went through Grandpa's foot.

Grandpa then proceeded to beat the crap out of the man. They had to carry the unconscious man away and Grandpa sat back down at the card table and resumed playing poker. Nobody knew that he was shot through the foot.

They played cards the rest of the night and when morning came he said, "Well fellas, would one of you mind taking me to the doctor's?" and that was when they realized that he was wounded. The doctor had to cut his boot off because it was filled with blood."

"You've got to be kidding?" Susan said. "That sounds like something you'd see in a movie."

"Yeah I know." Paul said. "He was definitely a larger than life character. Now my grandmother who was half Cherokee and half Irish was the opposite of my Grandfather in every way.

My mother believed that she was a saint. She was so calm and peaceful by nature and he was so hot tempered and fiery. But she was amazingly strong. My mother said that if she got you by the wrist, you might as well give up.

She told me that one time when Grandpa and Grandma were still courting he showed up at her place and pretended he was drunk. He came up her driveway staggering and shooting his gun in the air. But his joke backfired on him because Grandma, who was always a big woman, came flying out of the house. She tackled him, knocked him to the ground and sat on him.

Then to his shock, she grabbed the pistol out of his hand and tore it to pieces with her bare hands! She tossed pieces of it right and left. He said he never did find all of it."

"That's a great story." Susan smiled.

"Come on, its time to move on. I have so many relatives in here. This is my Aunt Lizzie's grave and over here is Aunt Janie, Aunt Edith and Uncle Jimbo." Paul said.

"How many siblings did your mother have?" Susan asked.

"My mother was the 12th out of 13 children. It was common to have very large families in those days. Only Uncle Robert was younger than she was. My father used to call him Katie's fourth son. Let me see if I can remember the order in which they were born. Birdie was their first born. Remind me to tell you another story about her.

Then there was Jimbo, whose real name was Charles Richard, so your guess is as good as mine where the nickname Jimbo came from? He was the family drunk. He never had any home. He just wandered between all his siblings homes his whole life. His siblings dreaded to see him but all the kids loved him.

Next came Uncle Willie, the tallest member of the clan. Then came Aunt Janie and Aunt Edith, Uncle Johnny, and Aunt Bessie who is the only one still alive. She lives on a farm in Elizabethtown, Ky. She's still riding horses at 90 I hear.

Then came Aunt Jessie, Aunt Florence, Aunt Lizzie-Pearl, my mother and then Uncle Robert.

"Ok what is the story about your Aunt Birdie?" Susan reminded him.

"Yeah, well she died very young, in her twenties. I forget why? Some illness I'm sure. So they buried her on top of a hill inside a concrete vault beneath the ground. A year passes and Grandpa kept having dreams about her. He dreamt she was drowning. So he began talking about digging her up and everyone thought that he was going mad with grief.

He kept on having the dream night after night. So his mind was made up. He was going to dig her up. His family and friends showed up to beg him not to do it, but he kept digging. When he popped the lid off of that concrete vault the coffin shot to the surface. The vault was filled with water."

"Oh wow! That's incredible." Susan remarked.

"Oh but there's more to the story. Grandpa wanted to open the coffin and the rest protested. After a year she should have been well decomposed, especially in water. But when they opened it she was perfectly preserved. She looked exactly the same way she did when she died. The women changed her and put her in dry clothing. She was taken elsewhere and re-buried in dry ground. Grandpa never had any more dreams about her after that."

"That's a pretty bizarre story." Susan remarked.

"Yes I know. Well it's time to leave." Paul said. They walked back to their van and drive away.

They continue on down Blue Lick Road. They leave Bullet County and enter Jefferson County. In a short time Paul points out a school on the right. "That's Blue Lick Elementary where I went to attended the 5th" and 6th grades.

They drive for a short way and then Paul turns onto a side street on the right. He stops the van.

"Where are we now?" Susan asked him.

"Maynard Drive. You see this row of homes on the right?' Paul points out.

Susan nods "Yes".

"Well there used to be a row on the left side as well. But as you can see it's just a chain link fence behind which is the now man made hill for the Gene Synder expressway to pass over Blue Lick Road. My boyhood home used to be on the corner of Blue Lick Road and Maynard Drive, where the hill is now at."

"That's too bad." Susan quipped. "I would like to have seen it. "

"You still can." Paul answered. "I know where they moved it to."

He starts up the van and they wind their way through the subdivision until they come to a dead end street. He stops the van.

"That's it, to your right." He says and then he unexpectedly jumps out of the van and rushes around to stand in the driveway. "Quickly, take my picture." He said.

"You can't do that!" Susan protested. "Someone is living there!"

"I know, I know! Hurry up!" Paul demanded. So Susan grabbed the camera and snapped his photo real fast. Paul rushed back to the van, jumped in and they drove off just as someone came out of the house to see what was going on?

They drive back to Blue Lick Road and drive until it runs out at Preston Hwy. "Wow!" Paul exclaimed. "I can't believe how much Okalona has grown!" Preston Highway was only a two-lane road when I was growing up here. Now look at it. It's 6 lanes. They turn left onto Preston Hwy and drive north.

Paul continues to play tour guide showing Susan all of the places he grew up with. "Okalona used to be a small town on the outskirts of Louisville but it's grown so much now you can't tell where One starts up and the other leaves off."

Oh! Look ovder to your left. "Paul points out. "That's Southern High School where I graduated from in 1974. Over on the right is St. Rita's elementary where I attended the first, second and third grades."

"Where did you attend the fourth grade?" Susan asked.

"Okalona elementary. It's further up on the left. They drive a little further and Paul asks, "Are you hungry?"

"Starving!" Susan replies.

"Ok good. Let's eat here." Paul says as he turns to the left into the parking lot of the White Castle hamburger stand. He parks and they get out to walk inside. "I practically lived on these things when I was growing up." They go inside and gorge themselves on the little square hamburgers.

Then they get back into the van and continue north on Preston Hwy. They stop at a red light and Paul gets a distant look in his eyes as he spots the street sign on his right, which reads McCawley Road. He turns right onto it and then left into the apartment complex. He parks and they get out.

"Where are we now?" Susan asks.

"Way back in 1959 when we moved away from here. None of this existed. McCawley Road was only a gravel road back then. Now look at it, two apartment complexes, a shopping mall and a factory of some kind. Hard to believe it's the same place." Paul commented.

"Looks like the developers have struck again." Susan said.

"Yeah. I liked it better before. Ok follow me." Paul said and began walking.

They walk to the end of the complex and see that the paved road ends and a gravel path continues. "This is part of the original road." Paul explains and they start walking down it. They reach a sharp curve to the right and Paul stops there.

"Straight down there is where we used to live. I see some of the woods survived." Paul tells her.

"Are we going back there?" Susan asks.

"Yes." He replied and she follows him as they begin to leave civilization behind. They walk a half a mile down the narrow gravel road as they approach the remainder of the woods. Soon they can see nothing but trees on both sides of the road. Most of the leaves have fallen off and crunch loudly beneath their feet.

As the trees close about them on each side of the narrow path Paul is carried back in time in his mind. Now McCawley Road begins to look and feel the way it did so long ago when he and his family lived there.

"These woods were called the Wet Woods back when my family lived here and they used to cover over 30 miles but as you can see only a few acres are left.

For 30 minutes they continue to walk deeper into the woods. Then up ahead they see that the road now ends and a large subdivision lies sprawling beyond that.

"Oh oh" Susan commented. "Looks like your old homestead is gone."

"No, not yet." Paul says as he stops about 50 feet before the road ends. "This is it." He says and he looks at the forest of trees to his left.

"How can you tell that?" Susan remarks, "It all looks the same now."

"You see these two trees?" Paul points at two large twisted trees near the road. "These two trees once stood in our front yard."

"Are you sure?" Susan asks, "You said you were only 4 years old when you moved away from here."

"Yes I know. But I still remember them. My cousin Rick, who is only 9 months older than me and lived here as well, was my playmate back here. We used to race between these two trees. They used to seem so far apart. Now I can practically lay down between them."

"Still are you sure these are the right two trees? It could just be wishful thinking." Susan replied.

"Ok I'll prove it to you. Follow me." He said and suddenly began pushing his way into the heavy brush.

"Where are you going?" She asked.

"I want to see if I can find any sign of our old house." Paul explains.

"But I thought you said it had been torn down years ago?" Susan protested.

"It was but we had a concrete basement, so when they bulldozed the house, you know they didn't dig up the foundation. It must still be here."

They break through the bushes and come to a clearing. "I'm pretty sure that this is where our house used to sit."

He begins brushing away at all of the fallen leaves on the ground and then shouts, "Here it is! I found it!" Paul then begins rapidly brushing away the leaves and now Susan can plainly see a row of concrete blocks.

The top of which are just barely sticking out of the ground. Paul stands and stares at the row of blocks. This was the left side of our house. Over to the left was our driveway and that led straight back to our garage which used to be about 30 feet back that way. I wonder if any of it survived?" He said. "Come on. Let's go see."

"But it's all bushes and tree limbs!" Susan protested.

"Yeah but we can make it. Come on." Paul said as he leads the way. They push their way through the growth and after a few minutes Paul stops. "Here it is! I found the floor of our old garage."

Susan sees him standing on a concrete surface. Various concrete blocks are strewn about its perimeter.

"The floor of our garage is still here under all of these leaves." He announces as he kicks some of the leaves aside.

"Well I'll be ... " Susan muttered.

"Back over there sat our old dump and beyond those trees is Fern Creek where Grandpa, Donnie and Pat used to fish. Hmm ... I wonder if any of Uncle Robert's old house still survived. He built it on the edge of our property. It would be straight over to the right of our house. Let's go see."

They trek through the grove of trees for 5 minutes. "All of these trees have grown up since we moved away. This was all field when we lived here." Paul explains.

Just before they come to the fence, beyond which subdivision now lies, Paul spots a large rectangular shape made of old concrete blocks.

"This was it." Paul said. "This was Uncle Robert's house. Apparently the. subdivision begins just beyond our old property line. Let's go back to the site of our house."

They again push their way through the undergrowth and just before they get to the site of the house Paul stops her and points to the ground. "Look it's our old well." He says.

"Oh my God!" Susan exclaimed. "It's wide open! We could have fallen in."

"Yes. It used to be boarded up but I guess they uncovered it when they bulldozed the house." Paul said.

"You see these bricks lining the well? My grandfather did that. Well, it's time to go."

Susan followed Paul through the twisted brush until they made their way back to McCawley Road. They walked back down the old country road in silence and Susan could see that Paul's mind was swimming with a thousand distant memories. They emerged back at the apartment complex.

"Let's see if we can rent an apartment here." Paul spoke up. "We have to stay somewhere for the next 3 months. It would be a real treat for me to live on McCawley Road again after all of these years. Kind of like coming full circle."

"If that's what you'd like to do, then do it." Susan replied.

They both got back in the car and drove over to the office for the apartment complex. They were informed that there was a one bedroom unfurnished apartment. So Paul paid the 250 dollar rent plus the 200 dollar security deposit and he and Susan moved in to the empty one bedroom apartment.

They didn't need that much to stay there. They brought in the four foam cushions from the sofa like seats in the back of the van. By placing them end to end on the floor and covering them with a fitted sheet they had a nice little bed to sleep on. They brought their portable black and white tv/radio to watch at night in bed and hung up their clothes in the closet.

"This will do nicely for the next 3 months. I see no point in getting any furniture since we're only staying 90 days. Now there's one more place I'd like to visit before we call it a day." Paul told her and Susan followed him out to the van.

They drive back to Preston Hwy and turn north. After 15 minutes or so they come to Evergreen Cemetery. They drive in and see row after row of gravestones. Paul drives about half the way back and stops the van. He gets out and Susan follows him. He looks through row after row for a few minutes trying to find a particular marker.

"Here it is." He commented and Susan walks up to where he is standing. She sees the tombstone says "Michelson".

"Your parents?" She asks.

"Yes" he replies. The tombstone reads "Louis J. Michelson; Born July 31st, 1913-Died November 3rd, 1983" and next to it, "Katherine E. Michelson; Born April 22nd, 1919-Died January 21st, 1979".

"Right next to her is Uncle Robert's tombstone. "Robert Murray; Born April 13th, 1923-Died March 16th, 1973". As you can see his wife Aunt Jean is still alive.

"Before we leave we'll pay her a visit." Paul is silent for a few minutes saying a silent prayer. Then he speaks. "I never told you much about my father because I don't really know that much about his life. He never talked about himself. When I did ask questions he'd only give me short one-word answers. He was a very private man and getting any personal information out of him was like pulling teeth. But I'll tell you what I know. His parents were German Jews. I don't know their names or how they died. But I know that a Catholic family adopted him at a very young age.

He mentioned being part of a street gang as a young man. I could never picture him doing that. He mentioned he had a job in his teens jumping off of a milk wagon, delivering bottles of milk early in the morning. He told me that after his adopted father died of pneumonia he joined a Benedictine Monastery. He received his education there. That was where he learned to speak Latin.

He was studying to be a priest when World War II broke out. He told me a funny story. He said when he a couple of other monks left the monastery to join the army, they were getting their induction physical at the recruiting station and the doctor noticed that all 5 of them had these large calluses on their knees.

After the 5th one in a row had his physical the doctor approached them and said, "Look fellas, I have to ask. Do you guys shoot craps for a living?"

Now some time after he joined the army but before he went overseas he met and married my mother. I do know that my father was acquainted with my cousin Ruth who happened to be an ex-nun. I remember my mother saying she told him once when he came over to the house that Ruth wasn't at home and he said that was alright because he was coming over to see her not Ruth.

That's about all of their courtship days that either of them ever discussed.

I know that Donnie was a little baby when they met. I had no idea for years that Donnie had a different father than Pat and I and I still don't know what his biological father's name was? We never used the term half brother and Dutch was the only father Donnie ever knew so I'm sure he never thought of Pat or me as half brothers either.

I remember my mother saying that Donnie's father was a sailor and she caught him cheating on her so the marriage only lasted a year when she filed for divorce.

I mentioned that my father and mother were opposites in every way. He was a college graduate who spoke 6 languages fluently and she was a farm girl with only an eighth grade education. But between the two she was the one with the most common sense. They were also the original odd couple. He was one of the sloppiest men who ever lived and she was obsessively clean.

That woman would get up at the crack of dawn and start cleaning and she cleaned all day long. She was the first one out of bed and the last one in it.

One thing that he did that used to drive her mad was when he would get up in the middle of the night to raid the refrigetator and leave all the cabinet drawers and doors open.

When she would get up in the morning she'd find all of them open. The madder she got the funnier she was. I heard her stomping down the hallway toward his room early one morning and she flung his bedroom door open and in a loud voice she said, "When you die we're going to leave the coffin lid open! And let them throw dirt right in your face!"

"Oh man! I had about half my pillow shoved in my mouth to keep her from hearing me laughing at her. But I couldn't help it."

"That's a riot. Your mother must have been something else." Susan smiled.

"You have no idea. She was the strongest person I ever met. She had a will of iron and whenever she made up her mind to do something, she did it."

I remember once that Donnie, Pat and I decided to surprise her for her birthday by painting her kitchen. The tricky part was getting her out of the house. Donnie's wife Barbara pretended to be sick and asked my mother to come over and clean her house for her. When she left we started moving the furniture out of the kitchen so we could paint it.

It took all 3 of us to move that refrigerator and you've never met them but Donnie and Pat are not little shrimps like me. Donnie must weigh 275 and Pat at least 180 at the time.

So it was sometime later that it occurred to me that Katie used to move that refrigerator to clean behind it every weekend all by herself. I'd seen her push that thing around like it was on wheels and she was only 5'2". But she was all will power.

Well let's head on back." Paul said and they make their way to the van began their drive back to their apartment on McCawley Road.

Susan commented, "You poor thing. You seem to know more dead people than living ones."

Paul said, "You know I've got an idea. My cousin Rick has a video camera and a copy of my handwritten book that I transcribed my mother's ghost stories into. I'll see if I can borrow them and I'd like to make a home made

documentary. I'll get you to be my camera man, or person and I'll read the stories on the actual sites where they took place. What do you think?"
"Sounds like fun." Susan smiled. "But maybe you should see about finding work first."

"Yeah, I'll go out in the morning and see what I can find."

They go home and sleep in their new apartment. Paul opens the window and listens. He hears the sounds of crickets chirping. A sound he hasn't heard in years.

The next morning Paul looks in the yellow pages under Nursing homes and finds one not too far away called Westlake Manor. He drives over and asks to see the D.O.N. She lets him in and he tells her that he just moved here from St. Petersburg, Fl. And needed a job. It just so happened that a nurse just resigned that week and they were short handed. So he got the job. He would be working 12 hour shifts on the weekend's from 7pm-7am. Which was perfect as that left Monday through Friday for Susan and him to explore his hometown.

So many sites he wanted to show her. They visited Churchill Downs, the Museum of Science and Art, the 4th street Mall where they saw the Louisville Palace which was a restored 20's theater. They took a ride on the Belle of Louisville, the old original paddle boat of the 1800' s.

They also attended the St. James Street art fair. Three blocks of gothic style homes have their streets closed to traffic and artists from all over the world bring their artworks to sell on the streets.

They visited the amazing Cave Hill cemetery where the rich and famous are buried. They saw the graves of George Rogers Clark, and Colonel Harlan Sanders among others.

It was a wonderful vacation and no sign of Simon, until the first night of the full moon in September and then he came out at work and seduced the C.N.A. who he worked with on the night shift. Paul never mentioned this to Susan. It would only upset her and he brought her here so she could have fun and get away from their stressful lives.

CHAPTER 7
Tales of McCawley Road

Paul and Susan are standing outside in the apartment complex parking lot. It is a cold windy day in Kentucky. As promised Paul has borrowed his cousin's video camera and they have decided to begin filming their homemade documentary.

"Ok I will stand here next to the street sign. I want you to zoom in on the street sign that says "McCawley Road" and then pan slowly back until you see me standing there. Then I'll do the opening speech. Got it?" Paul asked.

"I'm ready." Susan replied.

"Ok action." Paul said. As requested Susan focuses on the close-up of the street sign until the name comes in clearly and then slowly pans back until Paul can be seen from the chest up. He is wearing his black hooded coat as the wind whips past him. Then he speaks.

"Good evening. It's October 16th, 1995. It's been 34 years since my family and I moved away from our home on McCawley Road.

As you can see, there is a sprawling apartment complex here now. But in 1959 McCawley Road was only a gravel road that started over there at Preston Hwy and made a sharp left turn to where I am standing, and then past me to the end of the apartment complex.

There it made a sharp right turn and then straight on back into the woods. Our house was about a half-mile into those woods. Ok come with me now as we walk down McCawley Road."

Paul begins to walk to the end of the paved road as Susan follows him with the camera. When he reaches the end of the pavement he turns to the camera and says, "Now as you can see the paved section of the road ends here. This gravel section is what the entire road looked like when we lived here. Up ahead is the second curve in the road that turns to the right.

Of course there was no factory back then as you can see now." Paul walks to the bend in the road and Susan follows filming as she walks. He goes around the bend in the road and Susan follows. Then he turns and speaks to the camera again.

"As you can see the road continues straight on back and into what is left of the woods. I'll cut it off here and we'll pick it up again at the former site of our old house."

Susan turns off the camera. "I think we should film the whole road." She comments.

"I would but I'm afraid we won't have enough battery power. We'll try and film the road on the way back." Paul explained.

He and Susan trek the mile into the woods again. This time the trees are completely bare. The long, grey branches reach up into the equally grey sky. After hiking for 30 minutes the pair reach the former site of the house.

Paul says, "Ok get ready to shoot. 3 ... 2 ... 1 ... action" Paul speaks to the camera.. "We're at the site of our old house now. As you can see behind me McCawley Road ends about 50 feet away and beyond that is now a sprawling subdivision. Our old house use to lie between these two old twisted trees.

The driveway was about here and went straight back to our garage. We moved away from here when I was only 4 years old. But my parents first moved here in 1941. A lot of strange things happened back here. I grew up listening to all of the stories that were told to me by everyone who lived here. I'll share some of them with you today. But first I'd like to point out something I noticed the other day.

In the 1960's scientists conducted some experiments with plants. They took identical plants and made sure they received identical sunlight, water and nutrients. With one group of plants they spoke tosoothingly and to the other group they shouted at them angrily daily. The first group grew up healthy and the second group grew sickly and died. The point of the experiment was to prove that plants could be effected by strong emotions.

I bring that up because I noticed something odd about the trees that have grown up here since we moved away.

Notice that all of the trees to the right of where our home once stood grew perfectly straight, but the trees and vegetation that grew over the site of our former home grew twisted and formed a tangled mass of limbs. The difference is really quite startling. I hope that shows up on tape as obvious as it is in real life. Ok we'll cut off the camera here so we can make our way to the former site of our old home."

They cut off the camera as Paul leads the way through the thick undergrowth. After a few minutes he and Susan are back at the site of his old house.

"Ok here we are now at the site of our old home. As you can see this row of concrete blocks we've uncovered was part of the foundation of our old home.

On the left would have been our old driveway leading back to our garage. We'll go back there in a while but for now I'll read to you a few of my mother's stories standing here in the site of what was probably our old living room.

As I told you I grew up listening to the strange stories that were told to me primarily by the mother. Years later I managed to secretly tape-record her when she was telling them and years after that I transcribed the tapes into this book that I am holding. It's a good thing that I did as the tapes themselves were destroyed in a house fire in 1988 but luckily the book survived.

Here you can see a drawing I made of our old place. (Paul shows a sketch of his former home that he drew to the camera)

It was big two story wooden house. The boards were painted white. The roof was black roofing tile. It had 5 large concrete steps that led up to the concrete front porch. Four concrete block pillars held the roof up over the porch. There were 3 windows showing in the upstairs portion and 4 windows downstairs, two on each side of the front door. It also had a long wooden back porch with wooden stairs leading up to it and brick chimney that went through the center of the house.

Ok let's begin with the first story shall we?" Paul says as he opens his book. "The stories are a series of questions and answers between myself when I was a young boy and my mother. I asked her. .."How did you ever find our house and why did you move back there in the first place?

She replied, "Well at the time me and Dutch hadn't been married for too long. We were living in a duplex downtown on Chestnut Street. Me and Dutch lived in two rooms and Johnny and Mildred lived in the other two."

I asked her, "What year was that?"

She replied, "Let's see ... Donnie was only one year old. So it was 1941. It was February. Well one day Daddy came over and he was all excited about this house he'd found.

He worked for this old real estate man who would buy run down houses and hire Daddy to fix them up for him. Then Mammy and Daddy would live in it until it was sold. Then in between homes they would stay with one of their kids. At that time Mammy and Daddy and Robert was living in LizziePearl's basement. So Daddy caught the bus in town to tell us about this house. He said it needed a lot of work but that he was sure he could fix it up.

I told him we'd all go take a look at it on the weekend whenever Dutch got home. He was stationed at Ft. Knox then but he had already gotten his orders to go overseas soon.

Well the weekend came and me and Dutch caught the bus to LizziePearl's and we asked her husband Joe to drive us to see it and we all ended up going. We went in Joe's old pick up truck.

He and Lizzie were in the front seat, Mammy and Daddy were in the back seat and Robert, Dutch and me rode in the back. I left Donnie at home with Johnny and Mildred cause it was winter and I didn't want to take him out in that cold wind. I was afraid he might get pneumonia.

So we turned off of Preston Street, it was only a two-lane road in those days and onto McCawley Road. McCawley Road didn't even have gravel then. It was an old horse and buggy trail.

Well we rode and rode and it was a bumpy ride as the rode was full of potholes as wide as the rode and I kept thinking, "Well Goddamn! How much further?"

Finally we got to the house and I took one look at it and I was ready to leave. The boards on the house had never seen a coat of paint and they were black from the weather. Every window downstairs was broken out. There was no electricity or indoor plumbing, only an old well on the back porch for water.

We went inside and the floorboards were all horribly warped because you might as well say there wasn't any roof! The rain just came straight on through and had for years. Spider webs and cobwebs were a hanging everywhere.

I remember I had Mammy by the dress tail and I said, "You ain't going from one room to the other without me!"

The more we looked it over the more disgusted I got. So finally I spoke up and said, "Daddy! I know you said it was run down but. my God! This ain't a house, it's a shell!"

He said, "I know it. But I'm sure you can buy it for practically nothing and I know I can fix it up nice. You know how good I am with my hands. What do you think Dutch?"

Dutch said, "How much do you think he will be asking for the house and the 5 acres it sits on?"

Daddy said, "He wants $4,200.00"

Dutch said, "Well the 5 acres it sits on is worth the money but I can probably talk him down to less due to the bad condition of the house."

Then Lizzie's husband Joe spoke up. He laughed and said, "If I know you, you'll have him paying you to take it!"

Dutch said to Daddy, "Listen, I'm going to be going overseas soon. If you're sure you can fix it up I'd like you and Katie's mother to live here with her for as long as you'd like."

Daddy said, "Well by God, what do you think I'm showing it to you for?"

Dutch liked to have died a laughing.

So then the old real estate man showed up and Dutch talked him down to $3,300 for the house and the five acres. You might as well say we just bought the land as the house wasn't worth a penny.

That was in February, but it took a month to close the deal. So we moved there in March. March 29, 1941.

On moving day we rented an old cattle bed truck to move our furniture which we had in storage. Wouldn't you know it decided to pour down rain. You know it was dangerous to take a car back there when it was sunny let alone in the pouring rain. So about half the way back we got stuck in the mud and we had to carry our furniture the rest of the way.

The first damn thing I did was to tear some boards off of the old barn and nail them over the open windows of the basement because it was so flooded and Donnie was just a little baby then and I was afraid he'd fall in and drown.

Me and Daddy worked on that old place a little everyday. Dutch went on overseas and then Robert joined the army too. So that just left me and Donnie and Mammy and Daddy.

I asked, "How long did it take you to get it fixed up?"

She replied, "For two years we could only live in 3 rooms. It had eleven rooms and the basement but we could only use the living room, dining room and the bedroom that led from the dining room. We took the glass out of the upstairs frames and put it in the downstairs windows and then we nailed cardboard over the windows upstairs.

Daddy put a patch job on the roof so we wouldn't drown. We used the fireplace in the living room for heat and cooked on Mammy's old wood-burning stove. Kerosene lamps were the only lights we had. I gave Mammy and Daddy the bedroom and me and Donnie slept on a feather bed on the living room floor. The fireplace kept us warm and Mammy and Daddy had a kerosene heater."

I asked, "Where did you bathe and go to the bathroom?"

She replied, "Well we had an outhouse out back for that and to bathe we used a washing tub. We'd get our water from the well off of the back porch and heat it up on Mammy's wood-burning stove.

Also to wash our clothes. I had an old scrub-board for that. Then I would hang them out on the clothes line to dry. That was how we lived for 2 years until Dutch came home and re-mortgaged and re-modeled the place."

"So how did you find out about the history of the place? When it was built and so on." I asked.

She said, "Well one day there was a knock on the front door and there stood a woman. She was in her forties and she said, "How do you do? My name is Esther Wilkins. I'm your neighbor from down the road. I brought you some housewarming gifts."

I said, "Well isn't that nice of you. Come on in." So I invited her in and took her into the kitchen to meet Mammy and Daddy.

We were all sitting around the table and I offered her some coffee. That was when she told us that our house was the house that she'd grown up in. She said her Daddy had built it. That it was 45 years old and that she was born in it. She said her mother had died in childbirth and she was raised by her father.

She ended up telling us her lifestory. We heard that she eloped with the boy who lived downthe road named Jacob Wilkins and her father disowned her because of it. Then we heard how her father was a moonshiner in the 20's.

Daddy spoke up and told her that he'd made his share of whiskey back then himself. She said that her father got caught by the law making it and he had to sell the house and property to pay off his lawyers. She said the house has stood empty for 15 years. Then she told us her father was dead now. He'd died two years ago.

Daddy said he'd lived in this area all of his life and wondered if maybe he knew her father. Right about then I handed Daddy his cup of coffee and just before he took a sip of it he asked, "What was your father's name?"

She said, "Floyd Hobbs."

And Daddy spit his coffee halfway across the table and got so choked that Mammy had to beat him in the back to unchoke him.

Well I saw Esther get a funny look on her face and she excused herself and said she had to leave.

So I showed her to the door and after she left I turned to Daddy and I said, "What on earth was that all about?"

He said, "Oh Goddamn! If I'd had known this was Floyd Hobb's old house I'd never have set a foot on it!"

I said, "Why?"

He said, "Child that man was a witch! The whole county was scared of him!"

So I said, "Oh Daddy, that's just plain silly. There's no such thing as witches."

He said, "Is that right? Well sit down I want to tell you a story."

This happened to me and Emma a long time before you were born. We hadn't been married too long. Emma was pregnant with Birdie at the time. We were living in a log cabin that I had built. It was winter time. I started noticing that every morning when I would go out to the barn I'd find the horses all sweaty and lathered up like somebody had been riding them all night. Their tails would be knotted up too.

So of course I thought maybe somebody was stealing them and riding them at night and bringing them back in the morning. I couldn't figure out how they were doing it without me hearing or seeing them?

Well before I could set up a trap to catch them I got sick. I started having nightmares all night long and in the morning I was paralyzed. I couldn't move a muscle. I had to yell for Emma to come pick me up. Then I was fine. I could move again.

That started happening every morning. I kept getting weaker everyday. I thought I had some disease and was dying. We couldn't afford no doctor. So I just kept hoping I would get well.

Well after a month of this, one night there was a knock on our door. Emma opened it and there stood an old Indian. Real old. He asked if he could spend the night. Emma was afraid of him but you know I don't believe in turning anyone away from my door.

So I told him we don't have any bed, he'd have to sleep on the floor. He said that would be fine. He lay by the fireplace. Emma said she never slept a wink all night. When she wasn't up a doctoring me she was keeping an eye on him. She said he never moved a muscle. He slept with his hands behind his head.

So the next morning he got up and we invited him to have breakfast with us.

Then he said to me, "I could tell you what is wrong with you and I could tell you what to do about it?" He didn't call it bewitched, but that's what he meant. He gave it an Indian name but I knew what he meant.

He told me that demons were riding my horses at night. He told me to urinate in a bottle and hang it in the fireplace. So I did. Then he prayed for a long time in his native tongue. When he finished he said, "If the bottle boils dry the party that's cursed you will die. But if the bottle breaks it will break the spell but it won't kill them".

Then he left. Three days later the bottle broke and after that I didn't have a thing wrong with my back and my horses weren't sweaty anymore. Well I kind of forgot about it until one day I was out in the woods hunting.

The nearest house to us was about a mile away. That was where old man Hobbs lived. He was an old hermit and everybody thought he was an old witch anyway. He was standing in his doorway when he spotted me and he said, "Well Dick, you almost got me."

I didn't know right away what he meant but later on I remembered that about a month before I got sick I was out hunting that day and I stumbled across him and two other men standing around their still.

They had the drop on me but I told them I wasn't the sheriff and I had made some moonshine myself from time to time. I bought a jug off of them and that seemed to pacify them. But after I thought about what he said I knew that he was the one who put the curse on me?"

Then Mammy spoke up. She said, a couple of years ago when he died, the undertaker was a friend of ours and he asked me to go with him to help lay him out because none of his help would go with him. They were too afraid.

So I went to the funeral home and honest to God, his whole body was twisted up like a pretzel. The undertaker had to break every bone in his body to straighten him enough to get him in the coffin. I'll never forget the horrible look on his face. He looked like he'd seen the Devil himself."

My mother said, "I listened to their story but I just thought it was a lot of superstition you know. So every day me and Daddy worked on that old place trying to make it livable.

We tore down the old barn, the hen house and the meat house and cleared away the mess. Most of the lumber was still good. The ends were rotten of course, so we sawed the ends off and stacked the boards. We started tearing up the warped floorboards each day and we replaced the ones that were too warped to use. It took us two years to completely straighten out the floor."

I asked her, "What was the first really strange thing that happened back there?"

She said, "Well like I said we moved there in March and this happened in May. Spring finally arrived and I decided it was time to plant flowers around the house. It was odd but once the snow melted you could see that for about 3 feet all around the house nothing grew. Not even weeds. I tried to spade up the ground but it seemed like it was as hard as a brick. The ground was a strange greenish-black color when the sun would shine on it. Still I kept trying to plant flowers there. I kept soaking the ground with well water, trying to soften it up.

So after I planted my bulbs I went in the house for awhile and when I came back out to hang up my clothes I almost dropped them in the dirt! I was so shocked at what I was looking at. Over in my flowerbed the ground was bubbling up some strange looking stuff. I took a closer look and now the wet soil looked reddish-brown in color and you could see pools of this strange stuff bubbling out of the ground. I knelt down and wiped some of it up with my hand. It smelled like rust or something.

Well I was so mad I went in the house and I said to Daddy, "Come out here and look at this! I think some dirty son of a bitch has poured something in my flowerbed! After the hell that I went through to spade it up too! It was as hard as concrete when I started!"

So Daddy knelt down to take a look at it. He rubbed some of it between his fingers and smelled it. Then I saw him get kind of pale looking. He didn't say anything to me he just shook his head and went back in the house. Mammy could tell something was bothering him, but I was too mad to notice. I kept carrying on about it for a week. I kept thinking about it and raising hell about somebody pouring something in my flowerbed.

So finally he said, "Well child, I'll tell you. I don't want to scare you, but that's blood all the way around this house."

I said, "What do you mean? What kind of blood?"

And he said, "I don't know. I guess it's where the Indians had their battles. It's the only thing I can tell you."

I'd have heap rather he said it was a hog farm or something. It was about 3 to 5 feet wide and went all the way around the house. When the sun would shine on it, it would be a greenish-brown color but when it rained it would bubble up a reddish brown color. You could wipe it up with your hand. I tried everything to get rid of it. I'd dig and dig and dig and turn the dirt over, but it would still come through. I finally ended up planting some bushes around the house so I wouldn't have to look at it!"

"Now bring the camera over here." Paul said to Susan. Paul began brushing the leaves away from the ground.

"As you can see the ground here is still the greenish-black color she was talking about. Notice too that no weeds, nor grass, nor anything is growing in the dirt on this side of the concrete foundation of the house.

Because I grew up hearing these tales of the supernatural I began reading all I could find on true ghost stories and hauntings to see if I could find any parallel stories that mirrored the strange things that I heard about this place.

"How could your mother and grandfather be sure it was really blood that they were seeing?" Susan asked.

"Well remember that both of them were raised on farms so the smell of blood is something that they would be very familiar with. Nor is blood unusual when it comes to paranormal events. Many haunted house stories including the famous Amityville house dripped blood from the walls. In some rare poltergeist cases blood as rained from the sky. There have also been many unusual religious paranormal blood related events, like bleeding statues, or the stigmata.

Here's one I wrote down. In Marinagar, India a family found red liquid oozing out of the floors of their kitchen, bathroom and veranda. It oozed out from between the tile joints for about 30 minutes.

Forensic tests revealed it was human blood."

Susan comments, "It too bad we don't have the money to take a soil sample and have it analyzed."

"Yeah" Paul agreed, "I would be interested in hearing the results. Ok let's continue now with the tales of McCawley Road. It was still 1941 when we left off.

So I asked, "What was the next strange thing that happened back there?"

My mother replied. "Well a couple of strange things started happening at the same time. But fixing up the house kept me so busy and tired I really didn't pay much attention to the little things. Daddy put a patch job on the roof so the kitchen became usable. We moved Mammy's wood-burning stove into the kitchen."

"What did you use for a refrigerator?" I asked.

She said, "We had an icebox. We put it out on the back porch and you know how cold it is 9 months of the year. During the winter Daddy would chop blocks of ice out of the creek and keep them in the basement."

"How did you keep them from melting in the summer?" I asked.

She said, "Oh you pack them in sawdust. That's an old trick. You know people used to live just fine before they invented electricity and indoor plumbing Paul. Daddy and Mammy lived most of their lives without it and I lived a good portion of mine.

So it wasn't all that strange to us to live without it there. But sometimes it did make things easier. Remember I told you the basement was flooded when we moved in. One of the first things Daddy did was to go into Okalona and rent a gasoline-powered generator.

Then he talked some friends of his whom also fixed up homes for a living to drive back there and use the electric pump to pump the water out of the basement. Once we got the basement dried out Daddy used it to store ice for the summer.

We had to chop wood for the fireplace and stove. Daddy would do a lot of ice fishing to help feed us and he brought the ice home for our ice box in the summer time.

Also each day I had to pump water from the well on the back porch to wash our dishes in the dishpan. I also needed to pump water to wash our clothes and ourselves. Plus I had 3 meals to cook and Donnie to look after. He was one going on two. Once he learned to walk and then run he was a handful all by himself."

I asked, "What did you do for entertainment? It sounds like your life was all work and no play."

She said, "Well Mammy loved to read and Daddy made his own fun. He would go into town every weekend to play cards, drink and see his girlfriends. He was in his 80's with snow white hair and he'd take shoe black and blacken his hair before he went into town. Then he'd kiss Mammy goodbye and say 'I'm going in town to see my girlfriends but you're the one I love." And she'd just smile. I'd say "Why don't you take a baseball bat and knock his head off?" And she'd just laugh at me."

I asked her, "What was the next unusual thing that happened back there?"

She said, "We had this 3 sided cupboard in the corner of the kitchen and it had 4 doors, two at the top and two at the bottom. Just when you weren't expecting it all the dishes inside would just jingle. Mammy kept telling me it was mice. I never saw any mice but I set some traps anyway.

It was around June that the laughing sound started. By that time we had most of the downstairs livable. So Mammy and Daddy slept in the bedroom by the kitchen and me and Donnie in the one by the dining room. One night at about 3am I woke up hearing the most horrible sound. It sounded like an old woman laughing.

He he he he hah hah hah hah. I mean it made chillsgo up and down your spine! I was laying there awake thinking "What in the Hell is that?" and then I heard it again.

So I got up and I met Daddy coming out of his room. He was hearing it too. We both went out on the back porch and the sound was coming from a tree. Do you remember that great big tree that stood between the house and the old barn? Well it was coming from there.

Mammy told us to come on back to bed. She said it was a rain crow. I said, "Well let's load the shotgun and blow that tree to pieces and kill that son of a bitch!" It just got on my nerves you know. She knew it wasn't any crow because no bird ever made a sound like that! She just didn't want me outside at that hour cussing and throwing rocks up in that tree.

So we just got used to getting up at that hour and putting on the coffee at 3am. Because it started that damn laughing sound every night at that time and kept it up until dawn. We were sitting there you know and those damn dishes would rattle in the cupboard occasionally. I'd check to see if any traps had gone off but I never saw any sign of any mice.

Then one morning that first summer we lived back there, Daddy had gone fishing and Donnie was asleep. I was washing dishes and Mammy was sitting in her rocking chair looking down the hallway. She was in the kitchen but she could see all the way to the dining room.

Well it was real quiet day. Mammy was reading and all of a sudden we heard a loud crash come from the dining room. I said, "What in the hell was that?"

Mammy said, "You won't believe this but that big marble ashtray you bought just leaped into the air and hit the floor!" So I went in the dining room and there it lay on the floor broken in two! I had just bought it. It sat on the end table in the dining room. I wouldn't let anyone use it because it was the only new thing we had.

That was the moment that I changed my mind about Daddy's stories and began to believe he was right about that old place being haunted. So I tossed the ashtray in the garbage can and tried not to think about it. Like I said we were so busy trying to get the house in shape that I just ignored a lot of the little things. They didn't really scare me. They just annoyed me. So all summer long we put up with that laughing sound and rattling dishes."

Paul closes his book and says, "Cut. Ok I guess that's enough filming for today. We'll come back tomorrow and film some more. Susan follows him back through the brush until they make their way back to McCawley Road. They make their way back to the apartment complex and call it a day

Chapter 8
Tales of McCawley Road- 1942-1944

Paul and Susan rise early. After they eat breakfast Paul checks to see if their battery is charged for the camera. They put on their heavy coats and once again make their way out of the apartment complex and walk all the way down McCawley Road until they reach the site of his old home.

Paul leads the way and Susan follows him through the brush and they make their way to the clearing that was once his old living room. Susan aims the camera at him and Paul opens his book to wear he left off. Then says, 3-2-1 action."

He speaks to the camera, "I asked my mother what happened next back at our old home?

She replied ... " "By 1942 we had the house in pretty good shape. At least we had all of the floorboards straightened out. Donnie turned two years old. One night Daddy was out with Tommy Jones the real estate man he worked for and me, Mammy and Donnie were by ourselves again.

Jimbo showed up at our house drunk as usual so I let him in and made him get in the washing tub and I heated up the water for him on the stove. I let him sleep in my room and I slept in the dining room on one of the old cots we had.

I had gotten Donnie a little pair of leather boots. Every thing he saw Daddy do he's have to copy. Every time Daddy got drunk he'd have to dance.

So Donnie was dancing like Daddy in the dining room. Mammy had gone to bed and I said, "Come on Donnie get in the bed." Well he sat down on the steps that led upstairs and crossed his legs like Daddy used to do. Daddy used to think that was so funny.

Anyway, he looked towards the living room and he never was a kid to be easily scared, I wish to hell he had of been, I could have kept up with him a lot easier! Well all of a sudden he jumped in my bed and started screaming. "The man's going to get you! The man! The man!" and he had me around the neck so tight it was almost choking me. He carried on like that until he finally went to sleep.

Mammy heard the commotion and came to see what was going on? Finally at about 2 in the morning he dozed off. Mammy said, "Now in the morning, don't mention this to him and see if he remembers it." Daddy got home around that time and he and Mammy went on to bed.

At 3am the damned laughing sound started but I was so tired I just put the pillow over my head and went on to sleep. At dawn Jimbo got up and Daddy too so I got up and made them breakfast.

Jimbo said, "I ain't hardly slept a wink since 3am. Did you all hear that noise?"

I said, "Yeah but we're kind of used to it. You want some coffee? The cups are in the cupboard." So when he got up from the table to go to the cupboard all of the dishes inside started rattling again.

Jimbo said, "What in hell caused that?"

Me and Mammy both said "Mice" at the same time.

"They must be wearing combat boots then!" He said.

He opened the door to the cupboard and got his cup. A little later I heard Donnie waking up. mammy went in to put his clothes on him and the first thing he did was to look toward those glass doors that separated the dining room from the living room and he said, "The man's gone home." So he did remember it."

I asked her, "Didn't Donnie see the old man again?"

She said, "Yes. That was about 2 weeks later. Me and Mammy were sitting in the kitchen. Donnie wasn't supposed to go upstairs by himself but he sneaked up anyway and he was on his way back down when he fell. I was sitting so I could see him when he hit at the bottom of the steps.

At that time there was a doorway to the stairs in the kitchen as well as the dining room. Later we closed up the kitchen entrance. Anyway we both ran to him. Naturally he was screaming and crying because he landed on his knee.

We took him to see Dr. Bates and he said that he had pinched a nerve in his knee. So he could hardly walk for two weeks. It took him that long to get calm enough to tell us why he fell. That's when he told us about the old man that he saw. He showed us where he was standing and everything."

"Ok" Paul commented, "This next story was taken from a separate tape where the same story is told by the one who experienced it, my older brother Donald Michelson.

Donnie said ..."They say I wasn't over two years old but I remember this like it was yesterday. We all lived downstairs and we had the upstairs vacant. We owned a little brown and white dog named Skippy. She was upstairs eating and I slipped upstairs to see her.

Well, I got a funny feeling when I started down the stairs. I remember I was holding onto the wall watching how to go down them and then I saw somebody standing about half the way down.

I looked up and I saw a real tall old man. He was dressed all in black and had one of those stove pipe hats on. I remember he had the most horrible look on his face. It scared me so bad it cut my voice off. I couldn't scream. Then I remember that I was trying to hold onto the wall so I could get by him and that's when I fell."

Susan asks, "Do you think he saw the ghost of old man Hobbs?"

"Yeah, I think that's exactly who it was! The stove pipe hat like they wore in the 1800's would fit his time period as well. Not only do I think that's who it was but of course Grandpa thought so too when he heard the description."

"Before we continue I would like to point out that many books on parapsychology state that houses in which apparitions are seen rarely also have poltergeist like moving of objects. Yet at McCawley Road we seem to have had both types of phenomenon at the same time.

The flying ashtray is a classic example of a poltergeist effect and the appearance of the old man is a classic apparition. The blood around the house and the dishes rattling also are classic poltergeist effects." Paul explains.

"Couldn't the dishes have just been mice?" Susan asks.

Paul said, "I don't want to get ahead of my story but let's just say that it gets much worse than just rattling."

"What do you make of the laughing sound?" Susan asks.

"Yes of all of the paranormal cases I've read about the one with the most similarities was the Bell Witch case. I'll go into that in more detail later but since you brought it up, the Bell Witch was heard by all who attended John Bell's funeral to laughing hysterically. So even the laughing sound has its parallels in other hauntings. But let's move on and return to our story."

I asked her, "So what happened next?"

She replied, "In 1943 Robert came home early from the Army. He had a heart attack and the doctors said he had a hole in his heart and gave him an honorable discharge. I don't know who was the happiest to see him, me, Mammy or Daddy.

I knew he'd be such a help to us with all of the work that needed to be done around there. Since we didn't have any heat upstairs I made him a bed on the sofa in the dining room. I kept my bedroom door open so we could share the heat from the kerosene heater.

At 3am that damn laughing sound started. I just went on and got up as usual. Robert was sitting up on the sofa when I came out of the bedroom.

"What in hell is that sound?" He asked me.

"Something you'll have to get used to." I told him. Daddy got up too so I made them both breakfast. At 5am they decided to go fishing.

Robert was such a help to us. Daddy was getting kind of old to chop wood everyday so Robert took over that chore. Robert went out everyday looking for work. He ended up getting a job at International Harvester. He worked the 3pm till 11 pm shift so he didn't get home until midnight usually.

Now this next thing that I'm going to tell you I didn't find out about for a long time until he finally told me about it. He said one night when he got home everybody was in bed as usual and he lay down on the sofa. The only light was the light of the moon shining through the living room windows, which he could see through those glass doors in the dining room.

He said he was still wide awake. He hadn't been sleeping yet. It was so quiet that you could hear a pin drop. At first he thought he was seeing things because he saw what looked like white fog begin to seep out from under the sofa. He lay there watching it and ever so slowly the fog began to take shape.

He said he was too scared to move or even blink. He said it rose up about 4 or 5 feet tall and took on the shape of a white ape. Then it began to cock its head back and forth looking at him. He said its eyes were just coal black.

Well, he said that's all he saw of it as he jerked the cover over his head so he wouldn't see it anymore. Then after a minute he peeked out from under the cover and he didn't see it anymore in the dining room.

Thinking it was gone or maybe he dreamed it, he sat up on the sofa and then he saw it again. But now it was in my room. I didn't have a real bed yet. All I had was a feather bed on the floor. Robert said he saw it squatting over me. Then it raised up and looked in the mirror on my dresser.

Before he knew what to do it got harder and harder to see and then it disappeared altogether. But then he heard me making choking sounds in my sleep. Like I was having trouble breathing. So he came running over and yanked me up and when he did I was ok again.

I said, "What happened?"

Well he said, "I guess you were having a nightmare. He didn't want to tell me what he saw because he didn't want anybody to think he was crazy.

I said, "Yeah ...I couldn't breathe. I felt like something heavy was sitting on my chest." Donnie slept through the whole thing. Robert didn't say anything the next day. He told me later he figured he must have dreamed it.

It was also a big help to us that Robert owned a car. I could get him to drive us to the store in Okalona. So we didn't have to walk or take the bus so much.

One morning Robert took Daddy into town for some reason. It was about 9 in the morning and the dishes started rattling in the cupboard again.

Even louder than usual so I said to Mammy, "And I'm getting damn sick of that happening too! We never have seen any mice. Not a single trap has gone off."

Mammy just changed the subject. She knew it wasn't mice making the dishes rattle but that place was the only decent home she'd ever had and I guess if she admitted it was haunted she was afraid I'd up and move out."

"Next in my transcript I asked her to tell me the story about those choking sounds. This is what she told me." Paul commented.

"One night about ten o'clock at night there was a knock on our back door. I looked out the window in the kitchen and I said, "Oh Goddamn! It's Jimbo again and he's drunk as usual."

Daddy said, "Be nice. He's your brother too you know."

I said, "Don't remind me!"

Well I opened the door and Jimbo stumbled in. He tried to hug me and I pushed him away.

He slurred "Katie ... my favorite sister."

I said, "Oh get off! What in the hell are you doing here?"

He said, "I...I came to see you."

I said, "Drunk as a skunk and you're still the biggest bullshitter I ever knew!"

He said, "I... think I'm going to be sick."

I opened the kitchen door and shoved him out on the porch. I said, "Goddamn it! Get out there and do it!" I was so mad I was cussing under my breath. I said, "Why the hell did he have to show up?"

Mammy said, "Now Katie you can't turn him away."

I said, "Oh alright Mammy. For your sake I'll put up with the old fool." And I said, "But I don't know where he's going to sleep? The upstairs is as cold as the outside and we only have the three heaters."

By this time Robert had taken one of the rooms upstairs as his bedroom and he had his own kerosene heater now. Daddy said, "He'll be alright. He sleeps outside half the time anyway. So I'm sure he'll be all right upstairs if we pile enough blankets on top of him."

So I cleaned the old fool up again and helped him upstairs. There was an old featherbed on the floor in one of the rooms upstairs that was there when we moved in.

So I stuck him on that and we piled a bunch of blankets on top of him. The others went to bed and I was still too upset. So I stayed up waiting for Robert to get home.

Well he got home just after midnight and said, "What are you doing up?"

I said, "That damn Jimbo had to show up drunk as usual."

Robert said, "Oh well he never stays anywhere very long. I won't worry about it." I said, "We put him upstairs."

He said, "Well I'm heading on up to bed." I put out my cigarette and said. "Alright. I guess I better turn in too."

I fell right to sleep but at 3 in the morning I woke up hearing a horrible sound. I mean it sounded like somebody had a rope around someone's neck!

Well I jumped out of bed and I ran in Mammy and Daddy's room and I woke Daddy, I said, "Daddy I hear an awful sound." Then it hit me that Robert had a bad heart. I said, "Oh Daddy! I hope Robert's not having a heart attack!"

He jumped out of bed and we both headed for the stairway. He wasn't going fast enough to suit me so I went under his arm and beat him up the steps.

When we opened Robert's door, he was sitting up in bed on his elbow! He was hearing it too, see?

He said, "What the matter?"

I said "Are you alright?"

He said, "Yeah."

I said, "Do you hear that choking sound?"

He said, "Yeah. I was wondering if it was one of you all?"

So then we remembered Jimbo. So we all 3 looked in on him and he was sound asleep. But we could still hear the choking sound. Well since it wasn't any of us we started searching the whole house. We checked all 11 rooms and the basement and we couldn't figure out where the sound was coming from? You could hear it just as well in every room. We went outside and searched. But the further we got from the house the less you could hear it.

Then all at once it stopped just as suddenly as it started! I was the last one to stop searching for it. But finally I gave up and came back into the house. When I went to my bedroom there was Robert in bed with Donnie!

He was too scared to go back upstairs! So I went to Daddy's room almost beside myself in laughter!

I said, "Robert's in bed with Donnie! He's too scared to sleep alone!"

Daddy got to laughing and said to Mammy, "Well Emma don't you think we ought to wake Jimbo up and let him get between me and you."

We all got a big laugh out of that one. We went to sleep and we didn't hear the choking sound anymore. The next morning I was making breakfast for every one when Jimbo woke up and had no idea where he was at until he came downstairs and saw us at the kitchen table.

He said, "Good morning. That coffee sure smells good."

I gave him a cup. I said, "Jimbo I thought you were staying with Bessie in E-Town?"

He said, "I was but we had an argument and she run me off."

So I said, "Well you're welcome to stay here as long as you're sober. If you'd give up drinking you could live here with us."

Robert said, "I could probably get you on at International Harvester."

Jimbo said, "I've tried to quit drinking but I just can't."

He said, "Don't worry about me little brother. I'll get by. Life's too short to work yourself to death."

Robert said, "Well you can help me and Daddy to chop some more wood after breakfast."

Jimbo said, "Sure I'll be glad to."

After breakfast when the men went out to chop some firewood, me and Mammy went out to the well to get buckets of water to wash the dishes and clothes. Then the 3 of them went out to the old creek to do some fishing.

Mammy said, "I don't know what's going to become of that boy?"

I said "Boy? He's in his 60's!" I said, "Quit worrying about him. He's been drinking like that since I was a little girl and it hasn't killed him yet! He'll probably see all of us in the ground. I'm sure Bessie will take him back. She always does."

I started washing the breakfast dishes and Mammy went in to dress Donnie who just woke up. While I was standing there the damn dishes in the cupboard started rattling and shaking again.

By now everyone was so used to it we just ignored it. But not this time! Because all of a sudden all four doors flew open and all of the dishes inside flew out and crashed on the floor!

Mammy shouted from the bedroom, "Katie are you alright?"

I yelled back, "I'm fine Mammy." I went down in the basement and got the hammer and came back up to the kitchen and demolished the cupboard!

By the time I got finished there wasn't anything left but a corner! I swept up the wood and broken dishes and saved what wasn't broken. I put the rest in the garbage can.

Daddy came in and went to get a coffee cup and said, "Where the hell is the cupboard?"

I said, "It's gone! The coffee cups are in the cabinet now."

Susan laughed upon hearing that. "Your mother was something else!"

Paul replied "You've no idea! Well that was the end of the cupboard problem anyway."

"What do you make of that ghostly white ape thing or whatever it was? And what do suppose those choking sounds were?" Susan asked.

"I've given that a lot of thought over the years. The white ape thing is one of the strangest creatures I've ever heard about. The only category I can place it in is under demonic activity.

In the book "The Haunted" by Robert Curran the Smurl family encounters a couple of half beast-half men demons that physically attacked them. Also in the Amityville case there was a demon that took the form of a pig named Jodie. Ok let's continue with our story.

I asked her, "What else happened in 1943?"

She replied, "Well I started to notice that Robert would leave right after breakfast and go into town. Every time we asked him where he was going? He acted kinda funny. He'd say no place in particular" and he'd just get real quiet.

After he left I looked at Mammy and giggled and she giggled back.

Daddy spoke up and said, "You two want to let a man in on the joke or should I just wonder about it?"

Mammy said, "I think Robert's got a girlfriend."

Daddy looked up from his breakfast in surprise and said, "Well I'll be ... "

So we didn't see a lot of him in those days. He disappeared after breakfast and went to work in the afternoon. One day Robert said, "Katie, have you got any plans for that big pile of lumber out behind the old barn where you tore down the meat house and hen house?"

I said, "Not really. We got the floor straightened out now. Why did you want to use some of it?"

He said, "Well if it's ok with you and Dutch I'd like to build a house over in the field."

I said, "Sure. You can have it all if you need it."

About a month later I went over to see it and he had about half of it finished. I said, "My goodness. This is going to be nice. " I said, "Could you do me a favor? I need a ride in town. I've got some blankets on lay-a-way and I have to make a payment on them."

He said, "Sure. I'll take you. It looks like it's going to rain anyway."

So he drove me to Louisville and when he parked I looked across the street and saw a sign that said, "Fortune's told-one dollar."

I said, "Look Robert. Let's have our fortune's told."

He said, "No thanks. I don't really believe in that stuff. I'll just wait here with Donnie if you'd like to go."

I said, the last payment on the blankets is four dollars and all I have is a five dollar bill. Do you have any change? If that old fortune teller sees this five she'll try and swindle me out of it."

He said, "I'm sorry I don't have a penny."

So I said, "Well I ain't gonna let her see it. I'll stick it up here in my shirt pocket and I won't pay her until she's finished."

I walked up to the door and I started to knock on it and she said, "Come in Mrs. Michelson." Well I liked to have dropped over! I'd never seen this woman before in my life!

She had long black hair down to her waist and a big cat sitting on her shoulder. That was enough for me, the cat! I guess she knew I was afraid of it by the look on my face, so she put it down and then she said, "Are you willing to give me that whole five dollars in your pocket?"

Well that made me about half mad so I said, "Hell no I'm not. Your sign says one dollar."

She said, "Those blankets can wait."

I said, "Well they ain't a gonna." I said, "Are you going to read my fortune or not?"

So she looked at my palms and said, "I don't think I can tell your fortune. You're as strong as I am. But I do see that something is going to happen to your younger brother. Something to do with his feet very soon.

There's something else. There's something in your house. I don't know what it is? But it's evil and it's very old. Something the previous owner brought in. It's the cause of the strange things happening there."

I said, "Can you help me get rid of it?" She said, "I can try. But it's dangerous. I'll have to charge you 100 dollars." I said, "Well sorry but I don't have that kind of money. I'll just settle for the palm reading."

She said, "Your abilities are too strong. I can't see it. But my mother can tell your fortune. She's in the next room." I looked through the door and there sat the scariest looking old woman I'd ever seen."

So I said, "No thanks." I paid her the dollar and she said, "Oh before you leave your little boy is crying up a storm for you."

I said, "Oh like hell he is. He's sound asleep."

Robert told me that I didn't even get out of sight until Donnie woke up and cried the whole time I was gone. So I went and paid for my blankets. Robert said, "What did she tell you?"

I said, "Oh just a big bunch of bullshit you were right not to waste your money."

The next day Robert was out working on his house and Daddy stopped by to help him. He said, "How come you're making it only one story?"

Robert said, "Later on I intend to build a bigger one next to it and I'll make this one my hen house."

Daddy said, "Oh I see what you have in mind." They worked for about an hour and then Robert took a step backwards and stepped right on a nail sticking up out of a board. It went right through his shoe and through the bottom of his foot!

I heard Daddy yelling for help and I ran out there and helped Robert into the house. We washed Robert's foot and wrapped it. Then Daddy walked into Okalona and got Dr. Bates. He drove Daddy back and then he examined Robert's wound. He re-cleaned it and put antibiotic ointment on and re-wrapped it.

Then he gave Robert a tetanus shot. He told me to change the bandage twice a day and Robert to stay off of it for a couple of days. Daddy rode back with the doctor to Okalona and used a payphone to call International Harvester to tell them what happened and what the doctor said. Dr. Bates said he'd send me a bill later and to call him if we needed him.

That night Robert's temperature went sky high. I sat up all night putting cold rags on his forehead to bring his temperature down. By dawn his fever had broken, but when he tried to get up he felt dizzy and he had lost all feeling in both of his feet!

I kept changing the bandages twice a day like the doctor said to do. By the week's end both of his feet turned bluish in color and then the skin began to peel off the bottom of both of his feet. I kept soaking them and putting antibiotic ointment on them that Dr. Bates had given us twice a day.

Then one morning a knock came on the front door and when I opened it there stood this pretty auburn haired woman. She said, "Excuse me but does Robert Murray live here?"

I said, "Yes. I'm his sister Katie."

She said, "My name is Betty Miller. I was hoping to talk to him."

So I said, "Come on in. He's been laid up in bed for a week now."

She said, "Oh, I was wondering what why he stopped coming by?"

Betty visited Robert and he told her about his accident. I went in the kitchen and told Mammy and Daddy about Robert's visitor.

When she started to leave I brought her in the kitchen to meet them.

Then she left, so I went into Robert's room and said, "Well well, I guess we know where you've been going every morning."

Robert said, "I knew you'd make a big fuss about it so that's why I tried to keep it quiet."

Then he said, "How do you like her?"

I said, "She's wonderful. I hope it works out."

He said, "Well it won't if I lose my feet."

I couldn't help but remember what the old fortune-teller had told me. That something would soon happen to Robert's feet. So I told Mammy I had to go into town. I walked down McCawley Road and caught the bus into town. I went back to the fortune teller's and I knocked on the door.

She said, "Come in Mrs. Michelson."

I said, "I'm here because of Robert's feet! Something did happen to them just like you said. How do I know that you didn't put some kind of a spell on him to cause it?"

She said, "It's not me. It's the evil thing in your home. It killed the previous owner. It choked him to death and now it's after the you and your family."

She said, "I can't get rid of it but if you pay me 20 dollars I can protect your brother and his feet will heal." I said, "Alright. I guess I don't have much choice. You heal Robert and I'll pay you fifty dollars. But you don't get a penny until he's well."

"Very well." She said.

The very next morning the feeling came back in Robert's feet. Dr. Bates just scratched his head in puzzlement. He said, "I not only don't know what caused the problem in Robert's feet when he was only wounded in one of them, but now I can't figure out what cured it? Still I'm glad to see you better. Let me know if this ever reoccurs."

I said, "Thank you doctor. I'm sure it won't come back." True to my word I mailed 50 dollars to the old fortune teller."

I asked her, "What happened next?"

She replied, "Dutch came home from the war. He was stationed at Ft. Knox and came home every weekend. He remortgaged the place and we began to remodel it from top to bottom. It took months we had so much to do.

But eventually we had electricity put in, in door plumbing with a bathroom of course. A new roof put on. All thewindows replaced upstairs, a new kitchen sink downstairs with cabinets, a refrigerator and gas stove, new furniture allover the house. A bedroom suite, dining room table and a large radio for the living room.

Daddy and Donnie listened to it every night together. Donnie loved "The Lone Ranger." Oh and where the old barn stood we tore it down and started building a two car garage.

Finally it was time to paint the old place. I talked Dutch into hiring your Uncle Elmer. He was a house painter at the time. He'd been ill and needed the money. So we all helped him paint it."

On a Saturday, Elmer, his wife Mary and their daughter Tiny arrived with paintbrushes, buckets of paint and ladders. I stayed in to cook a big dinner for everybody while outside Dutch, Daddy, Robert and Elmer began to paint the house white.

It took 3 coats of paint, as the first one just soaked right on in like it was water. You can imagine a 45-year-old board that had never seen a coat of paint. When they got finished they were pleased with it. Our old house looked like a new one.

With all the workmen coming and going in and out of the house everyday and us picking out our furniture all of the supernatural activity seemed to stop. I figured that maybe whatever the old fortuneteller had done had broken the spell on that place and for the first time since we moved there I was happy and at peace.

Robert finished building his house. Then I discovered that I was going to have a baby. A few months later though Dutch was ordered to go back overseas."

Paul said, "Ok cut. That's enough for today Sue. Let's pack it up and head home. We'll come back out early tomorrow and film a little more."

"Ok" she said and they made their way through the thick brush until they got to McCawley Road, and began their long walk back down it to their apartment complex.

Chapter 9
Tales of McCawley Road- 1945-1947

Paul and Susan rise at dawn and after eating breakfast and making sure they have fresh tape and batteries begin their early-morning trek down McCawley Road to the site of Paul's old home.

Once again they make their way through the brush to the clearing and see the top of the row of concrete blocks sticking out of the ground. All that remains of the left side of his old home now. Paul opens his book to where he left off the day before and says, "Action." Susan begins to video tape him as he reads.

I asked her, "That brings us to 1945 right?"

My mother said, "Yeah but before Dutch went over left to go overseas he and I decided to throw a big party for Mammy and Daddy's 50th wedding anniversary. Now at the time all of Mammy and Daddy's kids were still alive except for the Birdie, the oldest.

So the big day came and the house was full of people. All eleven rooms and the yard was full. Bessie showed up from E-Town with her daughter Wanda June and Jimbo road with her. Elmer, Mary and Tiny came.

Willie and his wife Dorothy and their eleven kids, Florence and her husband Sam and Florence's daughter Dolores, who was the same age as Donnie showed up.

Lizzie-Pearl and Joe came by with their newborn son Joey. Janie came and her husband and nine kids, Edith and her husband and seven kids. Even Johnny, his wife Mildred and their son flew in from California for the occasion.

Of course Robert invited Betty. Everybody brought a dish so there was plenty of food.

Daddy and Mammy cut their anniversary cake. Edith worked at a bakery at the time so she provided the cake. Dutch hired a photographer but there were so many of us we had to shoot them in groups.

Then at the end of the evening Robert stood up and said he had an announcement to make. He said, "Betty and I were married today."

Well the tears started flying! Jimbo had sworn that this was one day when he wouldn't get drunk. But we saw him grab his hat and head for town. About ten o'clock that night Bessie was getting worried about him. Everybody else had gone home.

Then I heard Skippy barking at something down the road. It was a friendly bark not a hostile one. So I went out on the front porch and I looked down McCawley Road. All you could see was this white ball moving up and down about two feet tall. Plus you could see Skippy whose fur was mostly white dancing around it.

When it got a little closer, I could see it was Jimbo. He was crawling on his hands and knees. He was too drunk to stand up! It was his white hair we were seeing!

Bessie said, "Well let's load him into the back of the truck and we'll be heading home. Robert and Betty spent their honeymoon in the house that he had built for them.

Everyday after that when Robert went to work in the afternoon Betty came over to our house. We got to be really good friends. Dutch went on overseas and I started writing him every week.

Betty would stay until Robert would get home and she would fix his dinner in our place since they didn't have electricity yet in Robert's house. I'd usually got to bed about eleven o'clock and she'd wait for Robert to arrive.

One night in February Mammy and Daddy were sleeping in their bedroom next to the kitchen. Betty was still there waiting for Robert to get home from work.

You know how cold it is in February. I always get an itch when I get pregnant. I'd nearly scratch myself to death. It was my nerves is what it was, but I never did know what in the hell it was? Until the doctors at Ft. Knox told me.

Well like I said, "Betty would wait for Robert to arrive to fix him his late supper and she'd always come to my room to get a cigarette. Just about an hour before she usually came in I started itching.

So I got up and washed down in alcohol and crawled back under the covers. Well I forgot to turn off the light. I was lying there awake and I knew if I moved I would start itching again. So I thought. "I'll just wait until Betty comes in to get her cigarette and ask her to turn off the light."

Then I felt somebody standing behind me and I thought it was Betty. I didn't turn over and my back was to the door. I said, "Betty, the cigarettes are over there on the chair and would you turn out the light?"

I didn't get any answer and I thought, "She must have gotten mad because I didn't turn over." So I rolled over and there stood the most beautiful woman you've ever seen in your life, right up against my bed! Looking me right down in the face!

Well Goddamn! I alarmed the whole neighborhood I screamed so loud! It liked to have scared poor old Mammy and Daddy to death. I don't know which one of them jumped out of the bed the fastest and they got hung in the door! They thought I was having the baby, see?

I didn't want to tell them I saw a ghost and I was afraid they would think I was crazy so I told them I was dreaming. Well Goddamn! Daddy cussed all night long!

He'd say "Seven in the morning I'm leaving! A man can't even get no Goddamn rest around here!" He didn't go to bed the rest of the night.

I wrote Dutch about what I saw. I said, "I don't know who she is but she sure scared the pants off of me!" I'll never forget how she looked. She had coal black eyes, an olive complexion and the prettiest mouth I've ever seen. A long, slim nose and she was little featured. Coal black hair parted in the middle, which hung loose on her shoulders and was real wavy. She was wearing a bluish-green dress. She had her hands crossed and was smiling, looking me right down in the face.

Oh man! I liked to have had a heart attack! If she'd have been ugly I guess I would've!

Anyway ten years later, Dutch was overseas again and you were about 17 months old and we were sleeping in that same room. This time I was asleep, but I woke up talking to the same woman standing at the foot of my bed.

Dutch was in Germany and he wasn't scheduled to come home for a whole year in February. I woke up and went to ask her a question and she vanished.

All she said was "Don't worry about Dutch he's going to be alright. He's coming home in October of this year. He'll be awfully disappointed and hurt but just put up with him because it's for his own good."

Well I woke up and I went to say, "What's going to happen to him?" and she vanished. It was the same person.

Now that was in July of 56 and I sat down and wrote Dutch a letter. He's still got it. I said, "That beautiful lady has appeared to me again and told me that you were coming home in October of this year and not February of next year." And he made fun of me.

He wrote back and said, "Your beautiful lady's goofed this time." He said it wasn't ten days until he got a notice that he was to be cut from an officer to a master sergeant and they were shipping him home in October. He was so disappointed over losing that rank because they cut his pay too.

But before he came home, Dutch showed my letter to a priest over there. The priest believed that I had seen the Blessed Mother and he wanted me to come over and meet him.

I said, "Not on your life. I wouldn't cross that much water for nobody! But he can come over and meet me if he wants to." So I don't know if that's who it was or not?. I never did know for sure who she was?"

Susan asks, "So who do you think it was that she saw?"

Paul comments, "That's a good question. We know no one lived there before my family moved in except Hobb's and his wife and daughter.

Esther Wilkins said her mother died in childbirth, so perhaps her spirit was drawn to my mother because she was pregnant with Pat and you notice that she did not reappear until ten years later just after I was born. So maybe that's who it was? Of course I'm just guessing.

Susan asks, "Do you still have the letter she mentioned writing to your father?"

Paul says, "No. I wish I did. I moved to Florida with Lavonne when he died in 1983 and Pat was the one who handled his affairs. I think Donnie still has most of the photos and Dutch's personal things. But I don't know what became of the letter she mentioned?"

Susan said, "That's too bad. It would have provided some tangible evidence for the stories."

"Yeah, that's true." Paul commented.

"Well on with our story. I said, "We got a little ahead of our story. Let's go back to Pat's birth.""

She said, "Pat wasn't supposed to be born until May. But on March 22, 1945 at about one o'clock in the afternoon I started having labor pains. But I didn't tell anybody because I thought maybe it's my imagination. About five in the evening I thought, "Well by hell! I'm going to have to tell it!""

Florence and Sam were visiting. Dutch was stationed in Indiana then and he could only come home on weekends. We didn't have any telephone yet so Sam drove out to Okalona to get Dr. Bates.

Jimbo happened to have shown up drunk the night before. So when Dr. Bates showed up we had Jimbo take the kids Donnie and Delores who were both 5 years old at the time, into the living room and read comics to them.

Florence told me when she was in there to check on them, Jimbo was reading the comics to them but he had it upside down! He couldn't read! So he was making it up!

But it must have been interesting cause they were listening. They thought he was really reading. Florence said, she never said a word. She just closed the door.

Well Mammy was walking the floor and wringing her hands. I wouldn't let her into the room. No matter how much agony I was in, I wouldn't open my mouth because I didn't want to scare poor old Mammy and Donnie to death.

So anyway Pat was born two months premature. At 7 months old his stomach wasn't completely developed yet. We had to buy special milk for him and his was just so tiny I was afraid he wouldn't live. But he did.

Donnie always wanted a baby brother and I couldn't get that little shit away from the crib long enough to even get him to eat. Dutch got a 10 day leave and all he knew how to cook was eggs. I got two for breakfast, two for dinner and two for supper.

So after a few days I said, "By God let me out of this bed! I can't take any more eggs!"

Susan had to laugh at that. "Your mother was pretty funny. No wonder you enjoyed hearing these stories so often."

"Yes" Paul replied. "She was a natural storyteller. I used to hang on to every word. It was better than television to me.

Well back to our story. I asked her, "What was the next unusual thing that happened back there?"

She replied, ":Like I said, Jimbo had come to stay a couple of weeks with us. He slept on the sofa in the living room. One night after we were all in bed asleeep and Robert got home from work. Betty had his supper ready for him. Then she went out on the back porch to have a cigarette while he finished eating. It was real quiet and Robert heard a funny sound. It sounded like someone was having trouble breathing.

He listened in on Daddy's bedroom door to see if it was either one of them and then at my door to see if it was me or the kids. Then he heard it again and realized it was coming from the living room. So he opened the glass doors that separated the living room from the dining room and then he heard it plainly.

He rushed in and saw Jimbo was laying on his back on the sofa asleep and he could tell that he was having trouble breathing. So he ran over and jerked him up. He said real low so as to not wake up the whole house, "Jimbo are you alright?"

Jimbo sat up on the side of the sofa and rubbed his face. He said, "Yeah... yeah. I'm ok now. Heh heh...I was just having a bad dream. It was a doozy. I dreamt some ugly looking white monkey was sitting on my chest and I couldn't breathe."

Well Robert went pale when he said that. He knew that it was the same thing he saw that night and the same thing that was taking my breath. He decided to wait until morning to tell me. The next morning we were all having breakfast and he showed up after we ate. Robert spoke up and said, "Jimbo did you tell Katie about that dream you had last night?"

Jimbo laughed and said, "No I forgot about." He said, "I had a nightmare about some ugly looking thing like a white monkey was sitting on my chest and I couldn't breathe!"

Well I liked to have fell over when he said that. I said, "What did you say?" So he told it again. I said, "My God Jimbo! I had the very same dream one night and I couldn't breathe either! It was Robert that pulled me up then too!"

So Robert spoke up and said, "I should've told you this sooner but it was so crazy I was sure I must have dreamt it. But we can't all be having the same dream." So he told us about the smoke of fog that came out from under the sofa that night and formed into a big white ape right in front of him.

I said, "Oh Goddamn! I know I'm leaving here now!"

Daddy spoke up and said, "Now do you believe me? I told you this place was cursed cause it belonged to old man Hobbs."

So I said, "I know you did. Here's something I didn't tell you. When I went to see that old fortuneteller she told me that there was something evil in this place. She said that whatever it was killed old man Hobbs and now it was after us."

Daddy said, "I bet you that choking sound we all heard that night must have been the ghost of Floyd Hobbs re-enacting his death. We know he died in this house and Emma said when the undertaker took her to the funeral home to help lay him out they had to break every bone in his body to straighten him out enough to get him in the casket. I think whatever killed him is still here and I think it's time for us to move."

I said, "Daddy Dutch and I have sunk every penny we own into this place fixing it up. What about all the work you and I spent here breaking our backs just to make this place livable? We can't afford to move out and I ain't letting nothing scare me away.

Besides, what would I tell Dutch? He don't believe in nothing like this and he'd laugh at me if I told him this place was haunted." He said, "Well we have to do something. What if it attacks one of the kids?"

I said, "I already did something once. I paid that old fortuneteller to heal Robert's feet once and all of this craziest stopped for a time. But now it's starting up again. So let's make a pact not to hide anything from each other no more. If anything happens to any of us I want you to promise and come and tell me. But let's keep Mammy out of this. It would just worry her to know what we learned."

So they all agreed to that. The next day I went down to St. Rita's church in Okalona and I asked to see Father Donnelley. I had to wait about 20 minutes because he was seeing someone else at the time. I asked him if he could come and bless the house. He said he'd be happy to.

But he was going out of town and he'd tend to it when he got back. I didn't tell him about any of the crazy stuff that had been happening back there cause I figured he'd think I was a nut or something. So since he promised to come in the future that was good enough for me and I left.

At home I was so busy raising the kids I kind of forgot about it and I guess so did Father Donnelley because he never showed up."

So I asked her, "What happened next back there?"

She said, "Robert's marriage didn't work out. He and Betty got a divorce so he moved back in our house. Dutch was stationed at Ft. Knox once again and we only saw him on weekends. I guess the next thing I remember was when Robert had that vision."

I said, "What year was that?"

She replied, "My sister Jessie was pregnant with triplets and that was in 1946. One night when Robert was driving back from International Harvester, I don't know if you remember, but on McCawley Road you turn left and then about 50 feet later you make a sharp right turn and then it goes straight on back to our house.

Well when he got to that second curve he slammed on the brakes because he saw a Christmas tree appear on the hood of his car!"

I said, "Did you say a Christmas tree?"

She said, "Yes. Lights and all! He stared at it and it looked as real as could be. He opened his car door and got out of his car and it was gone.

Then when he got back inside, he could see it again. So he got out again and it was gone again. He felt all over the hood of his car. Nothing was there. He got back in and he could see it again.

He thought maybe it's the moonlight playing some kind of trick. He started the car and drove about half the way home with it still on the hood of his car. He stopped again. He looked down in his pocket to get a cigarette and when he looked up it was gone!

So he came on home and went to bed. The next morning we could tell he was shook up about something but he wouldn't say what? Finally I just asked him. I said, "Robert what is bothering you?"

Then he told us what he saw. Mammy said, "Robert, you know I'm half Cherokee and your Grandmother was full blooded. All of my life I've had visions like that. But they are usually omens or warnings of something bad that's about to happen. Usually when you see something like that, it means someone close to you is about to die."

I said, "She's right Robert. I've had visions like that as well."

Robert said, "Well I'm glad I told it now. I thought I was going crazy."

Susan asks, "So did anyone close to him die?"

"Yes" Paul replied. "Their sister Jessie died in childbirth not long after that. I asked my mother the same question and here is her answer.

"Jessie was going to have triplets. Well Lord have mercy, she'd already had five kids one at a time and a pair of twins. Nobody would ever have dreamed that she would die having a baby. But Robert had his vision about a month before she died."

I asked her, "Did you see anything before she died."

She said, "I had a dream about her right before she died. She had on a green skirt and a sweater and was sitting on the side of a chair. All I remember her saying to me was, "The only thing I hate about it is that Jean and Jeanette will be separated." They were her twins and she wouldn't even let the teachers separate them. They wanted to put one in one class and one in another and she wouldn't let them.

So when she died Jean and Jeanette came to me and asked me to take them in. But Jean said that she wanted to live with her cousin Leonard. So that was the separation, see?"

Susan said, "You told me your mother used to have visions before someone in the family died."

Paul replies, "Oh yes and the closer the person was to her the more startling and numerous the visions. The two siblings she was the closest to were Uncle Robert and Aunt Lizzie-Pearl. Unfortunately both of them died the same year, in 1973 and only a few months apart. Aunt Lizzie died in the hospital of kidney failure and Uncle Robert was murdered.

"Murdered?" Susan exclaimed.

"Yes. He was working as a security guard for an oil company and he was on the telephone with his wife, when some thugs robbed a convenience store across the street and saw him in the telephone through the window and shot him. He died instantly."

"How awful." Susan remarked.

"Yes. It was a terrible blow to my mother. Aunt Lizzie had died only 3 months before. About three months before Aunt Lizzie died my mother started having her visions. I was watching tv with her one evening on the sofa and she had the first one.

She was watching tv when suddenly she jumped up and looked behind her. I knew what had probably happened because I was used to it by now. I said, "What did you see?"

She said, "I saw two hands come down over my eyes like someone reached down over my head." But of course no one could have because the sofa was up against the wall.

Then a few nights later I was in my bed in my room and she was in hers and I heard her yell "Oh no!" So I jumped out of bed and ran to her room. She said she hadn't been to sleep and was lying on her side and when she rolled over on her back and saw a coffin floating above her head. Then she saw it open and it was full of flames. Then it began to turn on its side that was when she yelled out and it vanished.

Susan comments, "No wonder she yelled out!"

"Yes," Paul replied, "It's a small wonder she hated having this gift. Not only did she have to endure the shock of the visions whether asleep or awake, but then she had to worry about who was going to die?"

Susan asks, "So she never knew who it was going to be?"

"No", Paul explained, "She felt that she wasn't allowed to know so she couldn't warn them. She said the omens were only to prepare her for the impending death.

Anyway the visions kept coming. A few nights later she was awakened by the sound of big heavy wings beating over her bed. Which she took to mean a visit from the angel of death. About a week later she awoke in the middle of the night to see 6 men in suits, 3 on each side of her bed like pallbearers. She could see their shapes and sizes but not their faces as they were all in silhouette.

I knew something was wrong as I heard her get up in the middle of the night. I got out of bed to see if she was all right and saw her sitting at the kitchen table smoking a cigarette. So I asked her what was wrong and she told me what she saw.

Another night she awoke and looked up and she said she saw hundreds of hands sticking out of the wall behind her bed and waving around.

Susan asks, "What do you suppose that meant?"

Paul replies, "Most of the things that she saw were symbols of death, some were more cryptic than others. Years later I read that the "hand over the head" is a symbol of death in Tibet. Of course my mother had no way to know that.

The visions continued. One night she saw a woman's arm and had a blue sleeve come out of the wall behind her bed and then it pointed to the window to the left of her bed. Just down the street in that direction was my Aunt Lizzie's house.

Since Aunt Lizzie was already in the hospital at that time and not doing well my mother naturally assumed the omens were warning of Aunt Lizzie's death. Not long after that Aunt Lizzie passed on. My mother was sure the visions would cease as they had in the past, but this time they continued on. She started to wonder if she was going mad seeing these things.

The next week she was sitting at the kitchen table one morning, and when she looked up she said the kitchen wall was gone and she could see a hillside and on the hillside she saw a fresh grave all covered in flowers.

One night about a week later she had just gone to bed and when she looked over at her bedroom door and she saw what looked like green ribbon begin to wrap up her door. She sat up and watched it. It was about 4 inches wide and started at the bottom of her door and row after row of it began to appear. Climbing higher and higher on the door. She got out of bed and touched it. She said it quivered and vanished.

Susan asks, "How weird! What do you suppose that meant?"

Paul replies, "That one I have not figured out, nor the next one. She was lying in bed and she saw what looked like black leaves falling on the bed. They vanished too of course. Black is a symbol of death but I'm not sure about the falling leaves.

Then one day she was on the telephone talking to Uncle Robert's wife, Jean when she looked down and she saw someone lying in a pool of blood. In her vision it was me she saw, but of course it was a premonition of Uncle Robert's death. He too was talking on the phone with Aunt Jean when he was shot and killed.

Susan remarks, "How horrible."

Paul says, "I know. My mother was never the same after he died. But all of that took place in 1973. We need to get back to our story. We left off in 1946. Aunt Jessie had died and her daughter Jeanette came to live with our family for two years. She was 16 at the time.

"Did she have any strange experiences back there?" Susan asks. "You know I don't really know. I never had much contact with her and I don't know where she lives or even if she is still alive? Well back to our tale.

I asked my mother, "What happened next back there?"

She replied, "Pat grew stronger each day. The doctors didn't expect him to live being so pre-mature but he fooled them. I started to notice the haunting activity was getting more noticeable again but with two kids to watch over I just decided to ignore it. Little things would happen that would drive you mad. You put something down and when you went to get it, it would be someplace else. I can't tell you how many times that happened.

Then that damn laughing sound started up again. Three o'clock in the damn morning. I just got up and made coffee the first night it started and Daddy got up too. He didn't say anything but one look said it all. He knew it was starting up again and so did I, but moving was out of the question.

I asked, "What did Dutch think about all of this?"

She said, "That was the maddening part. Every time he was home, nothing happened. But all week long when he was gone it was active. So he didn't know anything about what was going on and I didn't want to sound like a nut by telling him, because I knew he didn't believe in anything like that."

So Mammy and Daddy could have more room, me, Dutch and the kids moved upstairs. We gave them the downstairs because they were too old to climb the steps. That was in 1947. We all still ate breakfast and all of our meals together downstairs of course. Pat turned two years old and Donnie was seven.

Daddy and Donnie started going fishing together. I don't know which one of them loved to fish the most. Well Pat was too little of course. One morning when Pat was playing in the dining room by himself and all of a sudden he come running out of there in screaming hysterics. I couldn't get him to go back in the dining room for a month. Every time I would start in there with him he would hide his face or look away from those glass dining room doors. All he would say was "The man ... the man."

I said, "So both Donnie and Pat saw a man in the dining room at the age of two years old."

She replied, "That's right. Well like I said, Daddy and Donnie would go fishing every morning and one morning when Daddy came to the house with the fish they'd caught, Donnie stayed by the creek and in between the creek and the garage was our dump.

So one morning Daddy and I were cleaning the fish they'd caught and I heard Donnie screaming bloody murder.

I ran out on the back porch and I seen him a running toward the house as fast as his little legs would carry him. He came running up the back steps and into the kitchen and he was so out of breath he couldn't speak. I couldn't understand a word he was trying to tell me.

I said, "Donnie! What's the matter?"

Finally he caught his breath enough to say, "Snake! Snake!"

I said, "Is that all? You've seen lots of snakes before."

He began shaking his head "No" and finally he was able to say, "Giant snake!!"

I started laughing at him. I said, "A giant snake? Heh heh. How big is it?"

Donnie said, "Honest to God mom ... it's as big around as a telephone pole!"

I said, "Oh come on! Snakes don't grow that big around here."

He said, "This one did."

So now I was starting to get worried. I said, "You wait here with your Grandpa. I'll go take a look." So I went to the closet and got my shotgun. I figured he must have seen something the way he was carrying on. But I was sure it couldn't be as big as he said. So I headed for the dump and I sat out there for about a half an hour, but I didn't see any sign of it. So I came on back to the house. Donnie said, "Did you see it?" I said, "No. Whatever it was it's gone now."

Paul closes his book and says, "Ok cut. We'll stop here for today." Susan turns off the video camera and they head back home.

CHAPTER 10
Tales of McCawley Road- 1948-1950

Paul and Susan rise early on October 19th, 1995 in their apartment on McCawley Road. After breakfast Paul checks his batteries to make sure they are charged and he and Susan prepare for their sojourn down McCawley Road once again. In an hour they are back at the site of Paul's old home and he opens his book and prepares to read more tales as Susan aims her video camera.

Paul says "Action" and Sue begins to film. Paul says, "So I asked my mother, "What happened next?"

She replied, "This happened in 1948. Dutch, Donnie, Pat and me were still living upstairs while Mammy, Daddy and Robert lived downstairs. Dutch was still in the army and he'd come home only on weekends. Donnie and Pat had their own bedroom. I made my living room out of the room with the 3 windows that faced the front of the house. My bedroom was right next to it.

One night I was sitting on the side of my bed. I was writing a letter to Dutch. You know how you can see out of the corner of your eye? I saw someone coming down the hallway right toward my bedroom.

I looked over to see who it was and my heart nearly stopped beating! It was a strange man! That would have been frightening enough, but I'll never forget how he looked? He was dressed like someone from the Middle East. He was tall and had a turban on his head, which was black on color and hung down over his ears. It had a silver band around it. His skin was olive colored and he had a long, black beard. His robes were purplish colored, more like a maroon and he had sandals on his feet.

Well I was too shocked to move or scream or anything at first! Just before he got to my room he turned and went down the steps. Well Goddamn! I jumped up and ran to the stairwell and he was gone! Nobody could have gotten down those steps that fast. But just the same I went downstairs and searched the whole house anyway. The doors were still locked so I knew it had to be a ghost or something."

Susan says, "What a weird thing for someone from Kentucky to see? What would the ghost of an Arabian man be doing there? What do you think she saw?"

Paul looked at Susan and didn't have to answer. The look on his face told her what he was thinking.

Susan replied. "Oh no! ... Don't even start with that Simon stuff! The doctor told you it was all in your mind remember? Simon's not real. You must believe that."

Paul says, "I guess you think it's just a coincidence that my mother and I experienced hauntings by a man dressed in Middle Eastern type garments?"

Susan shakes her head and says, "No, it's not a coincidence. You told me you grew up hearing these stories. Obviously she told you this one when you were very young and it stuck in your subconscious. Then when you were a little older you created this imaginary friend based on the story you heard. That's all."

Paul smiles, "If you say so."

Susan goes on, "You know who you remind me of? That James Stuart character in the movie "Harvey".

"You mean Elwood P. Dowd? Paul asks.

"Yeah! Susan laughs. "I think I'll start calling you Mr. Dowd from now on every time you start talking about Simon like he's real. He's not real Mr. Dowd. Harvey the rabbit is all in your cracked brain! Get it!"

"Ok, ok! I get it. But uh, just for the record. Harvey turned out to be real at the end of the movie, remember?"

Susan folds her arms and frowns at him.

"Do you want me to call Dr. Bornstein?"

"No, no! I'm ok." Paul said, "Well let's move on to the next story."

I said, "What else happened in 1948?"

She replied, "The same week I saw the ghost of the Arabian man I started having really bad nightmares at night. Then one morning at dawn I woke up and when I opened my eyes I saw these scary looking black hands weaving around over my face. Not human hands, they had long black, thin bony fingers, which were covered in black fuzzy hair. I only saw them for a moment when I opened my eyes and then they vanished.

Of course I didn't tell anybody what I saw? I just got up and made breakfast for everybody. Robert drove Donnie to school. I decided to call Father Donnelley because he never did show up to bless the house. But I got a busy signal. We had a telephone by that time. I got busy doing my housework and I forgot to call him back.

That night I had another nightmare. I dreamed I was fighting with something. Then in the morning when I opened my eyes I saw these scary looking black hands again for just a moment.

I noticed that I started to feel so tired all of the time. I just figured it was because I wasn't getting much sleep. Now this went on for over a month. Then one morning when I woke up and saw those hands for a second I then realized I couldn't move. I was paralyzed!

I yelled for Donnie. He came to my door and said, "Yeah mom?" I didn't want to tell him anything was wrong with me. I didn't want to scare him.

I said, "Go downstairs and ask your Grandpa to come up here for a moment. So he did. Daddy got dressed and made his way up the steps. I asked him to help me get out of bed. Once he pulled me up, I was all right again. I could move again.

That was when I told him about the scary black hands I was seeing.

He said, "By God child! Now do you believe me when I tell you somebody is trying to bewitch us?"

I said, "Yes, I guess I do. I didn't want to, but with all that's happening I can't deny something is going on?"

He said, "Back when this happened to me and that old Indian showed up I talked to him a long time about this kind of thing. He said a witch can use anything that was once alive to bewitch you with. Like leather or fur or feathers. Now since you're only paralyzed in bed like I was maybe the witch is using your feather pillow to bewitch you. I think we ought to try burning up your pillow."

I said, "Oh come on Daddy. That's just silly."

He said, "You ask me what I think you should do and when I tell you, you don't want to do it?"

So after a few more days of waking up, seeing those hands and not being able to move until Daddy pulled me up I was ready to try anything. I gave in and we took my pillow out in the field. I took a knife and made a little split in it and I ran my hand in there and when I did I felt something wiggle!

Well Goddamn! I liked to have croaked! I screamed and said, "Something wiggled in the there!" Daddy cut it open and inside we found two strange looking things. It was a piece of sheet torn into a strip and had feathers woven into that so perfectly that it made it round. There were two of these things, a big one and a little one. Both were shaped like the letter Y or like a slingshot. Plus we found a fan of feathers in 3 corners and in the fourth one was a partial fan.

Daddy said, "See I told you someone was bewitching you. I bet you if they'd finished that fourth fan you'd have died."

I didn't know what to think? So he tried to burn it. Now you know feathers should just go up in smoke. We tried to light that thing and it wouldn't even burn. We poured kerosene on it and it still wouldn't burn. Daddy ended up tearing it up into little pieces and dug a big hole and buried it.

From that day on I never saw' those hands anymore and I wasn't paralyzed anymore."

I asked her, "Anything else happen in 1948?"

She said, "The next thing I remember happening was when Elmer, his wife Mildred and his daughter Tiny came to visit. At dinner for dessert I served wild blueberries and Mary asked where I got them? I told her we discovered some blueberry bushes growing out by the creek.

She asked if they could go pick some to take home with them.

I said, "sure" and got them some baskets. Elmer and I went out on the front porch and we were talking. There was Dutch and me, Mammy and Daddy and the kids when all of a sudden we heard somebody screaming and hollering coming from the back yard.

Well we all headed out back and we saw Mary and Tiny a running toward the house as fast as they could go. When they got a little closer we could hear they were yelling "Snake! Snake!" They ran straight to their truck and Mary started it up. Elmer walked over and she said, "Get in! Or I'm leaving you here!" So he got in and Mary hit the accelerator and drove off as fast as they could go!

Daddy said, "What in Hell was that all about?"

Dutch said, "I haven't the foggiest."

Then Donnie spoke up and said, "Mom I bet you they saw that giant snake back in the dump!"

Dutch said, "Giant snake?" So I told him what Donnie claimed to have seen, but I never saw it myself. So when Daddy heard about it he went and got the shotgun and went out to the dump. He sat for hours but he never saw it either. Finally he came on in."

I asked her, "Anything else happen in 1948?"

She said, "Well the usual little things kept happening. Things would seem to disappear and you'd find them someplace they shouldn't be and stuff like that.

Then around Christmas time, one night I was washing the dishes at the kitchen sink when I saw a shadow go past the window. Thinking we had a trespasser I ran to the back door real fast and looked out. Just as I did I saw something in silhouette jump off the end of the porch. It looked just like a gorilla!

Well Goddamn! I closed that door in a damn big hurry too! So I ran to the closet and got the shotgun and headed for the front door. Mammy had already gone to bed. Daddy, Donnie and Pat were listening to some radio program. Daddy said, "What's wrong?" I said, "Stay here!" I went all the way around the house, then around the garage. I didn't find anything so I went back inside."

I said, "Ok, that brings us to 1949. What do you remember about that year?"

She said, "Your Uncle Willie came to stay with us for a short time. He had a fight with his wife so he asked if he could stay for a time.

I said, "Of course."

Well one day he went out to fish at the creek and I looked out the kitchen window and here he come a running toward the house as fast as he could go. That worried me because I don't think he was ever scared of anything!

When he ran in the backdoor, he said, "Goddamn! Load the shotgun! There's a snake back there as big around as a water bucket!"

So I said, "Oh no! It ain't no bigger around than a telephone pole."

He said, "You knew that son of a bitch was back there and you let me go!"

It scared nearly everyone who saw it into a heart attack. I got to laughing and he knew I was just teasing him. I gave him the shotgun and he sat back there for almost half a day hoping to kill it. I still hadn't seen it at that time. I didn't know what to think? I knew snakes don't grow that big in Kentucky, but I was starting to hear the same story from too many different people."

I asked her, "Anything else unusual happen that year?"

She said, "Well right after that was when I got sick. I got to where everytime I would bend over and then raise up, I would go stone blind for a few moments. There was no way I could hide that from everyone.

Dutch came home on Saturday. He always did the shopping because he got a big discount at the PX at Ft. Knox. Well it happened to me again when he was there and he had a fit. He said, "How long has this been going on?"

I said, "The temporary blindness just started this week. I didn't want to worry you."

He said, "You didn't want to worry me? You're my wife! You're going to the hospital right now!"

I said, "Oh no I'm not! Who will take care of Donnie and Pat?"

Dutch said, "You've got a whole house full of people who will take care of them! So no more excuses."

Daddy came in from outside and then said, "What happened?"

Dutch said, "Katie's ill. I'm taking her to the hospital."

So Dutch went upstairs and got my suitcase and packed it. I told Daddy I was just going to get checked out. Then I went in and talked to Donnie and Pat. I told them Dutch was going to take me to see the doctor but I would be ok. I said the doctor may need me to stay a little while at the hospital."

Donnie said, "How long?" I said, "I don't know yet. But while I'm gone you listen to your Grandpa and Grandma and Uncle Robert. You hear me?"

Dutch drove me out to Ft. Knox to Ireland Army Hospital and Dutch waited with me in the emergency room. Hours later I finally got examined. They did x-rays and blood tests. That was when I first met Dr. Neblett. He said the x-rays showed that I had five tumors and one of them was pressing against my spinal cord. Which is why I would go blind when I would bend over.

That was when he told me he would have to remove one ovary and maybe both of them. He said it was more than likely that I would never have children again. He insisted on immediately admitting me and they operated the next morning.

Ten days later they stopped giving me morphine and when I found out I'd been gone 10 days I had a fit! I said, "I'm leaving here right now!" Dr. Neblett said, "Well if you can walk you can go home." I said, "I'll show you I can!" I slid out of bedand my ass hit that hard floor. I said, "Well don't just stand there and laugh you fool. Pick me up!" That was when I learned they had removed one ovary and half of the other one. He said, "I wouldn't be able to have any more children."

I said, "Well I'm going home anyway. I've got two kids at home who need me." I called Dutch and asked him to take me home. He wanted me to wait until Saturday so he could take me, but I wouldn't wait that long. I called Florence and she and Sam drove out to get me. They put a featherbed in the back seat because I was still too weak to even sit up.

Well in the meantime Pat who was only four years old at the time asked Donnie, who was nine then, "What they had done to me?" Donnie said, "They cut her with a knife." That's all he told Pat, see? Cause he didn't really know either. I only weighed seventy pounds and I had on that long housecoat Dutch had bought me which went way past my feet.

Well when we came in the front door Sam was carrying me and Pat let out the most awful scream you've ever heard! Just as Sam went to lay me on the bed, I said, "Pat! What on earth is the matter?" He said, "Oh mom! They cut off your feet!" Well Sam just dropped me on the bed he was laughing so hard. If he hadn't have had me over the bed I guess he would have dropped me in the floor!"

Susan laughed at hearing that one. "Kids say the darndest things!" Paul smiled and continued to read.

I said, "What came next?"

She said, "In about a week or two I got steady on my feet again. Well one day these two old colored men drove their truck back there to our house and knocked on the door. They asked me if they could go back to my dump and collect the tin and stuff. I was glad to get rid of it, cause that wouldn't burn, you know. They parked their truck in the yard and carried the junk to it.

Well about 30 minutes went by and I heard them a coming in a run. They were both yelling "Snake! Snake!" When they got to the house one of them said, "My God woman! There's a snake down there, you'll never believe it! But it's 20 feet long and as big around as a washing tub!"

Now I knew that had to be a big bunch of shit! It couldn't be that big. So I said, "Oh hell, that's my pet."

He said, "Goddamn! You knew that son of a bitch was back there and you didn't tell us!"

Susan spoke up and said, "What the heck were they all seeing back there? I used to own a boa constrictor name Orion and he was five feet long and as big around as my bicep ... but come on. Twenty feet long?"

Paul replies. "Yeah I know. Plus even if it was an escaped pet I doubt it could survive Kentucky winters. Boas and Pythons are tropical animals. No, I think the giant snake, like the white ape and other strange animals you'll hear about that was seen back here were not natural animals. Again this is similar to the Bell Witch case, in which odd animals were seen by the Bell family as well. But let's continue on with our stories.

I said, "What happened next?"

She said, "Well I was supposed to go back to the hospital a year later and let them finish up removing those tumors. But in 1950 both Mammy and Donnie got sick. It started one morning. Donnie and Pat came down for breakfast and I noticed that Donnie seemed quieter than usual. I said, "Donnie are you alright?" He said, "No ... I don't feel so good. I feel dizzy." I felt his head and he didn't feel warm.

I said, "If you don't feel any better after breakfast. I want you to go lay down."

He said, "Oh I'll be alright." So after breakfast he got up and started to walk out the back door and his legs buckled and he collapsed! Daddy and me carried him to the couch and then he came to.

He started to get up and I made him lay down again. I called Dr. Bates. When he got there he examined Donnie and drew some blood for tests.

I said, "Can you tell me what's wrong with him?"

He said, "Not yet. It could be a simple ear infection or a million other things. I recommend bed rest and if he isn't any better in the morning bring him by the office."

I made him sleep in the downstairs bedroom and Robert moved upstairs. I didn't want him going up and down the stairs if he was feeling dizzy. The next morning though when he woke up, he couldn't move either of his legs. He was paralyzed from the waist down.

I had Robert carry Donnie and put him in the backseat of his car and drive us to Dr. Bates' office. Dr. Bates helped Robert put Donnie on his examination table.

Donnie said, "My legs ... Why can't I move my legs?"

I watched Dr. Bates take a pin and touch it to Donnie's feet in several spots and he couldn't even feel it. Donnie said he couldn't feel anything from the waist down. Dr. Bates asked me if Donnie had fallen?

I said, "No, only when he fainted yesterday. After 30 minutes of tests Dr. Bates admitted to me that he was stumped. He said it's time to move him to a hospital. I called Dutch at Ft. Knox and he called Ireland Army Hospital. Robert drove us out there and they admitted him and began their own tests.

I was there for 6 hours and finally a Dr. Manning came out to talk to Dutch and me. He said the x-rays showed no injury to Donnie's spinal cord. They tested him for polio, rheumatic fever, meningitis and all sorts of things. They couldn't find anything wrong with Donnie's legs.

Dutch spoke up and said. "Are you suggesting he's faking it?"

Dr. Manning said, "Oh no, no. He definitely has no sensation in his legs. You can't fake something like that." Dr. Manning said, "We'd like to have Donnie examined by Dr. Woodsworth."

Dutch said, "Is he a specialist?" Dr. Manning said, "No, he's the head of our psychiatric unit."

Well I went off then! I said, "Are you saying my son is crazy?"

Dr. Manning started apologizing then. He said, "No, no. We just want to rule out psychosomatic illness."

I said, "That's it! I'm taking him home!"

Dr. Manning said, "Mrs. Michelson you mustn't do that. We still don't know what's wrong with him?"

I said, "By God, that's why I'm doing it? You people with all your education and fancy equipment can't find out what's wrong with my son and you want me to leave him in your care? Nothing doing! He's coming home with me!"

Dr. Manning said, "Mr. Michelson please reason with your wife."

Dutch said, "On the contrary. I agree with her. If you've failed to diagnose the child then it's time to try elsewhere, not blame the child for your incompetence."

Robert drove us all the way back to Louisville and we took him to St. Anthony's hospital. Dutch had to stay at Ft. Knox. They admitted Donnie and I got permission to stay with him in his room. Then next he had more x-rays and more tests. Finally at 6pm the doctors asked me to meet with them. They had to admit they were stumped too. So they asked to do a spinal tap. I said,

"If it will get some answers then do it." I stayed the night again. They came to get him at 5am and by 4pm they asked to meet with me again.

They said, "I'm sorry to tell you that we are still unable to find the reason for Donnie's paralysis."

I blew up! I said, "I can't believe this! For God's sake! My son can't walk and no one can help him!" Then they suggested I put him in a nursing home.

I said, "Forget it! We're leaving here right now!" I called a taxi and got help loading him into it and we went home. We put him in bed and I made him dinner. We just started learning to live with it. Dutch bought him a wheelchair so he could get around. Robert and Daddy would help me lift him into the tub.

Then before the month was out, Mammy had her stroke. She was paralyzed on the right side of her body. Now I had two complete invalids to care for. Again Dr. Bates suggested that I put her into a nursing home and I refused. But taking care of them both nearly killed me.

Every morning I'd get up at 5am and bathe Donnie and change his sheets. I'd dress him and help him into his wheelchair. Then at 6am I'd go into Mammy's room and bathe her and change her sheets. Then with Daddy's help I would put her into her wheelchair.

Next I would make breakfast for the family. Donnie could feed himself but I had to feed Mammy. Then after breakfast I'd do the dishes and dry them. Then wash the linens by hand and hang them out on the clothesline to dry. By then it was time for lunch.

In between I would be helping either Donnie or Mammy on and off the toilet. I'd cook supper for the family, do the dishes again, sweep the floors, dust and fold the laundry. By 7pm Mammy was ready for bed and after I'd get her in the bed I'd go get Donnie and help him into his pajamas and into bed and this went on for almost 2 years. I don't know how I did it?

Mammy told me she prayed for the Lord to take her and cure Donnie. I told her not to do that because her life was just as special as Donnie's. Every night I'd collapse in the bed, I was so exhausted. There might have been haunting activity in the house but I was too busy or too tired to notice.

Daddy saw that I was reaching the end of my rope. He said, "It ain't fair that Emma and me had 13 children and you are the only one taking care of your mother. I'm taking Emma to live with each one of them for two weeks and that way they can each take a turn with her."

I said, "Daddy, Mammy isn't in any condition to travel."

He said, "I ain't just thinking of you. I want to get her out of this damned house!"

I said, "Oh Daddy! Don't start with that again."

He said, "What about what happened to you with that pillow? Did you forget?"

I said, "No."

He said, "What about what happened to Robert's feet? Now Donnie can't walk either!"

I said, "I know. I never told you this, but I went into town and paid the old fortune teller to break the curse on Robert that time and his feet healed up the next day."

He said, "Well why don't you go see her again? Maybe she can help Donnie and Emma."

I said, "It's been on my mind to try it."

A few days later I had Robert sit with Donnie. Daddy took Mammy to Bessie's for 2 weeks. I caught the bus downtown. I knocked on the fortuneteller's door. She opened it and said, "Come in Mrs. Michelson." I said, "I guess you know why I am here?"

She said, "Yes. But I can't help you."

I said, "You've got to. My mother had a stroke and my son is paralyzed from the waist down! You helped my brother. You've got to help them."

She said, "Please don't ask me. The last time when I broke the spell on your brother it nearly killed me. I was sick for months. I'm afraid to try."

I said, "Once you told me that my powers were as strong as yours. I'm not afraid. Teach me what to do and I'll do it myself!"

She looked at me and said, "You know, I believe you can do it." Then she taught me how to break a spell. I gave her 50 dollars and I left.

When I got home I asked Robert if he had any lead fishing sinkers.

He said, "Yeah."

So I said, "Bring me 3 of them and then go for a walk."

I didn't tell him what I needed them for? At 3pm he went for a walk like I asked. I took my old iron skillet and placed it on the stove. I put the 3 lead sinkers into the hot skillet and I began to pray. I said, "In the name of the Father and the Son and the Holy Ghost, if anyone has placed a curse on Donnie, let this break it."

As I watched the lead sinkers melted and ran together. Then a woman's face appeared in the lead. It was so plain I could see that she was wearing a bandana on her head. Then it melted again. This time it formed into a perfect cross. I poured water on it to cool it. Then I picked it up. I wanted to keep it to show Daddy but it jumped out of my hand and disappeared. I never could find it.

Well the next morning when I went in to Donnie's room to give him his bed bath. He said, "Mom! I can feel the warm wash cloth!" Then he bent his knee. He said, "I can move! I can move!" I said, "Oh thank God! Thank God!"

I called Dr. Bates and he came over and examined Donnie again. He scratched his head and said, "You're the luckiest little boy in the world."

Well about an hour after he left I saw someone coming up my back steps. I opened my backdoor and it was a woman with a bandana on her head. It was the same face I saw in the lead and she knew that I knew who she was!

She said, "I have to talk to you. I've done something terrible."

I said, "I know what you've done! Now get out of my sight! All I want to know is why? I've never even met you!"

She said, "Your neighbor down the road, Esther Wilkins has been paying me to put a curse on you and your family. I'm a fortune teller."

I said, "Why? I only met her once!" She said, "She wants you out of this house. She grew up here and wants it back. But you just say the word and I'll put a curse on her!"

I said, "I don't want any part of you or your curses. Now I said get out!"

Then I remembered that the fortuneteller told me that once I melted the lead, if it broke the spell the one that put it on Donnie would have to come to me and have me give something to them or they would die. I wasn't about to give her anything. So she ran over and took a big bite out of a head of cabbage I had sitting on the counter.

"I said get out!" I told her and she left. From that day on there wasn't a thing wrong with Donnie's legs."

Susan says, "Wow! That's some story!"

Paul replies, "Believe me. You haven't heard anything yet!"

Chapter 11
Tales of McCawley Road- 1951-1960

Friday October 20th", 1995, Paul and Susan rise early for their final day of filming. Once again after breakfast they head down McCawley Road. They arrive at the site of Paul's former home and once again Paul begins to read from his book while Susan tapes him. "Ok on with our stories."

My mother went on to say, "Mammy and Daddy left Bessie's and went to stay at Lizzie's so I went over there to tell Daddy that it worked and Donnie was well. He told me that I needed to get out of there as soon as I could. After I thought about it, I figured he was right."

Paul says, "Now this next story is taken from a transcript of a different tape. Once when Donnie came over I got him and my mother to tell me about this tale together. I asked, "When did you all hear those walking sounds?"

Donnie said, "Me and Pat was in the bathtub."

My mother said, "We were getting ready to move into town and we had all of the furniture upstairs."

Donnie said, "Mom was upstairs. I don't know what she was doing?"

My mother says, "I was getting your all's pajamas."

Donnie said, "So we were downstairs taking a bath and we were just getting out of the tub and it sounded like somebody took hold of all of the pipes in the house and shook them behind the wall. Well me and Pat took off upstairs as fast as we could go and we met mom coming down."

She said, "I'm gonna whup both of your all's asses. You done broke that. .. "

My mother interrupts and says, "It sounded like the back part of the toilet."

Donnie continues, "She said upstairs it sounded like somebody picked that up and just threw it down. I said, "No mom! No! It was upstairs. We wanted to get upstairs cause we didn't know what it was?"

My mother continues, "Donnie said it was upstairs and I said, "Like hell it was! It was down here!" So I went in the bathroom and the lid was still on the back of the toilet."

Donnie continues, "So we went upstairs you know and as soon as we got up there it sounded like somebody was walking downstairs. So mom said, "You all stay here. I'm going down to see." Well we followed her downstairs anyway cause we weren't going to stay up there by ourselves.

We were standing in that little archway by the steps while she searched the whole house. So I made it up with Pat, I said, "If anybody grabs Mom, I'll run out the front door, (starts laughing) and I gave Pat the long way. I told him, "You run all the way through the dining room and kitchen and out the back door!" I said, "They can't get both of us." "Ok" he said. He'd do anything I'd tell him.

Well we had these toy German pistols made out of cast iron. So we were standing there you know and Mom was going further and further. So me and Pat was going to get a head start. I got by the dining room doors and he got by the hallway. We were going to run in two different directions so they couldn't get us.

About that time we heard "Clunk, clunk, clunk ... " Sounded like someone walking in the hallway upstairs and around the banister. Mom said, "By God! I've got them now!" She said, "I'm going to get them. You all wait out on the front porch."

We went out on the front porch and we had the front door open and she went upstairs. If she screamed we were supposed to run for help. So there we were just kids, with those big iron guns and just scared to death. Then that big old dog that belonged to the Wilkins named Blue. He came up and stuck that big old nose of his right to one of us and boy we liked to have killed him! We clubbed him half to death! We beat him in the back, knocked him down and everything else, you know! We really went to work on him!

My mother says, "Well hell! I came flying down those steps cause I thought something had done got them from all of the noise!"

Donnie continues, "So we all went upstairs. Mom said, "We'll lock ourselves in the bedroom upstairs and they can't get us. If I have to I'll set you all out on the roof. So we did that and we were sitting on the side of the bed."

My mother said, "I wasn't scared. I was mad and puzzled. I was sitting on the side of the bed and Donnie and Pat were standing in front of me and then something pulled my hair! I looked around and there wasn't anything there!"

Donnie says, "Then Mom's complexion started to turn white. I said, "Mom you're as white as a ghost." She said, "Yes by God, and I think that's what we're looking for!"

So I had Pat by the hand and she had me by the hand and we were going down those steps lickity-split! We had to run all the way out the front door, all the way around the house and then all the way back to the garage to get in the car. So then we drove all the way out that old road. I'll bet we did seventy, to stay with Aunt Florence and Sam."

Susan remarks, "Wow! That's the scariest story yet!"

Paul says, "Yes, well they get even worse. But let's continue.

I asked her, "How did you explain moving out of the house to Dutch?"

She said, "I said since Mammy and Daddy were staying with her other children for the winter and Robert had moved in town, I didn't want to stay in this big old house with just me and the kids and have to walk out that road everyday to take them to school. So I told him I was moving in town. I locked up the house and I got a room on Second Street. The school was about a block away and we stayed there until May."

Paul turns the page in his book. "I asked her, "When did Uncle Willie kill himself?"

My mother said, "Well after Mammy and Daddy stayed at Bessie's, then Lizzie's, they went to stay with Florence and then Janie's. One night I went to Janie's to see how Mammy was doing? While we were there, Lizzie-Pearl showed up to tell us that Willie had killed himself."

I said, "What happened next?"

She said, "While we were living in town, it was about October or November, I said, "Robert, you've got to drive me out to McCawley Road to get Donnie and Pat's winter clothes and coats. Now Willie had done killed himself when this happened. This was still 1951.

Donnie and Pat was in the backseat and me and Robert in the front. I had to ask him to drive us because my car was in the shop at that time. So when we got to the house Robert said, "I'll go up and get them." He knew where I kept them.

Well Lord have mercy, the door didn't much more than get closed behind him, till it opened again and he was back out in the car!

He said, "Let's wait until tomorrow and get them."

I said, "Oh shit no. Since we're already out here let's get them now." I said, "I'll go get them." .

So by hell, I'm telling you, I came out faster than he did! Cause, when I got in that archway between the basement door and the bathroom, if I'd have looked in the bathroom I'd have seen Willie! Well I flew back out! I didn't say a word to Robert, I just said, "Let's wait till tomorrow."

You could just feel it! It was so strong. I mean it was strong! The strongest feeling I ever had! And coward me, I ran instead of looking. He might have told us who killed him. Damn shame we ran. Well like I said, I came out faster than he did. It was cold and they didn't have any coats.

I said, "They're not going to school tomorrow, they don't have any coats to wear, but I ain't getting them now. We're going to come back here in daylight hours."

Then we got about half the way down McCawley Road and Robert slammed on the brakes. I looked over at him and I said, "What did you stop for?" I said, "Robert you're as white as a ghost. Are you sick?"

He said, "No ... Why did you come back so fast?"

I said, "Well why did you?"

He said, "I don't want to say."

So I said, "Well if I'd have looked toward the bathroom ... "

He said, "You'd have seen Willie wouldn't you?"

"Well hell, I liked to have croaked! He finished it for me! We both felt the same thing. I said, "Yes! Lord have mercy, I wasn't ever going to tell it!"

He said, "No, and me either."

So I said, "We'll go back tomorrow."

We went the next day and I don't know which one of us was the most scared? I said, "You ain't getting more than an inch away from me and I ain't looking toward that bathroom either! We went upstairs and got Donnie and Pat's clothes. When we got downstairs we got to talking and he said, "Well it ain't here."

Susan remarks, "Ok I'm a little confused. At one point she said your Uncle Willie committed suicide and the next minute she implied he was murdered. Which was it?"

Paul explains, "Officially it was ruled a suicide, but his death was very suspicious. Willie was the tallest member of the family. He was found sitting at a table with a shotgun pressed against his chest. He had a screwdriver in his right hand that he supposedly used to pull the trigger. That was the first odd thing because he was left-handed. The other anomaly was that his arms were so long that they reached a foot past the trigger. So he wouldn't have needed a screwdriver to pull the trigger anyway. But no one was ever charged in his murder and the case was ruled a suicide.Ok back to our stories."

I asked "When did you move home?"

My mother replied, "In April of 1952 me and Robert went out there and found the basement was full of water. The house smelled like mildew. So we had to pay to have the basement pumped dry and we opened the windows. The curtains and bed clothes were all moist so I had to dry out the whole house. It took a month to get the place livable again.

So in May of 52 we moved home. I talked Daddy into bringing Mammy home because that was what she wanted. They were staying out at Lizzie-Pearl's again at that time. He didn't want to do it. It took me a whole month to talk him into it.

Finally in the middle of June they moved back in. We all just picked up where we left off. I got up early and bathed Mammy and got her into her wheelchair. Then I made breakfast for everyone and got the kids off to school. After June they were out for summer vacation.

With Donnie well it was not as hard on me as it was before and of course I was happy to do it. I took care of Mammy until November when she died.

I'll never forget that day. I went in to give her, her bed bath and we were talking when all of a sudden she just slumped over to the side. I thought for a minute she had just fallen asleep until I noticed she wasn't breathing. I yelled for Daddy and he came. He told me she had passed and I refused to believe it. She looked like she was just asleep. So I called Dr. Bates and he came and confirmed it.

But you know how dead people change color, get grey looking and usually in hours rigor mortis sets in and they stiffen up. I wouldn't let them take her until I saw some sign that she was really dead and not just in some sort of coma. Because her joints were as limber as in life and her color was the same.

We ordered a coffin and placed her in the living room and started calling all of the family. 3 days later Daddy and the others told me it was time to bury Mammy but I refused. I still couldn't believe she was really dead and I was afraid we'd bury her alive. So I said, "No. Not until there's some change in her."

I kept her a week and then her complexion finally turned white and I knew she was really gone. Then I agreed to let her be buried.

That was at the end of 1952. Daddy wasn't happy about being back in the "witch's house" as he called it. He only came back because Grandma wanted to and he'd have done anything she asked him. Then Lizzie-Pearl discovered something. In the back of one of her son Joey's school books someone had written, "Six more months to live." She showed that to me and I'd know Mammy's handwriting anywhere. She must have written that when she was staying there in June. From June till November is six months."

Susan comments, "Oh wow! She knew exactly when she was going to die and she must have wanted to die in your mother's care."

Paul replies, "Yes, that's right. Well that brings us to 1953. I asked her,"What happened next?"

She said, "Well with Mammy passed on Daddy decided that he was leaving that place. One day he told me that he'd found a house for rent, not too far away on Robb's Lane and he wished me and the kids would come with him. After thinking about it, I decided that Maybe he was right. The house was about a mile from our house on McCawley Road on the other side of those woods."

Paul says, "Now this next story I got on tape after my mother had passed on. I bought one of those microphones that you stick onto the receiver of a telephone and you can tape record both sides of the conversation. So I called Donnie up to ask him what he remembered about that house on Robb's Lane? I'll just read you the transcript of the tape word for word.

"Hello?" Donnie said.

"Hello Donnie." I said.

"Yeah?"

"Are you busy? I asked.

"No why?"

"I just wanted to ask you a few things. I was writing in that book you know and there's a few things that I needed to ask you about that house that you all moved into on Robb's Lane."

"Yeah." He said.

"You don't remember what year that was do you?" I asked.

"What year?"

"Yeah. I know it was you, Pat, Katie and Grandpa. But I don't think Grandma was alive."

"That had to be ... She died in "52" so that had to be "53" cause he died in "54". He said.

"Unfortunately I don't have Katie telling those stories on tape. I remember her telling me most of them but I wasn't born yet. So I thought maybe I would get you to tell me. If it was "53" you must have been 13 years old." I said.

"Yeah, that's right. It was two years before you were born."

"Mom said the house was L shaped, is that right?"

"Yeah, it had 4 rooms. The back bedroom, the living room and the kitchen were all back to back. Then there was a closed in back porch that Grandpa took for his bedroom." Donnie said.

"What happened there?" I asked him.

"Well the first thing that happened was when Uncle Jimbo showed up drunk. We put him in the backroom to sleep. We heard him carrying on and we thought maybe he was having a heart attack or something, so mom went in a jerked him up, He said something had him down and wouldn't let him up.

Well they thought it was just because he was drunk, see. But later on Robert came by to spend the night and the same thing happened to him. Well the next thing that happened was something started pulling the covers off me and Mom." Donnie said.

"Which one did it happen to first?" I asked.

"Me, I think. Pat and her was in the other room watching television and I went on to bed. While I was lying there, I hadn't dozed off yet; the covers started sliding off the bed. I thought it was Pat teasing me, you know. So I started fussing. I jumped up and was going in the living room to tell mom and I seen Pat and her was still sitting there!

So, I never said nothing you know. I just kept real quiet. Then it happened to Mom a few nights later. She thought it was me and Pat doing it. She came flying out of there raising hell and she seen we were both in there. So she grabbed a flashlight and went back in the bedroom looking around cause we didn't have a light in that room, see? So she came back in the living room and I asked her what was wrong, cause I already had a pretty good idea. When she told me, then I told her that it happened to me a few nights before." He said.

"She mentioned hearing walking sounds in the kitchen." I said.

"Oh yeah. Well Grandpa slept in the back room, the closed off porch. It was right next to the kitchen. He kept complaining that me and Pat were keeping him awake walking in the kitchen at night. Mom said that we were asleep all night. She said she heard it too and thought it was him.

Mom said, the next time you hear it you sneak out of bed and don't turn on any lights and I'll do the same on this end and we'll catch them in between us. So a few nights later they both heard it again. So they eased out of bed and they met in the middle of the kitchen floor! There was nobody there!" Donnie said.

Paul closes his book. "So obviously whatever was haunting my family at McCawley Road had followed them over to the Robb's Lane house. So since moving away wasn't going to do any good my mother and the rest decided to move back home."

I asked her, "What happened next?"

She said, "It was pouring down rain when we moved back home. I dropped off Daddy and the kids and I had to go back to the house on Robb's Lane to get the last of our things, clothes and stuff. Well it rained so hard we had a flash flood and I was afraid to try and make it down McCawley Road. You know it had pot holes as big as the road and it was hard enough to drive down it when it was sunny, let alone in the pouring rain. So I'll just take old man Lowe's Road. I knew he didn't want anybody going through there but I thought, "I'll just go this one time anyway."

I got about half the way back there and I spied a log across the road. I said, "Well that old son of a bitch has laid a log across the road so nobody can get through!" I said, "I'm going to go over the top of it!" And I did, but goddamn! It liked to have turned the car over. I looked in the rearview mirror and that log turned out to be that damned snake! It had curled up as big as a washing tub and its head was looking right at me! Boy! I liked to have had a heart attack! I gunned the engine and I bet I did 90 going down that old road!"

"Holy smoke! So she finally got to see it!" Susan remarked.

"Yeah, I don't know what it was but too many people saw it to have everyone's imagination run a way with them. Well back to our stories. I'll just have to tell you what happened next as I don't have a transcript of it." Paul comments.

" Life went on despite the haunting activity. Dutch came home with a surprise one weekend. Two spitz puppies, both mostly white in color. Donnie picked the girl puppy with the brown markings, which he named Lassie and Pat claimed the boy puppy with the black markings, which he named King.

Meanwhile Uncle Robert met a young woman named Jean who lived further down on McCawley Road. She had been previously married twice and had four kids. Ronnie Roberts who was Donnie's age, and Marcus Roberts who was Pat's age. She also had a four-year old girl named Carolyn Morris and a three-year-old boy named Bobby Morris.

Uncle Robert brought her over to the house to meet the family and her and Katie became fast friends and Donnie and Pat became friends with Ronnie and Marcus. Robert and Jean were married soon after and he moved in with them. Then later in 1954 Uncle Robert announced that Jean was going to have a baby.

Well you would have thought that my mother had gotten the news that she was going to have it, she was so happy for them. Grandpa was as excited as she was. Especially when he found out that the baby would be born in September because his birthday was September 29th. Uncle Robert was his favorite child. He always called him "Baby-boy" and now Baby-boy was going to be a father. So Grandpa couldn't wait. He used to walk down to their house everyday to visit them.

But he never got to see the baby. On June 30th Grandpa went into town. He was crossing the street when some guy ran the red light and hit him with his car. He was knocked 20 feet and the doctors said he wouldn't live through the night. So Katie had them bring him home. He lived for 3 days in a coma.

Then on July 2nd he came out of the coma. Katie said Grandpa told her that Grandma had come to see him and she said she'd be back at 4pm. Well at 4pm exactly he died."

Susan remarks, "Oh ... How sweet. She waited for him on the other side."

Paul replies, "Yeah that story always gets to me as well. So anyway that only left Katie, Donnie and Pat all alone in that big house. One day Donnie went out to feed the dogs and only King came up to greet him. He started looking for Lassie and he spotted her across McCawley Road in the woods.

He called to her but she wouldn't come to him. She turned and walked into the woods and he never saw her again. Not long before their older dog Snoopy had disappeared. Which brings us to our next story. Paul opens his book and begins to read. "My mother tells this one."

She said, "Donnie's dog Lassie and Snoopy disappeared, so we brought King in the house with us. One morning I was sitting up on the sofa. It was about 5 in the morning, just getting daylight. Well, Donnie and Pat got to squirming over in the bed. I looked over that way and I saw what looked like a white veil floating over the top of them!

Just as I saw it, King saw it too! He ran over and lunged on the bed. He grabbed their blanket and yanked it off of them. It was a grey wool blanket that was given to us by the county when I was a little girl.

You know we had washed it a million times. There wasn't a thing on it before. It was just plain solid grey. I threw it out in the front yard. Later when I went out in the yard when daylight came and spread it out and now that damn blanket had a great big red "W" on it and scribbly writing on it.

I said, "Oh oh! I'm burning that son of a bitch up! I sent Donnie and Pat to Okalona on their bicycles to get a quart of kerosene. So just as Donnie got back to the house with it, he dropped it and broke it.

So I said, "Go right back and get some more." But when he got back the same damn thing happened. So I thought "Well that son of a bitch ain't gonna out do me! I'm going this time myself!"

So I searched the garage and found a can I could use and I got on Donnie's bicycle. I left Donnie and Pat sitting on the porch. I said, "Yall stay here." Cause I didn't want anyone to steal the blanket.

I road the bicycle to Okalona and bought some more kerosene. I got home and poured the kerosene on that blanket and tried to light it. You know wool should just go up in smoke. I lit some newspaper and tossed it on there and it just smothered out. It just wouldn't burn. So then I got mad. I went in the house and got my bottle of Holy water. I came out and when I sprinkled Holy water on that blanket it went up into a huge flame and then green foam carne rolling out of that blanket all over the ground. So I burned it up.

I said, "Well since I got this shit started, I'm burning up everything I've ever felt funny about. So I went in the house and took every feather pillow I had and burnt them up too.

The next morning, Donnie and Pat were laying there asleep again and I saw the Wilkin's old hound dog named Blue peeping in the bedroom window at them. I remembered Daddy once telling me that a witch could use animals to put a hex on you. So I jerked open the front door and I tossed Holy water on it. I figured if it wasn't evil it wouldn't hurt it but it was it would kill it.

Three straight mornings he was peeping in their bedroom window and every time I would toss Holy water on it. Then they found that dog dead over in the field. They said there wasn't a scratch on him and they couldn't figure out what had killed him?

All of this happened in one month. Dutch had been transferred to Texas at that time. Well the next day it was pouring down rain and I was mad because I wanted to finish burning up things. So I said, "Well I'm not going to be out done. I'll just build a fire in the grate and burn them up there."

I didn't have any wood so I used this old vanity stool which had been in the house when we moved in. I broke up that stool and used that to start the fire.

Well my God! It like to have burnt us up! It got to popping and crackling and fire ran all over that living room! I used the 3-sided screen in front of the grate. I had to flatten it out and stick it right up against the fireplace to keep the fire from coming out on us. Donnie and Pat stomped out the little fires it started.

One of the first things I decided to burn was this white nylon blouse. I tossed it in the grate and green foam came out of that too! It was brand new! Well about that time it sounded like a shotgun went off in that living room. We didn't know what had happened at the time? But we found out later that the chimney had cracked from the ground all the way to the roof. A crack about 6 inches wide.

Well that blast kind of got to me, you know. Then I happened to look over in the window and there was the ugliest bird I've ever seen in my life! It was coal black and it didn't have hardly any beak. Its mouth was real wide from ear to ear and its eyes stuck out on each side of its head.

It didn't have feathers. It had hair! Black hair! Even up and down it's legs. It wasn't very big but I was afraid to touch it. Its wings were square looking! That thing would look at me and oh God! I thought I wasgoing to have a heart attack!

The windows were up but I had screens on them. The screens were hooked. I took a broom handle and unhooked the screen and pushed it out and it flew out and went across the road to those woods. Then I discovered the chimney was split from the ground all the way to the roof. I paid to have it cemented all together.

The next day I said, "Well since I got this shit started I'm going to finish it." There was a featherbed upstairs on the floor in one of the rooms. It was also there when we moved in. I'd already burned up all of the feather pillows and I happened to think about that featherbed upstairs.

When I started to go get it, King beat me up the stairs. His hair was standing on end and he was carrying on like he was crazy. He went straight to that door and started digging and scratching on it. Then when I opened it he went running in and jumped in the middle of that featherbed and started trying to tear it apart.

So I dragged it down the steps and took it outside. Once again feathers should just go up in flames like hair, but it wouldn't burn. We lit a tire and when it got to burning real good we put the featherbed on it and it smothered right out. I poured kerosene on it and tried to light it and still it wouldn't burn. Then I split it open and reached inside. I pulled out a little crocheted baby cap and yards and yards of blue ribbon. I thought, "Well I've seen enough." I went in the house and got my bottle of Holy water. I sprinkled Holy water on it and it went up into a big blaze.

As we were standing there watching it burn, we were on the side of the house. In the kitchen we had a 150 gallon electric water heater which was sealed with a chrome band. Well while we were outside that lid blew off of that hot water tank, blew across the kitchen and all the insulation blew out of the tank.

By the time Dutch returned from Texas we just about had the whole house cleaned out burning things up."

Paul closes his book and says, "My mother and Uncle Robert had a talk. Jean was about to have the baby soon. Katie asked Uncle Robert if he would consider moving into the upstairs of our house. They would have more room than where they lived and Katie would not have to live alone in that house with only Donnie and Pat. He agreed to it and so upstairs lived Uncle Robert, Aunt Jean, Ronnie, Marcus, Carolyn, Bobby and Jean's father. While downstairs lived Dutch, Katie, Donnie and Pat.

Uncle Robert built an outside staircase and made an outside entrance upstairs so his family could come and go without disturbing us downstairs.

Then on September 29th, 1954 Robert's son was born on Grandpa's birthday. So he named him Richard after Grandpa.

Right about the time that Rickey was born my mother started having her morning sickness symptoms. She went to see the doctors at Ft. Knox who insisted she could not be pregnant. They were certain that she was having a false pregnancy induced by the return of the tumors that she was supposed to go back to the hospital all those years before to get removed. But fortunately for me she made them wait 9 months to operate and I was born on June 13th, 1955.

Rickey being only 9 months older than me we were learning to walk and talk at about the same time. Actually I learned to talk before I could walk. My mother used to tell me a story about one of our relatives who came by and leaned over my playpen. I think it was Aunt Florence and said "My grandson Bobby is your age and he's walking. Why aren't you walking yet? I replied, "I'm a coward." She said, "Oh he can talk!" 1 was 18 months old then.

Susan said, "Really? It's hard to believe. You're such a quiet person now."

Paul said, "Very funny. Me thinks I detect a note of sarcasm there."

Susan laughs, "You think?"

Paul said, "Well back to our stories. Just as Donnie and Pat saw a man in the dining room at the age of two, so did I. Here is my mother talking about it." He opens his book.

"Me and Florence and her husband Sam were sitting at the kitchen table talking. Paul was two years old at the time. He was sitting on those dining room steps that led upstairs and he was writing a letter to Dutch who was at Ft. Knox at the time. Of course he wasn't really writing but he thought he was.

Then all of a sudden he let out an awful scream and came running out of that dining room and into the kitchen where we were sitting. He spotted the willow switch I kept between the refrigerator and the stove. He grabbed it up and ran back into the dining room. We followed him to see what was going on? He started hitting the steps with the switch and screaming "He tore my letter!" He cried for an hour because the man tore his letter. It was later on that I realized that all 3 of my kids had seen a man in the dining room at the same age of two years old."

Paul closes his book. Susan asks him, "Do you remember what happened?"

Paul replies, "I'm not sure if it's a memory or just part of a dream I had one night. In my dream I was sitting on the dining room steps. There were 3 wooden steps that led up to the archway and then the steps that led upstairs were on the left side of the archway. I was sitting on the second step and using the top step as my desk. I was scribbling on a piece of paper. I was so small the pencil in my hand seemed as big as a log. I could hear someone coming down the steps. I kept on writing.

Then the shadow of someone standing in the archway fell across my paper. Then a sandaled dirty foot stepped on my paper. I tried to pull it out and it ripped. I looked up and saw the man was wearing dark maroon colored robes. Then I saw.a black bushy bearded face with big eyes glaring at me. He was wearing a black turban on his head and had a horrible grin on his face. I screamed and that was when I woke up."

Susan says, "Well I'd say that was only part of your Simon delusion and not a real memory."

"Probably" Paul agreed.

"Did you tell Dr. Bornstein about it?" Susan asked.

"Yes. He said that I was projecting my fears which I've embodied into this Simon creation and that what I was remembering was a created memory. That my imagination substituted for my real memory. Which was erased by the trauma of whatever I really saw back then."

Susan remarks, "Doesn't that sound more reasonable to you?"

Paul says, "Yes, I suppose it does. Well back to our tales." Paul opens his book. Once when Uncle Robert was over to our house I asked him if he ever saw anything strange back there. He told me his version of the time he saw the ghostly white ape standing over Katie and the time he heard those choking sounds. The time he had that vision of the Christmas tree on the hood of his car and then he told me one I hadn't heard before.

Paul begins to read. "This was Uncle Robert talking ... " "We was sleeping upstairs, me and Jean and the family. I had a nightmare. At least I hope it was. There was a skeleton flying over me. His face looked like a skull but his wings looked like a dragonfly's. You know, black thin lace. Just hovering over the top of me. Great big wings, way out and I come out of the bed and hit at it and it disappeared. I don't know if I was asleep or not? But he was as big as an eagle and just a hovering over me."

Paul continues, "Then once I called Aunt Jean on the phone to ask her about a story I had heard my mother tell me. I used that microphone to record both sides of the conversation again. Here is the transcript of what she said ... " Paul turns the page and starts to read.

" I heard that after Grandma died someone who had moved in later and had never met her saw her ghost come into their room and cover Robert over. I thought it was you." I said.

"Oh yeah." Jean said, " I remember that now. I had never seen her, see? I had seen Mr. Murray but not Mrs. Murray. Yeah she came into our room. I described her to Katie. I told her she had a pin on her dress. Katie said, "Yeah she had a cameo she always wore." Then she went and got a picture of her and showed it to me and it was the same woman. Just exactly like her. She looked a me and said, "You'll be good for Robert."

"Wow" Susan exclaims. "That's amazing. I'm surprised she didn't appear to your mother."

Paul says, "Well my mother told me that one time after Grandma had passed she was moving the refrigerator to clean behind it and it got caught on a piece of tile and almost tipped over on her. My mother clearly heard her mother say "Oh Katie be careful!" But then she realized that her mother was dead. She said she was so shook up she had to go outside on the back porch and have a cigarette. She never told anyone about that incident."

Susan says, "Maybe your Grandma stayed around to try and protect your family from whatever was there."

Paul smiles, "Yeah. I believe she did."

Susan says, "So your father never did see anything back there." Susan asks.

"Well not directly but in 1959 he came back from the Korean War and ... well I'll just read you what happened. Donnie tells this one." Paul replies and then opens his book again and starts to read ...

Donnie said, "Back home, I don't know if you can remember it, but it was worse than England when the fog came in back there. You couldn't see the garage. So I was taking some hot food out there to King that I had warmed on the stove, cause it was winter time. I went out there to give him the food and I came on back in the house. I left the garage door open so later on I went back. Then I heard King fighting with something.

I thought he was fighting with that dog named Gypsy who lived down the street. Like I said you couldn't even see the garage in the fog. All you could see was a big blurred light. I spotted the hammer lying on the back porch so I picked that up and started back there. I took it in case he attacked me too. Well I got within about 10 feet of it and all I could see was a blur. I could see two white things moving.

Well I had the hammer drawn back you know and whatever it stood up and kept coming up. It was about 4 or 5 feet tall. They were on the side of the garage where there wasn't no light. Then I saw it cock its head back and forth trying to see me too! Well man! That's all I seen of it cause I threw hammer and all and I run!

I ran in the house and everybody but Dad wasn't home. He was sound asleep and I said, "Dad! Something is out there killing King!" So he jumped up and we both ran out there and there lay poor old King. He was alive but hurt real bad. We carried him into the house and discovered that he was bit in 4 places. He had 4 holes all the way across his chest as big around as a pencil."

Paul says, "Now I also have the transcript of my mother talking about the same incident.

She says, "Well when I got home Donnie told us what had happened and the next morning I went out to the garage and Dutch went with me. In the garage we had a gallon jug of kerosene and whatever it was had broken that jug and stepped in the oil and it looked just like an ape track. You could see the thumbprint and all. Then in the wooden rafters of the garage we found long course white hair caught on some nails. Dutch just shook his head. He didn't know what to make of it?

That was when I told him about all the stuff we had been through while he was gone. He said, "If it was that bad why didn't you get a priest to bless the house?"

I said, "I've been trying to get Father Donnelly to come out for years and either he puts it off and forgets about it or I would."

Dutch said, "Is that so? Well let's go pay him a visit this morning. He won't ignore me!"

So we drove over to St. Rita's. Dutch knocked on the rectory door and the housekeeper answered and said, "May I help you?"

Dutch replied "Please tell Father Donnelly that the Michelson's are here to see him."

She said, "Do you have an appointment?"

He said, "My wife made one years ago and he never kept it."

She said, "Father Donnelly is busy right now perhaps if you'd called ahead."

Dutch said, "You tell Father Donnelly that he will see us right now or we can all meet in the Bishop's office later."

She said, "I see. I'll relay the message. You wait here." She came back in about two minutes and said, "Father Donnelly will see you now."

We went into his office and he said, "Mr. and Mrs. Michelson! What seems to be the trouble?"

Dutch said, "The trouble is that you've been derelict in your duties."

He said, "I don't understand." Dutch said, "My wife asked you to come out and bless out home 18 years ago and you never showed up."

Father Donnelly replied, "So she did. You're absolutely right. I do apologize."

Dutch said, "We don't want an apology, we need to have the house blessed."

Father Donnelly said, "Well of course ... of course. I'll be there first thing in the morning."

Dutch said, "No. You'll come over right now and do it."

Father Donnelly seemed a little flustered and said, "Well I...I mean ...Oh very well, very well."

So he followed us over to the house. Father stood in the living room and prayed in Latin and sprinkled the room in Holy water. Robert was standing in the doorway and the moment he did that all of us felt like a cloud of pressure lifted up from the floor to the ceiling. When he left Robert said to me, "Did you feel anything when he done that?" I nodded "yes."

Paul closes his book. He says, "One month later Dutch sold the house to a real estate man who agreed to let Robert and and his family continued to live on McCawley Road for 3 more years and then they moved also because the activity started up again.

Aunt Jean told me that one night when Bobby was 12 years old he woke up screaming. They rushed into his room and she said his eyes were as big as saucers. She said, "What's wrong Bobby?" When he finally calmed down he told her that there was some kind of ugly looking monkey sitting on his chest."

I never got to interview Ronnie, Marcus or Carolyn but I'm sure they could add a lot of their own stories about that place. Bobby was killed in Vietnam in the 60's."

Paul closes his book and looks into the camera. He says, "That was 36 years ago. As you can see on one side of our property is a growing subdivision. On the other end is an apartment complex and factory and on the south end is now a Mall. Our property sits like an oasis in the middle of a growing community. I can't help but think about old man Hobbs and how he swore this property would never do anyone any good. Looks like he's still keeping his word. Ok cut."

Susan turns off the camera and they make their way out of the brush and back to McCawley Road. She uses up the remainder of the tape filming Paul as he walks down McCawley Road.

CHAPTER 12
Revelations

October 31, 1995; Paul tells Susan that Westlake Manor asked if he could work 11-7 on Tuesday. So at 10:30pm he starts to leave and she says, "Hey did you forget to put on your uniform?" He replies, "Oh I have it in this paper bag. They weren't even sure if they really need me tonight or not. It depends on whether a certain nurse who they think might have quit shows up or not. So I may be right back."

Paul goes out to his van and starts it up. He pulls out of their parking spot, but truthfully he is not going to work at all tonight. He only told Susan that so she wouldn't worry. He drives to the end of the apartment complex and parks out of sight. He sits and looks at his watch. 10:40pm. He sits in his van and waits until 11:10 pm. He then gets out of his van. The cold Kentucky wind whips through he weren't even wearing his winter coat and gloves. He takes his flashlight and begins to walk. He walks to the end of the apartment complex. Pausing as he looks back at the building where Susan is. "This has to work," he thinks. "For her sake as much as mine."

He looks at his watch. 11:1 pm. He begins to walk down McCawley Road. It takes him 30 minutes to walk down the old gravel road. Finally he reaches the familiar two trees which mark the sight of his former home. Turning on the flashlight he makes his way through the bushes until he breaks through to the clearing where the foundation of his old home is. He looks at his watch. 11 :45pm. He bends down and picks up a piece of wood from his former home.

"This will make a good makeshift wand." He thinks. Standing facing east he visualizes a beam of light erupt from the end of his "wand". Turning in a clockwise pattern he forms an imaginary circle of protection. Then he "draws" the giant double pentagram as he did 27 years ago tonight.

After so many years of practice he no longer needs physical symbols like real candles and incense as he did when he was 13. Now it is enough for him to visualize 5 violet candles. One on each of the large pentagram points. He then lights them mentally. He also imagines lighting the honeysuckle incense and placing the stick in it's holder between the bottom points of the pentagram.

Continuing to face east, he performs the magic ritual called the "Mystic Pentagram". Saying, "In the name of. .. " He touches his forehead with his right hand. "Earth" he says as he touches his right knee. "Water" as he touches his right shoulder. "Air" as he touches his left shoulder. "Fire" as he touches his left knee and "Spirit" as he touches his forehead again. He looks at his watch and presses the light up dial. 11.50 pm.

He must perform the protection ritual to prevent any interference from any spirits and he is sure there must be plenty of those in this cursed spot. He closes his eyes and pretends he is holding a box of salt.

He says, "By the power of earth" as he walks the perimeter of his protective circle imagines sprinkling the salt as he goes, "water" he says as he imagines he is holding a glass of water and sprinkles it as he walks the perimeter of the circle. "Air" he says as he imagines picking up his stick of incense and smells the smoke of it as he walks the circle.

"Fire" he says as he imagines picking up the candle and again walking his circle. "And spirit" he says as he points his wand at the apex point of the pentagram and turns in a circle.

Paul sits on the icy cold ground in his circle of protection in the center of his pentagram. He looks at his watch. 11:55 pm, 5 minutes before midnight. He has to time this perfectly. He lays down in the pentagram drawn in the center of what would once have been his old dining room area. He closes his eyes and visualizes rising out of his body until he is hovering above it. While keeping his consciousness in his astral form he must perform the rital for entering the Holy Sephiroth of Yesod.

First he visualizes a ball of violet light before him. Then he brings it closer until it engulfs him and the entire magic circle. Next he pictures a doorway in the light and opens it seeing the brighter violet light within. He steps through it mentally.

"Now for the hard part" he thinks as he takes a deep breath and while exhaling intones the God-name "Shaddai El Chai". All the while visualizing it coming from his astral mouth and not his physical one lying on the floor. He succeeds and then mentally intones the God-name as he slowly inhales. With every exhalation he verbally intones the God-name and with every inhalation he mentally intones the God-name. With every inhalation and exhalation he sees the light glowing brighter. He continues until he can no longer see the light any brighter.

Next he begins to intone the name of the Archangel Gabriel. Again verbally upon exhalation and mentally upon inhalation. But with every utterance of the Holy name makes the light grow softer, more opaque.

After a minute of this the light begins to shift and wave. It clears and now he is standing before the temple of his consciousness. He sees the two pillars and the altar. On the altar burns the lamp with the violet flame. This time Paul takes the lamp and places it on the floor and then lies on the altar.

He opens his mouth and begins to exhale grey smoke. He then visualizes the cloud of grey smoke above him begin to separate into white smoke and black smoke. The white cloud remains smoke and the black smoke forms into Simon in his black hood, robes and cape. Only the two burning red eyes show beneath the darkness of the hood. Paul then inhales the white smoke.

Behind Simon and behind the altar the curtains part and there is a door. It opens inward and inside a brilliant violet light can be seen. Paul visualizes holding on to the altar as a violent suction comes from the door as if it were an airplane door opened in mid-flight. He sees Simon sucked into the doorframe and trying to hold on it but he fails and is sucked through. The door slams shut and Paul rises from the altar and takes a wooden beam and bolts the door. Locking it forever in place.

Paul opens his eyes. He sits up and presses the button on his watch. The dial lights up and he sees it says 12:00 midnight. "I did it!" he thinks. He then has one more ritual to perform. In his mind he takes his wand and erases the smaller pentacle leaving only the larger one. He opens his eyes again.

The ritual is over but will it work? He gets up and brushes all the leaves and twigs of of him so no evidence of him having lain on the ground will show when he goes home.

Turning on his flashlight he makes his way his way through the brush and back to McCawley Road. As he walks down it he reflects on what he has tried to do?

Ideally he would like to have performed this attempted reverse invocation spell on the spot that it originally occurred. But the Gene Snyder expressway atop a man made hill of dirt lay above where his home on Blue Lick Road once stood. But when he saw the foundation of his previous home on McCawley Road still existed he knew that he must at least try.

After all, despite what Dr. Bornstein and Susan think, he knows that Simon, or whatever he really may be came from this very spot originally. His mother's description and his memory of seeing that Middle Eastern man on McCawley Road had to be Simon. He just knew it in his gut.

Plus the table that he performed the ouija experiment on was the kitchen table that once stood here in this house on McCawley Road. Maybe when they brought their old furniture to their new home they may have carried something with them. All the old McCawley Road furniture that they brought along they had put in their basement on Blue Lick.

The kitchen table, the refrigerator, their old telephone and the wooden table it stood on and even the kitchen clock were all in his basement at Blue Lick. He'd read that many people who move away from haunted houses often take the spirits with them if they take any of the furniture from the haunted house to their new one.

So maybe, just maybe by performing this reverse ritual of the one that first caused his problem, he may have found a way to free himself. The next full moon wasn't until November 6th though. So he would have to wait and see.

Paul walked back down McCawley Road and finally arrived at his apartment complex. He got into his van and started it. He turned on the heater and just sat for a time thawing himself. He was chilled to the bone from laying on that frozen ground. After a few minutes he started up the van and drove back over to their usual parking spot. He made his way up to his second floor apartment and used his key to get in.

The lights were out. Susan had gone to bed but she heard him enter. She said from the bedroom, "You're home!" He told her the other nurse showed up and he didn't have to work after all. So he joined her in bed.

They awoke the next day and started packing their things. The vacation was over but neither of them wanted to leave. This was the happiest time of their whole marriage so far. But Susan felt responsible for her son Levi and even though his father only allowed her to see him twice a year she still would feel guilty just moving away. So for his sake they had to move back to Florida.

They packed their clothes and tv and put the cushions back in the van that they had been using as their makeshift bed. They informed the office at the apartment complex that they had to return to Florida and then stopped at Donnie's and used his phone to call Westlake Manor and tell them also that he had to return to Florida immediately.

Donnie of course also did not want them to leave. No one in Paul's family wanted him to leave in the first place, nor did they understand why he was leaving again? What was he supposed to tell them? "I have to leave because I am possessed by an evil spirit and I fear he may harm you."

No better to let them wonder why? If only the rituals worked." Paul thinks to himself. Paul and Susan say goodbye to Donnie and get in their van. They drive away and just then they see the first snowflakes of the year. Paul hopes it is a good omen. Once again they hit 1-65 and begin their long journey home.

One by one Paul passes the landmarks he was so happy to see on their way there. He leaves Jefferson County and in a couple of hours passes by Ft. Knox, Ky. Then after that Cave City, Ky. where he worked those two summers so long ago. It seems.like it happened to someone else now. More like a past life experience than a memory.

They drive until they get to Nashville, Tenn. and then stop for the night at a Holiday Inn. They eat dinner at the Cracker Barrel next door and then retire. The next morning, November 2nd they leave at dawn and start driving the long, long drive through Georgia. Eventually they see the sign that says; "Now entering Florida".

Susan cannot repress her tears. She hates Florida and all of the bad memories that she has had to endure here. Paul has grown to hate it too. It's funny because he remembers the first time he came to Florida and how thrilled he was to come here. All the sun and palm trees and sand. It seemed like a kind of paradise.

But as with most tourist spots, Florida is a nice place to visit but a terrible place to live. The cost of living is very high. You must pay first; last and security even for a travel trailer there. That's because tourists come and go so quickly the landlord's have to be guaranteed more than one months rent. Then there is the weather. The idea of perpetual summer seems wonderful to a boy from Kentucky who knows what harsh winters feel like. But the common joke in Florida is that they only have two seasons down there, summer and December. The summer months down here are breathtakingly hot and it lasts for 9 months.

Paul didn't realize how much he missed the changing of the seasons until he moved home. Especially the autumn and the changing of the leaves. Paul misses the brown dirt and blue grass too, Florida is all sand and cigarette butts. Like living in a giant ashtray. Paul had come to call Florida "white trash Hawaii."

Paul and Susan make their way to U.S. 19. They pass Tarpon Springs, Clearwater, Largo, Pinellas Park and finally St. Petersburg. Their first stop is to their storage shed to check on their things and to make November's payment. They only paid for 3 months back in September when they left. All seems well so they check into in to the Suncrest Motel on 4th Street and collapse in bed. Susan calls Levi to let him know we are back.

The next morning November 3rd, he and Susan set out to find a new place to rent. They check the newpaper and see an affordable garage apartment on 11th Ave. N. not far from where they both used to live when they first met. They look it over and it seems acceptable so they pay the landlord the first, last and security deposit. Then it takes them the rest of the day to go back and forth to their storage shed and move all of their things in to the new place. Finally they finish and collapse in bed.

All is fine until early the next morning, November 4th and to their horror they discover that when the landlord starts up his car in the garage the fumes rise up into their bedroom. Close examination reveals that the boards of the floor have large enough cracks between them that they can see right down into the garage. Paul jumps out of bed and rushes to catch thelandlord. He manages to catch him before he gets away and tells him about the fumes.

The landlord tells him there is nothing he can do about it. Paul asks for his money back and he is told it is non-refundable. The landlord pulls away. Paul and Susan decide to move out anyway. They begin to re-pack their things into the van and it takes them most of the day to move it all back into the storage shed.

Unfortunately they are now too low on money to rent somewhere else. So they go back to the Suncrest Motel and spend the night again. On November 5th Paul and Susan leave the motel. They need to make some money fast so Paul goes and rents a pager and then goes to see his old nursing agency, that he used to work for. They are happy to see him and sign him up again right away.

Paul and Susan decide to just live in the van until he can raise enough money to rent them another place, They drive over to Cresent Lake Park and park for awhile. At 6pm Paul's pager beeps, so he calls the agency and they ask if he can work tonight 11-7 at a nursing home in Clearwater called The Pines.

He takes it and he and Susan drive to clearwater. They eat at a restaurant and then head over to the nursing home parking lot. They park and just hang out there watching their battery powered tv until it was time for Paul to go into work. Susan stays out in the van and sleeps in the sleeping bag,

The night passes by uneventfully and Paul listens to the Art Norry show on his pocket radio while he works. Tonight's show was on Roswell, New Mexico. At 7am he gives report to the on coming nurse and counts the narcotics. They sign his time-slip and he leaves. He goes out to the van and Susan wakes up when he opens the door. She gets up and they drive to the agency and Paul drops his time-slip through the mail slot.

Then he drives back to Cresent Lake and park. Susan explores the park while Paul tries to sleep a few hours in the sleeping bag. He sleeps till noon and then gets up. They drive over to the agency and pick up his paycheck, 100 dollars! The agency always did pay much more than being on staff. But not every nurse was versatile enough to be able to walk in a place cold and be able to function like he worked there all of the time. But Paul was a quick study. Maybe it was because he was used to having missing time and ad libbing his way through life,

They go to the bank and cash it. At this rate they will have enough money to rent a new place in about 10 shifts. They drive around to various places to kill time that day, At 6pm the pager goes off. Paul goes to the nearest pay phone and calls the agency, They ask him if he can work 11-7 tonight at St. Mary's nursing home on 4th Street.

He gladly accepts it. He and Susan go to eat at another restaurant and then over to St. Mary's parking lot. They hang out and watch tv until 10pm and Paul gets dressed for work. At 11 pm he gets out of the van and walks inside, Before he gets in he sees the orange rim of the full moon peaking above the horizon. He goes in and before he goes to the office he goes in the restroom and checks the color of his eyes, still hazel. That was a good sign. Maybe, just maybe he was free.

He goes in to the office and they inform him he will be working on B-wing. He is delighted, as it was his old unit when he worked there for 4 years. B-wing is the Alzheimer's ward and is a locked unit. He enters and is greeted by a familiar face. The 3-11 nurse Mary's face lights up when she sees him.

"Well look what the cat dragged in?" She said. She rises from thedesk and gives him a big hug. Then she gives him report and they count narcotics. He was amazed during report how many residents were still there and virtually unchanged since he worked there 2 years before. He felt like he was getting older and the residents stayed exactly the same. Like time had stood still for them.

Then his C.N.A.'s arrived and they too were thrilled to see him. He was glad to see them as well. Two of them he knew. Shelly Barnes and Betty Brown, but the third one was new to him. She was a young girl named Sharon Robbins. She had dark shoulder length hair and a pretty smile. Paul made out their assignments. They had 20 residents apiece. Then he made his list of midnight meds and then passed them.

He sat back at the nursing station and did his charting at 12:30am. By 1 am he was finished with his work. So he took out his pocket radio and earphone and listened to the Art Norry show. Tonight's topic was the prophecies of Nostradamus.

The nursing station on B-wing sat between the L shaped hallways. Betty's assignment was at the far end of one hallway and Shelley's was at the far end of the other. They both had seats on each end of their hallways so they could listen to make sure none of their patients started wandering the halls.

Most of the patients on B-wing were still in good shape physically but were mentally impaired. So sometimes they wandered out of their rooms and had to be guided back to their beds. Sharon had the middle assignment and so she sat at the nursing station with Paul.

They started to talk and Paul heard all about her life. She was 22 years old and this was her first job as a C.N.A. Paul said that it was ok if she wanted to put her head down and nap, as the next rounds weren't until 5am.

As with most mental wards it was best not to do the 3am rounds as once you woke the residents they were up the rest of the night and disturbed the sleep of the rest of the unit. So Sharon took him up on her offer and put her head down. Paul said he would wake her if any of her residents needed her.

Paul continued to listen to the Art Norry show but then at 3am it happened. It came on suddenly and with no warning. Before he knew what had hit him Simon took over his body. Simon rose from his chair and walked over to where Sharon was sleeping with her head down on the desk. He began to rub her shoulders. She awoke and said, "Hmm ... that feels so good. Thanks. You know I was having the strangest dream. You were in it."

Once again Simon continued to rub her back and then eventually worked his way up under her smock. Then moved his way up to rub her bare skin. Then he casually unhooked her bra and she made no protest. As he rubbed her neck with his right hand his left hand made its way over to her rib cage, pausing only for a moment as he reached her bra cup. Then he slowly slid his left hand under the bra cup and began fondling her left breast. Then blackness overcame him.

The next thing Paul remembered he found himself lying on top of Sharon. They were on the floor of the medicine room behind the nursing station. He quickly got off of her and she says, "What's the matter?" He looked away from her naked body and said, "I think I hear someone wandering around." He leaves the room and enters the restroom next to it. Looking in the mirror he sees his eyes are still cobalt blue.

"Damn it!" He mutters under his breath. The ritual was a total failure, Simon is alive and well and still living in his body. Sharon came out of the medicine room still adjusting her dress. Paul kept busy to avoid her. He looked at the clock. It was 5am. Time for Sharon to do her last round and for him to pass his morning meds.

That kept them both busy until 7am and he counted and gave report. They signed his time-slip and he went out to his van. Susan woke up and said, "How did it go?" Paul mumbled "Fine" and started up the van. He drove to the agency and dropped off his time-slip.

Then they drove over to see Susan's brother and stepfather who still lived in her boyhood home on 2nd Street. While she visited Paul got some must needed sleep in his van. He didn't wake up until 4pm. He went inside and asked if he could use the shower. Susan had already taken hers.

Then he and Susan left a 5pm. Then at 6pm the agency beeped him and booked him at another of his old stomping grounds Gardenia Court. It was the first place he'd worked when he first came to Florida. They booked him there the rest of the week.

So Paul and Susan drove over to 66th Street and parked the van in the nursing home parking lot. They walked to a pizza place not far away and got dinner and then back to the van.

At 10pm Paul got dressed for work and went inside at 10:45pm. This time he didn't recognize anyone, except some of the patient names were familiar. The office told him he was to work on Lifestyle 2 nursing station. There were 6 of them at this facility, 3 upstairs and 3 downstairs. Paul was at the middle station on the second floor.

Once again he received report and counted the narcotics. Then he made out the assignment sheets. He had 3 C.N.A.'s on this floor. Robert Price who was around 25 years old, Emily Owens who was in her 60's and Shanika Jackson a black girl in her 30's.

Paul was hoping there would be nothing but old ladies working there, but no such luck. Then he got a little break when he found out that Shanika's assignment was at the end of the hallway and she sat down there as well. Robert was at the other end and Emily would be sitting at the desk with him.

Gardenia Court was not as easy to work as St. Mary's. There was a lot of midnight meds, lots of treatments, lots of tube feedings to change. lots and lots of charting to do and many morning meds and insulin shots to give as well. Paul listened to his show while he worked. Tonight's topic was Alien Abduction. By 2:30am he had all of his tube feedings flushed and hung, meds passed, treatments done and charting done.

At 3am he felt the first symptoms of Simon wanting to take over. He began to pray and was successful at fighting it off for now. Then Shanika asked him to help her turn a patient. He asked her to ask Robert but she said he was on break. There was no way he could refuse. So he got up and followed her down the hallway to the patient's room.

He helped her turn the patient and then she went in the bathroom to wash her hands. Just Simon took him over. He followed her into the bathroom. She was standing by the sink washing her hands. Simon turned out the light. "Hey! What's the big idea?" Shanika asked him. She turned around and he stepped up to her. He pulled his erection out of his pants and took her by the hand and placed it in her hand. She gasped and he pulled her close and kissed her. Then Paul blacked out again.

He awoke back at the nursing station. It was 3:30 am. He'd only lost 30 minutes this time. At 5am it was time to start passing his morning meds. When he got to Shanikas hallway he saw her coming out of a resident's room. She winked at him. He turned away and kept working. Simon struck again. Not sure whether to be remorseful about another of Simon's conquests, or grateful she wasn't one of those who could resist his charms and then he would be in big trouble again.

At 7am he gave report to the on-coming nurse and counted narcotics with her. Then they signed his time slip and he left. Susan woke up as he got in the van and he had to act like everything was just wonderful. She knew him so well he dared not show the slightest inclination that something was bothering him or she would know. But somehow he got through it and then went to sleep once they parked.

The hard part for Susan was killing time while he slept in the van. So he parked in the Mall parking lot and she window-shopped all day. He woke up at 2pm and went inside. They ate in the food court and left. They drove to the old KOA campground and just drove in. The showers were located behind the office and so they used them and washed their clothes there. Then they left. The security guard thought little of another high-top van coming and going. They even waved to him on the way out.

That was one of the tricks Paul learned when he was living in his van back in 1989. Paul drove to the agency and picked up his latest paycheck. The money was accumulating so it wouldn't be long until they had enough to get a place to stay. That night, November 8th, Paul was booked at Gardenia Manor again. He went inside while Susan slept in the van again. The office told him he was to work on Station I on the first floor.

So he went down. He counted and got report. Station I was such a difficult floor that it had two nurses on each shift including 11-7. Each nurse had one side of the L shaped hallway. The other nurse he worked with was named Janice Wright. Paul recognized her right away. She worked there when he did back in 1983.

Despite the years he had not changed that much and she knew him right away. Between doing their work they caught up on old times. She was recently divorced. He told her he was married. He didn't tell anyone his wife was right outside in the van. The nursing home would not have approved of it and they had no where to go. Besides Susan never learned how to drive. She had a phobia about it. Janice was shocked to learn about Lavonne's death. They had worked together back then.

Paul kept busy and was not overly worried about Simon tonight as there were 3 C.N.A.'s and another nurse so he imagined it would be hard for Simon to seduce anyone with so many witnesses.

Paul kept looking in the clock and checking his eye color in the bathroom mirror. At 3:15am it happened again. Once again it came on without much prior warning. Simon took over his body. He rose from the desk and went down the hallway. Then he called for Janice.

She rose from the desk and followed him down the hallway. He said, "Where are the tube feeding bags? I'm going to need a new one." She said, "in the supply closet. I'll show you." He followed her down the hallway and into the big supply room. She went over to one of the shelves and was opening it when he came up close behind her.

He reached around with both hands and began caressing her breasts. She gasped in surprise and turned suddenly around. He grabbed her and pulled her close to him and kissed her almost violently on the lips. She then pulled away from him. She said, "Paul! Please don't...You don't understand." Simon said, "Is it because I'm married?" She replied, "No ... I'm gay."

Just then Simon left him and Paul was so relieved. He almost laughed at loud at his glee over Simon's bad choice. He apologized and she accepted it because they were old friends and she didn't want to get him in trouble. They returned to the nursing station and Simon did not show up the rest of the night.

By the end of the week they had enough money for 1st months, rent and the security deposit. All they needed was another month's rent. But fate smiled on them for once. As they were driving over to see Susan's brother again they saw a "For rent" sign at a place right around the corner on 27th Ave. N.

It was another garage apartment but the unusual part was there was no house in front of it. They decided to call and they met the landlady. She told them there used to be but it burned down and the people who owned it never rebuilt it. They sold the property and she bought it. One day she was planning on building a house in front of the garage but for now she was just renting out the apartment. Paul and Sue told her about living in the van and their predicament and she was willing to let pay the second's month rent later. So they finally found a place to stay.

They went to the storage shed and began moving their things in. The cool part was they could put it all in the garage and unpack it at their leisure. That night they collapsed in their bed exhausted.

Paul dreamt that he was back on McCawley Road and walking down it, but when he got to the site of the house it was there as he remembered it. It wasn't torn down.

He ran up to the steps that led up to their long concrete front porch. Then he opened the front door. He entered the living room and saw the fireplace with the 3 sided metal screen and over at the end of it was the long window box. He walked up to the glass doors that led into their dining room and opened it the door. He walked in and looked around. To his left was his mother's and his old bedroom. In front of him their old sofa and to his right the archway that led to the stairway upstairs. Then he heard someone walking upstairs. They sounded like they were headed for the stairway. Then heavy footsteps down the steps. He knew who it was before he ever appeared in the doorway. It was Simon dressed in his Middle Eastern garb

"So! It was you back then?" Paul commented. "Of course little one. Did I not tell you so?" Simon said. "I was hoping I was free of you." Paul told him. "You mean your foolish ritual on Samhain? Did you not know that if it were of any importance I would have come out and put and stop to it? But as you can see all is as I foretold you from the beginning. We are one now. Forever shall we be joined. Stop resisting me. Accept your destiny. I could have given you the power you crave. I still could. You could have your fame and riches. It is all yours for the asking." Simon said.

"All I want is my free will." Paul said.

"Alas that is the one thing I cannot grant you." Simon responded. Then Paul woke up with a start! He looked at the clock. It said 3am. He rolled over and tried to go back to sleep.

The next evening they had their telephone hooked up. Paul decides to call Dr. Bornstein and set up his next appointment. He takes the doctor's card out of his pocket and dials the number, the receptionist's familiar voice answers.   "Hello? This is Paul Michelson. I'd like to set up my next appointment please." Paul says.

"Mr. Michelson! We've been trying to reach you for months." She replies. "Yes I know. I had to go out of town for 3 months. Anyway I'd like to set up an appointment with Dr. Bornstein as soon as possible please." Paul tells her.

"Um ... that's right you don't know. Oh I'm sorry to be the one to tell you this Mr. Michelson but Dr. Bornstein is no longer in practice. I'm afraid he had a massive stroke not long after your last appointment with him. I'm sorry. But we do have a full staff here who has absorbed Dr. Bornstein's caseload. May I set you up with an appointment with one of our other doctors?" She asks.

"No ... uh, no thank you. I.. .I'll be in touch." He hangs up and tells Susan what happened to Dr. Bornstein. He doesn't tell her about the nightmare he had in which Simon attacked Bornstein. "What am I going to do now?" He thinks. "I can't risk another doctor's life. I'll just have to forget medical care as an answer."

The month of November and December pass. Simon came out during the full moon cycle of December as always. Then in January of 1996 Paul was booked to work at another nursing home on 11-7. This one was in St. Petersburg on Central Ave named "Serenity Cove". He got dressed in his uniform and kissed his wife goodbye. Then he got in his van and drove to

Serenity Cove. He went in and got report and counted the narcotics. Then settled into his routine.

At 1am it was time for the Art Norry show. So he put in his earphone and began to listen. The opening music fades and he hears Art's comforting baritone voice .

[Art] Good evening, this is Art Norry. Our guest tonight is renowned occult author and practicing occultist Constantine. Author of the book "Psychic Vampirism." Good evening once again, welcome back to our show.

[Constantine] Thanks Art. It's good to be here.

[Art] For those of you who are unaware of it Constantine was also the lead vocalist of the band "Witchcraft" and yes, Constantine is his real name. All right let's talk about your latest book, "Psychic Vampirism." What inspired you to write about this topic?

[Constantine] Legends I'd heard about from town in New York where I once worked and the personal experience of a friend who I also promised not to name.

[Art] All right then. I know that the New England area has a history of documented cases of Vampirism. So let's start there shall we? Most of our listeners are familiar with vampires only from the movies, books and tv series. How accurate is the Hollywood version of the vampire?

[Constantine] Most Hollywood vampires are just variations on the book "Dracula' by Bram Stoker. First you should know thatreal vampires come in 4 types. Immortal blood drinkers are the classic re-animated corpse type of blood drinking vampires. These type are also the least likely to really exist. But nonetheless must be included for the reason that throughout history, in many countries of the world there have been many intriguing cases. But these types bear little resemblance to the sexy young men and women portrayed in the movies and books. According to the stories and legends told by folk people these re-animated corpses are foul smelling, rotten corpses, brown, withered looking things that reek of the stench of the grave.

[Art] I once read a short story called "The Vampire of Croglin Grange." In that tale the vampire was a withered, brown corpse just like you just described.

[Constantine] Yes Art. The Vampire of Croglin Grange is one of the most well known of supposedly factual vampire stories in Britain. The story first appeared in fiction in a book called "My Solitary Life" by August Hare.

Now the second type of vampire is what I like to call "Mortal Blood Drinkers." These are living people who for one reason or another feel the need to drink human blood. This used to be a rare thing, a result of mental illness. However today thanks to the popularity of vampire fiction, a subculture of young people have risen that live in a vampire fantasy world of their own choosing. To these people, drinking blood has become a fashion statement

[Art] Oh yes. I know. I've actually had a few on as guests.

[Constantine] Yes, I heard that show. The leader of the cult that you had on sleeps in a coffin by day, had his incisors capped with fangs and lives on the blood of his followers as I recall.

[Art] (sighs) Oh yes.

[Constantine] (Laughs) Well moving on to our third type of vampire, we come to what I have labeled "Unintentional Psychic Vampires." These are also living people, but they have the unconscious ability to siphon the lifeforce energy from the living. Sometimes they are called "drainers". They can leave you feeling weak and exhausted by just being around them for a few minutes. These people do this unintentionally. Often the sick and the elderly become unintentional psychic vampires. This is because their own energy level has dropped so low that when they come in contact with the auras of the healthy they subconsciously reach out for the energy they need so.

But it is the fourth type that is the real subject of my book. They are called Intentional Psychic Vampires. They are the least known but conversely the oldest and most numerous type of vampire in the world. They are actually special types of ghosts who maintain their unnatural existence by siphoning the life force from the living.

[Art] Hmm ... Why would a ghost or spirit need to siphon life force at all?

[Constantine] As you know our physical bodies generate life-force energy. This creates within us an exact energy duplicate called the astral body. Now within that is the mental body or soul. When we die our astral body containing our consciousness or mental body is released. Now with a physical body to generate new life-force energy the astral body will soon begin to break up. The Egyptians called this "second death".

[Art] Second death? I've not heard that term before.

[Constantine] It's a natural process that happens to us all when we die. The astral body can break up as early as 48 hours after physical death.

[Art] What happens to us then?

[Constantine] But some individuals, usually sorcerers, have learned in life the secret of how to siphon the life force from the living to work their magic ...

Paul's mouth flies open when he hears that. "That's exactly what Simon told me that he used to do?"

[Constantine] ... and in death they continue to siphon the life-force from the living to prevent the break up of their astral bodies, thus rendering themselves immortal in a sense.

[Art] So by siphoning the life force from living humans they avoid second death. Doesn't that mean that they never go into the light then?

[Constantine] Exactly what they are trying to avoid Art. For if they do not go into the light, they never have to face their final judgement. They can remain earthbound. Walking among us but invisible to our eyes.

[Art] That's not a very comforting thought. I wonder how many of them there are?

[Constantine] No one knows except God. But I do know that one in five people are attacked by an entity of this type in their lifetimes.

[Art] One in five!! That's ... That's incredible! Yet you say that they are the least known of the 4 types

.[Constantine] That's correct Art. I can't tell you how many times I've listened to your show and heard callers telling you they were attacked. By the descriptions of the attacks I could tell that they were being attacked by a psychic vampire.

[Art] What are the symptoms of such an attack?

[Constantine] They can vary slightly but a typical psychic vampire attack usually includes the following symptoms. First- the victim often wakes up in the middle of the night feeling terrified for no reason. Secondly- the victim has the unshakable sense that something is coming. Thirdly the victim may hear disembodied footsteps. Fourthly- the victim finds themselves paralyzed and unable to move, except for their eyes. Fifthly- the victim sees a being appear in their room. Most appear as dark forms. These can be a silhouette of human beings. Some are seen with glowing eyes. Usually red in color.

[Art] This sounds like you are describing shadow people!

[Constantine] Yes Art. I heard your show on shadow people. Many, many of your callers were describing psychic vampire attacks.

[Art] Oh!. .. Well if that's the case. The one in five people statistic is not only accurate but might even be an understatement. I have never received as much response on any subject as I did on Shadow people.

[Constantine] I'm not in the least surprised Art. With that in mind listen closely to the final steps of psychic vampire attack and I'm sure they will seem familiar to you. Sixthly- the dark entity will come close to the victim or more commonly crawl on top of the victim. Seventhly- the victim feels a great weight on their chest and has difficulty breathing. This feeling is caused by the entity siphoning the life force from your heart chakra. Then suddenly it is gone! You can move again. You feel weak and drained, because you were.

[Art] Wow! That does sound familiar. I've had hundreds of calls from people over the years, reporting attacks just like the one you just described.

[Constantine] Yes I know, I've heard them. One of the most famous psychic vampires that attacks people mostly in Canada and the northern USA is called The Old Hag.

[Art] Oh yes. We've had many many calls over the years about the old hag entity. So you believe that she is one of these psychic vampires, eh?

[Constantine] Not only do I believe so but also I think I may know who she is? I'm sure you are familiar with Aleister Crowley.

[Art] Of course.

[Constantine] Crowley once got into a magical duel with a rival named Gregor Mathers. According to Crowley, Mathers reportedly sent one of his followers, a vampire, his words, to him. She appeared to him in the guise of a young woman of bewitching beauty. But he was able to defeat her and she was transformed into a hag of sixty, bent and decrepit.

[Art] That's interesting.

[Constantine] You also once did an entire show on a very famous psychic vampire. I refer to the famous "Entity" case.

[Art] The Entity case! Oh ... so you believe that it was also one of these psychic vampires. But that one did a lot worse than just sit on his victim's chest. Why would a psychic vampire rape a woman as that one did?

[Constantine] The heart chakra is not the only chakra that the life force energy can be siphoned from. Any of the 7 major chakras will do.

[Art] Sorry to interrupt you but perhaps we should explain briefly what a chakra is?

[Constantine] A chakra is an old sanskrit word for wheel of light. It is a vortex in the astral body that circulates the life force energy throughout the body. There are 7 major ones that run along the body from the top of the head to the base of the spine. This lowest one is called the root chakra and is associated with the sex organs. So you see now why the Entity raped the woman Carlotta Moran. First the sheer terror the act caused the victim's heart to speed up, adrenaline to pump, thus increasing the amount of life force energy her body produced. Then by penetrating into the woman's sex organs the Entity was tapping directly into her 7th chakra. Then he could drain her of life force during the sex act.

[Art] Oh...I see. That's an interesting theory.

[Constantine] You've had a number of people claim they were attacked sexually by Shadow People haven't you?

[Art] Oh yes, definitely.

[Constantine] Before we continue I should get into all of the methods a psychic vampire uses to attack its victims.

[Art] All right then.

[Constantine] A psychic vampire is not confined to nighttime attacks. They can attack you in broad daylight or even in public. They usually prefer to attack at night because that is when most people are sleep. Making them easy targets. The feeding process tends to develop through stages.

First-touch. In life these sorcerers learned that the flow of energy in the body is linked to breath, inhalation brings it in, exhalation expels it. Most Yogis agree that the energy can flow out of the body in the right hand and in through the left hand. By touching their intended victim a psychic vampire can leave a tendril of energy attached to their aura through which it can feed anytime.

Secondly, close proximity. Since the aura extends several feet around the body a psychic vampire need only stand close to or hover above the individual so that it's own aura touches the victims. Another more advanced feeding process is eye contact. Practitioners of Tantric Yoga will tell you that energy can be transferred by gaze alone. So any vampire that learns how to do that can feed on anyone within their sight.

[Art] I've had some caller's report hearing some of these entities whisper to them.

[Constantine] As for sounds, victims occasionally report breathing sounds, or whispered voice, always a windy sound.

[Art] Other than feeling really tired are there any side effects caused by this energy siphoning?

[Constantine] That's a good question. If a psychic vampire feeds on you only once, probably not. The body gets to work replacing the lost energy. But repeated feedings can lead to physical illness, mental illness or even death.

[Art] Death?

[Constantine] That's right. Ask any acupuncturist and they will tell you that all illness begins as a depletion of life force energy. Kirlian photography has even proven that a diminishment in the aura occurs prior to one's physical illness.

[Art] That's pretty disturbing news. You say that one on five people are attacked by one of these psychic vampires in their lifetime. That it can occur in broad daylight or even in public and that repeated attacks can lead to illness or death. [Constantine] Yes but the good news is I can teach everyone how to protect themselves from attack by a psychic vampire.

[Art] That is good news. Go ahead.

[Constantine] First forget about stakes, garlic, sunlight and crosses. Those only repel movie vampires. Remember a psychic vampire became what he is because they feared going into the light at death. The white light is the only thing they fear. So the best protection you can use is if you are attacked or even as a prevention of such an attack is called by spiritualists "The White Light Ritual".

[Art] The white light ritual?

[Constantine] Yes. Here is how you perform it. Simply say, "Lord send down your white light upon me. I thank you for all that you have done for me this day and I ask for strength, protection, guidance and health." Now visualize a brilliant white light shining down on you from above like a spotlight. That's all there is to it. I recommend you do it before you go to sleep and after you awaken and you'll never have to fear being attacked again by one of these psychic vampires.

[Art] But that's so easy. Still what do you do if you are an atheist? I noticed you asked the Lord to send down the white light.

[Constantine] That's no problem really. Simply substitute the word Universe for Lord or call upon whatever name you wish for the God force. It all works just as well. If that poor woman who was attacked in the Entity case had only known the White Light Ritual she could have driven off her attacker. But no one knew how to help her. Not the psychiatrists who were treating her for mental illness nor the parapsychologists who were there just to document the phenomenon ....

The clock strikes 3am and Paul's radio goes dead. He just bought new batteries for it so he knows it is not that. He smiles and says to himself. "You're too late Simon. Now I finally know what you are and how to protect my family and friends from you? You're finished. "

Suddenly everything that has happened to him finally makes sense. The psychic vampire theory fits his case like a hand in a glove. Like a revelation from God all of the pieces of this 40 year old puzzle now fall into place.

1. Simon Magus as a sorcerer learned how to siphon energy from the living to work his miracles while still alive.

2. In death he became a psychic vampire condemned to walk the earth rather than go into the light and face his final judgement.

3. As a psychic vampire he was drawn to those with the most powerful auras. Was he really the father of the most famous mystics and magicians in history? Perhaps or perhaps he just told me that to sell himself to me as he told me that he was my father as well. I just have to wonder if there is any truth to that one. Especially since I did have a near miraculous conception.

4. My mother was a powerful psychic and just the type to attract a psychic vampire like a moth to a flame.

5. If he really is Simon of Samaria how did he end up at our house on McCawley Road in Kentucky? I think Floyd Hobbs might be the answer to that. Did he try and conjure the spirit of Simon Magus as Eliphas Levi tried to conjure Apollonius of Tyana. Or was it because our home on McCawley Road was a vortex of psychic energy and he was drawn to it naturally.

6. My mother saw Simon in his Middle Eastern garb walking down the hallway at McCawley Road. No doubt it was because she was clairvoyant and could see what was invisible to others at times.

7. People who lived at McCawley Road heard disembodied footsteps, one of the symptoms of psychic vampire attack. Those same footsteps were later heard at the house on Robb's Lane, our house on Blue Lick Road, Larry Troutman's home, Lavonne's home on Miles Lane, and Gunsmoke Mountain where I worked.

8. People at McCawley Road felt something heavy sitting on their chests and had difficulty breathing. Just like Constantine just described psychic vampire attack. It happened to Katie, Jimbo and little Bobby to name only 3 and myself in dreams.

9. What were those strange animals back home really? The white ape, the giant snake the strange looking bird. The encyclopedia's I read said that the living Simon Magus could change his form into animals. Could he as a psychic vampire have been seeking to instill as much fear as possible? Fear makes the heart pump harder and the body to produce more adrenaline and thus to produce more life force energy which is what he fed on. A white ape sitting on your chest would not only disguise his true appearance but also create the highest fear level imaginable in the victim. So all of the creatures back there may have either been him directly or demons he conjured to instill fear in the victims.

10. What about all of the sickness and death at McCawley Road? Robert's feet, Donnie's paralysis, Katie's tumors, Grandma's stroke, all of it could be caused by Simon feeding off of them. Who was that woman who showed up claiming to be the one who was paid to put a curse on our family? Where does she fit into this? If Simon controlled me how many others might he be controlling? Was she real or a spirit also? In life Simon was the ultimate trickster in death he is no different. If she was paid by Esther Wilkins, how do we know that Esther herself was not controlled by Simon or influenced by him in dreams as he has shown he is quite capable of?

11. At age 13 Simon talked me into performing the spell of invocation. After that he possessed my body and fed off of everyone I came into contact with.

12. As a boy in High School he would come out and just stare holes through the girls. I never understood that until now. He was feeding off of them.

13. Then at age 19 when Lavonne became my first lover, he all but disappeared except during sex. He was feeding off of her every time we had sex.

14. She began to hear the walking sounds at her house and then saw the dark form with the glowing eyes. Two of the symptoms Constantine claims are symptoms of psychic vampire attack.

15. She also heard the breathing sounds on our honeymoon, still another symptom of psychic vampire attack.

16. Six months into our marriage she started getting sick. She'd never been sick a day in her life, save for common colds and flus we all suffer from. Now I know it was because he was feeding off of her.

17. My mother's cancer, my best friend Larry's cancer and even my dog's cancer. All of them died the same year. It wasn't a coincidence. It was because

he had been feeding on them all since I was 13. They were the 3 beings I was closest to.

18. When my sex life dried up due to Lavonne's illness Simon began taking over my body and seducing other women to feed on during the sex act.

19. What about the invisible hands Brenda R. felt attacking her in her car when she was coming to see me? It sounds just like the daylight psychic vampire attacks Constantine just described.

20. Constantine said energy flows out of the right hand and into the left. Once when Susan and I were holding hands I felt the change coming on. Suddenly she jerked her hand away and said, "My whole arm just went numb and cold."

21. I once read that Eliphas Levi claimed to conjure the spirit in his efforts to conjure Apollonius of Tyana. It touched his sword and his arm went cold and numb just like Susan's. Simon claimed that it was he that Eliphas conjured.

22. Did he really possess Rasputin? Was that why Rasputin seemed like two different men? One a pious Holy man and the other obsessed with sex. Maybe he really was two men, like me.

23. Did he really possess Aleister Crowley? Perhaps that was why he ended up a drunken, heroin addict almost completely mad and obsessed with sex? Perhaps as I resisted Simon's possession, he may have embraced it. He obtained the knowledge of magic he craved but at what price?

24. Of course he may not even be Simon Magus at all. He could have told me that just to sell himself to me. Whoever he is though, I have no doubt that he is one of these psychic vampires.

"It all fits ... It all fits." Paul got up from his desk and went into the restroom to be alone. "I almost wish I had never heard this broadcast. Now I know for sure that Simon has destroyed everyone I ever loved and it's my fault. I let him into my body and I did it gleefully. I wanted power and fame and instead I lost not only my free will but also caused the deaths of my loved ones ... Or did I?"

Simon walked the hallways of McCawley Road 10 years before I was born. I didn't put him there. No, it's not my fault. It's his fault! He killed them, not me. I am just another of his victims. But not anymore. Now I know his weakness. The White Light Ritual.

What about Susan? Six months into our marriage she went into early menopause. She was only 36. It was because he has been feeding on her as well. But not anymore. Now I can at least protect her. But how can I use this to free myself of him altogether? Maybe I can use the white light ritual to stop his take over of my body.

Time passed. Paul began using the white light ritual everyday to protect Susan and everyone he came in contact with. But when the full moon cycle appeared it was not enough to stop Simon from taking him over. That problem continued. But Paul refused to give up.

He learned from studying the kabbalah that the white light that people see at the end of the tunnel when they are near death is the white light associated with the sphere Kether. The highest of the Holy Sephiroth and the one the closest to the God force. Simon as a spirit belonged to Yesod the astral plane. Should he ever be bathed in the higher energies of the light of Kether he would be immediately dissolved into it.

That was why psychic vampires feared the white light. Perhaps by performing the Kabbalistic Ritual of entering the sephiroth of Kether on a daily basis and especially when he felt Simon about to take him over he could drive him off.

It was a good plan but it seemed to fail. Paul did notice though that it took longer and longer for Simon to be able to take over his body once he began to practice it. It gave him hope at least so he kept on practicing entering the sephiroth.

The cure came but not in the way he expected. When Simon possessed him at age 13 he became spiritually stunted at that age. He grew physically, he grew mentally but spiritually he was still 13 years old. But the Kabbalah was designed for spiritual growth. So the more he practiced it the more his spirit grew. It took 7 years but in 2002 he was finally totally and completely free of Simon's possession.

Today he lives a normal existance with no more missing time. No more embarassing behavior to explain. No more dreams of Simon visiting him. He looks back on it all and wonders if indeed he was truly possessed or whether Dr. Bornstein was right and Simon was all in his mind. Either way, he is just glad to be free.

THE END

EPILOGUE

The case of Paul Michelson remains an unsolved mystery. So many questions will never be answered definitely. Was he really possessed or merely delusional? If he was truly possessed, what was this entity which called itself Simon Magus?

Like most things in life the truth can often depend greatly upon your own point of view. To those who do not believe in spirits or possession then the only answer must be mental illness.

Indeed DID or Dissociative Identity Disorder does seem to fit all of Paul's symptoms as Dr. Bornstein pointed out. But can the mind alone really accomplish things like eye color change and brain wave pattern change as those who have studied it claim? The problem of course with such studies is that those who only believe in the scientific method examine the results. The problem with western science is that they only believe in what they can prove exists by empirical science. Therefore they examine only the mind and body. Since no one has been able to prove the existence of the spirit it is ignored and disregarded.

What happens when a western scientist examines a person whose may be possessed? No doubt he will find someone whose eyes can change color, the can switch off from left to right handedness, their handwriting may change, their brainwave and even voice prints may change.

Where does that leave an atheistic scientific mind except to relegate those abilities to some unknown aspect of the brain? Since no one has explained how the mind can affect the body in such ways then the spirit is just as valid and explanation as the mind. You cannot use one unknown to explain another.

But the reverse is also true. Since no one has proven the existence of the spirit it cannot be ruled out that the mind is indeed capable of such miraculous changes in the body. So let's take look at each theory separately so we can at least cover every possibility.

1. Mental Illness- I agree that this is the most obvious, down to earth explanation for what was happening to Paul Michelson. For no one can argue that absolutely anything can happen to a man within his own mind. Paul's troubles seem to have began at the age of 13 when he began to receive his ouija board message from Simon.

If this was truly mental illness though, how is it that it started at a specific time? After the spell of invocation. Paul experimented with self hypnosis when he was 13 as part of his experiments in seeking to tap into his psychic abilities. Could it be that when he performed the spell of invocation which involved both visualization and meditation techniques, it may have suggested to his subconscious that it was successful?

Perhaps his belief in possession was strong enough to trigger the Dissociative Identity Disorder, which created a separate but equal personality. Thus his belief in the white light ritual and the kabbalah may have reversed the problem. if true the whole thing could possibly have been all in his mind.

But the psychiatric point of view is not the only point of view. What would a parapsychologist think of this case? While there is no evidence that spirits are behind the phenomenon of this case, there can be no doubt that such cases do exist. Most parapsychologist would probably label it a poltergiest case.

Many of the experiences shared by not only Paul but also many of those who surrounded him, seem to thwart a purely psychiatric explanantion. Things heard by others like the walking sounds, breathing sounds, objects moving around by themselves, the feeling of invisible hands touching you, etc. All such phenomena are common in poltergeist cases.

In most documented cases there always seems to be one person that the strange phenomena seems to center on. In a haunting the family can usually escape by moving away but in a poltergiest case it follows the individual who more times than not turns out to be a troubled teen. Paul was a troubled teen. So perhaps he had more success than he thought about tapping into his psychic abilities.

But there are many problems with trying to explain this case as just another poltergeist case. For one thing poltergeist cases are usually short lived. But this one persisted from age 13 till age 47. Even more puzzling would be trying to explain how the walking sounds were heard at McCawley Road and the house on Robb's Lane years before Paul was born.

The only way poltergeist activity would explain it, is if there were 3 different cases of it. It could be possible that Donnie or Pat as they entered teenage-hood may have been the cause of the earier phenomenon. But such identical cases in the same family stretch coincidence pretty thin.

Another idea we touched on in this story is the idea that Simon may have been an egreggore. A created spirit. In ceremonial magic a spirit may be created by a magician to perform a specific task and then ritually destroyed. If it is not destroyed the created spirit grows stronger each day and more and more independant of the magician.

My question is that if this can be done deliberately, may it also not be done accidently? It was suggested in this novel that Betsy Bell may have created the Bell Witch accidently. If true, Paul may also have created Simon. Like Betsy Bell, Paul was also an abused child. Not sexually abused as she was, but physically, psychologically and emotionally certainly. Due to his mother's alcoholism. He was bullied at home as well as at school. Perhaps like Betsy Bell he too sought a savior. Someone powerful to protect him.

Also like Betsy Bell, Paul may have unconsciously created Simon. His desire for Simon to be a real entity on the ouija board and not just his imagination may have actually brought him to life. But once created as with the Bell Witch, he was independent and became Paul's worst tormentor.

If I seem to be going out of my way to not accept the story at face value, it does not mean that I can rule it out either. Simon may indeed have been exactly who and what he claimed to be? The spirit of the Biblical sorcerer who has wandered the earth for 2000 years now. Who in death became a psychic vampire feeding off of the lifeforce of the living to maintain his unnatural existance. Indeed of all the throries listed and despite how fantasic it sounds, it does seem to be the only one which fits all of the facts of the case from 1941-2002.

But as with the others it leaves as many questions unanswered as it answers. If indeed it was Simon Magus who Katie saw walking the hallways of her house on McCawley Road, what was he doing there? Louisville, Ky is a long way from Samaria where Simon was born or Rome, Italy where he died. Yet if it was not Simon, who was it? What was any spirit doing there dressed in middle eastern garb? Was he conjured by the previous owner? Was he drawn there by the vortex of psychic energy that seemed to surround the home?

The final explanation that must be considered is summed up in one name. Demons. Demonic activity could also account for all of the facts of this case. It could have been demons which caused all of the tragic and horrible events at McCawley Road. Those same demons could have followed the family to Blue Lick Road and possessed Paul at age 13. Demons are famous liars so it would be easy to believe that they pretended to be Simon Magus to lure the boy magician into performing the spell of invocation.

But those who are demonically possessed usually show specific symtoms like revulsion for scared objects and places, such as the woman in the Earling, Iowa case. But Paul seemed to have his faith deepened by the experience and it caused him to turn to prayer and devotion to God on a daily basis, where before he had only been luke warm about religion.

Finally both of the last two theories could be true. After all it is possible that Simon Magus went to hell when he died.

Well all of the cards are now lain upon the table. I will leave it up to you the reader to determine what you believe to be the truth behind this bizarre true case? Peace be with you, Samuel Spulman

To see photos of the real Paul Michelson and his family, including the mentioned "spirit" photos I have set up a special web site. There are over 50 photos and to have included them in the book would have driven the cost of the book up. This way you can view them for free. Simply go to...

http://shadowofsimonmagus.mulitply.com/

For those of you who would enjoy reading my fan fiction tales of the tv series Dark Shadows I'll include the url here.

Go to http://simonmagus.mulitply.com/